STEF ANN HOLM

"Holm's comedic flair is much in evidence
in this fast-paced story."
—*Romantic Times BOOKclub* on *Leaving Normal*

"Stef Ann Holm at her sexy and irresistible best."
—*New York Times* bestselling author Carly Phillips

"Nobody writes families like Stef Ann Holm."
—*New York Times* bestselling author Jennifer Crusie

"*Undressed* is a feel-good tale about people
who find love and happiness in
the most unexpected places."
—*Romance Reviews Today*

"Stef Ann Holm will make you laugh
and cry and fall in love again."
—*New York Times* bestselling author Jill Barnett

"*Pink Moon* is tender and funny."
—*Romantic Times BOOKclub*

Also by STEF ANN HOLM

LEAVING NORMAL
PINK MOON
UNDRESSED
GIRLS NIGHT

Stef Ann Holm

Lucy gets Her Life Back

MIRA®

ISBN-13: 978-0-7783-2344-0
ISBN-10:   0-7783-2344-7

LUCY GETS HER LIFE BACK

Copyright © 2006 by Stef Ann Holm.

www.MIRABooks.com

Printed in U.S.A.

I am blessed to have two ladies in my life who have made my world all the better for their existence. I'm proud to have their friendship and support, feel the grace they bring into everyday things that surround us, their respect and unconditional love. They are my wonderful daughters.

This book is for Whitney and Kayla, who have been by my side the past three years with smiles, kindness, late-night conversations, laughter, tears and hugs. You have both been incredibly strong and loving in the challenges we have faced, and you make my days bright. God gave me an incredible gift when He gave both of you to me.

I love you,
Mom.

Prologue

The *Mountain Gazette* would later report that virtually the entire population of Red Duck, Idaho had gathered in the Mule Shoe Bar to witness history in the making.

With heightened anticipation, gazes fastened on the big screen television during the world news broadcast. The aroma of coffee mingled with remnant tobacco smoke from the night before. Steady conversation filled the barroom as the sun began to rise.

A handful of those in attendance had barely let their bar stools cool down for four hours before returning at this early hour to support something really big.

There hadn't been this much excitement in town since Bruce Willis premiered his latest movie at the Mint Theater in Hailey. Second to that was when John Kerry ran for president and the majority of Democrats in Red Duck had to go over to the dark side and turn Republican. But that was a heated story, one that was often rehashed over shots of Jack Daniels.

"It's coming on in a just a few minutes!" P. J. Guffy said, aiming the clicker at the television to turn up the sound. "Quiet, everyone!"

The noise in the crowded room hushed to a soft murmur as the morning broadcast changed gears and moved on to the weather.

Red Duck had its own radio station and a newspaper that came out once a week. To tide everyone over until each Wednesday when the *Gazette* was published, gossip was exchanged over at the High Country Motel's lounge. The closest thing to local news in between was the TV stations airing from Boise.

The toupee-wearing anchor in a double-breasted suit filled the screen, animated hand signs indicating it was going to be another record-breaking day in the area.

But nobody in Red Duck cared about the barometer.

Sitting dead center in the room for the best view of the television was the soon-to-be local celebrity.

Fern "Spin" Goodey-Leonard had both hearing aids ramped up to full power so she wouldn't miss a thing.

One of her liver-spotted hands clamped down on the chair's wooden arm while the other held on to a coffee sweetened with brandy. She smiled broadly, but at no one in particular—just a double check to make sure her dentures were still firmly in place. She inhaled, sucked in her gut, the latex of her girdle constricting her effort. When she'd been a spry young woman, and tall as a barn post, she'd been nicknamed "Spin"—short for "Spindly" because she'd always been so thin. Now she relied on Playtex to keep everything in place. It was amazing how one could pour one's skin and flab into a girdle, and in a matter of seconds, elastic smoothed out all the wrinkles.

She'd been the seventh woman admitted to the Idaho Bar in 1924, quite a feat back then. Judges had been discriminatory in the courtroom, her cases having been especially trying when she was defending other women. It was amazing she'd lasted in a male-dominated business, her career spanning three decades. She gave up her practice in 1953 and moved to Red Duck with her husband, Wally. God bless him, Wally had died in 1956 in a bear-hunting accident. Having lived with the love of her life for the better part of thirty-two years, Spin had never remarried.

P. J. Guffy flapped his arms, cranking the volume higher.

A stillness fell over the room as Willard Scott's face filled the screen.

Applause rose and Spin wasn't even on yet. Willard was one of Spin's favorites. She'd tried for a few years to get his recognition and, finally, this was her year. She was glad she'd held on this long, because she didn't think she'd be around for next year's birthday. Her bladder was failing and her kidneys gave her trouble. Cataracts had messed with her vision and her oil painting skills had suffered in recent years. But her mind was still relatively sound, so thank God for that.

As Willard addressed the camera, photos of centenarians across the country flashed on the screen, each one bordered by the well-known checkerboard frame.

"And from Red Duck, Idaho, Fern Goodey-Leonard, who turns one hundred and three this week."

Cheers rose in the barroom as soon as Spin's name was called, and gooseflesh prickled her loose skin. She hoped her red lipstick was still on straight. Seeing her picture on the television made her so happy. She had lived a long time for this.

Holiday poppers exploded in the bar, with tails of streamers falling over her shoulders and catching on her rhinestone-rimmed eyeglasses.

And it wasn't even over yet.

The screen went from Willard Scott to blackness as Guffy turned off the set, and all of a sudden the bar was filled with big lights from the local news media. Channel 7 had been sent to Red Duck to do a follow-up on Spin's birthday bash.

The reporter, perhaps twenty-two if she was a day, shoved a microphone in her face.

"So, Ms. Goodey-Leonard," she stated, "how does it feel to see yourself on national television?"

Spin spoke loudly. "Good."

"You're almost an icon in Idaho. The seventh woman to be admitted into the Idaho Bar. How have things changed since you practiced law in the early years? There used to be some dissension between you and a Judge—" the reporter referred to her notes "—Judge Harrison."

Spin went into a bit of history of the Idaho judicial system, careful not to call Harrison an asshole, but she thought it just the same.

Big-ass asshole, male-chauvinist pig…asshole.
Asshole.

That last asshole thought made her brows pucker. She should have stopped while she was ahead.

The reporter asked, "Are you in good health?"

"As good as I can be for one hundred and three."

"You look wonderful."

"I feel so-so," she quipped. "But I can die fulfilled now that Mr. Scott has recognized me on his weather segment."

"The whole of Boise would like to recognize you, Ms. Goodey-Leonard."

"I'm glad to hear that, because I'm having my ashes returned to Boise when I'm gone."

This piece of bold news caused the woman to falter somewhat. She probably hadn't dealt with death very much at her young age. "Oh, I'm sure that will be nice for you," she managed to murmur.

"It'll be more than nice. It's my way of saying a final goodbye to Judge Harrison for all those years in the courtroom when he looked at me like a tomato rather than a lawyer." Before the anchor could cut her short, Spin grabbed hold of the microphone and continued, "I'm having my ashes baked into bread, then fed to the courthouse pigeons."

The anchor attempted to pull away the mike, but Spin held fast, her red lipstick grazing it as she looked directly into the camera. "Then when the pigeons shit on Harrison's statue in the court gardens, it'll be my way of saying goodbye to the asshole."

Stunned but good-natured laughter erupted in the Mule Shoe as the camera crew cut the film.

Spin didn't care if her segment aired or not.

She was one hundred and three tomorrow and she didn't give a good damn what anyone thought. She'd been on NBC. Coast to coast. And with the checkered Smucker border setting off the lace collar of her blouse, she'd looked peachy on TV.

She hoped her great-nephew, Morris Leonard, wouldn't give her too much crap about the interview. He was a prominent Boise attorney and a fine catch for the right woman.

By lunchtime, life in Red Duck had settled back to normal: the sheriff cited two speeders; Jacquie Santini from Realty Professionals sold a 4.6 million dollar home to an "unnamed" movie actor from Holly-weird; Sutter's Gourmet Grocery put buffalo meat on sale; and a benefit to improve the Little League field was announced.

That night, Spin's interview was edited and cut

to suit prime-time television. No surprise there. But the residents didn't seem to mind.

There was other news already brewing in Red Duck.

One

"That stretch of Timberline Highway by the golf course looks like a slaughterhouse floor." The blue Idaho sky with its popcorn-shaped clouds reflected in the sheriff's sunglasses. "I don't recall such a massacre so close to town before."

Lucy Carpenter grabbed her two sons by their shoulders and drew them in close. Her lanky sixteen-year-old, Jason, shrugged out of her protective embrace, while her twelve-year-old, Matt, stuck next to her as his mouth dropped open.

The deputy, a whipcord thin man wearing a cowboy hat and sporting a red Fu Manchu mustache, remarked, "It'll be one hell of a job scraping off the pavement."

The lump forming in Lucy's throat ached, making it more difficult to swallow. Her skin grew clammy. The band of her bra seemed to constrict and cause a thin line of perspiration to roll between her breasts. With one hand, she flipped open the top two buttons on her wool jacket, welcoming the chill air through her knit shirt.

Suddenly, moving to Red Duck seemed like a horribly ill conceived idea. How could these two men talk so casually about a dead body on the road?

Jason's voice regressed to a prepuberty squeak. "Mom, I told you Boise wasn't *that* bad!"

"I never said it was a crime capital." Lucy's response was a little too abrupt, and perhaps on the defensive side, when she didn't intend for it to be. "I simply said the city was a bad influence on you."

"I only smoked some pot. They kill people up here!"

That last part, or rather that first part, had both law officials looking at her son as if he were a notorious drug dealer.

"We don't tolerate any mary-wanna-go-to-jail in this town," Sheriff Roger Lewis cautioned, his small eyes narrowing to slits. He had a dark tropical tan that George Hamilton would envy. Silver hair framed his long face, and his teeth were a blinding white. He sported a felt-brimmed cowboy hat in the same silver color that accessorized both law-enforcement uniforms. And each officer had a very large revolver in a holster.

Lucy's eyes felt dry. She blinked and tried to focus.

The deputy ran his forefinger under his nose, scratched it, then shifted his weight to an exaggerated stance. "Back in the late nineties, a few bad apples from Boise brought some cocaine with them, and several fledgling businesses went up some noses." He traded glances with the sheriff, the pair obviously recollecting the damage. "The Iron Mountain Paragliding School was one of them."

"What Deputy Cooper's saying—" the sheriff hitched his pants to high-water level while looking directly at her son "—is we won't tolerate any big-city trouble."

The crispness in the late May day seemed to evaporate, Lucy's cheeks growing warm. Indignance threaded through her. She laid a hand on Jason's shoulder, drew him close. This time he didn't resist. "We don't smoke marijuana and I wouldn't dream of bringing any drugs into town."

But as she spoke, she recalled her firsthand encounter with drugs and her son.

Jason had been caught with a marijuana cigarette in his hall locker. He'd been put on suspension, but it wasn't his first violation in the nearly two years since her divorce. There had been the day he'd cut class to go fishing with his buddies, and received his second speeding ticket on the way home. He'd had his driver's license taken away for thirty days. His rebellious behavior after her ex-husband left them was why she'd made the decision to move her two boys to the small town of Red Duck.

The glossy travel brochures touted that tourists might flock to Timberline, but they played in Red Duck. Golf, biking, skiing. Red Duck had a year-round population of three thousand that swelled to six thousand depending on the season.

Nestled in a flat valley at the base of the Wood Ridge Mountains, Red Duck only had two traffic signals on Main Street. All the buildings had the same false-fronted design—from the old Mule Shoe Bar to the new Blockbuster on Honeysuckle Road.

"Mom, can we go now?" Matt asked, the freckles on his face prominent from being in the high altitude sun.

They'd arrived in town a good hour ago and, for the life of her, she hadn't been able to find their rental. She'd gone several miles beyond Main Street, even into the Timberline Resort, but the road she was supposed to turn on seemed to have vanished.

She drove the do-it-yourself moving truck with all their possessions packed inside, navigating the best she could, with her sixteen-year-old, at the helm of her beloved car, following behind. Each time she'd stopped to turn around, Jason had raised his hands in exasperation as if to say, "Where are you going?" Then he'd clamped hard on the steering wheel and accelerated far too fast for her comfort.

Against her better judgment, and for lack of an alternative driver, she'd let her son make the two hundred mile trip from Boise to Red Duck in the Passat. She'd insisted Matt ride with her so he couldn't distract Jason—who'd totaled his small pickup almost two months ago and was without a car.

In defeat and puzzlement, Lucy had brought the boys to the sheriff's department, hoping the law officials would know how to direct her. Now she regretted that decision. Being put under a microscope before she'd even unpacked a single dish wasn't how she had envisioned their arrival.

Lucy squared her shoulders. "I'm renting a house on Lost River Road and I can't seem to find the turnoff. I've been up before. I thought I knew how to get there, but for some reason, the street's missing."

Matter-of-factly, Sheriff Lewis said, "It happens in the spring. Snowmelt. You get some flash floods out that way from the Lost River."

The deputy added his two cents. "It's a river that comes and goes depending on the rainy season."

"The street was washed out last week. Nobody's gotten around to putting up a new sign yet."

"Aw jeez," Jason whined. "We live on a street that disappears, and they've got dead bodies here, too."

"Dead bodies?" Sheriff Lewis echoed, his hand falling too close to his holster. "Where's a dead body?"

Matt's voice came out in a quiver. "Timberline Highway. The big massacre."

The sheriff had the nerve to laugh. Lucy was about to tell him that it wasn't funny in the slightest.

"That's no dead body. It's a road-kill elk," Deputy Cooper supplied, his facial expression trying to remain neutral, but a grin cut across his mouth. "And a damn big 'un. What's left of the carcass and guts is spread out on both lanes, blood splattered from here to kingdom come. My guess it was a three-quarter-ton diesel that got it."

The sheriff cocked his hat. "I'm thinking a Hummer."

"Drew Tolman drives a Hummer," the deputy mused. "I haven't see it in town today."

"Too early." Sheriff Lewis gazed at the sun. "Tolman doesn't roll into Opal's for breakfast until noon."

"Unless it's Little League season. Then he gets there about nine. Orders the same thing every day. Steak and eggs."

"Sometimes he swaps out the steak for six sausage links. I saw him do that a few times."

At that, Matt said, "Mom, I'm hungry."

They'd been snacking on crackers and fruit in the car, and now that food had been mentioned, Lucy's stomach growled. She could all but taste her special roasted pepper omelet with seasoned potatoes.

"We'll get something as soon as we find the house." To the sheriff she queried, "If the road is washed out, how am I supposed to get there?"

"Cooper'll draw you a map on how get in the back way. What's the address?"

"346 Lost River Road."

Sheriff Lewis gave them each another long, skeptical glance. "That's Bud Tremore's teardown."

Lucy cringed, not wanting to have to explain that to the boys in mixed company.

"What's a teardown?" Jason asked, slipping away from her once more. While it was a physical distance, she'd been feeling the emotional distance as well. He wasn't her baby anymore, and she hoped this move would help their relationship retain some of the closeness they'd once had. Relocating would allow him to make new friends, boys who were boys and not young men who thought they were tough and knew everything.

The sheriff didn't give her the opportunity to elaborate. "A teardown is just what you think it is. A building that's going to be torn down. Real estate in Red Duck is so pricey you just can't buy good land anymore. You take what's a pile of junk, demo it and build new." Looking at Lucy, he arched his brows. "I didn't think Bud was renting out that place anymore."

He wasn't. Or wasn't going to until she'd convinced him otherwise.

On her scouting trip, she'd been quickly disillusioned. She'd learned through a Realtor that the people who worked here most likely didn't live here. They lived in Twin Falls or Shoshone and rode a bus to and from town.

Bud Tremore owned the Salmon Creek RV Park, and when she'd been at her rope's end, unable to find a place to live, she'd stopped in to use the restroom and put a dollar in the vending machine for a bottle of Coke. She'd got to talking to Bud, and ended up telling him her hard luck story—something unlike her. But it had been a long day of disappointment, and he mentioned having a vacant house he used to rent out before the foundation resettled and knocked off the right side of the porch.

She'd begged him to show it to her, and she'd made a deal on the spot for $1,500 a month. Dirt cheap. Rent in Red Duck was obscene. She couldn't even think about buying, not even with the proceeds from the sale of her Boise house. And Timberline? You couldn't touch a home for less than two million.

"We have to live in a piece of junk?" Jason's question broke through Lucy's thoughts.

"No. It's not bad at all. I really liked it and there's a view of the ski mountain."

Well, sort of. The trees blocked it off. But they could fix up the house and make it a home. It was the best she could do and still live in Red Duck.

"I never wanted to move here," Jason grumbled, flipping the key of her Passat open and closed like a switchblade. "Why can't we go back to Boise? All my friends are there."

She kept an assurance in her voice she hoped would convince him. "You'll make friends here."

Matt rubbed his belly. "I'm hungry."

"We'll get something to eat soon."

The deputy returned with a map. She followed his finger as he traced a road, showed her how to get to the house.

"Just what is your business in town?" the sheriff asked, puffing out his chest like a rooster.

Lucy stared at him a long moment. "My business."

Then she thanked the two for their time, put the boys back in their respective vehicles and began traveling on Honeysuckle Road.

Her hands gripped the wheel of the moving van, her stomach pitching. Not from hunger this time, but from trepidation. She hoped she wasn't making a mistake.

She'd spent hours, days...several weeks planning for this move and contemplating every angle of what could or would go wrong. The positives outweighed the negatives. She could work up here, make a nice living as a personal chef. She'd gotten that part covered and knew the business could be stable. But a piece of her was riddled with guilt. She'd taken the boys away from the only home they'd ever known. She'd sold the house she'd won in the divorce—a modest four-bedroom with a big yard, basketball hoop, skateboard ramp in front where all the neighborhood boys congregated.

Things would be different for them up here. But it would be a good different. She had to remind herself that this was for the best.

But as the house came into view, with its gray-weathered sides, a magpie squawking on the roof, the porch sloping and in need of repair, and a discarded truck tailgate in the front yard, she bit the inside of her lip.

Matt rolled down the window and stuck his head out as she let the truck engine idle. "Cool! This place looks like a junky fort."

Jason had gotten out of the Passat, stood next to

his brother at the open window. He gave Lucy a pathetic glare, then muttered, "I wish you and Dad never got a divorce."

Lucy wished the same thing, but her marriage bed could sleep only two people comfortably, and Gary had decided he liked his office secretary taking dictation in between the sheets. Her ex suffered from classic male menopause and had bailed to Mexico on an extended holiday.

"Well, we did get a divorce," Lucy all but snapped. "So now it's the three of us and we're going to make the best of it."

She spoke more to reassure herself than the two boys, whose gazes had slid back to the house just as the magpie dropped a present on the front steps before flying away.

Before the day was over, Jason knew he could find someone in Red Duck to hit him up with a bag of pot. His mom was dumb to think that this potato-land town didn't have drugs for sale. If a dude had some money, anything was for sale.

Buying weed and keeping a joint in his hall locker had been effing stupid. The Special Resource Officer at his old high school was like a canine. He had a nose that could sniff out a stale P & J sandwich locked tight in a binder. Getting busted had reeked. Jason had really screwed up. That had been the first time he'd smoked weed, and he'd paid a penalty for it, but he'd done alcohol and never got caught.

When Gary left them, Jason got drunk on purpose to make the hurt go away—a pain he didn't talk about, not even with Matt. His mom never found out about the drinking. He told her he was going to the skateboard park with his friends, but they ended up at Brian's house instead. Brian's parents had a wet bar stocked with any liquor you could think of. Brian put water in the vodka bottle to make up for what he and his friends drank. They took some Smirnoff Ice, too, since there were a couple cases of it in the garage refrigerator. Five or six missing bottles—it was nothing noticeable.

Thinking back, Jason remembered how he'd puked his guts up and had a headache all the next day. He'd lied, told his mom he had the flu. After that, he swore, no more alcohol. Just grass. But not regularly. Only when he needed to forget his troubles.

He didn't hate his mom. She was trying. And he knew that he was a shit to her sometimes. But he couldn't help himself. He had a lot of anger in him. Sometimes he just wanted to hit something. Like maybe Gary for running off to Mexico.

Gary was an effing bastard.

He only called on Sunday nights, and stayed on the phone for ten minutes before he said he had to go. And he always called at exactly 8:00 p.m. because that's when the rates went down calling from Meh-he-co.

Jason didn't know his dad anymore. Now he only thought of him as Gary. He couldn't call him

Dad because a dad was someone who didn't walk out on his kids.

"Can we go inside, Mom?" Matt asked.

"Sure. I've got the key."

Jason held back, not eager to go in. He was thinking about not having a cell phone to call Brian and his buddies. This really stunk. If they'd stayed in Boise, his mom would have likely got him a phone, since he was driving. Well, that was before he'd totaled his truck. Eventually he would have gotten a flip phone. Now he had nothing.

"Jason, aren't you coming in?" she asked.

She stood on the porch, sunlight shining off her brown hair with red shades that were natural. She had full lips and brown eyes. The boys at school called her hot, and it pissed him off 'cause she was his mom. Awkward hearing a couple of the football players say his mom was someone they'd like to make out with. He was glad he didn't have an ugly mom. But still. He'd once hit a kid at an assembly for saying something about her.

His mom was forty-five. Jason always thought she was beautiful, even when he was a little kid. The other kids always commented he had one of the prettiest moms.

Now she looked sad a lot.

Sun played across her face and she looked tired. He knew Gary had caused a lot of the tired stuff. But so did he. Jason took the blame for being a screwup as a son. He felt bad.

Life sucked.

"Yeah, Mom. Sure."

He didn't want to give her a ration of crap anymore. He was going to try and be nicer to his mom. But looking at this place where they had to live, he thought about firing up a joint and forgetting where he was.

Drew Tolman could drive left-handed even though he batted right-handed. It was one of those skills he'd perfected when he'd first gotten his driver's license—keeping his right arm free. In those days he'd always had a soft shoulder or breast to lay his palm on.

Bad Company's signature song blared from the Hummer's CD deck as Drew headed toward Opal's for breakfast. Hot air pumped through the space-age-looking heating and air vents, yet he kept the window rolled down. He hated to be closed in.

He drank coffee from an insulated cup, tapping his fingers on the leather steering wheel to the beat of the music.

An L.A. Dodgers ball cap rode backward on his head. His jaw hadn't been shaved for the past forty-eight hours, though he'd run his razor up his neck. Neck stubble was an annoyance. He felt comfortable in a pair of athletic sweats and a thick pullover shirt that had holes in the hem. It was his Sunday look, even though today was Tuesday.

The default ring on his cell chimed and he

snagged it, and just like he did each time, he made a mental note to change that stupid ringer.

"Tolman."

"Hey, babe."

"Hey, Jacquie."

"Are you at Opal's?"

"Heading there now."

"I'm in between clients. I'll meet you."

The line disconnected. Drew tossed the cell onto the black leather seat, the charger still plugged into it.

When Jacquie said she'd do something, she acted and it was a done deal. She was one of Red Duck's top producing real estate agents, and had been his on again-off again girlfriend for three years.

Right now, they were on again.

Jacquie Santini was an ethnic mix of Native American and Italian. Thin enough to fit sideways in a gym locker, she was five foot ten, with a thick mane of black hair that fell down her back and brushed the swell of her butt. What had gotten his attention when he first met her were her brown-black eyes and the dark brows above. They had this definitive arch to them as if she was raising them in a no-bullshit expression.

Appearancewise, she was more plastic than a Visa card, but she refused to have her boobs done since her nipples were her most sensitive body part and she didn't want to risk losing sensation for a pair of DD silicones. Her breasts weren't all that big, but he was okay with that. She loved sex, loved having sex with him. That worked.

When they broke up for short spans of time, it was because he usually did something to make her mad. Which he was known to do, and hell, it didn't take much. All he had to do was say something that set her off, and she was done. Yet somehow when they got around to talking it through, the talking part was mostly a facade and it was all about making up in bed.

He'd questioned himself why he'd kept her around for so long. He wasn't in love with her anymore. He had been at one time. He loved her now, but he wasn't *in love* with her. She was comfortable and they had good times. Both were from larger cities on the West Coast, he from L.A. and she from the Bay area.

Lately she'd been pushing to move in together. He'd been putting her off, changing the subject, but Jacquie could only be held off for so long before she knocked the hell out of his bachelorhood with an emotional curve ball. She'd start bawling.

Jacquie didn't cry very much, but when she did she might as well take a hunting knife to him. God, he hated when she cried. But it wasn't enough to make him change his mind and let her move in, or worse yet, get married.

Not now, not with Mackenzie being without her mother.

His seventeen-year-old daughter hated his guts,

and he didn't blame her. Up until six months ago, at her mother's funeral, he'd only seen Mackenzie a few times in her life.

He'd been back to Florida this past February for the Dodgers spring training camp—a combination business and personal trip, one he'd hoped would begin to change Mackenzie's mind about him. She'd let him take her to the ballpark, but Mackenzie had wanted nothing to do with him outside of nine innings worth of his company.

Cleaning up his forty-six-year old past, with one major screwup, was complicated.

Over the years, he had always kept that phone call from Caroline and the possibility of having a daughter in the back of his mind. He hadn't actually believed he was the father of her child, and he hadn't wanted to be trapped into something like that when his baseball career had just started to go places. He'd had phone calls like Caroline's before, so hers had been no different.

But Caroline Taylor had been different....

Not that he'd thought about that phone call very often, but some nights, when he'd been on the road with the team and lying in a hotel room, the possibility of him being a father had crossed his mind. Sometimes he'd pick up the phone to call Caroline, then cradle the receiver without ever dialing. He guessed he'd been afraid that it could be true. And if it had been, what was he supposed to do about it?

Caroline and her family lived in Kissimmee,

Florida, and he'd lived in Los Angeles during the off-season. How could he be a long-distance dad?

And then there were the years when his judgment had been clouded and he could barely take care of himself, much less a kid. In a selfish way, it had been easier to deny parentage rather than confront possible truths.

But today he was able to look at that rationale with sober clarity. Disgust filled his chest. What an ass he'd been.

Caroline had sent him pictures throughout the years, but Drew hadn't seen any resemblance. Yet he'd never thrown the photos away. He'd kept them all. In fact, several had been in his locker when he'd been with the Dodgers.

Memories surfaced and the coffee cup in Drew's hand felt cold. He didn't want to think about the call he'd gotten from Caroline when she told him Mackenzie saw his name on her birth certificate.

Pulling into the parking lot of Opal's Diner, Drew looked for an available spot, didn't see one, so cut a sharp turn and did what he usually did. He drove the Hummer up and over the curb, four-wheeled through the field and parked out back of Claws and Paws grooming.

Ada, the plump owner, walked a terrier who was doing its business on a fireweed bush.

Puckering her lips, she frowned. "Andrew Tolman, I told you I was going to call Sheriff Lewis the next time you illegally parked on my property."

"Only be a few minutes, Ada," he said, aiming the touch pad at the Hummer and locking it with a chirp. "When I'm done, I'll bring you over some of Opal's hot biscuits."

"I don't want any hot biscuits. I'm doing the South Beach diet and those carbs kill me."

"Sugar, you do not look like you need to lose a single pound."

Ada blushed, smiled shyly, then wrinkled her nose. "No, I'm not going to let you talk me out of it, Andrew. I'm calling the sheriff to have you towed as soon as Buster's done with his potty."

Buster had been leaving a little potty all along the back brush. The terrier was going to be awhile.

Winking, Drew added, "I'll get you some of her clover honey to go with."

"Now, Andrew. I mean it."

"Won't be but a minute, Ada."

He headed for Opal's, knowing pretty damn sure his Hummer would be there when he returned.

Two

Jacquie Santini was trying to give up cigarettes, but it was like asking her to give up sex. Her body just ran better on nicotine and orgasms.

The peppermint gum in her mouth was losing its flavor so she put the stale piece in a paper napkin, then replaced it with a fresh stick.

Drew hated sitting in the smoking section, and while it was killing her not to light up, she didn't feel like getting into anything with him today—except for his pants.

She sipped a glass of cold water with cracked ice and waited for Drew to show up.

Jacquie told herself she was every kind of pathetic to still be in love with him. She knew he wasn't in love with her anymore, but she just couldn't give him up. How she felt about Drew Tolman was the same way she felt about her best pair of shoes from Barney's. She still got a thrill out of feeling them against her skin. Besides, they were broken in and comfortable.

Reaching into her purse, Jacquie fingered the soft pack of Virginia Slims. If he didn't get here soon, she'd have to go out back and take a few drags just to settle down. Why her heartbeat still raced when she anticipated seeing him was amazing to her.

She was thirty-nine, going on forty next week. She considered herself reasonably attractive and knew she drew male attention. Lots of men in Timberline were interested and those wealthy Hollywood actors coming up to buy real estate had hit on her. She'd only made one slipup, and Drew hadn't found out about that. But what woman wouldn't have had sex with—

"Hey, baby." Drew slid into the booth across from her.

"Hey, Drew." Jacquie forgot about the cigarettes when she saw him. "You're looking good."

Most men didn't wear the scruffy look without coming off like pigs. While she preferred Drew in a dress shirt and slacks, the way he dressed when she took him to her real estate parties, she got an itch in her panties viewing him in his athletics.

The backward ball cap always cinched it for her. He looked every bit the ex-pro baseball player. A little arrogant, but very hot, very good-looking. Even the stubble didn't turn her off.

Slashes of dark brown brows framed his hazel eyes. There was something about those eyes. She could lose herself in them. The expression in those eyes was like that stinking puppy-dog effect. His appearance just begged a woman to lean in and lick his mouth with her tongue.

She wanted to do that now. She wanted him in her bed. She wanted to please him, make him love her again the way he used to.

Damn him.

Jacquie hated when she got like this. No man had ever made her lose her self-dignity, but Drew shook her up. Any woman in her right mind would have moved on to warmer sheets when she realized hers were only warm on her cue. When she thought about it, she'd been the one making passes at him lately. He no longer elicited sex from her. That irked and upset her.

She didn't think he was sleeping with anyone else. Then again, at night when she had insomnia, her mind ran wild. A few times, she'd thrown the covers off, gotten in her Jaguar and driven by Drew's house just to see if the Hummer was in the circular drive. It always was and that appeased her, but only for a short time.

The reality was, she was losing him.

And like a bad habit that a person's hung on to for so long, the very idea was like giving up her best friend.

Drew understood her. With him, she could be vulnerable and show him sides of her she'd never show in town or with others. To have to give up that comfort, to start over with someone else and to learn a new man's body and teach him how to do what she liked in an intimate situation...well, the effort was too great and she just didn't want to go there.

She liked the man she had now.

Opal brought over the coffee, topped off Jacquie's cup and poured one for Drew.

"Drew, you know anything about a backed-up sink?" Opal asked.

Jacquie gritted her teeth. Opal Harvey had to be a dozen years older than Drew, with Olive Oyl legs and peroxide-blond hair. A cigarette always dangled out of the corner of her mouth when she was in the fry kitchen, and she had learned to bark orders around it without a single cherry falling onto the grill. Why the owner had to always come out and wait on Drew personally agitated Jacquie no end. Holy Mary Mother of God. Didn't any woman in Red Duck or Timberline *not* find her boyfriend the best thing under the Christmas tree?

And what in the hell would Drew know about plumbing, anyway?

"No, sugar, I wouldn't know about a backed-up sink," Drew replied, pouring a healthy amount of cream into his coffee. "I'd call a plumber."

"I'll just do that. Good advice."

Rolling her eyes, her fingers rubbing together, craving a smoke between them, Jacquie decided Opal was a twit.

Good advice? Who wouldn't have said to call a plumber? Good Lord.

"Opal, I'm in a rush today." Jacquie piped up, tapping her shoe beneath the table before nudging the pointed tip up the leg of Drew's athletic pants. "Bring me a toasted bagel."

"What can I get for you, Drew?" Opal asked, her light blue eyes trained on him.

"Uh, let's see." He made a show of looking at the menu in the metal holder on the table. The menu's vinyl-coated surface had splatters of ketchup and sticky spots of syrup on it. Colorfully photographed meals on white plates appeared on the front and back, including breakfasts, which were served all day long. Little jelly tins and gooey bottles of flavored syrups sat in a rack by the menus, along with salt and pepper and Tabasco sauce.

"I'll go with a steak today along with the usual."

"Coming right up."

Opal practically ran to the kitchen to shake a leg.

Momentarily forgetting to watch her posture, which Jacquie usually made a habit of so her boobs wouldn't look smaller than they were, she plopped her chin on her hand and stared at Drew. He shrugged as if he didn't know shit.

He knew exactly how it was.

Everybody in town loved Drew Tolman. He was a star athlete, the man men looked up to and woman threw themselves at. It didn't matter that he'd left baseball in the middle of a season. Nobody, not even Jacquie, knew the real truth as to why. It had something to do with a big steroid scandal and him supposedly pumping up on the stuff, but whenever she'd got remotely close to prying, he switched the subject.

He leaned into the burgundy booth, put an arm over the back of it and stretched out real comfortable-like. Jacquie knew that beneath that old shirt was a smooth chest that just begged for a woman's palms to explore it. In the right light, every slab of sinew and muscle looked twice as defined. He had six-pack abs, a narrow waist and lean thighs that she just loved to straddle.

"So how's your day going?" he asked, leaning forward to clink a dishwasher-bent metal spoon in the chipped coffee cup.

Straightening, Jacquie thrust out her chest and smiled. "Great, thanks. What about yours?"

"Just starting. So far, so good. I'm heading over to the Little League field when I'm done here. Park and Rec said we were getting in some new equipment today and I want to check it out."

Drew lived for baseball. While he didn't play professionally anymore, he lived and breathed it, and, while she hated to admit it, she admired him for that. He had a passion. She understood that. She felt the same way about selling real estate. She got to go into homes she'd never see, list them for obscene prices, then watch the investment buyers line up and the money pour in. Not bad for a girl who started out her life in Cheyenne, Wyoming.

"When's the new season start?" she asked, not really caring, but wanting to be pleasant. She was hoping to get through this breakfast real quick, then take a spin over to her house for a ride on her bed.

"Next Wednesday."

"That's my birthday." She blurted out the reminder, then bit her tongue. Dammit, she wasn't going to mention it. A lady never dangled something like that in front of her man. He should know. It should be branded in his head. She wondered what he was going to get her. Last year he'd bought her hand-crafted jewelry that she really liked, and had taken her to Seattle for the weekend. Funny how that coincided with the Mariners game they went to. But she hadn't complained. She loved that crystal bracelet he'd got her from Sunshine's. Sunshine was a former hippy turned actress who'd retired from Hollywood and now sold one-of-a-kind things from her shop on Main Street.

"I know it's your birthday, babe." Drew drank his coffee and gazed at her over the rim. "You think I've got numb-chucks for a brain?"

"No." She slipped her shoe out of his pant leg when he didn't move to continue the game. This was getting harder and harder. She used to be able to seduce him without even trying.

She must have been pouting because he reached over, took her hand and kissed her fingers. "You look nice today."

That's all it took. She lit up inside like a Fourth of July display, and that got her through their breakfast with an optimistic smile that said they'd be having dessert at her place.

Opal cleared their plates, then topped off Drew's coffee. She went to do the same for hers, but Jacquie put her hand over the rim. "Opal, we need the check. We've got to get going."

Drew didn't say anything to the contrary. He pulled out his wallet, put his credit card on the table. Of all the days not to pay in cash. Now Opal would have to run the card.

"I got it, baby," Jacquie said, sliding the plastic back to him. "Business breakfast. Tax deduction."

She opened her purse, grabbed a couple of bills from her wallet and tossed them onto the table. Her butt was sliding across the crumb-dusted booth as she spoke. "I need your opinion on something at my house."

Drew didn't make a move to get up. "Yeah, what?"

"I'm hanging a new painting and I want you to tell me if you think it looks good over the fireplace."

"Hell, Jacquie, I don't know anything about decorating."

"Of course you do." She stood over him now, her hand reaching out to him. "You have an eye for everything. Your house is disgusting."

And she didn't mean that in a negative way. It was disgusting because the man had a knack for knowing just how to furnish and decorate without overdoing it. His home was made up of dark woods, four fireplaces and a kitchen that any gourmet would kill to have. And Drew could do a pretty good job of cooking, too.

The man was multifaceted, but completely irritating to her just this exact second. She was all but ripping her clothes off in front of him and he was dragging his feet.

"I can't stay long," he told her, acquiescing.

Bingo!

She didn't need a long time. He knew exactly what to do and he did it well.

As they headed for the door, Drew paused. "Forgot something."

From inside the kitchen, Opal's face appeared through the pass-through window. She was talking to one of the cooks, a lit cigarette wagging from the corner of her lipsticked mouth. Drew waved her over.

"Yes, Drew?" She all but panted, probably burned the rubber soles on her Keds to get to him so fast.

"I need you to bag up a dozen biscuits and throw in some of that special clover honey."

Hesitation marked Opal's heavily powdered face, her tomato-red lipstick glossy as if she'd just applied a fresh coat before crushing out her cigarette. "Now, Drew...if these are for Ada, she told me she's on South Beach and she can't eat them."

"Right. She mentioned that. So I'll tell you what, only bag up a half dozen."

Opal was appeased by the compromise, a broad smile breaking out on her face. "Now that's an excellent idea. I'll be right back."

Jacquie folded her arms beneath her breasts. Now she had to stand around and wait for biscuits. If she thought Drew would meet her at her house, she'd leave him and make a mad dash for her car to light up and smoke a quick one. But she knew from past experience that if she didn't hang on to him while she had him in her sights, somebody would come into Opal's, or wherever, start talking to him, and he'd get sidetracked at someone's table before he remembered where he was headed. And at that point, he'd blow off meeting her, knowing she'd be hot under the collar by then.

Sometimes Jacquie felt as if she couldn't win for losing, and the frustration was giving her early wrinkles.

Stepping in closer, she put her arm around Drew, gave him a hug and tried a different tactic. "You're so good to Ada to buy her biscuits. You know you burn her leather when you park on her property."

A lopsided grin caught on Drew's mouth. "Yeah, I know. But it's a love thing. She loves me. And I love her."

The way Drew could say he loved somebody so casual-like had Jacquie's arm slowly sliding down his strong and muscular back. Another fraction of an inch and she'd be disconnected from him. A part of her wanted to end this. Right now. She couldn't hang on for much longer. But every time she thought she had the courage, she thought about how much she'd already invested, and she hated to go back to square one.

The hideous truth was, Drew Tolman floated her boat. The man just did it for her…and at one time, she'd done it for him.

Maybe he didn't find her attractive enough anymore.

As she thought about booking a spa package in Timberline for the full works—facial, exfoliation, body wrap, manicure, pedicure and massage, the sleigh bells chimed over the diner's front door.

A woman and two boys came in. She had her hand on the youngest's shoulder, but when she tried to do likewise with the oldest, he shrugged away. The woman managed to keep her half smile, although it was looking a little broken.

Jacquie noticed other women. It was a project of sorts for her. Maybe eyeing competition in a town of three thousand just came naturally, she wasn't sure. Most of the time, she pegged a tourist right off the bat, and she'd swear that's what this woman was.

They walked past the cash register. Drew's nose was in the current copy of *Wood River County Homes and Land* magazine, a passing interest of his. He'd been talking about buying investment properties. She'd shown him a few things, but so far he hadn't done anything.

The little boy, maybe eleven or twelve—Jacquie couldn't be sure—looked intently at Drew. She'd never had kids and was no expert at figuring out how old they were, nor did she really care. The whole thought of kids… That subject was a bit touchy for her, anyway.

"Hey, mister, is that a Los Angeles Dodgers World Series cap?" he asked.

Drew tossed the magazine on the counter and turned. "Now, how'd you know that?"

"I seen the team emblem." He pointed. "Right there."

Taking off the hat, which was faded at the band by sweat, Drew held it out. "You want to see it?"

"Yeah!" The kid examined the hat every which way from Sunday, then hesitated, his hands shaking.

"You want to try it on?"

"Yes, sir!"

"G'ahead."

The kid put the hat on, turned to his mother and beamed. "Mom, it's a World Series hat."

"I see that."

Jacquie's attention refocused on the woman. She was very attractive, tall and with generous C-cup breasts. A natural beauty, something that had always eluded Jacquie, who relied on cosmetics to bring out the best of her features. This woman looked as if she only wore a tinted moisturizer, blackest-black mascara and champagne-colored lip gloss. Dangling silver earrings swept through her long hair when she turned her head.

The front of her coat was open. Her clothes weren't the latest style, but she carried them well for her body type, which was a cross between curvaceous and slender. A soft-stretch brown shirt with a V-neck and lower-rise jeans made her seem younger than she might have been. Jacquie could usually peg a woman's age. She wasn't sure now. Early forties?

"How'd you get this hat?" the boy was asking Drew, whose gaze had somehow gotten tangled up with the mother's.

A quickening fanned through Jacquie. She never got used to when this happened; it cut every time. Drew wasn't exactly a flirt; he didn't have to extend the effort. Women came to him. He liked the attention, but he wasn't a man-whore. He didn't sleep around, or at least not that she knew about, but his gaze had strayed on more than one occasion. Seeing him look at this woman, Jacquie didn't like the feelings erupting in her heart.

They went beyond jealousy. It was a primal fear. A deep and achy feeling that panicked her.

This was more than casual interest from Drew. And it was probably the first time Jacquie had seen him look at another woman like this.

His eyes grew hooded, sort of like that alpha-male dominant thing. The body language on him changed. He folded his arms, his chest grew broader, his smile seemed whiter and more disarming. The usual ease with which he carried himself appeared forced to her, as if he'd noticed something in this woman that he wanted to… Jacquie didn't know. Impress? Which was asinine, because Drew Tolman wanted to impress everyone.

"I got it when I played in the World Series."

"Oh wow—really?" The kid whooshed the words together, his mouth dropping open.

"Yep."

"What's your name?" The older one spoke up.

"Andrew Tolman."

The taller of the two boys was now interested. "You used to play for the Dodgers."

"Yes, I did."

"Awesome." The little boy looked up. "Mom, he's a real baseball player."

"Retired now," Drew said, just as Opal came toward them with the brown bag of biscuits, grease spots dotting the outside.

"Here are you go, Drew. I won't charge you for them since they're going to Ada, and she's going to kill me, anyhow. No point in taking money for my death."

Drew laughed, the sound rich and deep. "Thanks, Opal." Then to the boys, he said, "Do you both play baseball?"

"Yes, sir," the youngest said.

"Yeah, I played it in high school," the older one added.

"You on any leagues?"

"I was back home," the littler one declared.

"What's your name?" Drew asked.

"Matt. And that's my big brother, Jason." The younger boy took the woman's hand, brought her forward.

Jacquie watched carefully, making a fast mental note. She was a fairly good reader of people, since she worked closely with them on real estate transactions. She could pretty much ferret out most any situation. In this case, divorce. No question. The younger one wanted to be Mom's Helper, the man of the family. Jacquie couldn't quite peg the older boy. He had the look of a rebel in his eyes.

"And this is my mom," Matt stated.

Drew extended his hand. "Hi, Mom."

The woman blushed; Jacquie clenched her teeth.

"I'm Lucy. Lucy Carpenter." She took Drew's hand, gave it a polite shake, then retreated a step to stand with her sons. "We just moved here."

Just moved here. The information caused Jacquie's heart to miss a beat. This was no tourist. She was in town for the duration.

Shaking off a feeling of dread, Jacquie went on autopilot, took her card out of her purse and thrust her arm out. "I'm Jacquie Santini of Realty Professionals. If you need any assistance with anything, please don't hesitate to call me."

Lucy accepted the card. "That's a nice photo."

"Thank you." Jacquie felt guarded. She knew she wasn't all that photogenic, but the cards were top-notch. She'd spent a bundle on them.

Matt gave Drew his hat back. "Thanks."

"Sure thing." Drew settled the baseball cap on his head once more. "You guys need to try out for Little League. We're drafting players for teams next Wednesday."

He might have been talking to the boys, but his eyes were on Lucy.

Suddenly, Jacquie wasn't in the mood for sex anymore. She felt cheap for even trying to manipulate it. The biting heat of tears threatened, and in her mind, she swore every sailor curse she knew.

"Baby, I need to go meet my client now. The painting will have to wait."

Then, on an impulse, Jacquie threw her arms around Drew, kissed him soundly on the mouth, forcing herself not to linger and taste, to get her body revved up for nothing. The kiss wasn't for Drew's sake, or even her own. It was to show Lucy Carpenter this man was off-limits.

Jacquie stepped away from Drew and felt Lucy's gaze on her. She smiled an internal smile of smug satisfaction. Especially when she lowered her eyes to the fly of Drew's pants and saw that her little "goodbye" kiss had awakened him with a little "hello" that only she would notice.

"Well, it was nice meeting you," Lucy said, then took her two boys and guided them to a booth.

Walking outside, Jacquie found her Jaguar in the lot and took one last look at Drew, who was headed for his Hummer.

If she didn't love him so much, she would have cared that he walked away without saying much more to her other than he'd see her around, call her later.

Fingering a cigarette out of the soft pack, she lit up.

But she did love him, and damn if it didn't hurt like a bitch.

Journal of Mackenzie Taylor

I met Drew Tolman for the first time when I was twelve years old. Momma and I were sitting on the porch sipping Dixie Colas when a big, shiny car pulled up to our curb. She wasn't expecting him and she just about dropped the glass in her hand.

I remember him staring at me, then looking at Momma, then back at me and looking at me as if he wanted to turn me inside out, to have a better look.

I remember him saying he wanted Momma to take a test. She told him to go to hell.

I figured out something right then. If Drew Tolman was going to hell, I'd likely be going right after him. He was my kin, and I knew it.

I looked just like him, and the face in the mirror that stared at me every day finally made sense. We had the same muddy brown hair, the same hazel eyes, same mouth, and same skin color.

Before he came to see Momma that day, I knew his name was listed on my birth certificate.

I wanted to be his daughter, but he wasn't ready to be my daddy. I heard him tell Momma that he had to figure out what he was going to do, that he wasn't convinced on words alone.

Meeting him, I was convinced. I knew what he couldn't accept.

I didn't see him again until I was fourteen. By then, it was too late.

I didn't want to be his daughter anymore.

There are things about a person's biological composition that my teacher, Miss Oldenburg, says are genetics. You simply can't change what the good Lord gave us. Miss Oldenburg is of the theological theory, not Mr. Darwin's, when it comes to man's creation. I'm of the same mind.

Ever since I was a little girl, I liked playing softball. I don't know why I took to throwing a ball like that. I asked my momma and she said I was born to it. I never knew what she meant by that because my "daddy" was a long-haul truck driver and Momma didn't have an athletic bone in her body.

If only I hadn't found my birth certificate, Momma wouldn't have had to tell me the truth and I'd still be thinking Bobby Wilder was my daddy.

Before I knew he was my dad, I'd heard of Drew Tolman. When I was seven, Momma took me to Vero Beach to watch the Dodger's play a spring training game. After the last inning, she left me in the stands with my aunt Lynette and said to wait for her. Momma came back and I could tell she'd been crying. Her and Aunt Lynette spoke in quiet tones and I couldn't understand them. Momma never took me to Vero Beach again.

Now I know a little bit of what happened on that day. She told Drew she'd brought me with her and she wanted him to see me. He wouldn't do it.

What pain Momma must have felt....

If Bobby Wilder hadn't left Momma and me, things might have been different.

Bobby was nice to me and Momma for a time and I liked him. Then he took off one day and we never heard from him again.

After Bobby left, I decided to make

Momma a "feel better" card. She kept a big album of cutouts for scrapbooking. Pretty pictures from magazines. I looked in a book I thought had more clip outs, but it wasn't for scrapbooking. It had some records in it. Important documents.

And my birth certificate where I read "Andrew Tolman" for the Daddy part.

I called Momma up at work and told her she had to come home right away. She did and I asked her why she lied to me about my daddy.

She said she never wanted me to find out this way. She was going to tell me. One day.

I asked Momma if Bobby knew he wasn't my daddy and she said yes. I'm surprised Bobby went along with it for as long as he did. He wasn't a bad father, he just had his own set of troubles and he hated living in Florida. He drove trucks for a living and I heard Momma and Aunt Lynette talking that Bobby had a woman in Georgia who he'd been seeing on the side.

Aunt Lynette would say, "Now, Caroline, you always knew nobody could tame Bobby Wilder into the married life and you had him for ten years."

I don't know if Momma ever really

loved Bobby. I thought she did. And now I can't ask her. She's gone.

I miss my mother more than anything.

In February, when Drew came to Florida, I asked him two questions.

1. Why didn't you want to see me when I was seven?

2. Why did you quit baseball?

He answered both with the same one-word answer:

Stupid.

I'd agree:

Drew Tolman, you are stupid.

Three

Eighteen years of her life. That's how long Lucy was married to Gary, and the man left her for another woman.

It had been almost two years, and the burning reality still singed the skin right off her if she let the past fester. And sometimes she did.

Scrubbing the rust stains in the dingy porcelain sink, she thrust her best energy into the job, hoping to get the rejection out of her system. Sometimes it crept up on her, and she hated that feeling of helplessness, that weakness that made her doubt herself. She could tell herself Gary's leaving had nothing to do with her, but the honest truth was, Lucy still beat herself up over it at the most inopportune times.

Right now she was questioning this move. She'd thought it through with a lot of care before making the jump, so why this doubt was hitting her she couldn't exactly be sure. But it was there. And it wasn't going away no matter how hard she jerked a sponge with cleanser over the rust.

Her life was like this sink. Tarnished in some spots, but without chips. She had survived, intact and whole. Or as whole as she'd ever been.

Gary had been the love of her life, her high school sweetheart. They'd met in the tenth grade, dated through graduation, had a parting of ways, lived independently until they got back together and married in 1987. For the most part, her marriage had been wonderful. She'd been so happy, especially after she'd had the boys.

Her husband doted on them and was a good father. But then, as the years passed, and one or two of his business ventures began to fail, he lacked the confidence she'd once found so attractive in him. He began to stay out a little later, go into work a little earlier. Five years ago, he'd had his first affair, and it about killed her.

The boys never knew what happened, but the tension in the house was so thick it was like an insecticide bomb that began to choke the life out of her marriage. She and Gary went to counseling, got more involved in their church, and things seemed to smooth over.

But Lucy never fully forgave him for the affair. Even though he said it only happened the one time. He'd been at a nearby bar and just gotten uninhibited after a night of drinking. Since he'd never really been a drinking man, she believed his story.

Now she wasn't so sure.

Gary and the new woman Diane, lived a party lifestyle, always going out to clubs and bars, and then packing up and moving across the border—something Lucy was still suspicious about. Diane had plenty of money, so Gary didn't have to worry about business capital and ventures anymore. Nor was his income what it had once been, so Lucy's child support was practically nothing.

The state of Idaho based child support on an 80–20 custody arrangement, even though she had the boys one hundred percent of the time. It wasn't fair. Gary's $346.00 a month for two children didn't stretch far. By the time they were done paying off some credit card debt with the equity in their house, the asset balance didn't leave her much extra.

She'd taken every cent from the sale of the house and socked it away in the bank to tide herself over until she started getting some clients.

Falling into the personal chef field had been a fluke. One of her neighbors knew she liked to cook, and had asked Lucy if she could fix a meal for a party in her home. Lucy jumped on the opportunity, and it was a huge success. Word of mouth spread, and within six months Lucy had been cooking for nine families. The money wasn't rolling in, but it had kept her and the boys in the black, and she'd made ends meet.

She could have made a reasonable living in Boise if Jason hadn't taken a wrong turn. Maybe she was jumping the gun, but her son had changed when

Gary left, and she was worried about him. The marijuana in his locker and the other incidents were ones she looked at very seriously. She'd had to make a choice. Leave him in a city where he had memories of a father who'd disappeared, or take him out and start them fresh.

The latter seemed her best option.

She liked Red Duck and she hoped things would turn around. Before she made the decision to move, she'd consulted with the only personal chef in town to get his take on potential business.

Raul Nunez was firmly established and had a heavily booked clientele list. He had his hands full, but he'd fitted her into his schedule and had met her for coffee. He'd been very flamboyant, very over-the-top and extremely candid about how much he made and who he cooked for. She'd found his personality rather saccharine. Artificially sweet to the point that her teeth ached as she listened to him go on and on about himself. But clearly, he had a knack for business, and had more than he could keep up with.

Funny how he hadn't viewed her as a threat. She'd thought about it, and after the fact came to the conclusion he didn't think she'd give him a run for his money.

She was here to prove him wrong.

In the Timberline area, cooking in people's homes was like a fast-food drive-through to high schoolers at lunchtime. Many of the wealthy didn't want to fight reservation lines in the town's high-end restaurants when the tourist season was in full swing.

While she didn't have any clients lined up yet, she'd left flyers all around town and on the grocery store bulletin board. So far, she'd received two calls. One from a woman who wanted to know if she could make Raul's famous chicken adobo Friday night because Raul was already booked. And another asking her if she knew where Raul was, he wasn't picking up his cell.

Certainly not the most promising leads, but while she'd had them captive, she'd mentioned she was available Friday night and made a delicious tuna Cozumel and beefsteaks with mustard-herb rub.

No takers. Not yet, anyway. She'd get them. She knew it only took one client to put the word out.

"Mom, where's my skateboard?" Matt asked, standing in the living room surrounded by boxes.

She smiled at him. Her boy. He went with the flow, adapted easily, and he had such a good heart in him. Shaggy brown hair fell over his brows and he had a smattering of freckles on his face. He wore a pair of Levi's and skater shoes, his T-shirt front dirty with the purple juice of a Popsicle he'd eaten after dinner.

"I'm not sure, honey. Try the porch."

"That porch freaks me out. Is it going to fall down?"

"I hope not."

The inside of the house was just as bad as the outside, and now that she was in the midst of it, Lucy could easily become overwhelmed. She hadn't wanted to move in much of their furniture until she got things cleaned up.

Calling her rental a house wasn't exactly accurate. It was more like a shack on the outskirts of a subdivision, but she tried to make it sound like an adventure to the boys. Matthew was young enough that he bought into it; Jason thought she was being lame.

The front room had a thick log pole in the middle to support the second-story loft, which was one large area—enough space for two twin beds and dressers. A balcony was attached to the loft so the boys could step outside and view the stars. The downstairs was comprised of a living room, kitchen, master bedroom and the only bathroom. The walls were in bad shape and needed paint. The pan on the hot water heater showed signs of rust, and when she turned the kitchen faucet on, the pipes reverberated through the wall of missing tile on the backsplash.

They had a wood-burning stove situated on cinder blocks, and it looked to be in decent shape. Bud had left firewood inside, as well as a woodpile toppling over at the side of the house. It would come in handy this winter. The floor planks were rough-hewn and, in spots, uneven. She'd have to figure out how to make the sofa not wobble once she brought it in.

In the bedroom, her girlie vanity appeared out of place beneath the elk head hanging on the wall. She didn't have a ladder or else she would have taken it down.

But overall, the house wasn't as dire as Jason had made it out to be when they were eating lunch today at Opal's.

Lucy just hoped and prayed Jason would adjust and fit in. She wanted more than anything for her oldest son to rebuild his life after Gary. She'd had Jason in family counseling with her and Matt, but it hadn't helped. People only got from counseling what they put in, and Jason had just sat on the chair and didn't say a whole lot. He was filled with rage. She knew it, she sensed it. She didn't think he'd do anything stupid, but she knew it stemmed from a deep-rooted hurt.

And the irony was—she, more than anyone else, understood. Because that's how she'd felt about Gary's leaving—but Jason couldn't see through his own pain to reach out to her.

Patience, Lucy kept telling herself.

Patience and love.

She was here for her boys. She tried to remain upbeat and optimistic, even when she heard the crash outside.

Wiping her wet hands down the front of her shirt, Lucy ran out the front door.

Matt stood on the edge of the porch, his hands over his head to ward off something falling.

"What happened?" She made her way quickly to him.

He silently pointed.

The support post lay in the front yard, and the

porch above him sloped dangerously low. Yanking him out of the way, she brought him toward the entry.

Jason filled the screen door, hands on the frame. He had that annoyed look on his face—the one that sometimes reminded her of Gary. She wanted to smack it away, but of course, she refrained.

With Matt safely tucked next to the cabin, Lucy went into the yard. "Jason, come out here and help me prop the post back up so the porch doesn't fall down."

They managed to get the post shoved back into position and as secure as she could wedge it for now. She'd have to tell Bud about it, or maybe get out her tools and try and fix it herself, since he already knew about it, and the deal was she was getting this place "as is."

"What'd you do, you idiot?" Jason barked at his brother.

"Nuttin'! I just leaned on it looking for my skateboard."

"It's in our crap for a room."

"Jason, that's no way to talk," Lucy exclaimed, reprimanding him.

Jason's hair fell past his T-shirt collar. He glanced at her before stuffing his hands into his pockets, but didn't apologize.

"Excuse me?" she said, waiting.

"Sorry," he mumbled. Then, as if the hostility of the world were on his shoulders, he blurted in a snappish tone, "But Matt was being a butthead to lean on the porch. This stink-hole place sucks the big one. I hate it here."

Inhaling, Lucy counted to three. She knew if she spoke the first thoughts that came to mind, she'd regret it.

A moment later, and calmer now, she said, "Jason, I'm sorry you don't like that we moved, but it was for the best, and I'm sure once we get settled in and you meet some friends, you'll enjoy the change of pace."

"No, I won't. We don't even have an Internet connection."

That was true. The house was wired with an old, three-prong telephone system. Corded phones were anchored in the kitchen, master bedroom and even the bathroom. They weren't connected. Thank goodness for cell phones. Maybe she'd have to get one for Jason. She'd been meaning to do so in Boise, but then he'd crashed his pickup. The insurance settlement should be in the mail soon, but it wasn't much, since the truck had been a beater. At least she'd be able to replace the truck with something else, and he could drive Matt to school in the fall when she was working. But she was reluctant to get him a cell phone because that only meant he could tell her he was one place when he was at another. She'd have to have a land-line rule. He'd have to call from the place he was at when he checked in with her.

"Well, maybe I can see about having the house

updated so we can hook up the computer." She knew that was unlikely, but she wasn't in the mood to get into it with her son.

It had been a long day. She was exhausted. The last thing she needed was to end her night with a confrontation.

But Jason knew just how to push her buttons sometimes, and he didn't let up.

"No, you won't. You're just saying that so I'll get off your back." He picked up a rock in the yard—if you could call the span of gravel and rickety carport a yard—and threw it into the bushes. "You never follow through except when it's to your advantage."

Gritting her teeth, Lucy stood there. When he was little, she would have given him a spanking. Tears burned the backs of her eyelids. When he was little, he would never have talked to her this way. Her sweet baby boy had changed when he hit puberty, and he'd gotten worse, so much worse, after Gary left.

Damn Gary. Damn him to hell and back for doing this to them, to their sons. The man was an insensitive jerk, a loser with a bimbo for a girlfriend. He never saw his kids, never took them for pizza, or a sleepover, or any of the things a father should do.

Lucy knew if she stayed here, she'd lose it. She'd snap at her son and things would only get worse. Rather than say another word, she marched into the house, grabbed her purse and keys and went back outside.

Jason's attitude put her in a mood that made her fight to stay sane. He was just so *angry* at the world and he wore her thin at times.

Matthew followed after her. "Where ya going, Mom?"

"To the grocery. I'm all out of cleanser."

"I wanna come, too."

She opened the car door, realizing she'd forgotten her coat and it was cold outside. Not taking the time to go back in and get it, she slid onto the seat. "No, you have to stay here."

"I don't want to. He's being a brat," Matt said, talking through the open window.

"Jason, you go upstairs and unpack those boxes in your room. I want it done by the time I get back. And don't you go picking on your little brother or else you'll be sorry."

Without a word, Jason stormed into the house. Matt stayed in the yard as she put the car in Reverse. His chin lowered a notch to his chest.

The tears she'd been forcing back threatened to fall as she watched her youngest son in the rearview mirror. He sat on the steps of the porch and dropped his chin in his hands. She should have taken him with her, but she needed some alone time.

Guilt assailed her. She had to be there 24/7 for her boys, but there were times when she just couldn't do it all. She was only one person, and if she didn't have a moment to herself, she wasn't any good to any of them.

When she turned the corner, a thicket of pines blocked her view. The road had a patch of dirt from the river wash, and the front-wheel-drive Passat forged over the rough spot. She wiped her cheek with her fingertips, then switched on the heater.

If she hadn't left her cell phone at home, she would have called her mother. Her parents lived in Sun Lakes, Arizona, and visited only during the warm seasons. They hated the cold winters in Idaho.

When Dad had retired from the telephone company, they'd moved from Boise to Arizona. It about killed Lucy to lose them, and it was the same for her parents, but they'd lived all their lives in Idaho, and now it was their turn to do what they wanted. Lucy didn't think they'd ever fully moved past the death of her older brother; he'd drowned in an irrigation canal when he was four years old. Idaho was only a sore reminder to Mom and Dad.

Lucy drove past the High Country Motel, its lot filled with four-wheel drives. Bud had mentioned that was the place to trade gossip in town. With all those vehicles taking up spots, something good must have happened. For a moment, Lucy was vaguely curious. Then again, anything in a town like this could be made into something big just for the sake of conversation.

Sutter's Gourmet Grocery came into view and she circled the block, still getting used to the parking setup. There were some empty spots down the middle of the low-traffic block, but she had to make sure she wasn't facing the wrong direction.

Snagging her purse, she crossed her arms over herself to ward off the cold air of dusk. Inside Sutter's, she was met by the aromas of soups in the deli section. Lentil among them, if she guessed right. She loved this grocery store. It was intimate, quaint and it lacked for nothing. The prices were on the steep side, though. No supersaver chains in Red Duck.

Near the entrance was the floral area, and the sweet fragrance of roses mingled with the heavenly scents of the soup. A newspaper rack lined the wall, along with the latest paperbacks.

She'd already been here once today, purchasing a few things for the house: toilet paper, milk and bread. The boys had wanted candy—and she'd given in. A box of Popsicles, cereal, and the cold cuts they'd eaten for dinner tonight.

Lucy could get lost in this store. She walked the aisles once more, taking in all the products, her mind working on special menus for special occasions. The place had a fabulous import section, from minicorns to oils and olives. The deli made nice appetizers.

Wandering toward the espresso bar, Lucy checked the glass-fronted bulletin board to make sure her notice was still up. It was. Now if only her phone would ring off the hook. And with calls for *her*, not Raul Nunez.

The fact that people would actually call her looking for him, or to ask her if she had his recipe…it made her reconsider the man's influence in town. He had more than she'd realized. During their meeting, he'd been arrogant, but friendly. In hindsight, maybe too friendly, as if he knew something and she didn't.

Shrugging, she found herself gravitating toward the meat case. It was extensive, with a vast array of fresh seafood. Her boys were such picky eaters, they wouldn't touch a filet of salmon or a halibut steak. They wanted fish sticks.

Cooking for the three of them, she was limited in what she served. When she was married to Gary, he'd loved her cooking, couldn't eat enough of it, and she could get real creative at home. The boys grumbled, so oftentimes she'd made them a grilled cheese sandwich on the side.

She wished she had someone at home who would appreciate her efforts. But as soon as she thought about it, she envisioned a man at the table. Where that thought came from, she couldn't guess. She hadn't gone out on a date since her divorce had been finalized. It wasn't as if she hadn't been asked. She had. She just hadn't been ready. Bitterness didn't go well with a glass of wine or a movie.

But lately, she'd contemplated going out on a trial run. Nothing daunting, where she'd be stuck for hours. Coffee, maybe. But then Jason got into trouble at school and her idea about dating changed. She had to focus on her son rather than some romance that would probably go nowhere anyway.

Checking out the help-yourself seafood baskets of

mussels and steamer claims, Lucy was lost in thought and didn't readily hear her name being called.

"Lucy. It was Lucy, right?"

Her chin lifted and she stared into Drew Tolman's face. She took a step back. The man was so tall, he filled her view and then some as she gazed at him.

When she'd first seen him in Opal's Diner, his good looks had definitely gotten her attention—until it became quite clear he was a hard-core charmer even though he was taken. That brunette he was with had laid one on him and clearly stamped his mouth as her private territory.

If it weren't for the fact she needed Jason to play Little League, Lucy wouldn't have given Drew another thought. But it was important her son be involved with sports right now, and unfortunately, Drew was the coach.

Gazing at him, she willed the wayward lustful thoughts out of her head immediately. Although with her standing this close to him, a few snuck back.

He was gorgeous…simply gorgeous.

The way his hair was mussed gave him a casual air that suited him. He still wore the sweats and Sunday-worn shirt he'd had on earlier. The ball cap was missing, which attested to the messy hair. But he still looked good. Too good.

And he knew it in a nonconceited way.

She'd come across his type before. Jock men who just thought they were too fabulous for words. Every woman under one hundred would throw herself at them if they held their arms open wide. And Lucy was sure this man had held his arms open for quite a few ladies.

A former professional baseball player. She read magazines and all those tabloids. These guys usually had women in every state.

What was he doing in Red Duck, Idaho, of all places? She may have wondered, but she wasn't going to ask him. She didn't want to get personal with the man.

"You're right," she finally replied. Then she said something so stupid, even she cringed. "You're Drew and your girlfriend's name was Jacquie."

So much for staying impersonal.

For a scant second she wondered if he was going to counter her claim about the girlfriend. Call it a woman's intuition, but suddenly Lucy recognized there was trouble in paradise for that couple.

Not that it was her business—nor did she care.

Thankfully, he let the comment pass. "So, how are you liking town so far?"

"I like it. It's different than Boise, but a good different. I'll be glad to get settled in."

"Where are you living?"

She paused, not sure if she should answer that. In Boise, she would have given a cross street as a general response. In Red Duck, when everyone proclaimed to know everyone's business, chances were that Drew could easily find out.

"Lost River Road," she said simply.

"Nice area."

Some of it was. Their teardown was in an off-shoot of a ritzy neighborhood a half mile away. Surrounding them was an overgrown horse pasture and rickety farm, with no sidewalks for skateboards. Bud kept a bunch of old Airstream coaches and dusty RVs on the adjacent property. It was surely no white picket fence scene. No wonder the boys were embarrassed. The idea of Drew seeing where she lived wasn't one she wanted to imagine.

"Doing some shopping?" he asked.

He held a handbasket with a thick steak, big russet potato and a bag of spring mix inside. His soft leather, black wallet and key fob were tossed inside. Her hands were empty.

"Actually, I just needed a break from unpacking. And I wanted to see if my notice was still up."

"Notice for what?"

"I'm a personal chef."

His stance changed and he grinned. "I like anything personal."

The big flirt. A real player, and not just at bat. Lucy held on to a frown. "It's nothing like you're thinking…whatever it was you were thinking."

"I only said I like things personal."

She opened her mouth to add something, then snapped it shut. If she had banter experience, she would have been more apt to have a fast comeback. As it was, she floundered, but quickly willed herself to regroup. "I cook for people in their homes."

"I know what a personal chef is. Raul Nunez cooks for me sometimes."

Lucy bit the inside of her lip. Who *didn't* Raul cook for?

"Well, if you know of anyone who'd like my services, it would be great if you could mention my advertisement, which will be in this Wednesday's newspaper, or the bulletin board here."

His posture was casual, his fingers hooked loosely around the basket's metal handle. "I can do that. What's your specialty?"

The way he said it had her questioning his intentions. He was playing around with her now that the shark girlfriend wasn't next to him! Lucy fought against rolling her eyes.

"I don't have any one specialty," she said, not taking his bait if he meant to lead her into any kind of sexual innuendo.

She was so rusty in this department, she wasn't sure if she was coming or going. He knew the game and she didn't have a clue to the rules. She didn't like this.

He smiled and her heartbeat snagged. "Maybe I'll have to tell Raul I've hired you."

The prospect both excited and dismayed her. She needed the business, but... Working for this man would be a challenge at best. He was way too confident and laidback about his presence. He had to know good and well what effect he had on women. My goodness, she'd seen Opal practically jump out of her panty hose to please him with those biscuits.

A man like Drew got whatever he wanted. It was a given. He just had to smile and he received.

Lucy opted to let his suggestion go. If he were serious, he could give her a call.

"So are you divorced?" he asked, the question taking her by surprise. He didn't stand on ceremony, and she wasn't sure if she liked his approach or not.

"That obvious?"

"No wedding ring, but that doesn't mean diddly these days."

"Yes, I'm divorced. And you?" She hated that she asked, but the question was on the table before she could shelf it.

"Never married."

Bad news. A man his age who'd never married wouldn't know how to spell the word *compromise*.

Perhaps his lack of matrimonial commitment was what caused that blank expression that suddenly appeared on his face. Maybe. Maybe not. But he did seem a little bothered by the status or, at the very least, self-conscious about it.

His broad shoulders captured her attention when he shifted his stance again. "How old are your sons?"

"Twelve and sixteen."

"Tryouts for summer Little League will be at the Park and Rec field by Wood Creek."

"I'll have them there." She'd always been an advocate of sports for her boys, and thankfully, they enjoyed participating. It kept them out of trouble, for the most part, and centered their focus on a team activity.

"If he makes the cut, I'll be coaching Jason's team."

"He'll make it." Lucy's conviction was steady. "He's good."

Drew nodded. "When he registers for school, make sure you get him on the high school team, too. We practice before the fall semester starts, so he'll have to be there in August."

"How could I find out more information?"

Drew set the basket on the end display of gourmet coffee, reached for his wallet, then handed her a card. "Give me a call."

An indecisive arch lifted Lucy's brows. She didn't call men, but she guessed she'd have to make an exception. For the boys. Only for the boys.

The card was straightforward. Bold. Masculine. The type set blocky.

Andrew Tolman
Little League Coach and H.S. Athletic
Director
Wood Ridge Team and Red Duck
School District
P. O. Box 935
Timberline, Idaho 83691
Cell: 208-555-9452

"Call me anytime. I'll make sure you're sent the paperwork to have him play for Timberline High." Drew tossed his wallet back into the basket, then added, "I'll need your phone number."

Lucy blurted, "What for?" Images of an indignant Jacquie Santini scratching her eyes out came into Lucy's mind, yet for some idiotic reason, she lost her head and wished he wanted her phone number to ask her out on a date. *Stupid!*

Drew gave her that crooked smile of his. "How can I refer clients to you if they can't call you?"

Flustered, she changed her posture and took back control. She was being an idiot, and just as ridiculous as Opal and her fast breathing at the diner. Even knowing she'd momentarily lost her common sense, Lucy staved off an untimely blush.

She recited her cell number—which was a moot point. It was on her business card, which was on the grocery store bulletin board.

"Okay," he replied.

"You don't need to write it down?" She didn't know why she asked him that. She told herself she wanted to make sure he got it right so she could get the referrals.

Biting back a groan, Lucy wanted to just crawl into one of the mussels and close the shell on herself. She was so out of practice in the art of male-and-female conversations, she called herself every kind of pathetic. Why was she letting this guy get to her? He was bad news.

"You think because I'm a jock I don't have a memory?" he asked, but he did so with humor.

"Uh, no. I just…well, my memory's not what it used to be the older I get. So I just…well, I'm sure you'll remember it."

"I'll never forget it."

The self-assured way in which he spoke evoked shivers through her that she prayed like crazy he wouldn't notice.

"How old are you?" he asked, breaking through her musings.

Recovering, Lucy had no problem in this department. "Forty-five. And I've earned every wrinkle and dimple."

And that was the God's honest truth. She was proud of being forty-five, and actually, she thought she looked better at this age than when she'd been in her thirties. She was at a time in her life when she felt free enough to speak her mind, was secure enough in her looks not to apologize for anything a younger woman may have that she didn't, and she was darn well a lot smarter.

"You don't look forty-five," he responded, giving her a smile that was genuinely complimentary.

Why his flattery made her feel so alive was a mystery. One she didn't want to explore. But she couldn't stop herself from asking, "How old are you?"

"Forty-six. My joints are a little stiff on a cold morning, but if you ever repeat that to anyone, I'll say you're full of shit."

The fact that he could reveal a truth like that and curse at the same time both fascinated and annoyed her. She liked to pride herself on keeping her language clean. There were times when a word slipped out and she rued it, but sometimes nothing better sufficed.

It seemed as if they'd run the gamut of small talk, and Lucy had nothing further to say. She suddenly felt awkward.

"Well...I need to get going." She stepped away, and yet she couldn't tear her eyes from his. They were a compelling hazel that just made her want to melt.

Why, of all the men she'd encountered since her divorce, did this one have to pique her interest? That Jacquie would tear her hair out from the roots if she suspected Lucy was remotely interested.

And besides, a man like Drew was the very last type she'd ever pick for herself. She wanted someone stable and family oriented. A hard worker. Someone who'd be her life partner, who'd rub her feet after a long day and watch a movie with her. In turn, she'd fix him candlelight dinners, put on sexy lingerie and...

Lucy felt her nipples harden and a tingle catch hold of her between her legs. Her plain panties felt tighter, more constricting. She blushed, backed away farther and put a hand out to steady herself, on a display of Idaho wines.

And what did Drew do about that?

He gave her a half grin, walked toward her and took the bottle right out of her hand.

"Good choice. I'll add it to my wine rack." Dropping the bottle in his basket, he drawled, "See you around, sugar."

Lucy couldn't find the words to reply. She stood there like a lump and watched him retreat, her gaze sliding down to his behind. The man had a firm butt like nobody's business.

Blinking, Lucy straightened her posture, waited a moment until she was sure he'd gone through the checkout, then dashed to her car and turned the engine over.

Going past the High County Motel's lounge, she wondered how many stories of Drew Tolman had been traded inside.

Lots and lots…or so she thought.

A man like him would most definitely be the talk of this small town. She didn't even want to know the half of it.

Four

Dean Martin sang for one night at the High Country Motel's Celebration Lounge. He'd been vacationing in Timberline without any of the Rat Pack, was feeling no pain, and ended up taking the mike right out of Burt Gunderson's hands.

Burt had been leaning in to croon a love song to Spin Goodey-Leonard. Sitting straight on the studded leather seat, Spin had been half into her third martini when Dean's face suddenly came into her view. She'd pushed her rhinestone-rimmed eyeglasses up her nose and focused on him, thought he was dreamy and grabbed his crotch.

It was the last time Spin ever got drunk.

The legend of Dino's solo that night was retold for many years, and to this day, every once in a while, it surfaced. And always with a more snappy ending. Sometimes Spin and Dino checked into room 69 for some sixty-nine action. Other times, Spin and Dino ran off to Lost Wages and had a secret wedding ceremony—performed by an Elvis impersonator, no less. Once, someone guaranteed that Spin had Dino's love child. None of it was true, but the story made good entertainment when gossip fell short in Red Duck.

Which, on this particular night, it did not.

Lucy Carpenter's name floated off the lounge walls, along with the mirrored reflections from the disco ball.

Sheriff Roger Lewis wanted to know more about her, and had just come in, off duty, to sniff out information. Opal Harvey smoked unfiltered cigarettes at the bar, sitting alongside Bud Tremore, who wore a lumberjack's red flannel shirt.

The sheriff smirked, headed toward the duo and thought to himself, *Yahtzee!* Just the two people who'd know about Ms. Boy-Zee Carpenter.

Roger had run a little check on her, wanted to see if she had any priors. Nothing. Her record was clean as a whistle. But still, Roger always did a double-detail.

"Bud," he said, sliding onto the stool next to him. "How's it going?"

"Good, Roger, and yourself?" Bud Tremore's middle filled out beyond the cinch of his belt, but he wasn't portly. Just big. His bald head shone and his shoulders were broad as a barrel. Bud was a decent guy. Straight up. Good citizen.

"Not too bad." Roger touched the brim of his felt hat. "Opal, how're you this evening?"

"Sheriff, some some-bitch jimmied the lock to the back of my diner. They didn't get in, but I'm telling you, they tried." Her red lipstick was creased on her full lips. "I told Clyde about it, but he said there was nothing he could do. This town—it's getting out of control."

Roger ground his back teeth until they ached. Opal could be sweet as apple pie to Drew Tolman, and snippy as cuss to him. Truth be told, Roger once had a thing for Opal, but he'd never let her in on it. She'd been involved with someone else at the time, and when that pooped out, Roger had just met a gal up from Provo and the two of them did a little spooning. But that ended last year.

"Clyde told me, Opal. I'll come on by your place tomorrow to check it out."

"I'd appreciate that." Opal sipped on a ginger ale, its bubbles fizzing to the top.

Settling in, Roger asked, "So, Bud, what's up with this Lucy Carpenter renting out at your place?"

"She needed something and she talked me into it. That teardown's just been sitting. It falls under subdivision covenants now, but it used to be zoned for commercial. I've got more restrictions on selling it than the trouble it's worth. I hate bureaucratic paperwork. She said she didn't care what condition it was in."

"Did you run her credit?"

Bud scratched his jaw. "No."

"Why not?"

"No need. She paid me a check on the spot."

"How did you know if it would bounce or not?"

"Didn't." Bud took a chug of beer, a crescent of foam staying on his upper lip. "But look at her. She's got the nicest face of any woman coming into town these days. Who wouldn't trust her?"

Roger frowned. "Opal, she say anything to you when she came into the diner the other day?"

"No, Roger. She just talked to Drew a short time while he was waiting on me to get Ada some biscuits."

"I thought Ada was on South Beach."

"She is. Doesn't look like she's lost a pound, but if you tell her I said that, I'll say you're a damn liar."

"So what's this Lucy Carpenter's business in town?" Roger grabbed a handful of Spanish peanuts and let them trickle into his open mouth.

"Cooking," Bud replied, nudging his chin a little higher to rid himself of its double sag. "She cooks for people. You know—like Raul Nunez."

"Raul makes a mean scalloped corn deluxe. He won't give me the recipe." Opal crushed her cigarette.

"He still cooking for that actress—what the hell's her name?" Roger's mind drew a blank, and he swore at the senility of old age setting in, even though he was barely a day over fifty-five. "That one who did the movie with Tom Cruise."

"Yep, he does," Bud said. "She's still in town for the summer. I seen her Mercedes at the yoga studio the other day."

"You think this Lucy'll give Raul a run for it?" Opal lit another cigarette, blew the smoke away from the men.

"I hate to say it, but she has spunk," Roger commented, then let his thoughts wander as he ordered a drink.

Time would tell what Lucy Carpenter would contribute to Red Duck—and if that boy of hers would get himself into any trouble.

The rest of the night was spent debating who served the best burger in town, Woolly's or the Mule Shoe. That ran its course at ten forty-nine, and then the conversation drifted to who might still be playing poker at the barbershop.

It was just another night in the High Country lounge.

Five

Matt walked down Main Street with his big brother. They'd gotten up early, had breakfast and helped move furniture, and now Mom was using their computer for work. She had to print out her cooking stuff for some people. She said he and Jason could check out the main part of town—as long as they were back in an hour.

Matt didn't see much wrong with living in Red Duck. He had a few friends back in Boise, but he never really had a best friend like he'd had in the first grade. Tommy Olsen moved away in the fourth grade, and Matt hadn't played with anybody else who thought it was funny to squish the guts out of night crawlers under the tires of a Tonka truck.

Shading his eyes against the afternoon sun, Jason stopped to look at a group of boys across the street.

"Jason, come on."

"Yeah, I'm coming." His brother pushed ahead,

his hair sticking up at his forehead. He'd put some jelly stuff in it today to make it spike.

Matt stepped inside a comic book store and Jason followed.

Jason didn't read them anymore, he'd only come along to get away from the house. Matt glanced at the rack. "Look at all these."

"Yeah, I see 'em." But Jason was staring out the door.

"Jason, come here." Matt didn't like the feeling he got, and he worried his brother thought about doing something dumb right now.

"I'll be right back." Jason was walking outside.

"But—"

"I'm just going across the street for a second."

"Only a second?"

"Don't have a cow—I said I'll be right back."

Stepping off the curb, Jason stuffed his hands into his jeans pockets and slumped his shoulders. Matt stayed in the doorway and watched his older brother talk to the boys. Jason thought he was hot stuff, but he wasn't. He wasn't anybody important in Red Duck. In Boise, other kids thought he was cool.

One of the boys lit a cigarette and Matt watched his older brother take a puff. Stupid. Mom was going to find out.

"Can I help you find something?" a man's voice asked.

Matt turned around and saw a bald guy smiling down at him.

"Uh, no, sir. I was just looking at the comics."

Matt took one, flipped the pages, then skimmed through a few others until he got lost in one. When he finally glanced back to the street, Jason and the boys were gone.

Matt racked the comic book and stepped outside. He passed a sandwich shop, then read a sign that said the Mule Shoe Bar. The tall and narrow windows on either side of the door were too dark to see through. Matt cupped his hands around his eyes and looked inside a few of the other shops. His brother wasn't in any of them.

Wandering around the corner, Matt tried not to worry. If he stuck around here, Jason would have to show up.

He saw a funny-looking lady walking a dog. She had one pink curler in her hair right on the back of her head. Her hair was gray, and she was like the dough boy on TV—plump and looking like her clothes were too tight. She had a happy face, though. She reminded him of his music teacher.

The dog she was walking was really cool. He was big and black and he kept pulling her down the street toward a fire hydrant.

"Hey, boy," Matt said, getting closer to the dog. Then, looking at the dough lady, he asked, "Can I pet him?"

"If you can make him stand still."

The dog's tail was wagging so hard his butt was shaking. Matt reached down to pet him, and his hand got slimed with dog tongue and spit as he licked.

Matt giggled when the dog piddled on the sidewalk.

"He's just a big puppy," the lady said. "I've got to get back to my shop, and Harley is being uncooperative."

"His name's Harley?"

"Actually, I call him the Devil Dog, because he doesn't mind me."

"He's your dog?"

"No, I'm just grooming him."

"I think it would be fun to wash dogs."

"Not so much fun as it is wet." She smiled at him. "What's your name?"

"Matt Carpenter."

"Do you live here?"

"Yes, ma'am."

"So polite!" Her face lit up as her arm jerked and Harley went to sniff the hydrant. He didn't lift his leg. He just stood there.

"Would you like to see if you can get him to piddle for me?"

Matt took the leash and talked to Harley.

The lady said, "My name's Ada. See that building right there?" She pointed a half block away to a shop that had an awning on it with dogs and cats painted on the ruffle.

"Yep."

"After he goes potty, walk him back to my shop."

She left, and Matt walked Harley up and down the street. He finally half lifted his leg on the drugstore's shopping cart return. He also decided to do something else, right on the sidewalk crack, and Matt just stared at it, wondering what he should do about the poop.

He decided to forget about what he saw, and walked fast back to Ada's dog place. Inside, she smiled at him and took the leash. "Did Harley go?"

"Yes, ma'am."

"Such a good boy!"

At first, Matt thought she was talking to him.

"And thank you, Matt, for your help." Her pudgy index finger pressed a key on the cash register. The drawer shot open and he could see money in there. She gave him a dollar.

"Thank you." He was really happy about that dollar. He could go buy one of the comics.

"Do you have a summer job?" Ada asked.

"No, ma'am."

"Would you like to work here and help me if your mother says it's okay? You do have a mother, don't you?"

"How do you think I was born?" he responded.

Ada laughed so hard, her big chest was jiggly. "Oh, you are just so precious. I mean, I'd need to check with your mother first to make sure it was all right." She shoved a business card at him. "Have her call me and we'll work out the arrangements."

Dogs were barking in the back, and Ada made a noise with her tongue and teeth, put her hands on her hips and called, "Coco, if you did a doo-doo in your cage…" And then Ada disappeared.

Matt shoved the dollar into his pants pocket.

Jason was inside the comic book store, scowling, when he returned. "Hey, where've you been?"

Happy to see his brother, and filled with relief, Matt forgot to be mad at him. "Where'd you go?"

"Nowhere." Jason was acting strange. He kept trying to stop himself from laughing, but he couldn't, so he laughed through his closed lips until they opened and spread into a big smile. There was nothing to laugh at. "You better tell Mom we were with each other the whole time. Okay?"

Nodding, Matt swallowed hard.

He didn't like to lie to Mom, but if she knew what had happened, she'd get real upset.

Matt suggested, "We better walk outside for a while, then go back home."

"I want to look at comics," Jason said, snickering.

"No, Jason." Matt caught the sleeve of his brother's coat and dragged him away from the rack. "You gotta walk outside for a while so you don't smell funny no more by the time we get home."

Six

Drew made eight o'clock dinner reservations at Indigo in the Timberline Lodge for Jacquie's birthday. After tryouts, he'd have enough time to leave the baseball field, go home, shower and put on a dress shirt and slacks. Given the uneasy state of their relationship lately, he hadn't been sure what to buy her, so he went with a stock gift that any woman would like—a bottle of expensive perfume he picked up at Christina's Boutique. It was a brand they sold at high-end department stores. The fragrance smelled good to him and it suited Jacquie. Spicy, not flowery.

The feminine scents of women's perfume were forgotten as Drew walked across newly mown turf cut on the diagonal. Its freshly shorn blades crushed beneath his tennis shoes, filling his nose with the pungent mustiness of meadow and earth.

He loved the smell of baseball turf, especially

when he wore spikes and was suited up. There was nothing better than digging his heels into the soft, red dirt of a field and sliding into home plate.

A new coat of green paint refreshed the Wood Ridge Memorial Clubhouse, its composite roof getting a few replacement shingles this year as well. Chalk lines marked the diamond, and the elevated pitcher's mound was raked to perfection.

An upcoming season always got under Drew's skin like a bottle of Tabasco sauce. He was so hot for the game, he felt on fire. He lived for baseball season.

He'd never been into football, not even in high school. He'd gone to the home games, only to see who'd hook up with whom and where the best parties were going to be that night.

Reflecting on his youth, he furrowed his brow, and the thrill of an expanse of turf was momentarily forgotten as memories took him back in time.

His parents had had to get married because his mom was pregnant. Drew wasn't sure if they were ever in love with each other, even in the beginning. He'd been born in Alhambra, California, in 1960. They'd moved around a lot. His parents never got along, his dad going from one job to the next, always thinking that the new and improved place of employment would be the key to his happiness. Employment satisfaction was never there, and his mom would get so angry with him she'd sometimes disappear for a day or two, leaving the neighbors to watch Drew.

He'd always wished he had a big brother, someone he could look up to. But that wasn't the case, and he'd had to learn early on to fend for himself.

Pop hadn't instilled a hard work ethic in him, and the male-slanted values he'd learned held little weight. His dad had been a British Petroleum firefighter in Carson—a job that nobody ever quit from because firefighters were heroes. But Pop said the pay was lousy for having to smell oil refineries all day and being in one of the most dangerous jobs in L.A. County.

It had been true. A main pipe busted and the place practically blew the Port of Los Angeles into the ocean. But Pop had been long gone when that happened; he'd gotten excited about making more money at Union Oil—which made no sense, since he'd said he hated the smell of petroleum. He eventually quit that because he disliked working a long shift. Ending up at the Department of Water and Power, he spent more years working for them than any other company. In fact, he'd put in a good word for Drew, and reading water meters had been his first job.

Drew's childhood had been pretty much just an existence. He was a body at the dinner table, a mouth to feed. Sometimes he was forgotten about, sometimes he stayed overnight with a neighbor when his mom took off and his dad was working the night shift. Not having a close family had never allowed him to warm up to people, to trust and to expose his emotions. He kept things locked inside, not one for sentimentalities.

But he'd known at a young age that he was special. Special in that he had a charm about him, and when he turned it on, that charm could get him pretty much anything he wanted.

Friends' moms would have home-baked cookies fresh out of the oven on the days they knew he was coming over after school. If he needed to be somewhere, a ride was always available. When he had a question about homework, someone's dad had the answer.

Puberty hit and he was the most popular boy in school. Never mind that he had no home life. He hid the fact that he was lonesome and didn't have parents who cared. Frequently, he steered kids away from his house and went to theirs so nobody would see how he lived.

When Drew got his first girlfriend, he didn't know what to do with her. He'd been eleven and she was thirteen. She'd already had sex and had hinted she wanted to experiment with him. One day they ended up under the crawl space of her house, on the dirt, and she took off her dungarees and let him look at her.

She'd had a patch of downy soft hair between her legs and he recalled being excited about it. Seeing her had given him a woody like he'd never experienced with his dad's bathroom magazines. He never had sex with her, didn't have the education to really go about it. Looking back, he thanked God he hadn't; he'd been way too immature to consider it. He lost his virginity two years later, to Stacy Ritter, a middle school cheerleader who'd taken one look at him and said to her friends, "I've got to get me some of that."

Ever since, women had been looking at him like he was the best eye candy on the block. And sometimes he felt like just another piece that was made to satisfy.

Early on, when he started dating, he never did stuff alone with a girlfriend unless it was to have sex in his car, or her bedroom when her parents weren't home. He always made sure they went out with other couples. It saved him from dealing with being in a relationship and dealing with real stuff. He had no experience with forming an emotional bond.

Eventually, his mother left one night and never came back home. They figured out where she was some ten years later. She'd remarried, which was illegal, since she was still married to his dad. The details of exactly what had happened were never explained to Drew. Only his dad had the answers, and he'd died a couple of years later, just before Drew signed on with the minors.

If it hadn't been for baseball, Drew would have had a lost life, drifting in and out of one thing for another—just like his dad.

Sports saved him.

The love of the game was what pulled him up, took him into a world he didn't fully understand.

Baseball made him a man.

Some would debate just what kind of man. He'd done so many things he regretted while playing for the majors, but a person couldn't reverse the clock and take everything back. It was a part of who he was, what had molded him.

If it hadn't been for that steroid story breaking wide-open—

Drew's cell phone rang, the melody making him grimace. He really had to change that ringer.

Pushing the talk button, he said, "Tolman."

"Drew, it's Lynette."

Drew stopped heading for the stands, where the parents and kids had begun to arrive.

Every time Caroline's sister called, his pulse slowed and felt thick in his veins. Lynette took in Mackenzie after Caroline died. He always wondered if this would be the call that would send his daughter to him, and he could try and make things up to her.

"Lynette, how're you doing?"

"Fine. You?"

"Good enough. Starting Little League today."

"That's nice for ya'll," she drawled.

He switched the cell phone from one ear to the other. A pause lingered, Drew rubbing his jaw and feeling the grit of stubble. The dead span of time was more than he could take.

"Has she changed her mind?" he asked, his chest tight.

"I told her you have a ticket for her to fly to Idaho

whenever she's ready, but she doesn't want to come. I'm sorry, Drew."

Not the news he wanted, but he'd expected as much. He knew he'd really screwed this one up, and fixing it might never be an option. But he wasn't going to stop trying.

"I sort of figured."

"I wish I could make her, but I think that's the wrong way to go."

"Agree."

"I'll keep talking to her about it. I've tried to get her thoughts about your trip up here in February, but she doesn't say much about it. I know getting you two together is what Caroline wanted, and that's what I've been telling Mackenzie, but she's headstrong, Drew. She's a lot like you."

He adjusted the bill of his ball cap. "Yep. No doubt."

More boys were arriving, and Drew forced the emptiness from his heart. He was always surrounded by people, and needed that social company, but nobody would ever know how badly he missed family. He continued to hope his daughter would give him half a chance to be in her life. Only Jacquie knew about Mackenzie. Nobody else in Red Duck would have guessed he had a kid, a girl who looked like him.

Some secrets were easy to keep, especially when the secret wanted nothing to do with him. If Mackenzie would only give him a chance, maybe she could see he wasn't such a shit.

He'd already set up a bank account for her, and had been giving Caroline and Lynette child support money for years.

"Keep on trying, Lynette." Drew made another adjustment on the ball cap, flipping the bill forward and checking to make sure his polo shirt was tucked in. He hated dressing like this on the field, but he had to.

"I will."

"'K. I gotta go."

Drew cut the call and turned his mind onto autopilot, making Florida seem a distant memory.

It was time to play ball.

Lucy had had to insist Jason try out for Little League. All he'd done was complain about it. He hadn't wanted to, even though he loved to play. She knew he just didn't feel like making the effort to fit in. This was the last year he could even be on a team. He'd be on the Senior League again. She knew he'd make the cut.

She'd kept after him, finally giving him an ultimatum. No baseball, no replacement car. She hated to use leverage like that, but it had been the only way. She knew what was best for him and this was it.

Matt, on the other hand, had been dressed in his athletic gear before he'd come to the breakfast table.

They arrived at the field and parked along with the other SUVs and cars. She watched her sons head out on the grass. Because of their age differences, they had to try out on different parts of the field.

Draping a blanket over the cold metal riser, Lucy settled in.

The day was pleasant for the first week in June. Cool, but not too cold. A blue sky cupped the baseball field like a catcher's glove.

Lucy wore a lightweight jean jacket, a pair of Levi's and Doc Martens. She'd never been into fashion, preferring comfort and durability. Or course, she did have a feminine side that liked to put on a cocktail dress and heels. Only she hadn't had any cause to do so in the past two years, except for a Christmas charity party she went to last year with one of her neighbors.

"Hi, I'm Susan Lawrence," a woman said, introducing herself. She wore her hair in a crisp bob, parted in the middle. Its color was silver-gray, with some natural brown left. Interestingly, it looked quite flattering on her and not aging. Her eyes were a friendly blue, her lips frosted with lip gloss.

"Lucy Carpenter," Lucy responded.

"Another season. I feel my wallet shrinking, but my son sure likes to play." She nudged the man who took a seat next to her. "Honey, this is Lucy Carpenter. Lucy, this is my husband, Dave."

"Nice to meet you," he stated, shuffling a camcorder and binoculars.

Susan met Lucy's eyes. "This is your first year here."

"We're new in town."

"Well, you'll like it. We'll have to exchange phone numbers and use each other as backup to drive our sons to practice." Susan's personality was easy to warm up to. "How old is your son?"

"I have two. Twelve and sixteen."

"I've got a sixteen-year-old. That's him right there."

Lucy followed Susan's gaze. The young man was tall and skinny as a stick, and even from this distance, Lucy noticed he had a prominent Adam's apple. The seat of his baseball pants drooped and his shirt seemed a size too large.

"Hi, Vince!" Susan waved, and her son slouched, half waved back, then turned to a group of boys his own age. "Where are your sons?"

"That's Jason right there, almost next to your son. And that's my Matt with those boys."

"They're nice looking."

"Thank you."

"Honey, did you charge the camcorder? I can't get it to power up." Susan's husband got that helpless-man look on his face and handed over the equipment to his wife.

Susan made a few adjustments and the camera turned on.

Dave leaned in and gave her a kiss on the cheek. "Thanks, honey."

For some reason unexplainable to Lucy, observing the affectionate couple made her feel hollow. Empty. There was no reason to remotely have that pang of loneliness. She'd been doing great on her own, keeping busy and making a life for herself after Gary left. But strangely, since coming to Red Duck, she'd had a few bouts of single-blues. Maybe it was because the town was so small and intimate and, as a stranger, she sometimes felt like an outsider. Who was to say? And it was silly to waste time dwelling on it.

"There's Drew!" Susan exclaimed. "He's the best coach our sons have ever had. He's doing seniors, and you're just going to love him," she repeated. "We all do."

Lucy had gathered that all the inhabitants of Red Duck could see no wrong, find no flaw, in Andrew Tolman.

She still had his card in her purse, never having called him. She'd found out on her own when to sign Jason up for baseball at the high school, so she had no reason to contact Drew personally. Although that card had burned a hole through her wallet leather. She'd taken it out a few times, looked at the script and the phone number, then slid it back inside.

As he strode onto the field, she couldn't help admiring him. He was a very handsome man, one who drew her undivided attention. Tall and broad, he filled out a polo shirt and khaki pants like nobody's business. He wore a newer, blue baseball cap, his eyes unreadable beneath the shade the bill provided. But his lips were in full sunlight, looking soft and wide. Made to capture and settle over a woman's mouth. It thrilled her to think about what they'd feel like next to her own.

"So what do you think?"

Lucy snapped out of her decadent thoughts, turned to Susan and blurted, "About what?"

"About Red Duck."

Wayward fantasies about Drew kissing her evaporated—thank goodness. They had no place in her mind. Why she even contemplated how his mouth would feel over hers distressed her. She was far too sensible to fall for a man with Drew's shameless charms. "I like it, so far. It seems like a nice place to bring up kids."

"It is. I've lived here all my life. My father bought property back in the seventies. It's the only way Dave and I could afford to build."

Lucy had wondered. "What does your husband do?"

"He's in landscaping. He's quite busy."

"I'd imagine so with the resort and golf course expanding."

Whistles blew from the field as the boys were taken into groups for practice. Lucy tried to keep her gaze equally on each of her sons, but found her eyes straying toward Drew.

Sitting up on a bleacher and having a full view of him almost felt wicked. She could watch him for hours. Lucy hated to admit she was just as infatuated with him as the entire town. What was it about the man that got so many people to smile? She took a harder look at him.

He walked with a masculine stride she couldn't help but notice—relaxed and void of arrogance. He stood out in a crowd because of his height, which was perhaps about six feet four. But what was it? What was it beyond the superficial? She couldn't peg it, not at this moment. But it was on the tip of her tongue, like a thought or a memory one went after that hung around the edges, illusive and niggling. So Lucy stopped trying to figure it out and settled in to watch the tryouts.

But a long moment later, the answer hit her. The reason Drew caught her attention was that he wasn't looking for it. He was secure enough in himself that he didn't try to get women's attention. Women went out of their way to get his.

And, she realized, she was no different. She wanted it, too.

The covered dugout smelled like paint; the plywood bench was cluttered with athletic bags and discarded tennis shoes. Bats and mitts were strewn on the concrete floor. The boys suited up in gear and wore turf shoes with rubber darts. Water jugs with last names printed in marker were thrown into the mess. Getting kids up this early was almost like having them play hungover. They wanted to be in the game, loved it, but more than likely, most had been up half the night playing video games.

Drew gave them a little intro speech, then told them to hit the field and warm up.

He tucked a clipboard underneath his arm, assessed the kids who were returning and those who were new. This year, he hoped the seniors would make it to the play-offs. He had his eye on Jason.

The kid wore attitude like it was a shirt—untucked. Nothing seemed to get him excited or interested, and he wasn't taking practice swings like the other boys.

Walking over to him, Drew stopped just shy of getting in his face. "Do you want to be here or not?"

Jason looked up through slitted eyes, the bill of his cap making his hair seem longer across his forehead.

"Not really."

"Then walk your butt off my field and don't waste my time."

His upper lip curled. "I wish I could, but my mom's making me."

Drew glanced up at the bleachers, noticed Lucy sitting next to Nutter's parents. He allowed himself scant seconds to watch the sunlight picking up red in the brunette strands of her hair. He couldn't ignore the pull he felt toward her. He hadn't been able to pinpoint why, he just felt it. Had from the moment he first saw her, even with Jacquie right next to him.

Staring back at Jason, Drew growled, "Well, then you better do your best not to make my team. Swing and miss, run like you've got rocks in your shoes. Make it good, because if you're going to be a loser, you better act like one."

Then Drew focused on the other players, turning his back on Jason Carpenter. Drew felt his blood pressure throb in his head. He didn't like getting in a kid's face, but looking at Jason reminded him of himself at that age, when he'd thought life had shit on him, too. A part of him wanted to take the boy by the shoulders and shake him. To tell him that baseball could make him lose the chip on his shoulder.

Playing ball was a good outlet to get a lot of steam out of their system when they were filled with resentment. That boy had more self-imposed injustice in him than Drew had seen in a long time. Maybe he had a right to; Drew didn't know the whole story. But somewhere along the way, that boy had been victimized by a bad parental call, or a bad parent. Period. And seeing how he'd already met Lucy, Drew didn't think it was her. It was a dad. And God knew how Drew could relate to having a dad who didn't give a good rip.

The tryouts got underway. A batting cage had been built on the far corner; the pitching machine was plugged in. Boys went into the cage, chased after some balls and took swings. Drew had his group of boys hit five pitches from an Iron Mike in the cage.

When Jason was up, he took a halfhearted swing, the ball catching the tip of the bat and fouling. But there was something in his stance, an act of defiance, as if he hadn't fully reconciled to failing on purpose.

"Put some mustard on it, Jason. Come on!" Drew shouted, as he cheered the boy on, encouraging him.

The machine spat out a ball and Jason held back,

then swung and missed intentionally. Drew didn't let up, clapped and told him to try again.

"It's easy to miss the good ones, harder to hit the bad ones. I think you can go after one. Your choice."

Then another ball spewed from the machine. This time, Jason grabbed wood and hit the thing so hard the ball slammed into one of the cage's metal poles with a metallic ring before bouncing back and rolling on the ground.

Drew met Jason's gaze. The boy had poker eyes— expressionless and unreadable—but his body language spoke volumes. Cocky and sure. There was a confidence in his stride when he turned to leave his place on the diamond.

"If that's how you hit when you want to hit like a loser, then we are going to the state series when you give me your best," Drew said.

Jason looked down, then gave him a half smirk and a snort.

The other boys rallied during their turns, having to catch three pop flies. Then Drew had them hit grounders so the outfield could get some practice in throwing to the bags.

Last year, Ryan Hall had been a cherry pie, but his parents sent him to a winter baseball camp, and damned if the kid wasn't hitting the ball with the meat of the bat and with a lot more confidence. Cal "Brownie" Brown's fielding was a little loose, but his throws to first were pretty good. Even Nutter had improved. His real name was Vince Lawrence, but he'd taken a few nut balls that dropped him to his knees, and had ended up with a nickname that stuck.

"Don't let that ball find some leather, Nutter."

"Yeah, Coach. I'm trying not to."

"You're doing good. Much better than last year. Great job."

Drew had them slice a few dewdrops, slow balls that the boys could connect with. Then he gathered the kids around. "All right, any of you who want to try to pitch, we're having a pitching tryout. Line up."

Drew kept his gaze on Jason, wondering if that was the boy's position. He had a hunch. And that hunch played out. Jason got in line to pitch, and when he was on the bump, he threw a high, hard one that about took the hat right off of Ryan.

After Jason delivered his sixth consecutive strike, Drew walked out to the bump. "What have you been doing with that pitching arm?"

Toeing the rubber, gazing down and then up, Jason shrugged. "Throwin' rocks at tin cans."

"Think you can throw a slider?"

"Yeah."

"Give it to me."

Jason threw a slider that was smooth as glass, and Drew knew he had himself a team-winning pitcher this year.

Stuffing his fingertips into his waistband, Jason looked over his shoulder to watch Matt field-

ing grounders. He ran so fast and hard, his cheeks
got red.

His younger brother struggled with playing good
baseball, but he wanted it really bad. It didn't seem
fair that it came so easy to Jason, when Mattie was
the one who really wanted to be on a team.

Jason glanced at Drew, wanting to hate him, but
not quite being able to. He'd razzed him on the field,
told him to play for shit, but something in Jason
wouldn't let him.

He knew he'd made the team. He was an ace
pitcher, had been on the Senior League in Boise last
year, and they'd dusted the competition in the play-
offs. The experience of winning had been a rush, but
going to the games and knowing his dad wasn't
watching had sucked.

He'd wind up, look over his shoulder, catch a
brief glimpse of the stands, and damn if he didn't
hope to see his dad sitting next to his mom each
time.

But it never happened.

Digging the toe of his tennis shoe into the grass,
Jason wished he was eighteen so he could do what
he wanted. As soon as he was of age, he was moving
out.

Movement caught his attention from the corner
of his eye. Some little kids were just about wetting
themselves trying to throw pitches. Peewees. A
bunch of wannabe Little Leaguers. You could tell
this was their first year. Jason had watched them

when he was in the batting cage. The peewees' mouths dropped open as the Iron Mike spat out balls, and it seemed like an effing new tricycle to them.

He noticed the majors were pretty good. Mattie might be in for a shot. Some of those guys were throwing the ball pretty hard. Maybe too hard.

Jason ducked as a ball sailed toward him. "Hey, shit-head," he said as a boy ran over to pick it up.

"Sorry!" he mumbled, and ran back to the group.

Shifting his stance, Jason tucked his hands in his armpits and slouched.

Come on, let's go. I wanna get outta here.

"All right," Drew said, pulling Jason from his thoughts. "Tryouts are over. Pick 'em up."

Jason sniffed, rubbed his nose, then took off his plastic helmet and bent over to pick up the baseballs on the field and collect them in his hat.

I hate it here and I'll never like this bass-awkward town. Rednecks and losers with shit for brains. Brian's probably at a party tonight. I wonder who's there. Probably got a bag of—

Those were his last conscious thoughts as something slammed him—*hard*—in the base of his skull, dropping him to his knees. And then the world went black.

Seven

Jacquie stubbed out her cigarette and ordered another gin and tonic. Drew wasn't here and she hated drinking alone.

Indigo's was dimly illuminated by a back light above the glass shelves containing bottles of alcohol. Oil candles on the mahogany bar flickered.

She was all dressed up for her birthday, but the sexy picture she made was ruined by a frown on her carefully lined lips.

Drew wasn't coming.

Anger boiled within Jacquie. Every curse known to man welled inside her, potent and strong, begging to be released. Her thoughts were jagged and painful. Hurt and disappointment clashed within her heart, and she couldn't begin to sort out which one she felt the most.

When she gazed at her reflection in the back-bar's mirror, she saw a woman who looked older, stressed out. Tired.

How dare he stand her up on her fortieth birthday?

He'd called from St. Joseph's Hospital's emergency room. One of the boys he coached had taken a skull ball—or that's what Drew had called it. The idiot kid had been hit on the head by a baseball, knocked out cold. And now Drew had to stay there and make sure he came around. He'd said he'd have to miss dinner, but he'd call her when he was leaving the hospital.

Damn him!

Damn him and baseball and kids.

On a day like this, she was glad she was unable to have kids of her own. She'd had a hysterectomy at age thirty-two, and at the time it had devastated her. Over the years, she'd talked to a therapist about it and was pretty much reconciled that it was for the best. She really didn't have a good mothering instinct, although there had been a boyfriend she'd had at thirty-four who made her regret being unable to conceive a child. After six months, he'd broken up with her based on the fact she was "broken" in that department.

With Drew, having kids was never an issue. He didn't want any more. He had a daughter he was trying to establish a relationship with, but frankly, if Jacquie were Mackenzie, she wouldn't have anything to do with Drew, either.

When it suited her, Jacquie did have a moral thread in her composition, and knocking up a woman, then denying paternity, was a crappy thing for a man to do. And Drew had done it.

Jacquie had always looked the other way. She preferred to see Drew the way she wanted, not how he was.

She drank her gin and tonic, sulked and gazed about the room. Couples made up most of the dining crowd, a sore reminder that she was by herself. If it hadn't been her birthday, she wouldn't be so upset. She still would be clenching her teeth, but not with such a bad taste in her mouth.

My God. A woman didn't turn forty every day. And Jacquie was having a hard enough time with it. She'd picked up the phone today and called a plastic surgeon's office for a boob job consult, but then promptly hung up without making the appointment. This getting older thing sucked. She felt as if she was looking tired. Like maybe she needed a mini-everything. Face, chin, neck—lift it all up.

Running her freshly lacquered fingernails down the column of her throat, she thought the skin still felt smooth. But for how much longer? She knew smoking was killing her, but she had to have one vice. She lived a pressure-filled life, thrived on it, and nicotine was like high octane in her blood. It just kept her going and going, as if she were that energizer bunny.

Fingering a filtered cigarette from her soft pack, Jacquie stuck it between her lips. She was reaching for her lighter when a butane flame flickered to life in front of her face.

She lifted her chin and caught a view of her reflection and the tall man standing behind her. His extended hand held a lighter, its orange-blue flame wavering as she breathed, slowly in, slowly out.

Jacquie leaned forward, brought the tip of her cigarette to the offered light. "Thanks."

He didn't say anything in return.

She blinked a moment, brought him into focus. He wore a red-plaid flannel shirt and, without her turning around to check, what appeared to be snug-fit Wranglers. His short hair was barber-buzzed, sandy blond and clipped tightly against the sides of his head. He had a ruggedly square jaw, wide mouth. Green eyes, as far as she could tell in the bad lighting.

"I've seen you," he said, his voice a deep baritone.

She swiveled on the bar stool, looked directly into his eyes. She had been right. Green, a very deep shade. "Really?" she remarked blandly. He wasn't her type, and this sort of thing happened. Men were drawn to her, especially when she had on heels and showed off her legs.

"At that house up on Shore Lodge in Timberline."

"The Kent Estate."

"Yeah. I was there doing the electrical."

So, he was a construction worker. Any interest she might have had was no longer piqued.

"Hmm," she responded noncommittally.

"Are you here alone?"

"Yes, um, no. Well…" She momentarily lost her verve. "Yes, I'm alone."

It was pretty obvious, as no one else had joined her as she sipped her gin and tonic at the bar. She'd almost finished her second one and, on an empty stomach, they were making her light-headed, messing with her perception.

It would serve Drew right if she left with another man. He'd stood her up. And on her fricking fortieth birthday.

She didn't want to be alone.

When she'd started dating Drew, she'd alienated herself from the handful of girlfriends she had, choosing to spend time with her boyfriend instead. That was a big mistake women often made when entering into relationships. They threw all their energies into a man, then lost sight of what was around them.

For Jacquie, work as a Realtor was number one—she flourished on the deals and the big commission checks. Drew and their relationship had fallen into the number two position. Time for herself had been relegated to number three. Bad move on her part.

"I'm Max Beck," the man said, slipping onto the seat next to hers. The scent surrounding him was unlike any cologne she recognized. It was a masculine scent. Pure male. Nothing from a bottle.

Her nostrils flared, and she felt hot even if he was a construction worker.

Jacquie sat straighter, thrusting out her breasts,

hoping to emphasize curves that were barely there. "Jacquie Santini, Realty Professionals."

"I knew who you were. I asked around."

She arched her brows. "Should I be flattered?"

"Sweetheart, you should be glad I came over here and sat next to you. A woman who looks—" he leaned closer "—and smells like you shouldn't have to sit by herself."

Tingles rose across her bare arms, the plunging vee in her dress allowing cool air to caress her cleavage. She shouldn't have had that second drink without eating. Her nipples grew to hard points; her legs began to ache.

The alcohol was flowing through her body, making her languid and careless. She threw her head back and laughed, a throaty sound that she knew drove men crazy.

"Well, I wouldn't have been alone for long."

"That's why I came over." Max rapped his knuckles on the bar. "Vodka on the rocks," he ordered.

Casting all caution to the wind, throwing out all reason and succumbing to the anger toward Drew that lingered around the edges of her mind, she put a hand over Max's. Their eyes met and held. "No. Don't order a drink here. I know of a place where we can go dancing."

He didn't move, but his hooded gaze lowered to the bare skin at the base of her throat. "I don't dance."

She rose to her feet, a little unstable. She put her hand on the bar to steady herself. Squaring her shoulders, she felt more like herself now that the blood was moving through her body. "You do now. It's my fortieth birthday," she laughed, "and I feel like celebrating."

Max flashed her a grin. "Well, then hell, just call me Fred Astaire."

"We got the CAT scan report back and it looks good." Dr. Berg stood before Lucy and Drew, giving them the news.

Relief pooled through Lucy, making her labored breathing ease to a more steady rhythm. She hadn't realized she'd been holding it ever since she saw Jason lying unconscious on the field. Everything had happened so fast. She'd been talking to Susan, had looked away for a moment, then saw Jason, and Drew running toward him.

After taking a look at Jason, Drew had reacted quickly. He'd called 911, and an ambulance was on its way before Lucy had time to think. She had no idea where the nearest hospital was, nor the quickest method to get her son there. Drew had taken care of everything, alleviating a portion of her stress by driving Matt to the hospital while she rode in the ambulance with Jason.

When Jason was brought in, he was still out cold. This wasn't the first time one of her sons had been injured playing sports, and it would likely not be the last. But each time, Lucy was paralyzed with fear that the damage would be severe or permanent. Matt had broken both arms—and he wasn't even a teenager yet. Jason had had two concussions prior to this one.

The team of doctors had checked him out, taken him for an image, and Lucy paced in the waiting room with Matt and Drew.

It seemed like it took forever.

Dr. Berg was reassuring, his tone soothing. "Your son will be all right. He woke up in radiology."

"Oh, thank goodness!" Lucy exhaled in relief.

"He's going to have a bad headache, but I don't see any serious problems. He's lucky."

The younger doctor wore his white coat well, and Lucy noticed he was smiling sympathetically at her…almost too much so, as if he knew something more. But he didn't elaborate.

"Is there something else, Doctor?" she asked, almost unable to utter the question.

He paused, then said, "If I could talk to you alone."

Tension wound tight within her, making her unable to move. Drew put his arm on her shoulder. "G'ahead. I'll stay with Matt."

Lucy walked behind the doctor, a knot working its way around her heart, squeezing, with unanswered questions plaguing her every step of the way. It was worse than the doctor was letting on. Jason was going to have some damage. Her son was going to be…damaged.

Oh, God…

Dr. Berg led her to a small alcove where two upholstered chairs faced one another.

"Mrs. Carpenter, take a seat."

"It's Miss." Why she made the correction, she had no idea. It was an automatic response. Knitting her fingers together, she worried her thumbs. "It's bad, isn't it? You couldn't tell me in front of my youngest son. What's wrong with Jason—really?"

"Nothing but a concussion, Miss Carpenter." His eyes were kind, a soft brown that made her feel comfortable. But the stress was still wrapping her in its taut cocoon.

"Then?"

The word echoed between them, suspended, as the doctor's expression became regretful.

He reached into his lab coat pocket, then opened his palm. "When we took off your son's clothes, I found this in his uniform pants' pocket. Do you know what it is?"

Lucy wished she could have been shocked and said she had no idea what the thing was. But she knew. All too well.

"It's for pot," she said in a monotone.

Dr. Berg nodded, "A roach clip."

"I thought so."

He gave it to her and she held on to the metal clip as if it were poison. Biting her lip, she looked away.

How could Jason have disappointed her so? She had had a long talk with him about this the last time, and he'd promised her he'd stay out of trouble. They'd been through this in Boise. Things were supposed to be different here. How could he?

How dare he?

"I'm not going to report this because I didn't find any drugs on him."

"Thank you, Doctor," she said, her voice barely audible.

"I'm sorry, Miss Carpenter." The doctor rose to his feet, and Lucy followed suit. "I've got to see my other patients. I'll be back to check on Jason shortly. He's resting right now. You'll be able to take him home tonight, but I'm not sure when."

"Thank you." The words sounded wooden, hollow.

Lucy didn't immediately return to the waiting area. She held back, fought the tears that threatened to fall.

Apparently there was no safe place for her children. She knew Jason had no pocket money, so he must have met up with some boys in town who shared hits from their joint or offered him something as a trade or…something. She shuddered, the unknown raising gooseflesh on her arms.

At this point, all she had was speculation, but the roach clip was enough evidence that her son had broken his promise.

How had she failed so miserably?

Everything she had done, everything she had planned for in Red Duck, now seemed misguided. A waste of time and energy.

Walking in the opposite direction from where she'd come, Lucy followed the signs to the chapel, found the small room with its faux stained glass and took a seat.

The pews were cushioned and soft, and she wondered how many people before her had come to pray about loved ones who were on the cusp of dying. Tragedy struck lives, took lives. And here she was… Her son would recover, but would she? Could she emotionally handle this?

She damned Gary. Then felt badly for doing so in the church.

But if he'd been around, she'd have help. She had no doubts they would have divorced, and at this point, she couldn't care less if he was with Diane. She *did* care that he was hundreds of miles away, as if he didn't have a responsibility in the world. The raising of their sons fell exclusively on her shoulders, and she needed help.

God help me….

The tears began to fall.

I need help.

Lucy quietly cried, lowering her face into her hands and letting out the sorrow of many months. She couldn't recall the last time she'd actually let it all out. Probably too long.

When she was done, she dug through her purse, found a tissue and blew her nose.

A hand settled on her shoulder, startling her. She turned, only to see Drew Tolman in the pew behind

her. His big hand remained on her, warm and com-
forting, as if she allowed those intimate feelings to
surface. The rapid thud of her pulse sounded in her
ears. Her gaze left his, lowered to where he touched
her. As soon as she did that, he let her go.

"I didn't want to interrupt you before."

"Jason?"

"He's okay. I meant, I saw you crying and I figured
you need some private time."

For some reason, the fact that he'd watched her
unnerved Lucy. "You watched me cry?"

"Not for all that long. But it looked like you
needed to."

Her emotions whirled and skidded. One moment,
she'd been drawn by the raw sensuousness in his
eyes; the next, those thoughts all but evaporated.
She felt a little snappish, slightly annoyed with him.
But for the life of her, she couldn't figure out why.
Then it hit her: *He's seen me weak.*

She hated that, hated to be less than capable.
And now he'd seen her at her worse.

"I didn't think you'd be the type to come into a
church." She couldn't help the short response.

"Well, I did put on my asbestos underwear this
morning, so I think I'll be okay."

She clued in to the fact he was teasing, saying he'd
have gone up in flames if he hadn't been wearing
protection.

Unbidden, she smiled. "Funny."

"I've been in a church a few times."

She straightened, stuffed her wet tissues back into her purse. "I'm sure that's a stretch, but I'm not going to debate it with you."

He merely chuckled. Then his voice lowered an octave and she could tell he was looking at the back of her head. "You okay?"

"Fine," she lied, still facing forward.

"I saw the doc heading back without you."

"Where's Matt?" she asked.

"He's watching TV in the waiting room."

"I should get back to him." Lucy stood, smoothed the front of her shirt and put the straps of her handbag on her shoulder.

"Give yourself another minute," Drew suggested, standing behind her.

"Why?" she asked.

"Because you look like you've been crying."

"It could be because I'm upset about my son getting hit in the head."

"Could be, but that's not the reason. Want to tell me?"

She walked past him, through the chapel doors and into the hallway. "No."

"I was once his age. Nothing would surprise me."

"I'm sure it wouldn't."

Drew matched her stride, fell in step with her. "If you change your mind, you've got my number."

And you've got a girlfriend!

Why she was suddenly aggravated about his circumstances...why the anger welled, knowing he was "taken," just when he appeared to express real concern for her and her son…she just didn't want to address it.

So she said nothing further.

Later that night, Drew dropped her off to pick up her car from the field. Lucy brought Jason home, put him to bed, but she didn't bring up the roach clip. She needed to sleep on it, figure out how she was going to deal with him, what the consequences would be.

Perhaps she'd been naive when she thought she'd never have to revisit this again.

The reality settled like a weight on her shoulders. It was going to be a long night.

Journal of Mackenzie Taylor

I graduated high school! Peabody Marsh sat in front of me and he lit off a smoke bomb just as the ~~valley victorian~~ valvictorian was giving her speech. Principle Walton had a conniption fit.

I kept looking in the audience and I only saw Aunt Lynette. I wished Momma was sitting right next to her. I started crying and I had to hide it so my mascara wouldn't run.

When the commencement was over, everyone threw their caps in the air. Then a streaker ran across the gym. He wore a Sponge Bob mask, but we all knew whose bare behind it was. Our best pitcher on the baseball team. Brad Smith. He was gone before any of the teachers could catch him. I would have known that butt anywhere. I've had a crush on it for the entire semester. Brad and I went to prom together.

I've always had a thing for baseball

players. Funny how that works out...considering.

I got my diploma and my picture taken next to the United States flag. I guess I am now officially done with school.

Some friends and I spent our first days in the real world by hunting crawfish. Brad and I made out on the beach. We didn't do anything, but kiss. I love how he kisses. All of us ended up going swimming to start our summer.

Now I've got my whole life ahead of me. I'm not sure if I can last four years in college, but Aunt Lynette says I need to try. A girl without a degree won't go far. But I like to do hair and make up and look at how much money the cosmetologists to the stars make.

Besides, college costs big bucks. But Aunt Lynette said not to worry about that because my "daddy" said he was paying.

Drew sent me a graduation present and I almost didn't open it. I let it sit on my bureau for three days. I didn't want it to ruin my big day. Just in case it was something bad.

So I opened it this morning.

I keep staring at the present, wondering how he knew. I asked Aunt Lynette and she swore she never said a thing about it.

That Drew did it on his own. I asked Aunt Lynette to get out her Bible and swear on it. She did. So I know she's telling the truth.

Drew got me a diary.

How he knew, I can't guess. Must have been a lucky guess, though. Or he probably asked the clerk in a store and she made a lucky guess. In any case, here I have it and what am I going to do with it?

I can't stop looking at my present from Drew and I decided I might as well keep it. It's just too nice not to use.

The diary the finest leather I've ever seen, and so smooth to touch. My fingertips glide over it. On the front, my name is inscribed in a really cool gold foil font. It only has my first name. He probably can't stand the thought of me having only momma's last name and not his.

Inside, the pages aren't lined. It's all fine white paper, really thick and nice so if I want to do a sketch or drawing, I can. The edges are a gold foil, too. It's about the nicest diary I've ever seen.

He gave me a graduation card and a check for $1,000.00. I never seen that much money in one check in my life. I *don't know what I'm going to do with it, if I'll even spend it. I should probably give it back...but last night I couldn't sleep for thinking about how much fun it would be to take that kind of money to the mall and just blow the whole thing. Aunt Lynette says I should spend it wisely, but I don't feel like being wise. I'm seventeen. I'm supposed to be reckless. Hah hah.*

I suppose I need to write him a thank you card. Or maybe I should call him up. I have to think about it. I can't remember what his voice sounds like. But I remember exactly what he looks like since he looks like me.

I have one of his pictures in my desk drawer, but I haven't pulled it out in a long time.

I did this morning. And it's on my bed next to me. And I'm thinking maybe I should call him and say thanks. But I don't know how to say it.

I don't know him.

I don't know Drew Tolman at all.

Eight

Lucy was running late.

She'd stayed up until well after midnight preparing for today. Then a bad case of insomnia kept her up as she lay in bed going over various scenarios about her son.

When this happened in Boise, she'd gone online and read as much information as she could find, talked to the school counselor and principal, as well as her general practitioner. Armed with what she needed to say, and how to go about it calmly and unemotionally, she'd sat Jason down and told him she loved him, but his choices were unacceptable in her home. She was there to listen to him, and wanted to be part of the solution; unfortunately, he'd only mumbled some excuses and said he wouldn't do it again.

She'd tried to get him away from the influence of his friends, had talked to their parents. Some were in denial and that was no help whatsoever. So she'd used the resources she had and made the best decision she could at the time.

Now that decision wasn't floating above water. She felt as if she were sinking.

With a sigh of frustration, Lucy went through the house with unorganized thoughts as she collected everything she needed for her job interview. Into her briefcase she stuffed her menu notebook and testimonials from previous clients, vision statement about her services, and the client agreement—along with the empty plastic containers for entrées and side dishes just in case they hired her. She'd printed a sampler menu, a spring theme centering around some lower fat options, as well as a few decadent indulgences. Desserts weren't the norm for her, but she was desperate.

She was meeting with prospective clients this morning, the first couple she'd actually have a face-to-face with. She'd fielded several calls in the past few days, but they hadn't garnered any appointments—just more curiosity about who she was and if she knew Raul.

Hearing all about how great Raul Nunez was was getting on her nerves. The resort area was in dire need of another top quality personal chef and Lucy wished people would be more open-minded. Raul couldn't handle everyone; he'd even said as much to her when she'd had coffee with him before moving here. But he'd also implied he'd put in a good word for her. Apparently he hadn't, or else she would have been on her way to establishing a client base by now.

Thank goodness the Greenbaums were willing to give her an interview. They'd read her ad in the *Mountain Gazette*. Ted and Shirley Greenbaum lived in the Knolls, an exclusive Timberline neighborhood. If they liked the sound of her menus and pricing, she was praying they'd hire her. She wished she could bring them the dishes to try, but it was against the personal chef regulations to cook in her home and carry it out.

"Where's my—?" She ransacked the kitchen, moving pots and pans stacked on the counter, not finishing the question because her mind was already focusing on what she was looking for. A tiny book with notes. But she couldn't find it.

"Mom," Matt said as he came down the stairs. "Are you going to drive me to Ada's or am I going to walk?"

"Drive you where?"

"So I can walk the dogs."

Lucy had forgotten about that. She'd spoken to Ada several days ago and had even gone to Claws and Paws to meet her. She was a genuinely sincere woman with a good heart, and she needed some help in her shop. Although Matt was young, Lucy felt he had enough maturity and a grasp on responsibility that he could handle the job, since it was only a few hours a week. She wasn't sure about the legality of hiring a twelve-year-old, but how could this be different than if Matt was mowing lawns? He'd be paid in cash.

"Of course, yes." Lucy found her notebook and grabbed the loose papers that threatened to fall out.

But then Lucy paused. Jason. That meant Jason would be left home alone.

Not a chance.

"Jason!" Lucy rummaged through her purse and fished out her car keys.

"What?" His muffled response came from the loft. He'd been in bed all morning, a place she let him stay after the concussion. Normally she babied him, let him miss school and watch TV or play video games.

He'd been so out of it last night, he'd fallen into bed and gone right to sleep. When she woke this morning, he'd been out cold and she'd worried. She'd put her finger under his nose to feel him breathing. He was. And steadily. But then she toed the wheel of the bed frame just enough to jar him awake. He'd opened his eyes, looked at her, then groaned and put the covers over his head.

He'd live.

That had been about thirty minutes ago and he was still up in his room.

"Put some clothes on," she said, finding her keys. "You've got five minutes to get downstairs."

"Why?"

She didn't answer. She let herself out the front door and began loading her car. When she returned inside, Jason sat on the second step of the loft stairs, his hair sticking out, still wearing the gray sweats he'd put on to go to bed.

"Get dressed," she commanded.

"What for?"

"You're going with your brother to walk dogs."

"I can't. I have a headache." He rubbed his temple and made an exaggerated face.

Maybe he did have a headache, but frankly, she didn't care. She wanted to shake him, to knock some sense into him.

"I'll give you some aspirin. Get dressed."

"I don't want to."

"It's not a matter of what you want or not." Her tone was strong and severe. He gazed at her through the loft spindles, saw she meant business, and rose to his feet. With his hand on the railing, he suddenly stopped, looked at her through the fringe of his hair.

"Where's my baseball uniform?"

Lucy's lips clamped together. She'd left it at the hospital so they could throw it away. Clearly, Jason just had a recollection of what he'd been hiding in his pocket. She wanted to make him fret about it, worry…wonder if she knew or if she didn't know.

"They cut it off you and it got thrown away."

"Where?"

"In the garbage. Now get dressed." Pivoting on her heels, she turned and went outside before he could ask her what garbage and where. She could already imagine him rifling through their trash out back, sorting through the wilted vegetable skins and the pan grease she'd discarded.

Minutes later, she had both boys in the car and was dropping them off at the curb near Ada's.

"Jason, you're to stay with your brother the entire time. If I hear you've left, you're going to be in big trouble."

He glowered at her, his brows dark slashes. "Where am I going to go?"

She glared back. "You tell me."

Straightening, he stuffed his hands into his pockets and went into Ada's with Matt.

Lucy pulled away, her mind running in circles without a set direction. On an impulse, she dialed a number, but regretted it as soon as she heard the voice on the other end of the line.

"Hullo?"

"Gary, it's Lucy."

"Hey, Loose."

She wouldn't allow his pet name for her to distract her from the situation at hand. He'd always called her that, and why he chose to do so now only annoyed her.

"I don't even know why I'm calling you," she said, running the sentence tightly together. "You're not here for the boys and there's nothing you can do."

"You called just to attack me? I'm going to hang up."

Swallowing, Lucy blurted, "No. Wait." She couldn't apologize because she meant what she said, but since she had him on the line, she wanted his input. "I'm calling about Jason."

"What's the matter?"

He sounded somewhat interested, in spite of the music blaring in the background. It made her wonder if he were wearing a straw hat and sitting on a bar stool at a beach bar while Diane suntanned. Neither one of them did much of anything by way of working, and it chapped Lucy's hide that he could get away with the meager child support he sent. But that was another story and she didn't feel like revisiting it now.

"Jason was smoking pot again," she said. But she bit the words off, wishing she'd never spoken them.

Gary knew about Jason's troubles in Boise, and in fact, Gary had been the one to tell her the city was a bad influence on their son. But Gary had no clue about how to fix the problem, he only liked to impose his opinion.

"You catch him?" Gary asked.

"No. He had a roach clip in his pocket. I found it."

"Maybe it wasn't his."

Lucy turned the steering wheel, hoping she was headed down the right street. "And maybe it was, Gary. I mean, come on. What are the odds? Trust me, it's his. Our son has a problem with pot."

"Then call the cops on him."

Gritting her teeth, Lucy tried to remain calm. "I can't do that."

"Why not? If he's screwing up, let him think about it in the slammer."

A few deep breaths and Lucy's pulse was under control. "I understand what you're saying, but I don't think that his problem is so severe he needs to be put in jail. Gary, he's a minor."

"A minor pain in the butt. This isn't his first screwup. He needs to be taught a lesson." Gary mumbled something to someone, then chuckled before returning his attention on their phone call. "I'll talk to him."

"No!" Lucy exclaimed. "You'll only make it worse."

"Well, then why'd you call me if you don't want me to do anything?" Gary's dander rose and she could tell he was clenching his entire body. He got like that these days. Combative and edgy if she so much as critiqued him.

"Gary, I don't want you calling him. Please promise me you won't tell him you and I spoke. I only called you because…"

At this point, she had no "because." In a moment of complete delusion, she'd thought she could count on him as an ex-husband and a father to their son. She was wrong.

Gary being Gary flew off the handle, was unreasonable, didn't think anything through, and he just plain irritated her.

"Never mind." Lucy flicked her blinker on, made a turn into Timberline. "I'll figure something out."

Even though he made a slight attempt to put his hand over the mouthpiece, Lucy heard him say, "I'll be there in a minute, hon."

It made her stomach roil to hear him speak to Diane like that. The pain of the affair still festered in her sometimes, and she wanted to scream. He was a deadbeat jerk.

"I have to go, Gary. I'm late for an appointment."

"Yeah, okay. But I think you should call the cops on him."

Lucy thought about Sheriff Lewis, his hick-town demeanor and the curl to his lip. She thought not. No calls to the law officials in Red Duck, thanks.

"I'll handle it," she said, then disconnected the line and prayed Gary would make good on his promise not to call Jason and talk to him.

Chances were he wouldn't. It would take too much effort and actual memory capacity to put his son on his radar.

Lucy drove through Timberline, the spacious estates large and looming, metal rooftops peeking through the thickets of pines and aspens. She couldn't imagine living here. What must these people do for a living? They couldn't all be investors, politicians and movie actors. Maybe some got their money the old-fashioned way. They earned it.

Her mind drifted to the expenses that Jason had just incurred on her insurance plan by having a hospital stay. Her deductible was a killer, since she was self-employed. Gary was supposed to pay fifty percent of the fees, but he was sporadic about it, and then she had to call Child Support Services and get them involved. It became a nightmare at times when she had to pay the bill up front, then wait for Gary to reimburse her.

Lucy *needed* this cooking job with the Green-baums.

But when she started working, who was going to keep an eye on Jason for the summer while school was out? He was beyond needing a babysitter, but he needed supervision so he wouldn't make more bad choices. At the very least he needed a full schedule so he couldn't have time to get into trouble.

Lucy glanced at her cell phone and wondered if she should call Drew to see if he'd made the team. If Jason got on the seniors, part of her worries would lessen. Baseball would take up a fair amount of her son's time, keeping him out of trouble.

Just as she contemplated making the call, the phone rang and she answered.

"Lucy—Andrew Tolman."

She didn't know why she felt such relief. His voice instantly comforted, soothed. She was glad he had her phone number.

"Drew. Hi."

"How's Jason this morning?"

Trying to drive, talk and read the directions she'd written down for the Greenbaums, Lucy replied; "He's got a bad headache, but he'll be okay."

"I won't be able to let him play without a doctor's release."

With Drew's words, finding the correct turn took a back seat. She knew her son was good, but she hadn't been completely sure he'd make the team until this moment. "Thanks, Drew. He'll do a good job for you."

As soon as Jason got involved, he would do his best. She knew her son, and no matter what he was struggling with, he always put his whole heart into playing ball once he was on a team.

"I know he will," Drew replied with a resonant laugh that got her attention and evoked shivers across her arms. "He's got attitude and a chip on his shoulder that's good for throwing fast balls."

She turned right, then started looking for the entrance to the Knolls, but her focus wasn't fully on the street signs.

Then it hit her: she was contemplating confiding in Drew about Jason and what she'd found last night.

What was she thinking?

It would be crazy to involve Drew, who she *knew* would be bad news in her life—but why did it feel so automatic to want to blurt out the truth?

Gary was all but useless, and there were times when Lucy was desperate to talk to another adult male about an issue with her son. She had a feeling Drew would understand because of the way he'd talked to her at the hospital, implying he had knowledge of rocky paths and teenage boys. But how could she tell Drew about the drugs? If Drew knew her son smoked marijuana, he'd be out of Little League without a half second to spare.

Lucy groaned, dismayed over the dilemma. The one man she thought she might be able to talk to about this was the very last man she could turn to. Thoughts about talking to him were banished.

Seeing the natural rock pillars for the Knolls, Lucy turned into the community. There was a berm that ran down the center of the road, and homes seemed to be built on five-acre lots.

"Yes…he definitely has an attitude," Lucy responded into her cell phone. "And I—"

Lucy cut herself short as a stealth-gray Hummer, its window down and Drew sitting behind the wheel, drove toward her on the exclusive lane. She slowed, just as he did, then pressed the button of the driver's window.

Lucy disconnected the call, staring at Drew.

"Hey," he said, his smile easygoing and warming her to the core. "You looking for me?"

She had to fight a battle of personal restraint, remind herself he wasn't available, was all wrong for her. She still didn't care for his image, not to mention he was her son's Little League coach now. Awkward, to say the least, if they ever dated.

Still, that knowledge did little to stave off the rush of heat to her cheeks when she looked up at him in that monster-size vehicle with its glossy chrome grille and testosterone-fueled accessories.

"No…sorry." It was the best she could offer without giving away the fact her heartbeat had sped up considerably, leaving her all but short of breath. "I'm looking for the Greenbaums." Gazing away, she briefly referred to her notes while collecting herself. "They live on Saddle Road."

He let his arm rest casually on the open window

frame as he leaned his head out a little. His short hair was slightly windblown, the hazel in his eyes looking more gold in the sunlight. She noticed his forearm was tan, a golden contrast against the white T-shirt he wore.

She tried not to get too hung up on his appearance, willed her reaction toward him to calm down. This was insanity. She knew better.

Drew's voice was just as buttery as the honey color of his skin. "Go down four houses, turn left. They're on the corner."

"Thanks."

She kept her foot on the brake, unsure what to say next. She gazed at him, willing herself not to stare. It didn't work.

The man looked great. There was no question. His hair just beckoned a woman to smooth it out. He moved his arm. A titanium watch encircled his wrist, a wrist that he now rested on the steering wheel. She could hear rock and roll softly playing out of the speakers.

Vaguely wondering what he was doing here, she was about to ask when he said, "I live across the street from the Greenbaums. They're good people."

Of course he lived in here. A former pro-ball guy could afford most anything in Timberline if he'd invested his money wisely. He'd been retired for more than a few years—at least that's what Susan had said.

"I like the neighborhood," Lucy remarked,

glancing at the big home to her right. The drive was circular, the stonework stunning.

"Me, too. You ought to come over sometime. Bring the boys and I'll show them my baseball stuff. I've got a bunch of team balls and autographed jerseys in my office. Lots of photos."

That he could casually invite her to his house put a ridiculous skip in her pulse. Why in the world would he be interested in her when he had a girlfriend? That just proved her point. He was involved with one woman and flirting with another. Then again, maybe he was sincere about showing her boys his baseball memorabilia.

But she'd seen how the women in Red Duck threw themselves at him, and perhaps he expected her to do likewise. She'd watched the baseball moms, even the married ones, hone right in on him on the playing field. It had been ludicrous the way they drooled over him. She wasn't like that. Not at all—

He was smiling at her and she forgot her train of thought.

"I'm sure the boys would like that."

What was she thinking, responding with that answer? She was losing her mind.

"I could show you the creek that runs through my property. I have the kids out and they fish in it. Never really catch anything."

And Lucy didn't want to catch an infatuation for the town's single, and too-good-looking-for-words, coach. Especially since he seemed to forget he was taken.

"How's Jacquie? Your girlfriend?" she added bluntly.

"She's good." His voice didn't change in inflection, as if it was no big deal. Perhaps Lucy had wanted to see if she could get him to shift in his seat, make him uncomfortable. But he didn't display any signs of discomfort.

"Well, I better go," Lucy said after a moment, more upset with herself than anything else. "See you around."

"See ya, Lucy."

The way he said her name gave her an involuntary shudder of pleasure, and she grimaced that she could be so easily charmed by him. She accelerated, forced thoughts of him from her mind, then found the Greenbaums and gathered what she needed to make her presentation.

Once inside the lovely home, she immediately liked the couple and felt confident she could sell herself and her menu.

Cooking was Lucy's passion. When she was a child, she'd watched PBS Saturday cooking shows rather than cartoons. Most of her recipe inspirations came from the Internet or cookbooks. She was always trying something new, enjoyed discovering wonderfully delicious flavors in restaurants, then putting her own twist on the dishes. Lucy especially favored hole-in-the-wall cafés with cooks who looked a little disreputable. The food served there was usually handed down through generations, and owners were almost always willing to brag and share.

Her parents loved her cooking, and whenever they were in the same city together, Lucy did all the meals. In awe of her talent, her mother asked Lucy how she could do what she did for a living. Lucy always smiled and said because she'd learned it from Grandma. Most of the basic recipes she had in her folder were family-related, passed down from her grandmother and great-grandmother before that.

She showed the Greenbaums her entrée catalog, explained how her services worked, what they would be required to do, and she showed them the fact questionnaire they'd need to fill out.

Ted and Shirley Greenbaum gave praise to the creativity of her nut-crusted turkey breasts, basmati rice pilaf and the spring salad. In case they had special dietary needs, she made sure they were aware she could prepare Atkins and vegetarian options.

"I'm all for it," Ted said, nodding his head.

Lucy had learned he was an avid golfer and liked to bring Shirley onto the greens with him. He was a retired stockbroker, living on investments. The couple had been married thirty-four years, their children both living in Los Angeles. Their fifth grandchild would be arriving soon.

Shirley smiled. "I will say you're more subdued than Raul."

Reining in her frown, Lucy kept her expression

pleasant. "I've heard Raul's roulades of beef is fabulous, but mine's great, too."

She had to land this account.

"Your menu looks delicious, Lucy. Raul favors heavier flavors, some with almost too much of a Basque flare." Shirley gazed at her husband for his opinion.

"Shirley, I've never liked Raul and I only tolerated him for you. I think he's too splashy and the man wears a cologne that spices up our house every time he's come over." Ted looked to Lucy. "I've been telling Shirley for years I was ready to give Raul the boot."

"Yes, but there's never been anybody else remotely as good as him in town." Shirley shrugged. "A few personal chefs have come and gone, but I think Raul runs them out. He's a little eccentric like that."

Lucy maintained a personable air, listening to the couple talk about her rival. It was rather enlightening.

"Well," Ted exclaimed, rubbing his hands together. "I guess we have ourselves a new cook!"

"Thank you so much," Lucy responded, grateful beyond words and just thrilled.

After the paperwork had been filled out, Lucy received her deposit check and a date to begin. She felt much better about her future. So much so that she glanced out the home's massive multiwindow front to see if she could catch a glimpse of Drew's place.

There was a house, but it was recessed too far for her to make out more than the chalet-style roofline.

Drew had definitely been generous in inviting her and the boys over. Perhaps she could put her opinion of him aside. After all, she didn't know him well and was only going on gut instinct—which was like cooking a recipe for the first time. Until she put the ingredients together and sampled them for herself, she wasn't sure if she'd like the blend of flavors or not.

In that regard, Drew could be a good influence on Jason. She had seen him around her sons and he did seem to care. Matt thought he was the greatest thing since his Roger Clemens card. Perhaps Drew could be a positive roll model for Jason, a man he could look up to. Unlike his absentee father.

Lucy decided to go "fishing"—and not in Drew's creek.

"I was talking to Drew Tolman on the way in," she said in a manner she hoped sounded casual as she put away her notebook. "He's my son's baseball coach and he mentioned living across the street."

"Tolman is a hell of a good guy," Ted said, resting his arm on Shirley's shoulder. She was wearing a cardigan sweater, a string of pearls around her neck. Both husband and wife had matching silver hair, groomed neatly, and both were dressed with style and chic.

Shirley touched her pearls. "I like him, too. Although, Ted, I'm not too fond of that girlfriend of his. Sometimes I see her drive by late at night."

Lucy's interest piqued.

Ted chuckled. "That woman is a pistol. He needs someone who'll appreciate him for more than his looks."

Lucy couldn't argue about Drew Tolman's looks, and any woman who had a pulse would notice that about him first.

She stood. "I'm sure Drew was quite the player in his day."

"Oh, he's still a player." Shirley laughed at the offhand comment. Lucy hadn't meant it like that.

"I mean baseball," she clarified, although she knew the other interpretation was probably just as apt.

"He was the best. Too bad about the drugs." Shirley's response froze Lucy to the spot.

Before she could close her open mouth, Ted explained, "They say he shot himself up with steroids all the time, was a real big user. I don't buy it, but then who knows? I mean, why did he quit the game when that steroid scandal broke? Makes you wonder."

"But I still like him, Ted." Shirley stood, her husband following, and the pair walked Lucy to the door. "People make mistakes."

Ted guided Lucy onto the stoop and they all stared across the street to the sprawling home of the man in question. The house appeared to be bigger than the *Titanic*, barely seen behind the curtain of white pines and the graveled circular drive that led up to what seemed to be a massive overhanging porch.

Drew was a former drug user....

Lucy couldn't think clearly.

Ted said, "I agree, Shirley. Tolman's the best. I don't care what the rumors are. He still gets aces in my book."

Smiling halfheartedly, Lucy said her goodbyes and left the porch. She got into her car, turned over the engine and drove away without another look at Drew's house.

And definitely without another thought of bringing her boys over to get to know him better.

Nine

Drew spent the better part of the morning in his batting cage slamming baseballs.

The sky was cloudless, and mature trees with heavy branches shaded half his house, keeping the interior cool and ready to absorb the mild afternoon warmth of June as the calendar made its way to summer.

A crisp chill hung in the air and he worked up a good sweat, got out some pent-up energy before walking back into the house to shower.

He ate breakfast at home instead of at Opal's Diner. He made oatmeal and drank half a pot of black coffee until he felt a jittery edge start to give him a headache.

Jacquie had called him just after seven and, in her cigarette-raspy voice, said they needed to talk.

He knew what was coming and, frankly, he didn't want to hear it. There was nothing he could do about last night and missing her birthday. He'd left the hospital, driven Lucy and her sons to her car, come home and given Jacquie a call. All he got was her voice mail greeting. He'd left a message, then went to bed. He never heard from her all night. When he woke and realized she hadn't gotten back to him, he'd thought about how he'd make it up to her, but the bite in her tone this morning quickly washed out those thoughts.

This relationship merry-go-round was getting old. He was done. Enough was enough. They should have been finished long ago, but for his own damn comfort and the familiarity he had with her, he'd let things ride. Way too long.

He'd postponed meeting her at the time she'd suggested, said he was busy until ten. She had an appointment and countered with ten forty-five. He didn't want to make a public scene, so when she suggested they meet at her house, he agreed.

Driving out of the Knolls, he'd run into Lucy and was glad for the chance to see her. He'd been telling himself that his reasons for wanting to end things with Jacquie had nothing to do with anyone but him and her. But Lucy's face had crept into his mind, filling his thoughts as he'd fallen into a hard sleep last night.

He remembered how upset she'd been at the hospital. He was pretty sure something was going on with her son, but without her talking about it, he could only speculate. Watching her cry, losing her emotional composure like that, had gotten to him. But he'd held back and refrained from placing com-forting hands on her because he hadn't wanted to add to her misery in case he didn't do it right. He wasn't sure he had a consoling gene in his body.

He couldn't console Jacquie when she was crying. It undid him when she let the tears flow, and he itched to be out of her company. Why Lucy's state of tears felt different to Drew, he could only speculate. When he thought about it, it bothered him that he could be cool toward one woman's emotional struggle, yet want to respond with his heart to the tug of another.

What did that say about him?

Drew was used to lots of testosterone, playing baseball with the guys and coaching boys. When you got hurt, you stood up and shook it off. You didn't let hurts linger, and you sure as hell didn't cry over something unless it required a minimum of fifty stitches or a broken bone that needed to be set without a shot of anesthetic.

Guys were different.

But they liked their women to be soft, sometimes helpless and weak. They wanted to feel needed. And that's something he was finally figuring out about Jacquie that just didn't make their on-and-off relationship work for him anymore.

Jacquie Santini didn't need anyone.

She was very capable, could handle anything. Hell, she even owned a gun, and if anyone was stupid enough to break into her house when she was home, he had no doubts she'd shoot him in the nuts.

Sometimes he wondered if Jacquie even had a

soft side. If she ever felt vulnerable. Yeah, she could cry about a bruised ego, but was it an act? He wasn't sure anymore. If she did feel despondent, she didn't show him. Either that, or he just hadn't clued into that part of her personality.

The interesting thing was, what drew him to Jacquie was the very thing he now questioned.

He'd liked that she was strong, assertive. But it left him with little to do. She had no use for him other than hot sex, and for him to take her around town to her black-tie events and show her off.

A time or two, Jacquie had called him shallow. Now that was the umpire calling a strike a ball. For the most part, Drew brushed her words off. Nobody could get to the Tolman-ater. Or so he thought. Jacquie had begun to rub him wrong with her stubborn streak, her attitude. Forget about using each other for good sex.

For a change, he wanted to feel needed by a woman.

He'd felt good about being able to help Lucy Carpenter last night, however small a role he'd played. She had needed him to be there. That male instinct was alive and well in him, and it was something he wanted to explore.

Wind blew through the open window of the Hummer as Drew listened to loud music. He loved rock and roll, loved how it vibrated through him, made him sing lyrics that brought him back to the days when he was in high school. He couldn't carry a note out of a choir hall, but that didn't stop him from singing.

Drew pulled the large SUV into Jacquie's drive and grabbed his cell phone and keys. She answered the door before he could knock.

Jacquie looked as if she hadn't slept all night. Her long black hair was twisted and pulled into a claw at the base of her skull. She looked presentable enough to have met with a client this morning, but he knew her better. Carefully applied cosmetics only hid so much.

Viewing the gray shadows beneath her eyes, it hit him—she'd probably tied one on. She liked to party on special occasions, and a birthday was a big deal to her.

He felt a moment's regret he hadn't made more of an effort to track her down last night. He knew her turning forty was a dicey event, one she hadn't been looking forward to. She'd wanted to spend it with him, to make it memorable.

He wondered what she'd done, where she'd gone. And without him. A sharp feeling assaulted him, and he ignored the jealousy that rose, but quickly ebbed and faded to nothing.

"Come in," she said, her voice low.

She stepped aside and he entered her well-appointed home. A color palette of black and green made up the entry and led into a very spacious kitchen. Jacquie decorated with flare, an occasional spot of red in a pillow or lamp to make a statement.

The house smelled like espresso and stale perfume, along with the stagnant odor of smoke.

The large window above the granite counter and kitchen sink was open, but it didn't do much to ventilate the air in the house.

On high heels, Jacquie walked to the breakfast bar and grabbed a pack of cigarettes. She knew he didn't like her smoking around him. But he had no say-so in her home. And once in a while, he hated to admit it, but the smell of a burning cigarette was a temptation. He used to smoke many years ago, and the draw of a nicotine fix could sometimes flare up.

Knowing their conversation was going to get rocky and that she'd probably get histrionic on him, he was halfway to asking to bum one off her when she blurted, "I was unfaithful to you last night, so we need to end things."

Drew held back, felt as if he'd been hit by a ball. He'd been prepared for one kind of pitch and didn't see this knuckleball coming.

Folding his arms over his chest, he asked, "Do I know him?" It was all Drew managed to say.

"No." Jacquie flicked her lighter to life, lit the cigarette and blew a stream of smoke out the crack in the window. "I don't even know him." Keeping her posture straight, she looked him directly in the eyes. "I'm sorry, Drew."

The expression on her face was one of true regret, a tired gaze he almost didn't recognize on her. She was usually so put together, so all-knowing.

He wanted to feel anger. Pissed off. Resentment. Something. But the emotions just wouldn't come.

"How come you're telling me? I doubt I would have found out unless you did it in public."

"Give me more credit than that." She took another hit on the cigarette, her face silhouetted by light from the window.

Neither one of them said anything for a long while.

The details of what had transpired with her and some other guy were inconsequential to him. That truth made him snort and think this really sucked. He'd come over prepared to break up with her, and she was breaking things off with him, and rather than feeling like shit about what she'd said, he felt relieved. How screwed up was that?

"We can't pretend anymore," Jacquie said, turning toward him. "You and I both know this has been a long time coming."

"You're right. Things between us haven't been going too good lately," he said, taking a seat at one of the stools at the breakfast bar.

His words put her on the defensive, as if suddenly the failure of their relationship fell solely on him and he was the only one to blame. "You think I didn't notice?" she all but bristled.

"Hey," he retorted, finally feeling the sting of her betrayal. The resulting heat of anger shocked him. She could say whatever she wanted about him, but he'd never once been unfaithful to her. And he'd had a lot of opportunities over the years. "You sleeping with another guy is not my fault, babe."

"If you'd showed up, none of this would have happened."

"I had a kid in the hospital!"

"He has a mother and you aren't the father," she sniped, her face contorting.

Her tone made his muscles tighten, and her high-and-mighty demeanor irritated him—enough so that when his cell phone rang, he answered for the distraction and just to annoy Jacquie while refocusing his attention. "Yeah?" he growled. "Tolman here."

Dead silence.

"Hello?"

Whoever was there clicked off and ended the call. Drew didn't have the desire to check the caller ID log.

Collecting his thoughts, he was quiet a long moment. This was an ugly way to end things, not the way he had envisioned. He had to own up to his part. He'd been distancing himself from her lately, doing his own thing when he knew she wanted to spend time with him. He found lots to occupy himself, wasn't available to her when she called. She'd come to Opal's—a sure way to run into him.

He knew this was coming, and now that he had a moment for a reality check, an unexpected sadness came over him. Three years was a long time to spend with someone.

He knit his fingers together, looked at his clean fingernails. "Jacquie, I'm sorry."

And that's when she began to cry.

And that's when he felt slugged in the gut. But

that's when he also knew he couldn't go backward. This was the old pattern. Her pushing, him pulling, her grabbing, him taking.

It was done.

"I'm sorry, too," she uttered with a sigh, trying to stop the tears and get herself together. "I wish things had been different for us. I loved you, Drew...I still do."

He couldn't reply. He knew she wanted him to at least say he still loved her. But he didn't.

Maybe he was a shallow asshole.

Since he said nothing, she pushed herself away from the counter and snubbed out her cigarette. "Can we remain friends?" she asked, her voice cracking.

He didn't have to think about an answer and replied with the truth. "Sure." A little lingering tie to her was not quite severed, and he still wanted her in his life. She knew things about him that he'd never told anyone else, and he knew she'd keep his confidences, even in a breakup. Jacquie did have integrity, and if she gave him her word, she meant it.

Her gaze locked onto his, dark skepticism filtering through the brown depths of her eyes. "Do you really want to remain friends or are you just saying that?"

"I really do, Jacquie. We had some good times."

"Okay. I appreciate it." Her shoulders trembled and she was having a hard time keeping herself together.

"No problem."

She sniffed. "Is there anything else you want to say?"

He had lots to say. But none of it mattered. "No."

"Well…all right then."

Without another word, he got up and left the house. Jacquie didn't come after him. He sucked in deep gulps of air, blinked in the bright rays of sunshine and tried to remember if he'd left his sunglasses in the Hummer.

He was barely out the front door when his cell rang again. Only this time he didn't bother to answer it.

Drew Tolman didn't feel like talking to anyone.

Journal of Mackenzie Taylor

I shouldn't have called him.

Ten

Drew swore.

He hit Redial for the number that showed up on his missed call list, waited for someone to pick up. Lynette answered.

"Did you call me earlier today?" he asked, knowing in his gut before he asked that she hadn't. Lynette always left him a message.

"No, Drew. I didn't."

He ran a hand through his hair, then rested his wrist on the steering wheel. He'd taken a drive to Burnt Mountain after leaving Jacquie's. That had been three hours ago. Now that he had call service again, being closer to Timberline, his phone had beeped to remind him he'd missed a call. As soon as he'd checked the ID log, he was pushing Redial.

"Mackenzie called me," Drew said, exhaling the tight breath in his chest. "Is she there?"

"Yes, Drew. She's out back with some friends."

"Get her for me, Lynette. She phoned."

Lynette's sigh was wispy. "Well, for heaven's sake. Yes, I'll get her. Hold on." The receiver was plunked down and Drew waited.

A tense silence enveloped the inside of the Hummer, the big motor idling softly.

For a moment, he thought Mackenzie wouldn't talk to him. But then a girl's voice carried over the line. "Hello?"

"Mackenzie, it's Drew."

"I know. Aunt Lynette said."

Drew's pulse quickened into sharp beats. He hadn't spoken to her in four months, had been waiting for the day she would call. Now that he had her attention, he found reason draining from his thought process. He had too much to say, and felt unable to round it up into something coherent.

Seventeen years was a long time for a girl not to have her real dad in her life. Drew couldn't say the wrong things and mess up their relationship further.

A crazy mixture of hope and fear collided in his chest.

When he'd brought her to the February spring training game, she'd hardly said anything to him, so he'd taken her lead and hadn't pushed. But now he felt like maybe she was ready to give them a chance—that maybe that was why she'd called. Only he didn't know how to talk to her, what to say without making her retreat.

Sitting stiffly, Drew forced himself to speak slowly.

"How did your graduation go, sugar?" The Southern endearment slipped out and sluiced across his tongue like honey. He instantly regretted his use of it on his daughter. He'd spoken the word casually for years. He sensed Mackenzie knew where it came from.

"Good." The monosyllable word hovered.

"I wish I could have been there." But he and Lynette had talked about it and decided Mackenzie wouldn't have wanted him to come. He hadn't wanted to ruin that milestone for her. He'd done enough damage already.

Mackenzie needed time to get used to his acceptance of her, even though it had been two years since he'd apologized to her and to Caroline. He hadn't gone into details as to why he'd behaved the way he had so many years ago. Once he gained her trust, he could tell her what had happened.

The scars of truth ran deep, were thick. Drew never discussed it with anyone. Only Jacquie.

The line was quiet. He could hear his daughter's soft breathing, almost smell the way her skin was perfumed with that fruity spray she wore. He'd never once given her a hug. Never told her to her face that he loved her. She wouldn't believe him if he did, and if he touched her, she'd bolt. Not even at Caroline's funeral had he come close enough to make her feel threatened. He'd waited. He would bide his time.

"I called…" she said, stopping herself as if to lick her lips or to think about what she wanted to say "…to thank you for the diary."

Relief hit Drew, warming his muscles, relaxing him. He'd guessed right. He knew Caroline wrote stuff down and he took a chance that Mackenzie would be like her mother.

"You're welcome."

"My old one was getting full."

Damn him, but he needed the reassurances, no matter how nonpersonal, so he asked, "So you like the new one?"

"I do."

But once more, a cold static carried from Florida to Idaho. The only sounds were the soft rasps of breathing.

Drew couldn't stand it. He had a resolve of steel, but when it came to Mackenzie, he wanted nothing more than to have the chance of being her father. "Mackenzie, have you thought any more about coming to stay with me for the summer?"

He tensed. Waited. Long minutes.

"I don't know."

It was the first time she hadn't flat out said hell no. Drew went on quickly. "You'd have your own room and I'd show you around town. There's lots to do. We could go out on my boat and I have four-wheelers at my cabin. You'd like it."

Silence. Then she murmured, "I don't know."

Disappointment settled heavily on his shoulders, but he wasn't ready to give up. "Think about it, Mackenzie, and get back to me."

"Okay. I gotta go now. My friends are here."

"Yeah, okay, Mackenzie." He sucked in his breath, his chest tight. "Thanks for calling."

"Sure."

The line disconnected, and Drew sat there a long while, parked at mile marker 9 out on Timberline Highway.

Large white clouds drifted overhead, fast enough for him to absently watch them move across the sky while he replayed the conversation in his head.

Stuffed buffalo heads hung on the rustic pine walls of Woolly Burgers, famous for their half-pound hamburgers. The smell of grilled onions filled the air, making a person's mouth water, along with a pungent scent of hops from draft beer. White restaurant dishes clattered in the kitchen, sounding as if someone had dropped a load of them onto a metal countertop. The booths were timbered by cross-cut sections of pines painted with clear enamel to a glossy shine. Country music played from a jukebox.

A waitress came to the Carpenters' dinner table to collect the empty cups leftover from the previous patrons, and to clear the rest of the mess before snagging her tip.

"I'm sorry," she said, half-breathless. "We lost our busboy tonight and we're shorthanded. Can I get you something to drink to start?"

The boys ordered soft drinks and Lucy ordered an iced tea.

It was Friday night and the place was packed.

Cheerful chaos abounded from the staff, and each time one of them moved into the pass-through door, Lucy caught a glimpse of the cooks. They stood over sizzling grills, wiping their foreheads with the back of a hand as their chef hats drooped on their heads.

"So what are you boys hungry for?" Lucy asked, smiling at the two of them. They sat next to one another across the table from her, their noses buried in their menus.

She'd taken them out to dinner as a celebration for making the Little League teams they'd tried out for. It was a positive note in the aftermath of a dark discovery. She'd yet to talk to Jason about what she'd found in his uniform pocket, instead taking several days so she could act reasonably rather than emotionally.

Lucy had told herself she'd been down this road before, and she knew how it could wind its way into unforeseen turns. She also knew that there had to be an end to the tunnel, a way out.

And a plan had come to her yesterday. She hadn't told Jason about it yet, but she was going to after their dinner. It might not be the perfect solution, but she was tackling this in a different manner this time. Rather than "take" something away from Jason as a form of punishment, she was going to "give" to him.

"I want the plain cheeseburger." Matt closed his menu and folded his hands on top of it. His chin was mere inches from the massive tabletop. He'd yet to hit any kind of growth spurt, while Jason sat a good five inches taller.

Jason scanned the food selections, and she observed him with an ache in her heart. Right now, at this moment, he seemed so normal. Happy. A regular boy. Just like he used to be.

"I'm going to have the bacon cheeseburger with fries."

"Mom, does mine come with fries?" Matt asked.

"I'm sure it does."

"Can I have coleslaw instead?"

The corners of Lucy's mouth turned upward, and she smiled fondly at her twelve-year-old. "I'm sure they can do that."

The young waitress returned with their beverages, then got out her order pad. "Have you decided?"

The boys ordered, then Lucy made the correct modifications to Matt's before requesting her own cheeseburger. She was starving and a burger sounded good. The waitress hurried off to post their orders in the kitchen.

"You think Coach Drew is going to show us some pitching, too?" Matt asked Jason. "You're the lucky duck for getting on his team."

Jason shrugged. "He probably won't."

Matt gave a disappointed frown, but it was quickly replaced by a toothy smile. "Hey, 'member that time we had Coach Steve for baseball camp and Bolthouse said *shit* so Coach said real loud, 'Bolty, what word did you just say?' But Bolthouse said nuttin' back and Coach said, 'Does your mother know you talk like that, Bolty?' And Coach said it loud enough for Bolty's mom to hear and she yelled at him?" Matt giggled, then looked at Lucy. "Mom, that wasn't me saying shit for real. I was just telling a story."

She laughed. "I got that part."

Jason laughed, too, then playfully socked his brother on the arm. "You're such a kid sometimes."

"Yeah. Takes one to know one." Matt took a sip of his soda, his large tennis shoes kicking the bench he sat on. Then he drew himself taller. "Hey, Mom. I made ten bucks walking Ada's dogs."

"He gave me three bucks of it," Jason said, his expression one of gratitude.

Lucy briefly wondered what he was going to do with the money, but she didn't want to ruin the moment. This was like old times, and it felt good. Both boys were horsing around like they used to, getting along, cracking jokes.

"I'm saving up to buy lots of candy, and I'm going to see if I can find a Drew Tolman baseball card and have him autograph it for me. You think he would?" Matt asked.

Shrugging, Lucy made no comment. She didn't want Drew as her son's role model. Now that she knew about the man's sordid past, she'd rethought her judgment of him—and it wasn't favorable. It was one thing when she thought him a flirt, a man about town who could get away with anything on looks and charm. Quite another when she knew he'd used drugs and ruined a baseball career because of it.

"He would," Jason stated. "I saw a new kid ask him to sign his glove and he did."

"Bang-o-rang!" Matt's face lit up. "I hope Ada's got lots and lots of dogs for me to walk all summer long."

Jason slouched. "How come Dad never sends us any money?"

Lucy refrained from rolling her eyes. "I think you know the answer to that."

"Because he's a jerk."

Matthew's lively expression fell. "Yeah…he's a jerk."

"I know you boys are mad at him, but you have to admit he does pay child support." On a sour note, she added, "Most of the time."

She hated to bash Gary, tried not to in case one day he stepped up to the plate and was actually a dad to the boys. Once they were spoken, she couldn't take negative words back, but sometimes they just slipped out.

"How come we can't have the child support to buy comics?"

"Because it goes toward food and electricity."

"I don't want electricity," Matt grumbled, stacking his fists and lowering his chin on top of them.

Lucy smiled. "But you use it every time you leave the light on in your bedroom." She drank a swallow of iced tea. "Dad helps, so I don't want you to think he doesn't do anything."

It was important to Lucy that the boys didn't hate

their father, even though he was an absentee dad. Sons looked at adult males as role models, and Gary Carpenter was surely no role model. So Lucy had to improvise and make him appear a level better than he was.

His lack of being here still annoyed her in that he didn't participate in Jason and Matt's lives. There was no excuse for Gary to be down in Mexico with another woman. He should have stayed in Boise, been there for her sons and been a dad.

But Gary had his own agenda and there wasn't a darn thing Lucy could do to change how her ex-husband thought. She'd wasted enough time on that over the course of their marriage.

The food came, and she and the boys enjoyed a family dinner together. It felt good. Right. She forgot about past hurts, the wrong choices, and just enjoyed. She even let the boys order dessert, and just as they were finishing off the last spoonfuls of chocolate syrup in melted vanilla ice cream sundaes, Drew came into Woolly Burgers with the other Little League coaches.

The group stopped by the table and said hello to the boys. The coach Matt had was pleasant and attractive. Too bad he wore a gold wedding ring. The fact that she noticed had Lucy silently chastising herself. He complimented Matt on his fielding, then said he'd see him day after tomorrow. The men filled a table, but Drew lagged behind.

"How's it going, Jason?" he asked.

"Okay."

Lucy kept her gaze leveled on Drew, wondering about his past and wishing she knew more. How could he have tossed away a great career for an addiction? She'd never understand why someone would cave to the lure of drugs. She hardly ever took a pain reliever, unless she had bad cramps or a headache. Drew's past didn't make sense and perhaps the Greenbaums didn't know the whole story.

Drew shifted his stance, emphasizing the strength in his well-muscled thighs. The faded blue jeans he wore fit him snugly, but they weren't too tight. A striped, button-down Oxford shirt made his shoulders appear quite broad. He tucked the tails in, so Lucy could see his stomach was flat, and there wasn't an ounce of fat on him. For his age, he was in great shape. She couldn't help admiring him, and when she caught herself, she looked away.

"We'll be doing dailies at nine," Drew said to Jason, "but if you want to come an hour early, I'll let you pitch some balls to me."

"Yeah, sure. I could do that." Jason seemed to really want to, and it made Lucy take notice. He'd complained about having to try out for Little League, but when he'd found out he'd made the team, he had looked pleased. She knew baseball would be good for him. Too bad he had to be around Drew....

She wished she could figure out if he was fit or unfit to coach. Surely the Little League commission had checked him out. They were very stringent in their guidelines. So many parents sued now, it was ridiculous.

"Just make sure you bring your doctor's release." Drew's profile drew her attention—his nose and straight forehead, the shape of his mouth.

"I'll get it." Lucy crossed her arms, perhaps a subconscious move to ward away thoughts of him because she found her reaction to him vaguely disturbing.

His attention turned to her and he smiled. A tingle started in the pit of her belly. She hated that he could cause her to feel a little flutter. "How're you?"

"Fine."

"Everything go all right at the Greenbaums?"

"I got the job."

"You'll like working for them. They're good people."

Lucy wondered how good Drew would think they were if he knew they talked about his past, even with favor and sympathy.

"Hey, Coach." Matt, who had quietly listened to the exchange, finally burst in. "Do you think if I got one of your baseball cards, you could autograph it to me?"

"Absolutely."

"Gee, thanks!"

Drew glanced over his shoulder to the table where his friends sat. "I better go. See you around."

A moment later, Lucy paid the bill and drove the boys home.

Switching on lights, she closed the kitchen window to ward off the chill mountain air that had settled in. She looked at the stack of mail on the counter, and watched Jason finger through the envelopes. He didn't have to tell her what he was hoping for.

She'd gone to their post office box earlier in the day, and what he wanted had come.

He grabbed an envelope and waved it at her. "Sweet! My car insurance money. When can we buy me a replacement truck?" Jason's face lit up as if it were his birthday. She hated to knock the wind out of his sail, but he'd given her no choice.

"We aren't," she replied, walking into the kitchen and getting a glass of water.

"Whadda you mean?"

"I'm not buying you another truck, Jason."

"Why not?"

"Because you haven't earned it."

He lowered the envelope, stared hard at it, then stared hard at her. "That's bull. You said if I tried out for Little League, I could have another car."

"I did say that, yes."

"So you can't change your mind! It's not fair."

"No. When someone doesn't stick to their end of the bargain about something, it's not fair."

"Whadda you mean?"

She gazed at him for a long, long moment, giving him a look that spoke volumes. Only one other time had she looked at him like this.

Then suddenly, he clued in. His shoulders slumped, the light in his eyes dimmed.

"I will keep my promise, since you're playing baseball," Lucy said, then raised her tone an octave and infused hope into her next words. "But there's going to be a delay. I know of a way you can get your truck by summer's end if you don't mess up. On *anything*."

Her meaning was quite clear and he understood. Jason frowned, tentatively asked, "How?"

"You'll go to work. For me."

"Huh?"

"Starting on Thursday, you'll be delivering meals that I prepare to the Sunrise Trail Creek Seniors Home each Tuesday and Thursday. I've already cleared everything with the staff, and I'll be making food donations to the home on those days." Lucy continued in a light tone, but she'd thought this out well in advance and was quite succinct with her plan. "I want you to stay there for a couple of hours, serve the meals to the elderly and then clean up."

Jason made a face. "I don't want to hang out with a bunch of old people."

She raised her brows, put her hands on her hips. "The way I see it, you don't have a choice, Jason."

"Can't I do something else?" She saw the flicker in his eyes as his mind worked. "How about if I apply to be a busboy at Woolly Burgers?"

Lucy smiled, nodded with genuine enthusiasm. "That's a fantastic idea. You can do that along with the meals at Sunrise." She inhaled, pleased. "Between the Sunrise, baseball and Woolly's, you'll be so busy this summer, you won't have time for anything else, now will you?"

She let the question hang, hovering between them as if suspended on an invisible thread.

Jason's mouth pursed. "Okay," he mumbled, then climbed the stairs to the bedroom he shared with his younger brother.

Lucy stayed in the kitchen a long while, hoping her son would be able to prove himself. She remembered her little boy and how he used to be, and she knew he had it in him to do the right thing. He just had to believe in himself.

Last evening had ended on a note of promise, but Lucy's morning began on a chord of disappointment.

She received a call on her cell just after breakfast.

She pushed the talk button. "Hello?"

Shirley Greenbaum was on the other end. "Lucy, I'm so sorry but we're going to have to postpone."

Lucy's heartbeat slowed to molasses.

Postpone. No income.

Shirley went on, "Our daughter developed a complication with her pregnancy and we're flying to Los Angeles immediately."

"I hope it's nothing serious, Mrs. Greenbaum."

"The doctors are monitoring her. She had a similar situation with our last grandson. So we're optimistic. It's still scary, though."

After discussing a possible restart date, Lucy disconnected the phone.

Since it wasn't technically a breach of contract, Lucy had no recourse. The Greenbaums still wanted her to work for them, only she wouldn't be making any money for a couple of weeks until they returned.

With her mind running on overload, half numb with Shirley's untimely news, Lucy neatened up the slips of paper on the kitchen counter. A gas receipt for $37.85 to fill her tank. The Little League paperwork. Hospital release.

Looking at the restaurant slip for last night's dinner—$48.95 on three burgers, drinks and desserts, plus tip—Lucy had a surge of regret for splurging.

If things didn't turn around, she would have to get a real job with a steady income. Something she hadn't done since before the boys were born.

But a weekly paycheck was desperately needed. And soon.

Eleven

Spin's eyesight gave her fits and she ripped out a strong curse beneath her breath. She wore her rhinestone, horn-rim glasses, the filigreed chain around her neck.

Squinting so she could see better, she dabbed some oil paint on the tiny section numbered 45. Or was that 46? *For the love of mud.* Da Vinci must have had the patience of a saint.

It had taken Spin the better portion of a year to get this far on *The Last Supper,* only able to work on the paint-by-number scene for small increments before her vision blurred from the strain. But she was making progress. She hoped to finish it before she died.

The Sunrise Trail Creek assisted care home was located by a stretch of the Wood River and appointed modestly in neutral colors—bland walls in the foyer, the floor covered in speckled linoleum. Out back, there was a pond where the residents could feed the geese. Every now and then, Spin liked to watch them, but it saddened her at the same time. They could fly away, go wherever they wanted, and she was stuck here. Dying a little each day.

Her purpose in life was gone. Over.

Back in the old days, she was quite the catch, a real dish. But as time wore on and age faded her beauty to a map of wrinkles and a widow's peak that turned white-gray, she felt her value ebb.

She used to be a live pistol. Could cut a joke with the best of them, and had attention lavished on her. After Wally died, life in Red Duck without her beloved husband had taken a solitary path. By choice, she hadn't remarried. Perhaps if she had, she wouldn't be alone now. But the saying went that women outlived the men they loved, and if the inhabitants in Sunrise were any indication, that was true.

There were more women than men in the facility. And the men who hadn't lost their hearing altogether, weren't drooling or wetting themselves sitting in wheelchairs, paid her notice that she didn't care for. Perverts, the lot of them.

Spin dipped her Grumbacher paintbrush into the yellow-gold mix on her palette. Hand raised, she tried not to let her wrist shake as she put a dot on the canvas. She smeared it and landed a dollop of color on the number 123 portion.

Hell's bells!

Disgusted, she set the paintbrush down and took

a break. She left the glassed-in sunporch and walked outside to look at the pond.

She stood on the covered veranda, her liver-spotted, gnarled hands holding on to the railing. For some ungodly reason, hot tears pooled in her eyes.

She blinked.

Borrowed time. That's what she was on.

Inhaling, she took a deep breath of the meadow grass, smelled the fragrance of aspen leaves and wild columbine. She held it inside her frail lungs for as long as she could. She wanted to remember for when she got to heaven.

"Hi, Ms. Goodey-Leonard!" one of the staff called cheerfully. Spin turned to see that cute little nurse walking onto the porch with a tall woman following her. "How are you today?"

"I'm still alive."

The nurse giggled, her fresh-faced complexion golden in the indirect sunshine. "You sure are!"

Spin sized up the dark-haired woman, who wore attitude like a coat. She was pretty, but the look in her eyes was bruised. She was in self-torture.

"Ms. Goodey-Leonard, this is Jacquie. She's volunteering at the Sunrise for the next few weeks, and she'll be here to visit with you."

"Visit me for what?"

"Play cards, take a stroll in our garden, share a snack at our coffee shop, write letters for you—"

"Everyone I loved is dead accept for Morris, my great-nephew, and I talk to him on the phone."

"Oh, for crying out loud," Jacquie muttered, rolling her eyes and exhaling sharply. Then, in a soft tone to the nurse, she said, "I didn't volunteer for this job. Can't you assign me to someone else? Someone who's bedridden, in a coma, and I'll just watch television in their room."

Spin might wear small hearing aids, but they were hypersensitive and she could radio in on things that others might miss.

"You don't have to have a kitten. I don't need anyone to write a letter for me. I can do it myself."

Pushing the glasses farther up her noise, she took a hard look at Jacquie and made a fast inventory. She had the goods, but a bad attitude went with that. A woman scorned. That was obvious in the way her concealer didn't quite cover up the dark circles beneath her puffy eyes. Women didn't bawl like that over missing a clothing sale. A man was involved.

Spin perked up. Hearing about a love story gone wrong would kill half the afternoon. The painting could wait.

"I need a letter written," she said bluntly.

Jacquie's expression clouded. "But isn't there someone else I can—"

"Dear, I feel some abdominal gas coming on from that cabbage soup I had for lunch," Spin said to the young nurse, then feigned a grimace, clutching her midsection. "Get me something for it. I'd hate to soil myself. Hurry along, now."

The nurse hightailed it to the infirmary.

Spin's arms dropped as soon as the nurse was out of sight.

Jacquie's eyes widened. "If you're going to have an accident, go to the bathroom."

"So what was his name? Some sugarpuss—wasn't he? How long did you know him?"

"What are you talking about?" Jacquie demanded, her brown eyes hard with attitude. "I'm getting that nurse."

"Don't bother." Spin's grip was slight but firm as she grabbed hold of Jacquie's arm. "Sit down with me. I'm not going to shit my pants, but my knees are ready to give out. I've been standing at an easel for an hour."

Something within Jacquie reacted. Who was this old bird that she could bull crap her way to giving a nurse the slip? Then talk as if she were born in a naval yard, yet appear as frail as parchment?

It hit Jacquie. She reminded her of…herself.

Clenching her jaw, Jacquie wished she wasn't in an old folks home. Damn Sheriff Lewis and his fake-and-bake tan to hell. He'd pulled her over the night of her birthday, after she'd left Max Beck's place. The sheriff could have written her up for a DUI. God knows she'd been juiced. Instead of hauling her butt to jail, he'd arranged for Deputy Cooper to come out, get her and drive her home—but with two conditions. She promised never to drive drunk again, and she had to perform one month of voluntary community service. He'd done the picking. The Sunrise Trail Creek Seniors Home.

Along with a bitch of a hangover she hadn't been able to shake after Drew left, Jacquie had literally been taken for a ride. This was her punishment—sitting with an elderly woman who was staring at her as if she could read her mind.

"Are you sure you don't need to use the bathroom?" Jacquie asked, suddenly antsy and nervous to be here. She didn't like that undressed feeling that rose when Spin looked at her through those diamond-encrusted glasses.

"Don't insult me." Spin sat on one of the patio chairs and let out an audible sigh. "So tell me. Am I right? It's a man. You didn't shove his clutch anymore?"

Jacquie didn't respond.

"I'd been around the block a few times before I met my Wally, and it was no picnic. Men can be assholes." Gazing at her over the rim of the glasses, Spin asked, "Ever heard of a Judge Harrison?"

"No."

"Good. Because he was the biggest asshole of all time."

Jacquie needed something to settle herself, and longed for the soothing smoke of a Virginia Slim. "Harrison's a former boyfriend?"

"Humph!" Spin's spider-veined hands cupped the arms of the chair. She had yellow-gold paint on her fingers. "Get a pad of legal paper and come back here with a pen, too. You'll find them in the rec hall. Go on."

A moment later, Jacquie came back and asked herself why she was even doing what this woman asked. She sat down once again, pad on her lap. "Okay."

"Okay," Spin repeated. "Start writing exactly what I tell you."

Jacquie suspended the pen over the paper and began to write as soon as Spin started talking, slowly enough for Jacquie to get the words down.

"Way back when we first met, I knew you'd be a special person in my life. I fell in love with you and you said you loved me. You are the heart of my heart, and no matter what has happened, I feel like I have been cheated out of my future with you."

The pen in Jacquie's hand paused, and she slanted a glance at Spin. "Who's this letter to?"

"Keep writing," Spin declared, "or I'll lose my train of thought." In a resolved tone, she continued, "It makes no difference whose fault it is. But I find myself thinking about you constantly, even though I am to blame."

Jacquie abruptly set the pen down. "I can't write this." Tears swam in her eyes, stinging them. "You'll have to get someone else to do it."

"Someone else can't. They haven't lived it like you." Spin's gaze was all-knowing. "I was young once."

Swallowing, Jacquie couldn't trust herself to speak. How had her life gotten so screwed up? She'd loved Drew with all her heart, would have done anything to stay with him. But he'd fallen out of love with her. And she'd cheated on him. There was no going back.

"You need to write this letter," Spin said, her voice wizened yet wise. "For yourself. Never mail it to him, of course, because it only shows him your weakness for him, but it'll be the first step in getting over the relationship."

With those words, Jacquie silently began to cry.

"Now, now. I'll help you get through it." Spin reached out to the attractive woman, patted her hand and felt a breath of fresh air fill her lungs.

Spin Goodey-Leonard suddenly had purpose.

Twelve

Raul Nunez was ruining Lucy's life, what little there was left of it. When she took stock, she came up far short from just a year ago. Gone were her suburbia home, padded bank account and comfortable client list.

Now she lived in a teardown shack with rusting motorhomes in the back, her bank account was slowly dwindling, she needed an oil change on her car—but didn't want to spend the money—and the hospital bill had come and the insurance wasn't covering $895 of it.

Her life, in a nutshell, was in the crapper.

And that eccentric Raul Nunez was making her existence in Red Duck hellish. He had such clout that getting a cooking job was next to impossible. She found out he'd done this to other personal chefs who'd come to town to infringe on his private territory. It was ludicrous. No man could keep up with the work he had, and she was sick of people calling her to ask if she could make his famous lobster bisque!

The last time someone asked, she'd said of course—replicating recipes was her specialty. She was determined to meet with a client, even if it meant she'd do so under false pretexts. Once they sampled *her* lobster bisque, they'd hire her. No doubts.

But she never got the opportunity. Raul called her to say he'd sue if she so much as *breathed another consonant* about cooking a personal recipe of his.

She'd taken a day to be indignant over it, then decided this war had to come to an end. And she was willing to knock pride onto the chopping board. Lucy was waving her white apron. She *had* to have Raul's cooperation here.

She tried to reach him by phone, but he wouldn't pick up. He must have had her caller ID earmarked and was screening her out, the god-in-his-own-mind chef. Over a latte, he had mentioned he thought he was a god, touched by Apollo.

What a crock of stew.

But Lucy just couldn't think about Raul the Weasel right now. She wanted to enjoy today for all it offered, and the sun felt so good warming her face.

Sue Lawrence had invited Lucy and her sons to go "docking" on Overlook Dam. The Lawrences had a seven passenger Bayliner, and when Matt found out they'd be going on it, he could hardly wait. Jason and

Nutter played on the same team, and Lucy hoped the trip would help Jason cement a new friendship. Nutter seemed well-adjusted, and Jason definitely needed to hang around boys who were on the right track.

Lucy had insisted on bringing food for everyone. She'd made roasted chicken sandwiches for the boys and went gourmet for the adults. Olive-oil-grilled rosemary bread with fresh mozzarella, baby spinach and tomatoes. Sue packed chips and pop. Beer for Dave.

The water level on Overlook Dam had reached full elevation from the spring thaw, its surface like a rippling layer of teal-blue glass. Boats motored through the main body, leaving wakes from water-skiers daring enough to brave the frigid lake in wet suits.

June was too early for the water to have warmed to a decent swimming temperature, but the air temp had risen, with an unseasonably high 76 degrees predicted by noon. Anyone in Red Duck and Timberline who owned a boat had come up to the dam.

Lucy and the boys had driven up with the Lawrences in their white Suburban, and once at the launch site, Sue and Lucy loaded the boat before Dave backed the trailer into the water.

In short order, Lucy learned what docking meant versus going boating. Halfway into Big Eddy's Bay, a floating, square-shaped dock, with a middle section cut out for swimming, was anchored. There were already eight boats moored to it, and the dock itself was covered with coolers, lawn chairs and several dogs. Activity abounded; a father and son threw a football, while in the opposite corner, ladies gathered—some in bathing suits, others in shorts. A golden retriever jumped into the water to fetch a stick.

Dave docked the Bayliner and Sue set up camp on their part of the dock, while the boys joined a group of kids and hung out with them. Docking meant a day spent socializing. At times, a boat would cast off, take a water-skier out, but circle back and dock for more beer and chips, more talk about boat motors and life in town.

"Honey, do you want a beer?" Dave asked as he lifted the lid on the cooler.

"Sure."

"Lucy?" he asked.

"That would be great. Thanks." She rarely drank beer, but it sounded good today.

The heat felt delicious on her mostly bare arms. She'd put her tropical-print bikini on, with a pair of shorts and a T-shirt overtop. The bottoms didn't reach far below her navel, but the French cut flattered her curvy figure. For a woman her age, she supposed she had a decent body. After all, she'd been pregnant with two kids, but thankfully didn't have stretch marks.

A man came toward them and talked to Dave.

Sue said, "That's Lloyd Zaragoza. He's the mayor of the dock. He knows everyone's business."

"Oh." Lucy turned her head to glance at Lloyd. He appeared as if he'd swallowed a small watermelon, his full belly taut and round, his flesh already tanned even though it was the beginning of the season. He wore body hair like a sweater. She felt under the gun as soon as he slanted an obvious gaze on her.

Lloyd came right up to her. "You're new in town."

"Uh, yes," she replied.

"You need anything, look me up. I'm listed in the book under Z. Zaragoza."

"Uh, okay." She knew she never would, and she wasn't even sure how to take the gesture. He had to be near sixty-five, the hair on his head thinning to silver strands.

"Tell me your story," he said, but went right on talking. "I'll be sure and keep it straight. Maybe. Depends on what you tell me, and sometimes why ruin a good story by sticking to the truth?" Then he guffawed at his own joke.

"My story?" she queried, not quite following him.

"What do you do in Red Duck?" he asked, staring intently at her. There was genuine interest and actually a warmth in his blue eyes. "What's your line of work, sis?"

"Personal chef," she replied, having a moment's optimism. If this man was a busybody, he could put out a good word for her. It was apparent he liked to talk. To anyone who'd listen. "If you know of someone who needs a great cook, my card is on the bulletin board at Sutter's."

"Raul Nunez has done a few Christmas parties for me," Lloyd said, and Lucy staved off a groan.

Raul. Raul! *Raul!!!*

"Of course you like Raul's cooking, but mine's just as good." Lucy had come to a point where she was going to pull out all stops. "I'd be happy to set up an appointment with you and give you a sampling of my menu."

"I might just do that."

No firm commitment, but it wasn't an outright "no" either.

Lloyd's grandson, who was about four years old, ran past, water spraying off the wet ends of his hair. Lucy's body clenched, the cold droplets on her bare arms causing her to shiver. The boy waved a plastic flyswatter and slapped at the deck, then the rails to the steps that led into the swimming area in the middle of the dock.

Outdoor insect control.

The distraction was all it took for the mayor to refocus his gaze on a group of men who'd gathered to check out a new boat that had just come in. The back motor case was lifted and they all stared at the inner workings.

Sue laughed when the mayor made an abrupt departure to see the new arrival's beefy outboard engine. "He's been widowed for ten years. I wouldn't worry about him, but he is influential."

Lucy merely twisted the top of her beer open and took a long and thoughtful sip.

"So what do you think of docking so far?" Sue asked, reaching into the bag of chips.

Lucy had no opportunity to answer. A large jet boat bore down on them, with music blaring so loudly she could make out the rapper's bass line before she could even make out the passengers.

It seemed as if everyone on the dock paused in what they were doing, staring at the glittering horizon with hands shading their gazes, as the high-gloss black boat came into view.

Lucy recognized the musical artist as Usher—someone Jason listened to sometimes.

A chrome boom rose from the back of the sleek formula supersport boat. The diesel motor rumbled, a deep, throaty sound that ricocheted off the dam's gravel banks. Lucy was able to see there were bikini-clad women on deck. Five of them. Long hair flowed like dyed rivers in the wind. Boxed blondes and brunettes.

As the boat approached, she could make out the tall driver, who stood at the cockpit rather than sat. He wore a short-sleeved white shirt, unbuttoned, the open sides rippling behind him and exposing a muscular chest. Beige swim trunks slid low at his flat waist, resting on trim hips. A fat cigar was clamped between his lips.

Drew Tolman. Of course.

Wind blew the brown hair from his forehead as he slowed his speed to keep the wake low. Rap music blared, so loud the floating dock vibrated and seemed to bounce against the water's surface.

Dave Lawrence was already at the mooring area to help Drew dock the forty-one-foot boat. Every man on the dock perked right up.

Rejoining Sue and Lucy, the mayor held back, his glassy blue eyes fixated on that boat. "Damn, but the Tolman-ater knows how to live life. I get a hard-on every time I look at that cruiser." Then, remembering himself, he mumbled an apology beneath his breath. "Sorry, ladies."

It struck Lucy that nobody was really interested in the women onboard—they wanted a look at that boat. And Drew pleased them by powering up the covering over the entire mechanical workings, exposing the huge motor.

Drew didn't lack for assistance getting the nylon ropes tied to the dock cleats, everyone careful not to scratch the boat's expensive paint. In fact, he didn't have to do a thing to exert himself. Every detail was taken care of for him. Soon the ladies were helped off the starboard side and handed cold beers, bags of chips, sandwiches and even a football.

Gossip buzzed around the dock, and within a few seconds, Sue glanced at Lucy. "Laker girls. How did he manage that?"

Lucy shrugged, fighting to keep her cool. How could she have ever thought Drew might find her attractive? He cavorted with the Laker girls—they were gorgeous. He could have any one he wanted, *and* he had a *girlfriend*.

Funny how she forgot about her meeting with the

Greenbaums whenever she ran into Drew. Common sense seemed to desert her at the worst times. Ridiculous and reckless on her part. She knew he had a checkered past. Wasn't good material for a stable future, or a future, period. He'd never married. He'd never had kids, wouldn't understand the meaning of compromise.

Drew was wrong for her in every way possible.

Sue took a sip of beer. "Dave told me that boat cost a quarter of a million dollars."

Lucy's mouth dropped open. "You've got to be kidding."

"Nope. Drew's very well off."

"How is that possible?" Lucy stared at him, watched as his smile flashed while he took the cigar from his lips and brought the neck of a beer to his mouth to drink. She hated that her heartbeat thudded in her chest, that her mouth went dry, that her thoughts were scrambled. "He's retired. Surely he didn't make that much money as a baseball player?"

"He did very well in professional sports. He's smart. Dave is friends with the president of the Timberline First Savings and Loan, and he said Drew is a savvy investor. He's got more money than he knows what to do with."

Lucy licked her dry lips, hating to sound overly curious, but she couldn't help herself. "Do you know anything about the drug scandal?"

"Not much. Drew quit baseball in the middle of a season. He wasn't hitting well at all, and the press blamed it on steroids. There was that big scandal involving both leagues. Drew never received a deposition like the other players involved, so nobody knows for sure if it's true or not. It does seem strange that he'd quit while under contract. I think there was a lawsuit about it. I'm not sure. He was a really good player. But sometimes, he'd be out there on the mound and he didn't look so great."

"You watched him?" Lucy's curiosity was more piqued than ever.

"I've always been a fan of baseball. Dave got me hooked on it. I watched Drew play for years. I never dreamed I'd ever meet him. When he moved to Timberline, he was the talk at the High Country for months. He still is," Sue laughed. "You have to admit, there's just something about that man..."

Lucy said nothing.

The mayor of the dock came over, grabbed five beers out of Dave's cooler and juggled them against his gut. Ice water dribbled down his stomach and he flinched. Glancing at Sue and Lucy, he proclaimed, "Drew and Jacquie are off again. This time for good."

"Lloyd," Sue said, her tone skeptical. "We've all heard that before."

"No. It's true. Drew said so. They're finished." Slanting his gaze sideways and taking in a wide-angle view of Drew, the scantily clad women and the expensive boat, Lloyd added, "He's got Laker girls with him. That man sure has the knack. Found out they were up at the lodge on a calendar shoot and he invited them out on the dam for the day."

Lloyd scurried over to join the guys drooling over the motor.

Sue shook her head, smiling. "Lloyd is going to wet himself one of these days."

In spite of herself, Lucy laughed.

Nutter, Jason and Matt came over and wanted to know if they could take the raft and paddle it to shore.

Sue replied, "Yes, and take me along."

"Mom," Nutter whined. "It's just the guys."

"I need to go to the shore," she said, not elaborating further.

Nutter wrinkled his nose. "Aw, Mom. Can't you just go in the water?"

"No way. It's only fifty degrees." Sue held out her arm. "Help your mom up and take me to shore."

For a moment, Lucy shaded her eyes and watched as the three boys rowed Sue toward the rust-colored embankment. Pines dotted the tops of the ridges, a thicket of greenery that left a fringy profile.

Slipping out of her T-shirt, but keeping her shorts on, she smoothed sunscreen across her chest and arms, then removed her sunglasses. She closed her eyes, leaned back in the chair and lounged in the sun.

The disk changer in Drew's boat switched tracks and cranked out Foreigner's "Jukebox Hero." The bass line coursed through her, the energetic beat making it impossible to sit still. Eyes closed, she tapped her bare foot to the rhythm of rock and roll guitar riffs until she felt the sun's warmth blocked from her body.

She peeked up through the shadows of her lashes.

"Hey, sugar," Drew drawled above the music. "How's your day going?"

He stood over her, tall and broad. Her eyelids lifted a little more, languid and lazy as she viewed him.

His chest was void of hair, smooth and contoured. The color of his skin was rich and golden, his nipples like flat pennies. At the base of his throat, his pulse slowly jumped and beat steadily. He had on a pair of smoky Ray-Bans, so she couldn't see his eyes, simply her own reflection in the lenses.

The white of his shirt was a muted brilliance, the linen fabric looking soft, yet slightly wilted at the bottom. On him, it didn't look bad. The trunks fit him loosely at the hips. She noticed the line of dark hair that trailed past his navel and below the waistband of the trunks. She glanced at the closure, the soft bulge, then darted her eyes upward as soon as she realized he could read her expression perfectly. Because he had the nerve to grin.

There was no one feeling she could describe when looking at Drew Tolman. She was in the middle of a war with a physical urge. She tried to tell herself *no*, when everything else within her said *yes*. A woman couldn't force her heart to feel anything, but when it naturally did there was no stopping it.

Lucy realized she was in over her head with him.

He was the one man since her divorce who could make her feel, think and live. Not far behind that was the possibility that he could creep into the core of her soul. The very thought petrified her.

She didn't know him. Why was she acting this way?

"Good," she managed to reply, her voice sounding scratchy.

"Dave and Sue are good people," Drew commented, as if to give his stamp of approval on her new friendship.

She didn't need it.

The little boy with the flyswatter approached, running another lap on the dock. He swished the air, then playfully slapped Drew's butt.

"Don't!" he squealed as Drew tried to grab him, but without a lot of effort.

"Hey, squirt."

Lucy watched the exchange, ignoring the mocking voice in her head that screamed, *Don't ask*.

"Why did you quit baseball?" The question was out before she could stop it.

She had Drew's full attention once more. He grew somber for a moment, then grinned. "I wasn't any good anymore."

She didn't want to let him off the hook so easily. "Seriously, Drew. Why? There are rumors in town. You had to have heard them."

He grew quiet, his expression going blank as the music played. Lucy tuned it out and waited for him to answer.

She didn't think he would, then softly, he spoke. "I had some personal issues I had to take care of."

"Like what?"

"I wasn't feeling like myself, so I had to take some downtime. I just never went back. Shit happens." And that was all she got on the subject. He closed off, put the smile back in place, then, to Lucy's utter surprise, sat down in Sue's lounge next to her.

Lucy turned her head to look at him. All she could think to say was the only thing on her mind. "You have a big boat."

He roared with laughter, his smile white and bright. "Yeah, I do, sugar."

Why did he have to use that endearment with her? She'd heard him say it to other women in town, and its casual meaning shouldn't affect her, but it did. The way he drawled that word made her body warm, turning her heartbeat sluggish.

She willed herself to be calm, to not react. Gripping the arms on the chair, she stared straight ahead and clenched her teeth.

Drew gazed at Lucy and inwardly smiled. She sat stiff enough to be a team owner at the World Series. She fought him, fought the feelings he brought out in her; but he knew he could win her over.

Only this was no game.

If he wanted Lucy Carpenter, he had to want her for real. And for a longer time than a few minutes.

Drew knew he was a flirt. Didn't necessarily think that was a detriment. He wasn't devious about it. He lived a life of easygoing comments and caresses that women relished. He knew how to treat a woman right, how *she* wanted to be touched and held.

But he also knew that substance was rare. That deep feeling in his gut that said he wanted more. More than just a night, more than just a moment of friendly banter. Needing someone was a lot different than just being with them. It was too soon after Jacquie for him to fully sort out his thoughts on this. But he was sure of one thing: Lucy had a killer body.

She lounged back in the chair, her shoulders pressing into the canvas and her long legs stretched forward. She had long, shapely legs and a waist that was narrow and trim. Her stomach was flat and in good shape. She took care of herself. Pink polish was painted on her cute toenails. He like femininity. In fact, he loved it. Was very drawn to a woman who was girlie. But not showy.

Those twenty-something Laker girls on his boat—they were all show and no substance whatsoever. But good fun.

"Shouldn't you be getting back to your friends?" Lucy asked.

Drew frowned. "Trying to get rid of me?"

"Well…no. But I just thought—"

"Lucy, don't think too much right now. You've got creases on your forehead as if you're trying to figure out the formula for something. Enjoy the day. Enjoy life."

She sat a little straighter, shaded her gaze with

the flat of her hand. "Don't you ever take anything seriously?"

"Hell, yes. All the time. But not on the first day of docking." Then he grabbed the leg of her beach chair and slid her closer to him. That he could do the maneuver with the strength of just one hand set her heartbeat racing. His bare feet were so close to hers they almost touched. He got her attention, gave her a smile that he knew would melt her. He wanted to melt her, make her flustered in ways she'd never felt before. "You're a beautiful woman and you have to have noticed every man here has been staring at you."

She took a quick look around. "N-no they haven't."

"Pete, Joe, Steve, Randy, Adam—every one of them has been looking over here the whole time we've been talking."

"That's absurd. They're looking at those women you brought with you."

"They're just fluff. You're the real thing, Lucy."

A blush worked its way down the swell of her cleavage. He thought about what her skin would taste like. What she'd taste like. Her mouth. The intimate part of her body.

She couldn't keep her eyes on him, not that she could read his expression behind the sunglasses. She had to glance away.

He felt a strange satisfaction in knowing he could get to her. It had nothing to do with ego. It had everything to do with wanting the moment to be about *her.* Making her very aware she was a desirable woman. To him. To other men. He suspected it had been a long time since she felt that way.

"Why did you get a divorce?" he asked, leaning back in the chair and settling in for however long it took him to get answers to things he'd been wondering about her.

"Have you and Jacquie really broken up?" she countered.

Drew laughed. "So we'll take turns answering questions, is that the deal?"

"Maybe."

"Okay, I'll play." He snorted. "Yeah. We broke up for good. It was mutual and for the best. And you? Why the divorce?"

She stared ahead, her profile delicate, yet resolved. "My ex-husband cheated on me."

A sliver of anger cut through Drew. He could relate. "That's a bummer."

"It was. But I'm over it."

"Are you?"

"I think so," she said, and he appreciated the honesty in her tone.

"Okay, next. You got me at a good time. I'll answer anything within reason."

This time she smiled. The expression lit up her face, made her so attractive to him it was like a slam in the stomach.

"Why is it you've never gotten married?" she asked.

"Nobody asked me."

"You're full of it," she teased.

Drew arched his brows, then answered. "I've never been so in love that the woman was a constant thought on my mind, a place in my soul, twenty-four-seven. You need that to make it work."

After a long while, she mutely nodded.

"How long were you married?" he asked.

"Eighteen years."

"Long time."

"Very." She was lost in thought for a moment, then asked, "Did you love Jacquie?"

He wouldn't taint the memory of their relationship with a lie and cheapen it. "Yes."

"I'm glad."

"Why?"

"Because then you know what love is."

He slid his foot closer to hers, the warmth of his skin kissing the tips of her pretty toes. Lucy held still, sucked in her breath and slowly closed her eyes. "Sugar, I know exactly what love is."

Her face was colored by golden sunlight, her lips pink and soft. He absolutely loved the high arch of her brows; they gave her a don't-screw-with-me look at times. Dark hair fanned around her bare shoulders, and he fought the urge to take a thick strand, feel it between his thumb and forefinger. Her skin smelled like flowers, a faint hint caught on the wind, and he inhaled her scent, his nostrils flaring.

Slowly, she opened her eyes, kept her face forward as if she couldn't trust herself to look at him.

"Cook for me," he said bluntly.

She turned her attention toward him.

"I want to hire you. I heard Raul's been making your life rough around the edges and you haven't had any business."

"Does everyone know everything about me?" she said, half in disgust.

"I don't know jack about you, Lucy, except for what you've told me. It's easy to view the surface—that's all this town does. But to really look beyond that takes time. And trust." He inhaled, felt the warm air expand his lungs. "Cook for me."

He didn't anticipate her response. "No."

"No?"

"No."

"Why not?"

"Because. It would be a mistake. And I've made plenty of them to last me a lifetime."

"Why would cooking for me be a mistake? You need the work and I need to eat."

"But you're asking for the wrong reasons. I'm not a charity case." Conviction marked her tone.

"I don't think you're charity."

"Good—because I'm not. I'll get things going. In fact, I'm on the verge of some really big things happening for my business." She didn't elaborate.

He didn't readily believe her claim, but he wouldn't dispute it.

He wanted to talk further with her, get her to change her mind about cooking for him, but, to his displeasure, they were interrupted.

"Drew!" one of the girls called, and she came over with a cold bottle of beer. "You're missing the party!"

Lucy raised her brow at the Laker girl, that arch that spoke volumes.

With a half laugh, Drew resigned himself to the fact that this conversation was over. He rose to his feet, the moment with Lucy broken. He had a boatful of guests, and even though they weren't what he'd call real friends, he was a gentleman and tried to treat everyone in his life as if they mattered.

At that, he momentarily thought of Mackenzie. He wished she were here right now. She'd love this. He wanted to show her his world, a glimpse of what mattered to him. Friends, a sunny day, a ride in his boat and good company.

The corners of Drew's mouth lifted and he gave Lucy one last glance. "You look great in that bathing suit."

Then he left her behind, feeling her gaze on his back. It was a moment when he wished a woman would actually follow him.

Only Lucy Carpenter wasn't the kind to do that. And he knew it. And maybe that's why he wanted her. Because she was different.

Matt chugged his orange pop, while Jason and Nutter looked in the raft for spilled Cheetos. They'd pulled up at the shoreline, and were waiting for Nutter's mom to come out of the bushes.

As soon as they took her back to the dock, their

plan was to hit the shore again and look for stuff. Nutter said there were probably a bunch of Indians buried around here. Matt wasn't sure, but it made a good story and he thought it would be cool to find an arrowhead.

Jason and Nutter cracked the tops to their pop cans and came over to Matt. They stood in a row, the three of them gazing at the dock.

"Drew Tolman's got a boss-ass boat," Jason said, taking a deep swig of his orange soda.

"I know. That guy's, like, loaded with big bucks."

"I wish I was him," Jason commented. Then exhaled.

Matt squinted at his older brother, thinking Jason wished he were anyone but himself.

They drank their sodas, then Nutter belched. Matt giggled and Jason let a big one go. It sounded like a grizzly bear.

Tightening his chest, Matt burped.

Jason playfully shoved him. "Is that all you got?"

Matt laughed, drank a deep swig of pop and tried to swallow a bunch of air, too. Then he gave it his best shot. This time his burp was really loud and really long.

Jason and Nutter snickered, then his brother said, "Good one, Mattie!"

It didn't bug Matt that Jason called him Mattie. Because right now, Jason was like the old Jason. He was goofing around, not trying to impress anyone, just being…Jason.

Nutter ate a bunch of Cheetos out of the bottom of the bag and they passed them around. Then Nutter decided it would be funnier if they switched to farting.

So with hands orange from their chips, lips orange from their pop, the three of them had a contest to see who could fart the worst.

Nutter Lawrence won.

Must be all those nut-balls he'd taken had messed with his plumbing down below. Because he was rank, too.

"Good Lord!" Nutter's mom hollered as she walked down the steep hill between the trees, rocks sliding beneath her sandals, "I can hear you boys all the way up the embankment. Where are your manners?"

"We don't got any," Nutter said.

At that, the three of them cracked up.

Tears practically rolling down his cheeks, Matt didn't care that Nutter's mom called them gross. He thought it was funny.

Today was about the best day he'd had since coming to Red Duck. And it wasn't even over yet.

Journal of Mackenzie Taylor

Brad Smith is the biggest jerk I have ever met! My summer is RUINED thanks to him.

I never cheated on him, not one time! Since he and I hooked up this last semester, I've only had my eyes on him.

How could he do this to me?

How could Misty Connors do this to me?

I thought she was my friend! She made out with my boyfriend. And they...did it!

I found out today when we were all at the swimming pond. Misty and Christine were talking by the make out spot. The swamp grass grows thick there and they didn't see me. I heard every disgusting word.

Misty Connors went all the way with my boyfriend. At first, I thought she was lying. I couldn't believe Brad would do that to me. So I left and I went to his work and I confronted him.

He was pissed I came to the lumber-

yard and called him out to talk to me. He walked at me with purpose in his steps, started to tell me I was ~~embarassing~~ embarrassing him, and that's when I just flat out asked him if he'd slept with Misty.

He didn't say right out he hadn't so I knew. He couldn't deny it.

I hate him!

I hate him!

I hate him!

Liar! He told me he liked me! Maybe I should have done it with him when he was trying. But I said no. And now look what happened. He went to someone else.

I want to cry...

I want to get out of Kissimmee. I hate it here. I want to be anywhere... but here.

I hate my life.

Thirteen

Lucy sucked in her breath when she spotted Raul Nunez by the half basket of honeydew melons. With fierce determination and a heated shove of her grocery cart, she angled straight for him despite the wobbly front wheel. She had to rein in thoughts about knocking him into the banana rack.

She'd been shopping at Sutter's, roaming the aisles for discounted specials to make budget meals at home, since she had no one to cook for. Tossed in among the food items in her cart was this week's fat issue of the *Mountain Gazette*. As soon as she arrived home, she planned on reviewing the want ads.

The racket her cart made from that defective front wheel tipped off Raul. His head shot up from the honeydews, and his hand knocked a few melons to the floor. Lucy almost ran one over as she all but burned rubber and came to a stop. She was not letting him get away, so she pinned his cart to the fruit display.

"Raul," she ventured, her tone clipped. "I've been trying to get hold of you."

His coffee-bean-brown eyes widened with fright, the black hair on his head shining like a crow's wing beneath the energy-efficient lighting. "C'hew about gave me a freakin' heart attack."

He wore his hair slicked down with some kind of pomade, his complexion olive-toned. He had oversize upper teeth that were on the straight side, while the bottoms buckled. They were the color of white out. Clearly, he bleached.

Raul had a thick accordion folder on the child seat of his cart. It brimmed with food-soiled recipes, handwritten notes and coupons. He hadn't struck her as the coupon-clipping type.

"How come you haven't returned my calls?" she asked bluntly, now that she had him captive.

Brown eyes darted to the honeydew melons. "I don' know what c'hew talking about."

"Cut the crap, Raul. I've been leaving you messages for days and you haven't picked up."

"I've been bee-zy. I work for a living, c'hew know."

"Yes. And I'd like to work for mine." Lucy straightened, her spine stiff and shoulders thrust back. "How do you expect me to get any clients when you keep telling them not to hire me?"

"I did no such ting!"

"Oh, come on! Raul, you own this town. But when we had a latte that day, you said, 'There's more work than I can handle, c'hew come right on up and you'll be bee-zy.'"

Those big teeth looked ready to bite. "C'hew making fun of my English?"

She sighed, frustrated. "You have to help me out, Raul. Quit sabotaging my chances of survival in this town. I have two sons to support. I want to work. I *enjoy* my job."

"C'hew can do your job. Jess don' expect me to loose any of my clients, becuz you can't cook like the Raul."

"How would you even know?" she demanded, venting. "I'll bet you and I could have a cook-off and I'd win."

His stature seemed to pump up from about five foot eight to six feet. "Don' tempt me."

Raul Nunez was a legend in his own mind.

Lucy loosened her grip on the cart's handle, not realizing she'd been holding it so tightly. She'd once read that frustration and anger had the ability to snap even the strongest metal in two if one's nerves were agitated enough. And hers were at the breaking point. "So are you going to stop telling people not to hire me?"

"I have never don' any such ting."

She hated to call him an outright liar to his face, so she didn't. This was getting her nowhere other than giving her a headache.

"We'll see about all this, Raul. You haven't heard the last of me."

"C'hew have me quaking in my chef's hat," he

called after her as she pushed the cart away, its wobbly wheel rattling.

Lucy had no real destination when she left Sutter's until she saw the sheriff's Blazer parked at the High Country Motel's lounge. On an impulse, she signaled, made a sharp left and angled her Passat next to his.

She got out of the car, slipped her folded sunglasses into the vee of her shirt, then swung one of the double doors open.

The lobby was dingy, but clean; it smelled like detergent and bleach. Chlorine from the indoor pool seeped into the air, and she glanced through the sweating windows to her right to see several people in the pool.

Heading for the lounge, she wasn't sure what to expect, except to see the sheriff, since his car was parked outside. She hit a double jackpot when she found both Sheriff Lewis and Deputy Cooper sitting at one of the tables with Bud Tremore.

"Hey, Lucy," Bud said, seeing her before the lawmen did.

"Hi, Bud."

"I've been meaning to get out there and take a look at that porch."

"It's fine for now, Bud," she said, not really needing to go into that at the moment.

Sheriff Lewis tilted his chin at her, his tanned face even darker than she recalled. It amazed her he didn't have skin cancer lesions on his nose. His red-mustached deputy gave off a more subdued aura, but his gaze traveled over her, too.

"Sheriff, I'd like to file a citizen's complaint," she said, quite seriously.

Taking a sip of what looked to be iced tea, and not missing a swallow as he drank around a full glass of ice cubes, he asked, "What about?"

Deputy Cooper thought he'd be a comedian and interjected, "She's going to put one out on you, Tremore, for all them run-down motor homes on that property she rents from you."

Bud snorted. "I can park whatever RVs I want as long as I own that land, Clyde. That's not in the dang covenants where my teardown is."

"What kind of complaint?" Sheriff Lewis inquired, setting his glass down.

"Raul Nunez is slandering me." She refused to cower despite the small town sheriff's raised brows and annoyed expression. "I have been trying to establish myself as a personal chef and he's done nothing but deter my business opportunities."

"How's he doing that?"

"Well, by telling his clients not to hire me."

"Freedom of speech," Clyde offered. "I believe we voted that in, back when Betsy Ross was sewing the flag."

Lucy staved off a groan and a desire to kick the legs right out from under Clyde Cooper's chair. He tilted backward, fingers knit together over his narrow chest.

"Well, now, Miz Carpenter," the sheriff said matter-of-factly, "there's nothing illegal going on here. My hands are tied."

"Surely there's a law against someone slandering a name."

"How's he been slandering yours? What exactly has he said that's been detrimental?"

Lucy's mouth opened, then closed. She took a moment to collect her thoughts. "He hasn't exactly been saying bad things about me, but he hasn't told anyone to hire me. He assured me before I moved to town that there was plenty of work and I'd have more clients than I knew what to do with, and now that I'm here, he's gone out of his way to ensure he's the only one doing the cooking in Timberline."

"I fail to see how that's a crime, Miz Carpenter." Sheriff Lewis tossed a few Spanish peanuts into his mouth by way of his raised fist.

"But it's not free enterprise," she argued.

Clyde Cooper gave her a forced smile. "I think that's what that Democratic presidential hopeful wanted for our great state of Idaho, and we voted his ass out of Dodge."

The three men chuckled.

"Isn't it illegal to be in a bar while you're on duty?" she retorted, then clamped her lips together.

"Now, now," the sheriff cautioned. "We're off duty. There's no law in Red Duck that says we can't come into an establishment wearing our uniforms."

Lucy said nothing further, knowing she'd get no

help here. It occurred to her, after the fact, that Red Duck was a town where the justice officials only served those to whom they felt justice was entitled.

With a discouraged stride, she left the lounge through the lobby, giving that overchlorinated pool one last glance.

For a moment, she thought about jumping in and sinking to the very bottom of the deep end, because that's where her life was headed. Not that she really would, but it sounded dramatic. And right now, she was in dire need of something drastic.

A heavy sigh left her lungs and a thought came to mind.

There was only one option left.

And it was about the most drastic thing she could think to do. In fact, it was her only choice.

Fourteen

Wearing a plush white towel wrapped around his waist, Drew strode barefoot through his seventy-five hundred square foot home.

Late afternoon sunlight slashed through the tall windows.

The main living area on the ground floor was spacious and open to the second story, with heavily timbered ceilings. He used the entry area as an informal gathering place. The fireplace was massive, its stonework reaching to the rafters. A set of six long-paned windows, which he left without blinds, gave a panoramic view of the backyard. He didn't have fencing around his property. The back was private, screened with white birch, aspens and pines.

He preferred natural stone and earth tones on the outside of the house. The deck had several hunter-green Adirondack chairs angled to view the decorative landscaping boulders, and—in the distance—the creek.

Heading for the kitchen, he crossed terra-cotta tile that felt cool, yet good, after a hot shower. He didn't have a lot of clutter on the countertop. The large range, with its professional hood and stovetop grill were barely ever used. There was a cook island with a black-and-white-speckled marble top. He usually tossed his mail on the surface, and there it sat until he was ready to open it and pay a few bills or answer letters.

He still got fan mail diverted to his P.O. box. Technically, he was supposed to go to the Timberline post office and collect his mail, since the Knolls didn't have rural mail delivery. But Drew had made a deal with the postmaster—he got delivery to his home in trade for free home plate tickets to a Dodgers' game for anyone working at the post office and taking a vacation to Los Angeles.

There wasn't a whole lot Drew Tolman didn't get, and damn if he wasn't aware he could get away with most anything. He knew he had a way about him, but he didn't think he abused anyone. He did a lot for charities, hosted events at no charge. He made anonymous donations to causes he felt worthy—the local city center was one of them. The town had been short a few thousand to put in a fountain and he'd taken care of it.

He didn't need or want any recognition. He liked to do things for the sake of doing them. It made him feel good.

He stopped at the chef-size, stainless steel refrigerator with its two double-wide doors, took out the milk carton and drank from the plastic spout. The icy-cold liquid coated his parched throat. He'd been slugging balls before he came in to shower.

He only bought skim milk. Hated homogenized. It tasted like cream.

Glancing at the clock in the library off the kitchen, he noted he had fifteen minutes to get dressed.

His cell phone rang with a basic ring tone that echoed off the cold countertop where he'd left it. He'd finally had its settings changed. When he was at the phone store, he'd decided to add Mackenzie to his plan. He'd overnighted her the new cell, then had the clerk program his phone to play Kelly Clarkson's "Since You've Been Gone" whenever her number was incoming.

He'd asked Lynette what Mackenzie's favorite song was, and she'd said Mackenzie had just bought the Clarkson CD. Drew had checked it out, found that song on the playlist, and figured it was the perfect choice for his daughter's ring tone—considering he had been gone.

"Tolman," he said into the receiver.

"Drew, it's Jacquie."

He'd spoken to Jacquie twice since the breakup, but had seen her only once. She'd shown him some investment properties just before they'd parted ways, and he'd opted to buy one in Hailey. He saw no reason to get a different Realtor to complete the transaction, so he'd had Jacquie do so.

Their conversations started out strained, but always ended up a little more loose by the time they were ready to hang up. He didn't want her out of his life completely. Three years was a long time to throw away without even salvaging a friendship.

Since they'd broken up, he'd owned up to the fact that he had to take partial blame. He'd even mentioned failing the relationship by taking his heart out of it the last time he and Jacquie had talked on the phone—only she didn't want to discuss it. Just the same, he'd said he was sorry.

Drew didn't hate anyone, couldn't see himself never talking to Jacquie again. Polite exchanges would be inevitable. The town was small. They would run into one another.

"Hey, Jacquie."

Her raspy voice was seasoned, professional, as she continued. He knew her well enough to know it was an automatic response. "I have the counteroffer from the owners on Bear Creek. They made one minor change regarding the closing date, but I don't see it as a problem."

"Okay. If you say so."

Muted noise sounded on her end, as if she'd tucked the phone to her ear to read through the legal documents. "They're asking for a forty-five day escrow rather than the thirty you proposed. Oh, and comps came in higher than the asking price." She gave the Jacquie laugh, the one he recognized as a marketing strategy. "So you've already made money."

"That's cool."

She exhaled, obviously smoking a cigarette. "You're probably the only person I know who can be so indifferent about an extra twenty grand in your pocket."

"I wouldn't say that's true. I'm thinking about how I'm going to turn over the property and make even more money off it."

"I should have known." Then she must have smiled, because her tone changed. "So I'll need you to sign the revised offer. I have to present it to the agent first thing in the morning, and this has to be taken care of a-sap." She paused, almost hesitant. "I was hoping you'd be home tonight so I can stop by and get your signature."

"I'll be here."

"Good." She audibly sighed. "I'm still at my office, tying up a few loose ends for some other people, and I shouldn't be much longer."

"Whenever."

"Okay. Good."

The line went quiet, and Drew stared out the back windows to the expanse of green grass, tall trees and a familiar mallard duck walking up to his patio.

"How're you doing?" he finally asked.

"Busy," she responded lightly, casually, with no undertones of emotion. "Summer really heats up."

For a flicker of a second he thought about how her slender body heated up when he'd kissed her, made love to her. But the thought was gone before he could remotely grasp it, or visualize her naked, or even remember what her mouth tasted like.

They talked a few minutes longer, then Drew's doorbell rang.

"Oh, shit! I forgot something. Jacquie, I gotta go." He clicked off the phone, tossed it to the counter and strode to the front door, still wearing his towel.

He hadn't planned on doing this, and he realized how it would look. Maybe he should go down the hallway first and slip into some jeans, but his movement had been detected through the glass panels on each side of the massive front doors— because an oval face pressed closer. Neither side had a window treatment covering it.

She'd had to have seen part of him, his silhouette. No doubt.

When he started toward his bedroom, the bell rang again.

"Shit," he repeated beneath his breath, then backtracked to the foyer.

Standing back, he opened the door.

Lucy Carpenter stood before him, grasping the blue handles of two extremely large plastic totes. They looked like suitcases, and through the murky plastic he could see utensils, spices, pots and pans, and a bunch of other cookware he was fairly clueless about.

This was her first cook date at his house. He'd hired her.

She wore a pair of jeans and a basic pink T-shirt

that hugged her breasts. The shape of her face was delicately defined, with her hair pulled back in a claw to keep it off her shoulders.

There was a wholesomeness about her, a femininity that was a rare find. She liked the softer colors that emphasized her womanly curves in a tasteful way. He thought her sexy as all hell.

The shape of her mouth was pouty, her lips full and kissable. She wore very little makeup—mascara, lipstick, maybe blush. She didn't need cosmetic help. She was beautiful to him just as she was. The ivory column of her neck was smooth, beckoning a man's lips to trace her skin from her collarbone to the soft angle of her jaw.

She smelled good. Like flowers. Light, but softly feminine.

Her brown eyes traveled over his naked chest, then darted to his face. "I'm not early," she blurted.

"I know." He checked the tuck on his towel, making sure he wasn't going to lose it. "I lost track of time. I had a phone call."

Jacquie. And she'd be coming over soon. It had momentarily slipped his mind that Lucy was going to be here. Although looking at her, how she could slip his mind was beyond him.

She attracted him. More than he cared to admit. And deeper than just physical. He saw something in her that he'd been missing in his life. During the last few years, trying to reconcile with Mackenzie, he'd felt himself lacking in stability and self-assuredness.

Lucy possessed a strong character, something he admired. She was determined, he gave her that much.

He'd been surprised to get her call, saying she wanted to cook for him and would take him up on his offer. She'd wanted to come over and give him a sampler menu, but he'd told her whatever she wanted to make was fine with him. He didn't need a demo. She'd brought the contract, an application and a form for his menu selections to one of the Little League games, and he'd signed the papers, hiring her for the summer.

He had no clue what she was preparing tonight. His stomach rumbled with hunger, so he didn't care what was put on his plate.

"Come on in," he offered, stepping aside. "Can I help you with anything?"

"No," she said quickly. "I can manage. Why don't you…"

He was already heading to his bedroom while he pointed in the opposite direction. "The kitchen's that way. I'll be right back."

Lucy was left in the foyer to examine her surroundings. She gazed at the high ceilings, the backyard and the built-in bookcases chock-full of baseball memorabilia. Gloves, baseballs, a plethora of photographs. With her kitchen gear weighing her down and Drew in the next room, she didn't have the opportunity to look closer, but she recognized his face in many of the photos.

The handles of her travel cases began to cut into her palms, so she proceeded. Bringing all her supplies to a cook job could be an ordeal. If she'd been doing a week's worth of meals, she would have brought four times the amount of things. Today she'd consolidated everything into two bins with handles.

Taking the hardwood hallway, she passed a dining room on her right. It was decorated in rich tones of red, gold and ivory, with a huge area rug and a black dining table. The walls were a deep crimson, and the large light fixture was made out of twigs. It was unusual, but she liked it for its uniqueness.

Right past the dining room she reached a spacious kitchen with state-of-the-art appliances. The birch cabinets were accented with white, the walls a sage-green.

She loved the tone, the feeling. The comfort.

For some reason, acknowledging that put her on guard. This was a kitchen she could get used to. Several seconds of completely unrestrained fantasy followed, and she envisioned herself here, with Drew, cooking. Together.

Oh, dear Lord. *I'm in big trouble*.

Lucy deposited the heavy bins on the floor, taking out pots and pans and grocery items. Since the trip to Drew's house was short, she hadn't brought her canvas insulated cooler for the perishable food. She arranged everything neatly on the countertop.

Pulling out his folder, she sorted through the paperwork he'd signed, refreshed herself on the menu, then remembered she hadn't printed labels for freezer storage, since he was eating it tonight. She'd still had him pay her a $25.00 fee for the plastic containers for when she created several entrées and side dishes. In that case, she'd leave the reheating instructions on the fridge. Cooking only one meal the night of serving wasn't customary, but she had some clients who wanted that option.

She cooked clean, didn't like clutter or mess. Noticing the way Drew kept his kitchen, she appreciated his neatness and the feel of organization, although there was a starkness about the room, as if nobody lived here. Almost like one of those model homes where only the basic props were out.

Curious, she slid open a drawer. Silverware. Nice stuff, too. Not hearing Drew approach, she quickly peaked into a cupboard, finding shelves of dinner plates and cereal bowls. To her right, she glanced inside a cabinet. Spices. And more than she would have expected.

"Looking for the booze, sugar?" Drew's voice startled her and she jumped, slamming the cupboard drawer.

"Of course not. I bring my own."

With that, he laughed. A deep sound that made her want to melt.

"Not to drink," she explained, fighting off the heat of a blush that was working across her cheeks. That he could unravel her over the slightest thing made her bristle. "For cooking a dish. And I didn't bring any tonight. I won't be needing it."

Drew came into the kitchen wearing a pair of sinful jeans, and she couldn't help fastening her eyes to the way they hugged his butt as he walked away from her toward the wine rack. "Would you like a glass of wine while you're cooking?"

"No," she replied quickly. "I don't drink on the job."

"Sugar, you aren't working any job at my house. You're a guest and just happen to be using my stove—even though I'm paying. I'm nobody special. Make yourself at home."

Lucy noted the way his shirt draped across the broad width of his shoulders. He wore a lightweight knit pullover with a ribbed collar. It was a deep green and brought out the color of his eyes. His brown hair had a light gel in it, and spiked at his forehead. He smelled good, too. Not overpowering cologne. Maybe a musky deodorant.

What had she been thinking, calling him up to ask if she could cook for him? And for the entire summer?

This was all Raul Nunez's fault! If he'd kept his end of the agreement they'd had, none of this would be happening. Settling into Red Duck wouldn't have turned into such an ordeal. She would be getting clients the normal way—by her good business instinct and word of mouth—instead of latching on to the one man she really would prefer not to hang around.

She wasn't sure she could trust herself with him. But Drew had clout. She sorely needed something to draw in clients. Unfortunately, cooking for Drew was like the open stock sale at Williams-Sonoma. Even kitchen-handicapped customers wanted a pan or a lid because the deal was just too good to pass up.

Drew was Lucy's key to success. Once everyone heard he was her regular client, her phone would start ringing like crazy. Raul wouldn't be able to do a darn thing to stop the steady influx of clients headed her way.

The fact of the matter was, what Drew Tolman did in this town carried power. Power she couldn't afford to turn away.

So here she was. In his kitchen. With him looking yummier than a seven bone roast, and her with her confidence being tested. Could she actually go through with this and not botch it?

His presence got to her. Flustered her. She wasn't sure if she was coming or going. He walked past— more like brushed past—as he went to one of the cupboards and took out a glass. He smelled to die for. She couldn't place the scent. She just knew that she couldn't breathe in deep enough to take him inside her lungs.

"You sure I can't get you a glass of wine? Beer?" he asked.

She momentarily forgot herself, and was unable to reply. Then she muttered, "Uh, no. But feel free."

"I'm going to have OJ."

He poured orange juice, then slid out one of the breakfast bar stools and sat down.

Lucy stared at him, unable to move. "What are you doing?"

"I'm going to watch you."

Her reply was swift and steady. "But you can't!"

"Why not?" Indolently, he propped his elbows on the marble top as he casually rested his chin in his left hand. His brows furrowed, his forehead creased and he had an expression that made her want to kiss him. It was that adult-male, little-boy look.

"Because you just can't. I can't cook under that kind of—"

Pressure.

He grinned. "Lucy, do I make you nervous?"

"Absolutely not." The lie was about as bold as Colombian roast coffee. "Stay there," she insisted, backpedaling as fast as she could so he wouldn't sense her discomfort any more than she'd already shown it. "I don't care. You'll just get bored, anyway."

"No I won't. I'm interested in what you do."

Swallowing, she forced herself to take control. Be collected. Very unconcerned that his gorgeous gaze followed her every move. And then some.

She noticed he appreciated the outline of her breasts in her top. She'd chosen something subdued, nothing overtly sexy. But she did prefer feminine things, and that's what she'd picked. Pink. It was her favorite color.

Vowing not to let him bother her, she reached into her bin and took out a white chef's apron.

The fine hairs on the back of her neck rose when

she turned away to set a saucepan and sauté pan on the stove. It was almost as if he had touched her; she felt tingles across her skin and up her spine. Quickly slipping her apron over her head, she tied the bow in front, her fingers fumbling with the knot. She tucked a terry-cloth towel through the tie so she could keep her hands dry and clean as she cooked. Still, she didn't turn to face him. She couldn't.

He just sat there, watching. Gazing. Slowly. Feasting. It was all she could do not to shiver.

She forced herself to maintain indifference, willed him out of her mind. She was preparing a medallion of beef tenderloin with a roasted sweet pepper reduction, spring mix salad with apples and feta, and garlic mashed potatoes. Preparation time would be approximately fifty minutes.

Lucy clicked back a groan. Could she last fifty minutes?

"How long have you been doing this?" Drew asked.

She slanted him a quick glance. His hand grasped the orange juice glass and raised it toward his mouth.

"About five years," she replied.

He took a slow drink, his eyes never leaving hers as she watched him over the glass's rim. "How come you wanted to do it?"

"I love to cook." Lucy had to turn away. She focused on what ingredients she needed first. The red peppers, onions and shallots.

Spearing the peppers, she turned on one of the

range burners and began to roast them. She liked to do that first for flavor, then she cut them up and added them to the large pot of Spanish onions with the golden-brown peels still on. She sautéed everything in oil—peppers, onions, shallots, several cloves of garlic. She even threw in one carrot for sweetness.

"What are you doing?" Drew asked, and this time his voice was a lot louder because he stood directly behind her.

Lucy could feel his body heat surrounding her, and smell him when she breathed. "I…uh, I'm making a sauce."

"What kind?"

His eyes pierced hers, and she knew this was no accident. He was trying to shake her up, rattle her. Make her fall for him like all the other women in town.

He wanted her.

That became so utterly clear she almost laughed aloud.

My goodness—Drew wanted *her*? He could have any woman he wanted. Why her? Why now? Was this a game? What about Jacquie? Yes, they'd parted company—but when was that? It felt like only yesterday. He wasn't ready to start something new with someone so soon.

And yet he was definitely trying to start something with her as he leaned closer.

"A…roasted pepper sauce." Lucy fought her feelings, fought the magnetism that radiated from

Drew. She wanted to curse him, to shove him away. A whole summer of this? She wouldn't be able to take it. She'd break down and do something stupid.

She hadn't had sex with anyone since Gary—and even then, it had been almost seven months prior to their divorce being finalized. One night, they'd done it, even after she'd found out about Diane. Lucy had thought that maybe if she'd tried harder in bed… But it had been a disaster, and her last memories of intimacy were filled with shame and insecurity. Now she wasn't even sure if she knew how to make love.

There hadn't been anyone she'd dated, been interested in since becoming single. In hindsight, perhaps she should have had a one-night stand. A fling. Something meaningless to get the bitter taste out of her mouth. Her neighbor had wanted to set her up with a good-looking man she worked with, but Lucy had turned her down. She just hadn't been ready. Maybe she'd never be ready.

But with Drew standing so close, fantasy images of slipping his shirt off filled her head to distraction.

Smells of roasting peppers, a charred odor, caught her attention and she quickly took them from the stove, almost burning her hand over the blue flames.

"You okay?" he asked, stepping in closer to assess the peppers. His shoulder brushed her arm. It was all she could do to keep from screaming.

"You have too much time on your hands—don't you ever go to work?"

"Sure. I coach Little League in the summer and I teach high school baseball in the fall when the school term restarts. Anything in between is leisure time." He stared at her, the level of heat in his gaze almost making her tremble.

"Drew!" she finally snapped. "You can't watch me cook. I'm having a hard time concentrating with you hovering."

He stood back, smiled—slowly. "Well, sugar, all you had to do was ask me to get out of the way."

But he didn't go far. He went into the library off the kitchen and sat in one of the high-backed leather chairs. Propping his bare feet on an ottoman, he clicked on the television. The volume was a bit on the loud side, but she wasn't about to ask him to turn it down. She'd simply have to tune him out.

He flipped through the channels until he found a baseball game. The commentators' voices droned on and, with great effort, Lucy soon forgot he was there.

Within forty-minutes, she had everything done and was ready to clean up and get out of there. She plated the meal, which wasn't typical of a cook job. But Drew didn't want to be bothered doing anything himself, so he'd arranged for her to cook hot meals for him three times a week, and on special occasions if he requested her time in advance.

In exchange for her services, he had agreed to tell everyone he knew that she was working for him. But only if he liked her cooking. She didn't want him to say he was enjoying her service if he wasn't. Although that really was a moot point. She knew he'd love it.

The red pepper sauce, thickened with cream, went on the plate first. She arranged the grilled filet on top, put a twig of thyme over it for presentation. Then she shaped the roasted-garlic mashed potatoes, put them next to the beef. On a separate plate, she presented the salad. She had made this up—spring mix, thinly sliced Braeburn apples, candied walnuts, feta cheese and a simple grape seed oil and balsamic vinaigrette. It turned out perfect every time, and people were surprised to find apple in their green salad.

"Okay. It's ready," she said. "Where would you like to eat? In your dining room?"

"Not hardly." He came toward her and she sucked in her breath, refusing to succumb to the erratic beats of her heart. "I never eat in there. Only if I have company or something. Which isn't real often. I always eat here."

He motioned to the breakfast bar, so that's where she put the dinner. He didn't sit down right away, rather, he made his way to her as she turned to wipe off the stovetop.

In the half breath she took as he reached out to her, she forgot herself. Whatever he was doing, she didn't care. She leaned toward him, emotions colliding within and every sense on alert.

"You have something on your lip." He ran his

thumb across her lower lip, then brought it to his mouth. "I think it's that pepper sauce."

Mortified, erratic, unsteady, breathless—those thoughts and feelings crashed within her brain. "Y-yes...I tasted it to see if I needed more sea salt."

"You don't."

That he could stand there, mere inches from her, so tall and wide and strong and everything that any woman could ever want, was beyond comprehension.

Drew was the epitome of masculinity, of fantasies and bedrooms and nakedness...and sex.

Lucy groaned, unable to stop herself.

"Lucy," he whispered. "You're shaking."

"No, I'm not!" The denial was too abrupt. She tried to move past him, to leave. But where to go?

He caught her shoulders, stopped her, made her stand directly in front of him as he looked down at her face. His smile was gentle and kind. She saw his heart in his eyes, and a slight insight into his soul. He wasn't all that he appeared. He had feelings, depth. Complexity and character.

Had she misjudged him? Within those green eyes was loneliness.

The truth had her gravitating toward him. She fought winding her arms around his neck, wanting to soothe, to take away his emptiness. She knew it, because she felt it as well. She might live in a house with two boys, but at night, alone...in her bed it was a different story. She longed for arms around her, for lips to settle over hers.

And now they became a reality.

Drew reached out, cupped her cheek with his large hand, then tucked her flush against him with an assertiveness she hadn't known with Gary. Yet she didn't feel overpowered. She liked that he took control.

Even so, she resisted. "No," she moaned, trying to break free.

"Yes," he said simply, softly.

Their eyes held, locked and neither spoke. Then Drew's firm mouth covered hers, in a light, brushing kiss that immediately intensified and grew deeper.

She held on to him, the hard wall of his chest pressing into her breasts. His heartbeat thudded against hers, the tempo strong. She felt light-headed, almost as if this were happening to someone else and she was simply an observer.

His kiss was subtle, but commanding. He didn't have to think about it, he just did it. He took charge, control. And she let him. It felt too good not to fall into him, to kiss him back.

It had been an eternity since she'd been kissed, and never like this. She knew she'd curse herself in the morning, call herself every kind of idiot. But right now...right now—

Her slender hands roamed up his neck, felt the fine hair at his nape. He was so masculine, yet his hair was so soft. The texture was cool against her fingertips.

Lucy kissed him, opened her mouth to him, and

his tongue slid inside. His jaw was smoothly shaved, yet rough at the same time. It bristled lightly against the tender skin of her chin. She didn't care.

She couldn't think straight.

If it hadn't been for the doorbell's ring, Lucy didn't know how long she would have stood in that kitchen with Drew, arms wound around his neck, her body pressed tightly to his.

Or worse, how long it would have taken her to ask him to carry her into his bedroom.

My God.

Lucy backed away, trying to pull herself together. She grew immediately embarrassed, self-conscious. "I'm…" She let the thought trail off, and Drew instinctively finished it for her.

"Don't be sorry." He leaned in, kissed her quickly on the lips. "I'm not."

Then he went down the hallway to answer the door. In the time he was gone, Lucy made fast work of cleaning the counter and shoving her washed pots and pans into her totes, mindless of the clatter. She had to get out of here. Quickly.

In the middle of slipping her apron over her head, Lucy looked up and stopped cold.

Jacquie Santini.

Oh my gosh—Drew and Jacquie had gotten back together. And here she'd been kissing him.

Lucy wanted to die.

Jacquie looked down her nose at her, but didn't say anything. Lucy immediately went into rambling mode. "Hi, Jacquie. I'm only here to cook for Drew. It's nice to see you."

Not saying anything, Jacquie glanced at Lucy's cookware and the gear she'd brought in. While the evidence of professionalism was there, clearly Jacquie wasn't buying into the whole story. Probably with good reason. Lucy's cheeks were hot, flushed. Her lips felt full and plump, bruised from Drew's kiss. There was no denying what they had been doing before she came over.

Once more, Lucy wanted to die.

Drew didn't seem to be alarmed over the situation, or if he was, he sure could play it down as if nothing had happened. To read his expression, you'd never know he'd just had his tongue in her mouth. "Jacquie came over to have me sign some real estate papers."

"I won't keep you," Lucy immediately replied. "I'm done now anyway and I'll just—"

A cell phone rang—more like played a song that was familiar to Lucy; every radio station was airing it. "Since You've Been Gone" filled the kitchen, and Drew about took a header to answer that phone.

Lucy glanced at Jacquie, who glanced at her, then the two women settled their unwavering gazes on Drew. Perhaps they were both thinking they'd been fools to fall for a man like him, who kept women on a string like fishermen kept the catch of the day on lines. Neither said a word as he answered.

Neither cared to examine the gamut of emotions that rattled to life within her heart.

* * *

"Hello?" Drew answered the phone, forgetting about the two women in his kitchen.

"Hi, it's me. It's Mackenzie."

He knew who "me" was. She didn't have to say Mackenzie. "Hi, how are you?"

"I'm okay."

Drew didn't want to smother her. He'd rather she take the lead, talk at her leisure, tell him why she'd called. Surprised didn't begin to describe his reaction. It was more like relieved. He'd been hoping she'd use the phone he sent her. And to call him.

"Just okay?" he finally said, unable to keep silent.

The line was dead a moment, and he thought he might have lost her. "Hello?"

"I want to come spend the summer with you."

His daughter's voice sounded far-off, tired. Sad. But none of that immediately registered. All he heard was she wanted to come see him.

Drew didn't even ask why she'd changed her mind. He didn't want to know, didn't care. The fact was she wanted to come.

"I want to be there as soon as I can," Mackenzie said, a waver in her tone. "Please."

"All right. We'll get it all arranged. I'll take care of it. I can't wait to see you."

After a few minutes talking with his daughter, he disconnected the call.

He exhaled softly, grinning so widely he couldn't stop it if he'd wanted to. Looking up, he realized he wasn't alone. He'd forgotten about Jacquie and Lucy.

The two of them—so different from one another—stared at him and he couldn't guess their thoughts.

Funny how the women in Drew's life had a strange way of all being there at the same time.

Fifteen

Jason delivered his mom's food to the Sunrise Trail Creek old people home. This was his third trip here and he thought it smelled like mold and something dying or dead.

He didn't like this place.

His mom had dropped him off and he had to stay and help in the kitchen. He thought they would have their own cooks for this sort of thing, so why his mom was volunteering to provide food he didn't know. The residents liked his mom. They smiled when she came in.

Momentarily, he wondered just how many people lived here. When he got old, he didn't want to live in a place like this where it smelled gross—like B.O. and medicine combined.

Maybe it wasn't *that* bad, but he just didn't want to be here. When he turned eighteen, he was so moving back to Boise.

Little League ate up a lot of his day. And since

starting "work" at the Sunrise, he had no time to himself. He'd also got that busboy job at Woolly Burgers. That one, he didn't mind. It was cash-o-lah in his pocket. He worked there four days a week, and had to come here a couple times a week.

He had no effing life. That made his mom happy.

At least he was definitely trying. He hadn't been smoking any dope. When he was done with work, he waited for his mom to pick him up and take him home. Too tired from being at baseball, Woolly's and here, he didn't have the energy to track down the local supplier.

If only he could get out of doing this food delivery for his mom. It was really not something he could get used to. Old people freaked him out.

Not his grandma and grandpa, though. They were cool. When he and Matt and Mom had lived in Boise, Grandpa and Grandma would drive their motor home to visit them and park it in the front yard. They'd hook up to the electric, and he and Matt got to stay with them overnight. It was like camping on their block. Jason missed their old house and everyone in the neighborhood. The skateboard ramp, the basketball hoop in the driveway and his old school.

Red Duck was a po-dunk town.

After Jason finished in the kitchen he wandered out front to wait for his mom. When the receptionist saw him, she waved him over.

"Jason, your mother called." The lady had big hair and pink fingernails. "She's running late and said for you to sit tight and she'll be here as soon as she can."

Frowning, Jason stuffed his hands into his pockets and went to look out the front window. The only thing that kept him from losing it was the fact that this volunteer stuff she was making him do would pay off and get him his truck back.

He waited until he got bored, then wandered out the doors and onto the porch that ran around the building. The heat outside felt good after being in the AC. Following the cement walk along the side, where a bunch of flowers grew, he held back when he saw a woman crying. And pretty hard.

She was with another lady. He knew who she was. Her name was Spin. She'd been featured on the television for living to be over a hundred years old without croaking.

When the tall, crying lady turned, Jason recognized her from that day in Opal's when they had just arrived in town. He couldn't remember her name. She was Drew's girlfriend. Or something. Jason had seen her with him before.

She was kind of pretty, but she wore a lot of makeup. Black stuff smudged beneath her eyes. She had a tissue and she blew her nose, then said a four-letter word he'd never heard an adult say. At least his mom had never used it.

Jason inched closer, hiding behind a potted fern on the porch.

"That bastard is already taking up with two women before the sheets have even cooled down." The woman sniffled into her Kleenex, her shoulders slumped. "I mean, I know I was the one who screwed up, but still. For chrissake…"

Spin stood pretty tall for someone over a hundred. Confusion about her name gave him pause. It made him think of the spin cycle on his mom's washing machine, and he couldn't figure out why someone would name their kid after a washing machine.

Spin put her arm around Drew's girlfriend. "Jacquie, you've got to knock this shit off. First of all, it takes two to blame, so you are not the only guilty party. And second of all, the man isn't worth it."

Jacquie's chin lifted. "How do you know? Sex is worth a lot, Spin. Forgive me, but you probably don't remember what it's like."

"Oh, hell yes, I do. Wally and I went at it all the time."

Jason grimaced. He wasn't sure he wanted to hear this. The visual made him a little queasy. He knew exactly what sex was. Brian, his friend in Boise, had a porno DVD they got from a kid at school and they'd watched it. Gross. Awkward watching that stuff with another dude. They had only lasted about five minutes before turning it off and saying it was sick. But Jason had thought about what he'd seen.

Sex was kind of weird. He'd had thoughts about what it might feel like, but actually doing it…no way. He'd never even had a girlfriend.

"But, Spin," Jacquie said, "that was a long time ago. You had a love of your life. I thought Drew was mine. I mean—" she started to cry again "—I miss him. I miss how we were."

Jason figured he'd heard enough. He wasn't interested in the problems of adults. He had enough of his own.

Jacquie continued as he started to turn, and then he stopped.

"I...I never thought I'd be such a pussy about it. But when I found Lucy at his house—it really hurt me."

Lucy?

Jason knew his mom had started cooking for Drew Tolman. She'd told them it was going to help her establish her business here. Jason hadn't thought much about it. His mom cooked for people. That was her job. How come Jacquie was mad about it?

Spin faced the duck pond and her bony hands gripped on the railing as she stared at the water. "You know what I think? I think you need to give up men for a while. Stop using sex to get your way. Value yourself, Jacquie."

Gasping, Jacquie acted as if Spin had suggested she jump into the pond with the ducks. "Give up men?"

"Yes. You need to discover who you are without a man. Learn to live alone."

"I can't!" Jacquie fumbled with the opening of her purse and came up with a pack of cigarettes. Casting a quick look over her shoulder through the recreational room window to see if anyone was looking, she put a smoke between her lips and lit it.

The smell of burning tobacco drifted to Jason, making his nose tickle.

"Have you ever tried?" Spin asked, her voice sounding tired.

"Well…not really. I mean, I didn't have a boyfriend in grade school. Maybe not through the fifth grade. But then in the sixth, I had one." Jacquie grew thoughtful. "And in junior high. Through high school. Of course I had a boyfriend," she insisted, as if she needed to verify that. "What woman doesn't need one?"

"You don't."

"You're wrong, Spin. I do."

"No. You just think you do." Spin moved to one of the chairs and sat down.

Jason had to hop a few feet back or he'd be spotted spying on them. Unfortunately, when he did that, the fern wobbled in its pot and he had to reach out and prevent it from toppling. When he did so, he gave a little yelp. Busted.

Jacquie came right for him. "Hey, you!"

Jason was going to bolt, but he had no place to go. So he put on a defiant stance. "Yeah, what?"

"How long were you standing there?"

"I don't know what you mean."

"You were listening!" she accused, then she narrowed her gaze, reading him like a book. "You're Lucy's son."

"So?"

She didn't say anything else about his mom and he

was glad. He might have had some issues at home sometimes—maybe a lot lately—but he loved his family. She was a good mom. What Gary did to her sucked and it was wrong and she was doing the best she could.

In that moment, Jason wished that back in Boise he'd said he was sorry to his mom for all the crap he'd given her. He had said, "Sorry," but it wasn't something he'd really felt. Now he did mean it.

"You're that young man who delivers the food." Spin gave him a long look. "I had some of it today…and nothing came up on me."

He wasn't sure what she was talking about, but he figured she was meaning she hadn't puked or something. Gross.

Jason didn't feel like being razzed so he said, "I gotta go."

He walked away, the scent of cigarette smoke following him on his clothes, his skin. Great, this was all he effing needed. His mom was going to think he'd been smoking.

Once he got to the front of the Sunrise, he saw his mom's car pulling up. When he got inside, he was relieved she didn't ask him if he'd had a cigarette.

Her radio was playing and she was in a good mood.

"Guess what?" she said, smiling and not waiting for him to ask. "I got another client! Now I have two people to cook for."

"That's cool, Mom."

She told him about it and he listened, watching the smile on her face. When she was done, she looked at him.

"What?"

"Nuttin'."

Her brows rose and she smiled once more. He felt like crying, something he hadn't done in a long time.

"Mom...I'm sorry."

That's all he had to say. She knew.

When she leaned over and planted a gentle kiss on his cheek at a stoplight, he had a really hard time holding back his tears.

He loved her and he was glad she was his mom.

Sixteen

"If it's got tits or wheels, sooner or later it's going to give you trouble." The mayor of the dock, Lloyd Zaragoza, was on his third Bud and feeling quite profound.

"C'hew got that right."

Lloyd, Raul and Opal sat at one of the high bar tables at the High Country.

Opal took exception. "I beg your pardon. I ain't never given a man trouble." She thought for a moment about Sheriff Roger Lewis. Several years back she could have sworn he had a thing for her, but he'd never acted on it so she'd ignored him. Time had passed and the both of them had become involved with different people. Opal had nobody special in her life at the moment and she wondered if Roger was seeing anyone.

She hadn't heard any gossip, and surely she would have heard some at the counter of the diner. The early birds slung more loose-lipped talk than she cooked hash specials.

"Present company excluded," Raul said, sipping a bloody Mary. "I'm talking about that Lucy Carpenters."

"Carpenter," Lloyd corrected. "The Carpenters was a musical group."

"C'hew making fun of the Raul's accent?"

"Oh, hell, Raul," Lloyd snorted. "Don't go acting like you've got a couple French fries short of a Happy Meal. Get a grip. I was only making a casual comment."

Raul's hair gleamed from pomade, reflections from the slow-moving disco ball glittering across its smooth black surface. He felt as if he was coming down with some sickness. His stomach roiled from the tomato juice he drank. He worried his thumbs.

"That Lucy Carpenters got a client today," he said aloud, the words souring his already aggravated belly. "Did anyone hear about her sample menu?"

The sparse details annoyed Raul's stomach even further. He didn't lack for confidence, but if she got one client, she might get another....

"Why would we know that?" Opal asked.

Furrowing his brow, Raul said, "This town is like a gossip ship. Information lands in all ports—from the hotel bars to the ice cream parlor."

"I haven't heard," Lloyd commented.

Raul pursed his full lips glumly, trying to figure a way out of the creative slump he felt himself slipping into. This was totally unlike him to let a newcomer worry him.

Then a brilliant idea hit! Like an explosion of flavors on his tongue, he tasted victory. "I know what to do! I wan' you to book a sample menu night with Lucy and tell me what you think of her cooking. Get the recipes and report in to the Raul."

Grimaces abounded and Opal spoke first. "I don't need any personal chef, Raul. I cook all day myself and take home plenty from the restaurant."

Lloyd's palm rested on his generous stomach. "My doctor's putting me on a low-fat restricted diet to help me lose a few pounds."

Raul had never known Lloyd to be weight conscious. "What does that have to do with anyting?"

"All right then," Lloyd retorted. "I got a bit of a spastic colon issue and I can't be eating certain foods right now. I'm not about to have that pretty lady come over and me tell her, 'Sorry there, sis, but I can't eat that—it'll give me gas.'"

Raul frowned, but was not defeated. There had to be a way to get a sample of Lucy's cooking.

"So just who is this client she's going to be cooking for that has you all riled up?" Opal nibbled on a bowl of buttered and heavily salted popcorn that had been brought to their table. Microwavable with fake flavoring. Raul wouldn't touch it. Peasant food.

"A Californiano."

"A what?" Lloyd scrunched his face. "What the hell's that?"

"The Dickensons from Californias. They moved up

here with a big cash flow, but I don' know what he does for his job. He knows Tolman. Drew Tolman is like that freakin' E. H. Hutton guy on the commercials. He talks and everyone listens. Damn Californians."

"Yeah, damn Californians with all their bucks," Lloyd snipped, then remembered a tidbit. "Hey, Raul. Aren't you from California?"

"La Puente."

"Where in the hell is that?"

"C'hew don' want to know."

The three of them voiced various opinions on the Californians in Idaho, then tired of that topic and switched gears to discuss whether or not Opal should expand her parking lot.

Raul listened, but only when his name was mentioned did he add to the conversation. These Dickensons could be big trouble for him. If one went over, then another would follow....

And Raul Nunez had had the market on the chef business in Red Duck and Timberline far too long to let any of his clientele slip away. No. He was the best.

This was the Raul's town.

Seventeen

The Wood River Tigers were playing the Sun Valley Cubs in a doubleheader. Drew sat in the dugout and rallied the boys around for a pep talk. They'd just won the first game three-to-one and, with a break in between, they wolfed down fast food for lunch.

The red-clay floor was dotted with spilled fries, soda pop cups and empty wrappers. Drew's stomach growled. He hadn't packed a lunch, and didn't have someone to bring him in food like the boys did.

The parents were really good about keeping their boys fed, while the coach was on his own. Usually Drew stopped by Opal's and had her make him a sandwich, but this morning, his mind had been completely elsewhere. Not on Little League baseball, though he'd been doing his damnedest to keep it here.

Mackenzie was coming into town at 5:45 p.m.

Drew was nervous as all hell. He had to drive into Hailey to pick her up at the airport, and he didn't want to be late. If the second game went as fast as the first, he could be out of the field by 4:00 p.m., head home and shower, then make it on time.

"Nutter, good fielding," Drew said, clapping with enthusiasm.

Nutter nodded, stuffing a bite of Big Mac into his mouth, then talked around it. "Thanks, Coach."

"You've got mayonnaise on your face, dummy," Ryan said to Nutter.

Using the back of his stained uniform sleeve, Nutter took care of it.

For the next game, Drew needed two of his players to switch gloves. He was moving their positions in the hopes he could get the game moving and his players motivated…and all done quickly.

Jason Carpenter worked a pine tar rag over his bat handle and disregarded the lunch Lucy had made for him. Drew eyed the thick turkey sandwich and his stomach growled. He'd had her cook for him three times now, and he'd made a referral to some friends of his who lived in the estates. They'd hired her. She'd been grateful.

But not so grateful that she let him kiss her again.

He'd spent some time thinking back on that kiss. Actually, in the moments when he wasn't planning for Mackenzie's arrival, he did a lot of thinking about Lucy. He liked her. More than he cared to admit to himself, much less to her. Wanting to be with Lucy wasn't about his usual chase and catch, love and leave approach that had worked so well in the past. That had gotten him many women, but it had also come with a lot of emptiness the next day.

Lucy was different. He felt different around her. She wasn't a woman to screw over—not that he would intentionally do so. But if he was with her, it had to be for real and it had to be honest. At this point, he wasn't even sure what "for real" meant. He'd gotten used to Jacquie, and to the games they'd played with one another.

Timing sucked for him. He liked Lucy. But he was just out of a relationship and his daughter was coming to town. A tough mix to juggle, without adding one more thing.

So Drew told himself that he wasn't going to think about Lucy. But then he caught his mind drifting to her. Like now. And then he stepped back from the dugout, glanced into the crowd and looked for her.

She sat next to Sue, talking, and wearing a pair of sunglasses that framed her face. Her hair shone reds and browns, the skin on her face slightly more tan than the last game. She'd been out boating with the Lawrences the other day. Drew would have gone, too, but he had too much to do to get ready for Mackenzie's visit.

Lucy gazed in his direction, and he couldn't help the tightness he felt in his chest, and the constriction in his lungs. She clearly fought against smiling at him, then gave in with a subtle upturn of her mouth. It seemed to be a struggle for her to let her guard down around him, but he remembered the taste and texture of her lips. The way her tongue swooped next to his, and the feel of her hands running over his back.

He had to fight the lust that curled deep inside his belly, and the feelings she brought out in him. When she'd come to cook during the days subsequent to her first visit, he hadn't been home for one reason or another. It had been a busy week, with a committee meeting on the field's new turf for next year, a luncheon down in Twin for the fall athletics board, and having new linens and a few "girl" things ordered for his spare bedroom.

This week, when he'd pulled into the drive, dead-ass tired, Drew wished he would have found Lucy's car there. But she'd been gone and the meals were in the refrigerator with the reheating instructions.

Drew ducked back into the dugout and talked to Jason. "Eat your lunch, Carp."

"Not hungry. I ate all of Nutter's fries."

"They sucked. Too salty." Nutter's athletic bag was under his rubber-cleated feet, and he didn't seem to mind that he was dirtying up the canvas with clay, and dripping sauce from his Big Mac. Sipping a soft drink through the cup's straw, he let out a long belch.

Brownie ripped a fart.

Then it became a free-for-all, and Drew shrugged, went to his clipboard and did some fine-tuning on the lineup.

The second game began and Drew threw his mind into coaching mode, directing players, talking to the umpire once to make sure a fair ball was called.

When they changed innings, he talked to Jason. "You dropped your shoulder too far back when you were hitting last time. Keep your shoulders straight and you'll nail a line drive."

"Okay, Coach."

The boys sat back on the bench, Brownie up to the plate. The greasy smell of fast food permeated the sweat-stale air, giving Drew a second reminder he was hungry. His stomach made a noise.

Jason laughed, shoved his sandwich out. "Here. You eat it."

Drew snorted. "I guess I will."

He had to made fast work of the sandwich, getting in only two bites before he had to take to the field and question his other coach on a play decision.

By the time 3:30 p.m. arrived, they were only in the sixth inning. It was going to be tight. He nervously tapped his hands on a spare helmet, the drumming sound ringing through the confined area.

Jason sat next to him, gave him a scowl. "What's the matter with you? You've been a few laces short of a shoe all morning."

Nostrils flaring, Drew laughed. "Oh, yeah? And what made you the expert?"

"I dunno. I just seen you acting stupid. Like you're thinking about a girl…or someone."

Drew was surprised Jason had such a depth of understanding, but he couldn't exactly admit he was stressed out about picking up his seventeen-year-old daughter who he didn't know from jack. So all he managed was, "That obvious, huh?"

"Yeah. Who is she?" Jason's brown eyes regarded him, staring hard. Seconds ticked by, the thwack of a ball and bat on the field breaking the silence. "It's my mom, isn't it?"

Not anticipating that one, Drew didn't remark. His lack of a comment gave Jason free range to come to his own conclusion.

"I'm not stupid. I've seen how she is around you even though she tries to hide it. At last week's game, you and her were talking, I saw how she smiled funny. She doesn't do that for just anyone."

Drew didn't know what to say.

"So are you still hung up on Jacquie? Because if you are, I want you to stay away from my mom."

"No," Drew said abruptly. "I'm not seeing Jacquie."

"I saw her and she was—" Jason's expression grew markedly indifferent, as if he were contemplating saying something further.

His interest piqued, Drew asked, "Where did you see her?"

A shield went up on the boy's face. "It doesn't matter."

Drew couldn't get a feel for it, but there was something about Jacquie that Jason knew, and he wasn't talking. There wasn't anything Drew could do about it, and frankly, what Jacquie was up to now was none of his business. But clearly, Jason was worried his coach would do wrong by his mother.

"Jason, I like your mom," Drew said, in the hopes of setting the record straight, but without getting into personal details. "She cooks for me and I think she's doing a good job with you boys. You're lucky to have her."

"I know. You'd be lucky, too. Just don't hurt her or I'd have to get really pissed off at you," Jason said, before picking up his glove and running out to the field.

The boys took their positions and a long moment passed before Drew left the bench to stand on the third base line. The sixteen-year-old's concern was a sobering reality. The last thing Drew wanted to do was play an emotional game with Lucy, but he couldn't guarantee her, or himself, that he wouldn't hurt her, however inadvertently.

So maybe it was best if he let his feelings for her die down before he burned them both.

Drew waited, his stomach muscles tight.

Fear of the unknown knotted inside him. It gnawed away at his confidence. He could handle any situation, had been in almost every one imaginable. But this was new territory for him.

A quick and disturbing thought surfaced. What if he messed things up worse than they already were?

He didn't have an opportunity to consider that. Mackenzie came through the passenger area and walked toward him, a backpack slung over her slender shoulder. He stood far enough away, hidden by security screening, that he could freely assess her without her seeing him.

She was all Southern belle, his little girl.

And for a moment, he felt the pang in his heart ache to his core—a reminder of how he'd done her so wrong. He deserved her hell, her fury and her wrath. The very fact that she was here astounded him, for he had no reason to have been this fortunate. He wouldn't question that she actually wanted to see him. He just wanted to believe he had a chance.

A memory surfaced, flooding his vision. He saw Mackenzie at twelve wearing a pair of pink capris and barefoot, sitting on the porch with Caroline and sipping cola through a straw. Mackenzie's golden-hazel eyes had fixated on him while he walked toward her mom, stopping in front of Caroline, his palms damp from the humidity. Mackenzie knew then what he knew now.

She was his.

With his thin shirt clinging to his perspiring skin, his heartbeat pounding in his ears, Drew had come to demand a paternity test—but she had flat out refused. She'd said all he had to do was look at Mackenzie, and that was test enough. Caroline had said she'd go to purgatory before she ever let him put her integrity into question. Paternity had been determined when their baby had been conceived; the truth was still there twelve years later. And if he chose not to believe what was staring at him, that was his own stupidity and he could get off her porch.

At that time, Drew had already checked out of baseball to get help with a substance abuse problem he'd been having for most of his major league career. Through counseling, he'd learned to live life differently, to be a different man, a better person. But it wasn't until many months later that he'd been able to come to grips with his past.

Caroline had always been a decent woman. Honest, with a good heart. That he'd ever doubted her wrenched his gut. But there was no going back.

The feelings of failure faded as Mackenzie came closer.

Her tall body moved with grace and ease. She walked with a fluid stride, her hips forward and shoulders squared as if she were poised for battle. She didn't take any sass with that walk. It was all attitude, with just a little sugar mixed in.

A teenage boy walked past her and smiled, and she shot him a sweet curve of her lips that made the kid bounce off the news rack.

Mackenzie laughed softly—a sound he never thought he'd hear from her. Too bad she wasn't laughing with him, and that it hadn't been him who'd made her smile.

Her long brown hair fell over her shoulders and curled at the ends. He wondered if that was natural. He couldn't remember if it was something she'd inherited from Caroline. The summer color of her skin resembled Opal's home-jarred honey: smooth and golden. She wore jeans, slung low on her hips, with a belt. Purple flip-flops smacked the linoleum as she walked. She had on a white T-shirt; a pearl bracelet circled her slim wrist.

Heading closer, she spotted him. Her easy stride slowed and she looked wary. So he did his best to put her at ease immediately.

"Hey, Mackenzie, how was your flight?" he said, stepping away from the pole he'd been leaning against.

"Long," she breathed in one slow exhale.

"You have any trouble changing planes?"

"No. I could do it."

He gave her a half smile, thinking this was going to be harder than he ever imagined. She was going to challenge almost anything he said. "I figured you could. I'm just asking."

"This is a small airport," she commented, looking around.

"Yep. But it works out okay." He ran a hand through his hair, forgetting that he'd angled his sunglasses on his head. He slipped the temple into the front of his black polo shirt as they started for the baggage claim area. "You want me to carry anything?"

"No."

He let a moment pass where neither of them said anything, each sizing the other up in silent contemplation. She was going to have to get used to him, and he was going to have to get used to her.

He was clueless when it came to teenage girls. In desperation, he'd bought a *Seventeen* magazine at the Fill and Fuel Minimart. During a soak in his hot tub the other night, he'd read every last page. It struck him that teen girls thought they needed to be sexy. The slick pages were filled with ads for shiny lip gloss, mascara, nail polish, skimpy bikinis, seductive perfume, hair lighteners, hair removal for their bikini areas, deodorants and menstrual cramp relief pills. The many articles ranged from how to revitalize tired and boring makeup to embarrassing moments when a girl's maxi-pad fell off at a pool party.

If he'd been somewhat freaked out before to have a teenage girl at his house, after reading that magazine he wondered how he'd cope without adding to the few strands of gray hair that had been slowly coming in.

From the boys he coached, he knew firsthand that they talked about girls constantly, and they gave some healthy descriptions of a few in town who were fun to hang out with. The idea that he had a beautiful seventeen-year-old who boys would be thinking about totally unnerved him.

Mackenzie *was* beautiful. He was proud she was

his. But if any of his boys ever put a hand on her, got close to her, even asked her to a movie, he'd kick their ass.

At the baggage carousel, they waited for Mackenzie's luggage to slide onto the ramp.

"So everything went okay on the flights?" he asked, repeating himself, then silently cursing.

"Yes."

"How many bags do you have?"

"Two."

"Are you hungry?"

"Yeah…kind of."

"We'll get something to eat on the way home. What are you in the mood for?"

"I don't care." She shrugged. "A hamburger."

He'd take her to Rainey's, a small café on the main highway that was quick and easy; they served the food hot off the grill, not too greasy. He didn't know many people in Hailey so their meal should be quiet and uninterrupted.

He ran his hand through his thick hair again, not caring if he messed it up. Racking his brain for something useful to say, he finally voiced a thought that had been lingering in his mind for days. "Mackenzie, thanks for coming. Thanks for giving this a chance."

She gazed into his face, looking up at him. He appreciated her height and figured she had to be five foot ten. He was glad she was tall. Like him. Her eyes were green-gold reflections that he easily recognized, because he stared at them daily when he shaved—but their expression was unreadable.

Mackenzie's wide-eyed innocence was merely a smoke screen. He saw through the layers of hurt, the years that she had suffered, and it just about killed him. Her voice was low and composed, yet softly commanding as she countered, "I'm not promising anything."

Drew felt strangely comforted that she'd even offer that much. "I'm not asking. Let's just see how things go."

Journal of Mackenzie Taylor

Drew's house is gi-normous. Bigger than I imagined. All this space for one person. It's like a mansion. The rooms are never-ending, the backyard so big I can't see where it starts or stops. He's got a batting cage, a waterfall, a hot-tub and a creek. He showed me, and he wanted me to be impressed. I could tell.

I wish I hadn't been, but I was.

It's 2:04 in the morning and I can't sleep. You'd think with the time change, I would have crashed hours ago. But I've only laid here, in this big bed, the softness of fine sheets and smells of fresh linens surrounding me.

I keep thinking about Brad and Misty. About how they went behind my back. I could cry. But I don't have any tears left to cry anymore. It still hurts, though. Deep inside my chest. Such a betrayal...I want to scream. It's not fair. I loved him. At least I thought I did. I wanted him to love me, not sleep with Misty Connors!

But there's nothing I can do about it. And thankfully I'm gone for the rest of the summer so I don't have to see either one of them.

Me and Drew ate cheeseburgers in Hailey before coming here. I thought Kissimmee was backwoods. Red Duck is as small as a puddle, and Timberline isn't even a real town. It's nothing but a big parking lot.

When I first saw Drew's house, I thought it was a motel. The Silverwood Motel down by the Gaitlin River is half its size. The outside has a rustic feel that Momma would have loved. She always had a fancy for pine trees and laying in a hammock in the shade.

Drew gave me a tour and told me to make myself at home. Now how can I do that if this place isn't a home?

I noticed he doesn't have any family pictures up. Momma had tons of me and her, my grandma on my momma's side, Aunt Lynette and some of my cousins. Our Beagle, Sally, before she died. Pictures of our trip to Disneyworld, one of me and Momma with the albino gator at the Nature Reserve.

Drew Tolman only has photographs of himself. I don't think he's stuck up, but that front room, where the big bookcase is, all that's in there is stuff from a baseball career. Seems like that's all he has to show for himself. Him wearing a baseball uniform, or with other baseball players, team managers, some pictures of him at dinners and shaking hands with people.

I got a funny feeling in my chest looking at it. What a lonely way to live not to have family memories to remind you of all the love in your life.

Me and Momma, we had each other and I am so grateful I have Aunt Lynette now.

Seems to me, Drew doesn't have anybody.

I don't want to feel sorry for him.

So I won't.

We're going up to the lake today after we get some breakfast at this place called Opal's Diner.

When I got up this morning, Drew was sitting on the patio feeding a duck pieces of bread. He said it was Daffy, a mallard that hung around.

He let me feed it. Daffy takes the pieces

right out of your hand. We didn't say much to each other, then Drew got this look on his face and he said something to me that made my heart quiet down to a slow beat.

He asked me how I wanted him to introduce me to his friends, that people were going to ask who I am. He didn't want either of us to be uncomfortable and it was better we figured out an answer together.

I understood what he meant.

"Who's the mystery girl, Drew?"

We came up with a reply that we could both live with.

But as I'm getting ready to spend the first whole day with my real daddy, I realize that the simplest of truths might as well be a lie.

Eighteen

"This is Mackenzie. She's a family friend." Drew handed a rope line to Lloyd Zaragoza, who'd elbowed his portly body next to Drew's sleek boat to check everything out.

Lucy watched the exchange from a lounge chair beside Sue Lawrence.

"Welcome to the dock," Lloyd replied, his grin broad and big. "I'm the mayor out here and if you need anything, I'm the man to ask. Can I get you a cola from my cooler?"

Mackenzie smiled with a sweet innocence. "Ya'll don't have to go to any trouble."

"No trouble a'tall!" Lloyd snapped right back. He pivoted an about-face on his bare feet and made a beeline for his boat.

Sue shook her head. "Lloyd sure loves it when someone new comes to the dock. He can feed them stories and they're not going to tell him they've heard them all a dozen times already."

Lucy smiled at Mackenzie. She liked the look of the young girl. She had a fresh face, a beautiful pair of eyes, and her complexion was like a bowl of honeyed cream. She was tall and attractive, maybe Jason's age.

Jason and some of the boys from the team were on the other side of the dock batting tennis balls into the water for Dent Gaines's black lab, Harley. He was known as Devil Dog to those on the dock because his tail was like a whipcord and he was always nosing into a bag of chips or swimming in circles around the boats and springing up onto the upholstery.

As soon as Drew arrived, everyone paused and looked at that expensive, glossy black boat of his. Lucy couldn't imagine it being worth a quarter of a million dollars, but Sue insisted.

Drew hadn't readily noticed her, but now he gave her a glance. Lucy looked away. If she were smart, she would never let him come near her again.

Her rule of thumb should be that she never date a client. That might not have been in the personal chef handbook, but it was still an excellent—and wise—thought to keep in mind.

Yet on the flip side, she felt connected to someone when she talked to Drew—him, of all people. Thank God she had survived the mourning period after her divorce, where she'd been sad and hadn't wanted to deal with relationships. But within the last several months, she'd been starting to feel like her old self again. She noticed men more often, noticed how they looked into her eyes, how they bantered with her or spoke politely, what body language they conveyed while they had her full attention. She was definitely ready to find someone and start over, and not let her past heartbreak hold her back.

But should she invest, even marginally, in the town's former ball player with an extroverted ego and a smile that could win him anything he desired?

Not hardly. She was too aware of the troubles in store if she fell for him. There was a path of red flags waving—just like those on the street corners of the main highway that pedestrians used for crossing through traffic. A flag for his past, a flag for his cloudy drug usage—which he had not explained, yet somehow, she'd been relieved that, apparently, it hadn't been a totally hideous mess. A flag for Jacquie. Make that two flags for the Realtor.

Even so, Lucy's gaze drifted back toward Drew, making a long and leisurely examination of him through the discreet cover provided by her sunglasses.

He wore a pair of printed swim trunks and a straw panama hat that made him look more appealing than one man had a right to. A cigar was clamped between his lips, but unlit. He tossed the butt in the open cooler on his boat, then threw his head back in laughter at something Dave Lawrence said. Reaching for a cold bottle of beer, he cracked the top and handed it to Dave. The music boomed on his boat, classic rock and roll.

Drew's smile flashed and he stepped onto the dock, went to put a hand on the small of Mackenzie's back. But he immediately reconsidered, lowering his arm as if he remembered himself. Mackenzie slanted him a glance and didn't readily smile, and was clearly thankful when Lloyd all but ran up and shoved a can of cola at her after pulling the tab.

"Here you go, young lady!" Lloyd's barrel torso, with its curly hair carpeting front and back, glistened with sweat. "So where are you from?"

"Florida."

"Migh-tee fine marlin fishing out that way."

The light breeze blew her long brown hair around her face and she caught a slight strand and hooked it behind her ear. She had on a pair of silver hoop earrings. "My daddy used to go deep-sea fishing all the time when he wasn't out on a haul."

Drew had been skipping through song selections on the state-of-the-art CD player when his hand froze. His action wasn't enough to draw attention, but it was enough for Lucy to take notice because her gaze had been fastened on him. The lightness in his expression darkened. Mackenzie and he exchanged a quick look, but it was over in a matter of seconds.

"What's your daddy do?" Lloyd asked, the white patch of sunscreen on his nose starting to melt.

"He was a big rig truck driver. But he and my momma parted company some years ago."

"Divorce is as common as a fruit fly these days." Lloyd took a big sip of beer, a visible belch working up his throat, but he had the good grace to hold it there. "I've been on a first name basis with it four dang times."

Mackenzie's mouth curved into a smile. "Momma said one divorce was enough for her. She wasn't ever getting married again."

"Wise woman!" Lloyd smiled back. "Next time, you bring her on down here with you. I'd like to meet her."

With that, the brightness in Mackenzie's eyes paled. "My momma's passed on."

It was Lloyd's turn to blanch. "I'm forever sorry to hear that."

"H-hey, C-Coach!" Matt ran up to Drew, the ends of his hair wet and a map of goose bumps on his arms and chest. He'd jumped into the reservoir to swim with Devil Dog, but the water temperature was still below sixty degrees.

"Matthew, come get your towel," Lucy said, standing and holding it out for him. She wrapped his narrow shoulders in the soft terry and gave his upper arms a vigorous rub.

"That's good, Mom," he moaned, ducking away from her and reaching into an open bag of potato chips sitting on an empty deck chair. "Hey, Coach," he said, crunching, "this is a killer boat. Can you take me for a ride in it?"

Jason and the other boys showed up, less to look at Drew's boat and more to check out Mackenzie.

"Yeah," Nutter exclaimed. "Can we, Coach? You took us out last year and we haven't been on it yet this year." He said to Jason, with a gap-toothed grin, "Dude, he goes so fast, it's like we're freakin' hydroplaning and going to flip over."

"Drew Tolman," Sue said sternly, "you had better not be going that fast with these boys onboard."

"Can we, Coach?" Matt pressed.

Jason's eyes were on Mackenzie, something Lucy didn't fail to miss. Her son had never had a girlfriend, but he was at that age where he did like girls. He'd gotten the job at Woolly Burgers, and the few times Lucy had gone in to talk to him a moment, the teen girl who had waited on them that night was hovering around. Lucy had told Jason the facts of life, but she supposed it was time for a refresher. Times like these, she wished Gary were around so he could do the honors. But he was about as reliable as a Yugo.

"I'm Jason," Jason said to Mackenzie, shifting his weight to expand his chest a bit more. He wore navy trunks, no shirt, his pale chest void of hair. But his voice had dropped some time ago. He could use a haircut and a little more grace in the way he walked. He was gangly, all leg and limb. Lucy figured he'd probably top out at about six feet like his dad.

"Hi. I'm Mackenzie." The way she said "Hi" sounded like buttered rum and flowed just as warm through the air. There was definitely something appealing about a Southern accent, and Mackenzie wore hers with apple pie sweetness.

"Okay, get on." Drew motioned to Lloyd to loosen the anchor ropes from the cleats. "I'll take you for a trip to the dam. We can see what the water level's at."

"For real? Bang-o-rang!" Matt exclaimed.

The boys filed onto the boat, the white leather upholstery like a blanket of ivory. There ended up being five boys and Mackenzie. Drew took the helm, then to Lucy's surprise, glanced at her. "You want to come, too?"

She hadn't given it any thought until this moment, and her first reaction was to say no.

But Lucy had been bucking convention these days in ways she hadn't anticipated. And someone had to make sure Drew kept the boat at a decent speed. After all, her babies were onboard.

"You go, Lucy." Sue nudged her forward. "Keep him in line."

Lucy wrapped a lime-green scarf around her long hair to pull it into a ponytail. "All right, Drew. Someone has to keep an eye on you."

As she took his hand to climb on, he said beneath his breath, "Sugar, you can look at me all you want."

Drew moored the boat on one of the floating docks by Overlook Dam so the kids could take dives and run around.

There used to be an entire town underneath them. Back in 1898, they'd found silver along the old creek's banks. Big Eddy Murdock had struck it rich, but eight years later, the ore had been mined out, and the town had been fully deserted by the early twenties. Floods wiped out what was left, leaving outbuildings ruined by silt-laden waters. Murdock, Idaho, was abandoned until 1973, when the U.S. Army Corps of Engineers decided to construct a $327-million dam for flood control purposes.

Drew had told Mackenzie about the dam's history as they'd launched at Big Eddy's Marina. Backing the Hummer to the water's edge, the boat trailer's tires rolling underwater, he'd unhooked the cable, and on impulse, told Mackenzie to get behind the wheel and pull forward.

Seeing his slight daughter gunning the big engine of the four-wheel drive SUV had made him smile. But at the same time, made him sad. He'd missed being there for her driver's training classes, the day at the DMV when she got her license…and a boatload of other milestones in her life.

When she'd talked about Bobby Wilder being her daddy, there was nothing Drew could do but listen and curse himself for the jerk he'd been. The only saving grace was the fact that maybe, in time, he could make things up to her.

They had the whole summer, and he was going to do his damn best to get things right, to take his time, to listen to her, to be there for her if she needed him.

Sharing his world was top on his list, which was why he'd wanted to bring her to Overlook today. This was where his friends gathered, where good times were always had. He had a feeling she'd like it, and so far, she'd been laughing and smiling. A lot.

He noticed she took an interest in Jason Carpenter. At this point, Drew wasn't sure how he felt about that. Mackenzie might've had a boyfriend before. She was seventeen, beautiful, an easy personality to be around. Then again, maybe Caroline had frowned on that sort of thing. Caroline had been fairly strict, yet loving.

Hell. Drew didn't know diddly about Mackenzie's love life. Didn't want to. He'd have to give Lynette a call. There were certain things he'd always asked about—if Mackenzie were doing well in school; if she'd been sick; if she needed any extra money or wanted to buy a special something. But his daughter's dating habits had never been one of the things he'd inquired about.

"Good Lord, you couldn't get me in that water for anything," Lucy said, her voice breaking into Drew's thoughts.

While the outside temperature had to be in the high seventies, the water was still holding residual winter runoff from the snow. It was damn cold.

Drew leaned his butt against the side of the driver's chair, his arms folded over his chest. "You want something to drink?"

"Do you have any bottled water?"

"Yep." Drew pulled up the lid to the cooler and grabbed two.

Water from the cooler's melting ice dripped from the

plastic bottles. Lucy gave a throaty gasp when droplets ran down her bare, tan legs. Drew's gaze slid across the smooth expanse of her thighs, knees and ankles.

She had on a pair of lower-riding knit shorts and her bathing suit top. Her skin looked soft and his fingers ached to run over the hollow of her throat and trace her collarbone. The shade of brown in her eyes was like caramel-chocolate, the lashes sweeping upward with a light coverage of mascara. Probably waterproof. Until he'd read *Seventeen* magazine, he hadn't known something like that even existed. She'd put clear lip gloss or balm on her lips. They were shiny and very tempting.

He admired the shape of her sexy mouth, the top and bottom lip almost a mirror of the other. She didn't have a noticeable bow to her upper lip, but rather, a fuller mouth—like Julia Roberts. Actually, now that he thought about it, in some ways Lucy did kind of look like the actress. Same hairstyle, same mouth. But the eyes were very different. So was the nose.

Telling himself to stay away from her had been good in theory, so what was she doing on his boat, long legs stretched out in front of her, butt up against the hull, and sneaking looks at him as if he were the best thing since a pair of four inch heels?

The boys on the dock were horsing around, showing off for his daughter. Nutter pushed Brownie into the water, then Brownie laid his palm on the surface and fanned them with a wide arc of spray. Matt did a cannonball and almost landed on top of Brownie.

Mackenzie stood here, laughing and basking in the attention. Her smile went straight to Drew's heart. The flush on her cheeks was proof she was shy—to a degree. He was glad about that. There was so much he didn't know about her. Wanted to know. Sometimes he got shortsighted, frustrated with himself and the situation. He wanted to know everything, and to know it yesterday.

"She's very pretty," Lucy said, putting the mouth of the water bottle to her lips. "I see the family resemblance. Who's she related to?"

Drew swallowed, glad the next song on the CD player was loud and kick-ass. "You like KISS?" he asked, ignoring her question.

"I remember them," she replied, giving him a sidelong glance. A hint of a question lingered in her eyes. She was just going to have to wait. He had nothing else to add. What could he say?

He and Mackenzie hadn't thought that far in advance. He was an only child, so saying Mackenzie was his sister's kid wouldn't work. Maybe a cousin on his father's side. That sounded good. But right now, he wasn't sure if he could work out enough of the details to make it all sound credible.

The corners of Drew's mouth pulled upward in amusement. "Of course you do, sugar. You're only a year younger than me," he drawled, cranking up the volume and enjoying the beat of the song.

Music drifted across the water, catching on the sun-ripened ripples, and the day was good. Drew liked simplicity, and this was one of those times.

"You're a complicated man," Lucy said, coming closer and looking him directly in the eyes.

"No, darlin'. I'm just the Tolman-ater."

"You hide behind that, but there's more to you than meets the eye."

"Is there now?"

The pink-painted toes on her bare feet were so close to his, he could step on her foot and caress it if he wanted to. And he wanted to. But with Mackenzie and her sons, and the other boys right there, that was something he wasn't going to do. But he could think it.

He could even fantasize about it.

"You have a scandalous past."

Drew laughed. "Doesn't everyone?"

"I don't."

"None that you've ever let me see. Maybe you do, sugar, only I just haven't figured out that part about you yet." Drew inched his bare foot toward hers, his big toe meeting her pinkie.

To her credit, she didn't flinch or move away. She held strong and kept her chin up, brows raised. He thought she might be a little skittish after that kiss in his kitchen…and then Jacquie showing up.

Not something he wanted to think about. Damn awkward.

"Don't play with me, Drew."

"Well, hell, you got me." He lowered his voice. The cleavage from her bikini top was full and round. She had nice breasts, perfectly shaped for a man's hand. "That's exactly what I wanted to do."

"Funny."

She smelled like body splash, sweet and inviting. Her hair was pulled back in a green tie, silken brown strands having fallen out in a messy caress at her cheeks, tugged by the wind as he'd opened up the twin diesel engines. He wanted to tuck her hair behind her ear, kiss the shell and trace her lobe, slowly lick the side of her neck.

The fire in his eyes must have been blazing because she stood back, took a step away. She turned, gazed at the dock and refocused her attention. Probably more to get him out of her mind than to see what her boys were up to.

Absently, her hands rose to her hair and she pulled the tie out to redo it. As her slender fingers worked her hair into a ponytail, he came up behind her, knitted his hands with hers and said against her cheek, "I got that."

She went ramrod still, but didn't knock his hands away.

The texture of her hair was soft, and strands sifted through his fingers like sugar. He used his fingers to comb it back, then pulled the scarf around and knotted it.

"You want a bow?"

"Do I look like a bow girl?"

He smiled silently, made the bow. Her shapely body shivered, most likely out of control from his soft touch as he pulled the ends of the scarf. Then he grazed his career-scarred knuckles down the back of her bare neck.

Lingering, he fought the strongest urge to kiss her shoulder.

The bareness of her back aroused him, the thin band of her bikini top more sensual to him than if she'd stood there without it on. The idea of unhooking it teased far more.

So he stayed close, close enough that he could feel the heat off her body like a gym sauna, and feel their jumping heartbeats pulsing in the air around them.

"This Tuesday," he said softly, leaning closer, "when you come over to cook…I want you to…"

He let the sentence trail, let her think what she wanted. And he hoped it was the same thing he wanted.

Long seconds played out. He inwardly smiled.

"What?" she finally said, the word a breathy sound.

"I want you to…cook for two. I've got a house-guest for the summer."

Lucy's shoulders relaxed, a soft snort left her lungs. "Sure. I can do that."

She ducked away from him, stepped up onto the dock and did a quick pivot on her feet. A cool pink blush worked across her face, her cheeks.

He grinned.

Indignant sparks flew from her eyes, and he knew damn well he'd yanked her chain and gotten her pissed.

"You know what?" she declared in a tone edged with sass. "I never did like KISS. I always thought that group was for immature men who had tongue envy and complexes about their drumsticks." Then she strode to the kids, her hips swaying hotly. The shape of her back was sexy as all hell.

Rather than being annoyed with her, he wanted to take that luscious body of hers and show her just how good his tongue would be in all the right places.

"Dude, there's an ATV at Bomber's that has snow tracks on it," Ryan said. "You can spin donuts on it."

Drew had driven them around the reservoir in his badass boat, and now they were back with everyone on the main dock. The group of boys congregated at the corner, talking about nothing and junk; but all of them were looking at Mackenzie when they were talking. She stayed on other side of the dock, laughing with some girls.

"I spun donuts in my mom's car." Brownie shoved a handful of pork rinds into his mouth, some getting stuck on his braces.

"Dude!" Ryan exclaimed. "I did that once on the ice, pulled the e-brake. I about lost it and took out our mailbox."

The boys laughed.

"I was lifting weights in my garage," Nutter stated,

"and there was this time that I almost dropped a barbell on my dad's Suburban. He would have freakin' freaked out."

"How much do you weigh, Nutter?" Jason asked, dipping into the conversation.

"A hundred and forty."

"You're a hundred and forty?" Ryan challenged, grabbing the bag of rinds. "I'm one-sixty. I can bench-press two hundred."

"You're full of shit." Nutter grabbed the bag back.

Jason sat on his towel, the sun in his eyes, but he was just as interested in Mackenzie as the other boys. They'd all been horsing around, trying to get her attention at the dock by the dam.

Mackenzie had smiled at all of them, been friendly, but Jason thought she was looking at him the most. So he'd tried to play it cool.

Mackenzie was real pretty, and he liked how she sounded when she talked. He'd never heard anyone say "ya'll" before unless it was in the movies. When she said "dinner" it sounded like "dinnah." She told him his momma was making her supper. He didn't know what supper was, and she said, "Ya'll don't call the evenin' meal supper? Oh, then I'm meanin' dinnah."

Thinking about the quality of her voice gave Jason a flush on his warm, summer skin. He found himself extremely conscious of every move she made and every word out of her mouth. He could listen to her talk forever.

She was by Drew, sitting on a chair and talking to another girl on the dock. They were laughing about something, and Jason felt a little like toeing the rubber—showing off.

Effing A.

Jason never did anything stupid like this—have a head-banger over a girl. But Mackenzie wasn't just any girl.

She was like one of those magnolia tree flowers that bloomed in the park by the Boise zoo. She was different. And all of the boys making jokes, talking big and staring at her—they all knew it, too.

Nineteen

"Clyde, you are just downright wrong." Opal's insistent voice carried loudly enough to give a brass band a run for its money. "It was Burt Gunderson who had the affair with *Betty-Lay*, that waitress at the Timberline Lodge." Opal was adamant in her argument with the deputy. She remembered things like a womanizer, and Burt had been a real hands-all-over-you guy.

"Beverly wasn't doing no two-step with Dirty Burty. You've got it all wrong. That was Blanche who worked at the ski lodge. Them broads both have names that start with the letter *B*." Deputy Cooper gave a snort-laugh. "Though Beverly earned her nickname, I won't argue that. I recall Roger almost calling her *Betty-Lay* to her face. I-gad, now that would have been something."

Opal dragged a chip through the gooey nacho cheese sauce, ate it with a jalapeño and a green onion, then took a sip of her margarita. The coarse salt on the rim puckered her lips, but the tequila went down smooth. It was Wednesday—"Olé Night" at the High Country Lounge—and the drinks and appetizers had a Mexican theme.

"I'm telling you," Opal insisted sharply. "It was Beverly."

"I saw *Betty-Lay* suntanning at the dam last week. Holy God a'mighty, she's got to be in her mid-seventies now." Clyde pursed his lips in remembrance. "That tattoo she had on her breast has become a long stemmed rose, if you get my meaning."

"Unfortunately, I do." Opal was glad she'd never taken to any body art. It was bad enough her *girls* were drooping without having an artist's ink to accent nature's deficit.

Raul grimaced as he ate a nacho, then looked as if he was going to spit the chip out. "This cheez isn't real cheez. It's that piss-whiz from a can. Jess the taste of it insults my tongue."

"Raul, this is all-American Mexican food. You just haven't developed the right taste buds."

"The Raul has an excellent palate."

"Then go paint a mural." Clyde cracked himself up.

Raul didn't see the humor.

Sheriff Lewis came in through the doors, felt hat cocked at an angle and determination in his gaze. "Raul, you're parked over the line in the parking lot, gawdammit. I couldn't find a single space for my

Blazer, so I'm double-parked in back of Opal's Ford. Go out there and move your car, Raul, or I'm going to slap a ticket on it right after I order my beer."

"C'hew can't ticket me if you're off duty." Raul's dark hair was a perfect black wing, parted and combed on the side. "And if you're on duty, c'hew can't be drinking no beers."

"I'll call it in to Dispatch and the sheriff on duty can come on over and tow you."

"How do you know it's my car?"

"For the love of Pete," Roger said, sidling up to the bar. "Who else drives a 1985 Cadillac DeVille with CHEF4U personal plates?"

"He's got you there, Raul," Clyde laughed.

"That issa classic automobile," Raul intoned with indignance. "In La Puente, that cherry DeVille was borrowed for weddings and funerals."

"Well, go bury it in its own parking slot and free one up for me."

Raul muttered, fishing through his pockets for his car keys. "I don' like this town sometimes. Everyone knows everyone's business and it makes me sick."

"Speaking of business," Clyde offered, sliding the nachos down the sheriff's way, "you find out anything more on that young gal who Drew Tolman has staying with him? She really a family friend?"

"Far as I can tell, his story hasn't deviated." Roger Lewis took a long drink of his Coors. "I think she is."

"I cannot believe what I'm hearing," Opal said.

"You boys are actually thinking Drew would have some underage girl in his home and she ain't family? I'm shocked."

"Oh, hell, Opal, stop with the indignant look. Nothing shocks you." The teasing mirth in Roger's handsome eyes pulled at Opal's heartbeat like the choke on her old Ford Falcon.

"Now, Roger, you know I'm not a prude. But I think it's bad of you to talk like that about that young lady. Drew's brought her into the diner, and I think she's sweet as can be. If you put your glasses on, you'd see the family resemblance between him and Mackenzie. She's peach pie fresh and quite charming."

"I heard someone say she's his second cousin," Bud Tremore interjected. He'd been sitting quietly listening to the exchange with a big sombrero on his head. He'd won the raffle earlier on in the evening. All the beer he wanted as long as he wore a sombrero with OLÉ on the band of the crown.

Clyde refilled his mug with beer. "That's not what I heard. I heard she was his niece, only we all know Tolman don't have any brothers or sisters."

Biting her lip as long as she could, not wanting to talk out of turn about her favorite customer, Opal piped up and spilled. "I did hear something...but it was passed on several times over, and I can't tell you who started it...but I heard she was a love child he had with Goldie Hawn."

"No shit?"

"I'd believe it."

"Is that so?"

"I-gad."

Then someone tossed in the comment, "I saw Kurt Russell over at Starbucks a week ago. He held up the line by ordering a specialty coffee. Quarter-pump of chocolate syrup. Some people just can't drink a regular cup of coffee."

"I always had a crush on him when he was in those Disney movies." Opal got a dreamy look on her face.

Then the group grew thoughtful, and Roger's threat to have Raul's Cadillac towed was forgotten.

Wouldn't it be just like the Tolman-ater to have a love child with a famous Hollywood actress?

Twenty

Jacquie Santini had gone exactly seven weeks, six days and four hours without a man.

Turning onto Honeysuckle Road and Main Street, she frowned without regard to the lines she was probably putting in her forehead. "God didn't make Adam to have him end up alone," she reasoned to Spin, who sat belted into the Jaguar's passenger seat. "That's why he created the Eves and the Jacquies to handle all the men's needs."

"What a load. You haven't read the King James version if you came up with that." A stiff, black leather handbag rested on Spin's narrow lap. Running her bony hand across the gray upholstery, she asked, "Is this Corinthian leather?"

"No, Spin. You asked me that the last time. It's just regular leather and that's a black-walnut dash."

Lately, Spin's state of mind had concerned Jacquie. As well, Spin had also been saying her bladder was giving her trouble. Always as sharp as a shooting pistol, the woman was clearly degenerating. The horrifying idea of Fern Goodey-Leonard's possible demise clutched at Jacquie. She didn't want to think about it.

Jacquie's community service had ended at the Sunrise Trail Creek Home a couple of weeks ago, but during her time there she and Spin had formed a unique kind of friendship. Jacquie couldn't exactly describe it, but taking Spin out of the residence and to the beauty parlor, or sometimes to the Mule Shoe for a brandy, and even to a movie down in Hailey—gave Jacquie a much-needed purpose in her present, man-less life.

"Can't I just go on one date?" Jacquie teased, hoping to pull a smile from Spin and bring the old girl back.

Spin's profile grew rigid, the spunk back in her posture. "I told you, you're suffering from Goldilocks Syndrome. You just can't keep trying out man after man for size, hoping you'll get one to fit right."

"Don't tell me size doesn't matter." Jacquie parallel parked the sports car into a spot on the street.

"My Wally was a good-size man in that department and I had no complaints. That's not what I'm talking about." Spin put a hand to her chest, hammered back a burp of gas. "Take a breather on the men, Jacquie. If you keep doing things your way, you'll end up with some asshole because you aren't being picky."

"I am picky!"

"Not with Max Beck you weren't."

"But he was there, and he was good-looking."

"Humph! Good-looking is only as good as looking at a dead tree if there's nobody nesting in the branches."

Spin tried to undo her seat belt restraint, but she didn't have the dexterity to push the button in hard enough. Smiling, Jacquie did it for her. Spin smiled back, her lipstick a little crooked. Her eyes looked large behind the lenses of her rhinestone glasses.

"Go to the Timberline spa and get the works," Spin suggested. "It'll get rid of some of the tension."

"I know what would get rid of my tension."

Spin laughed, her eyes merry. "You're a bad girl, Jacquie. I like you. My great-nephew, Morris, he'd like you, too."

As Jacquie got out of the car she thought, as desperate as she was, even a geek named Morris sounded good. If there were such a thing as a testosterone detox patch, she could have cut out men without upping her cigarette habit to a full pack a day versus the half pack she'd smoked when she'd been dating Drew.

Spin had been on her case to quit. Jacquie couldn't give up men and nicotine at the same time. That just wasn't possible.

She helped Spin to the sidewalk and they walked past several shops.

"Hold on, Spin. I'll get the door." With a tug,

Jacquie swung open the door to the Shear Class Beauty Salon. "If the damn thing closes on you, you're going to bust your arm."

Inside the busy hair salon, the odor of perms, bleach and ammonia came at them in a strong wave. But the douse of cold AC was worth the stink.

July had slapped Red Duck like a bitch, hot and unrelenting. Nobody could recall it ever being so god-awful sweltering this early in the year.

Tomorrow was the big Fourth of July picnic at Overlook Dam. Big Eddy's picnic grounds would be overrun with kids, parents, lawn games, and when the sun set around 9:40 p.m., fireworks would be let off.

"Spin, are you sure you want a set and style? Why don't you try something a little different this time?" Jacquie settled her butt onto the vacant vinyl chair next to where Spin sat with her beautician. "Why don't you give her a dye job? I'm thinking red."

"I'm not going red. I like my silver."

"But silver's just so boring."

"I don't want to look like Lucille Ball in my casket."

The whole casket thing was a moot point, since Spin was dead set about being cremated.

When Spin talked like that about herself, Jacquie didn't like it. She supposed it was healthy to accept one's fate…but still. The thought of losing Spin…

"Well, maybe you could go blue," Jacquie said thoughtfully, in an attempt to get a rise out of Spin and get her mind away from funeral arrangements.

"Screw that," Spin snipped, gazing at her tired reflection. "I'm not going to be any blue-haired old lady."

As Spin got her hair done in its usual fashion, Jacquie settled back and read *Cosmo*.

The humming cone dryers warmed part of the long room with hot air, and the ink from a fresh shipment of *People* magazines permeated the smells of hair products.

Gazing from her magazine over to Spin, who sat with her eyes closed while getting a helmetlike dose of hair spray, Jacquie wondered what she'd be like if she lived to one hundred and three.

Chances were, if she kept smoking, she'd die at fifty.

Shit on a stick. Maybe she should give up her cigarettes.

When Spin was finished, Jacquie walked her to the door. She was unsteady on her feet from having sat for so long, and she tucked a hand into the crook of Jacquie's arm.

"I got it," a man's voice said, and the door was pulled open.

Jacquie's mood lifted from gloom to boom as her eyes fastened on the UPS driver. He wasn't the regular. This guy was about six foot two, brown eyes and brown hair all wrapped up in a nice brown uniform—quite a package.

"Hey," she said, thrusting out her meager breasts and standing taller. "Thanks so much."

"No problem." His smile was white, his tan appealing.

Spin passed through the door, gave Jacquie a quirk of her brow, saying, brassy as tacks, "When we get home, dear, don't forget to take your antibiotics for that little problem you have."

The door was let go and the UPS guy headed straight into the salon without a backward glance.

Jacquie stood on the sidewalk and put her hands on her hips after slapping a strand of hair from her eyes. "I cannot believe you just said that. How totally embarrassing is that?"

"Very embarrassing."

Digging inside her purse, Jacquie found her Virginia Slims and got a cigarette. She stroked her lighter to life. So much for being worried about dying at fifty.

She helped Spin into the Jaguar, the smell of tobacco and hair spray overpowering the scent of the leather upholstery. Cranking the AC, she cracked the window and pulled away from the curb.

The two sat with electric hostility sizzling between them.

Spin wanted to shake Jacquie and make her realize she was an attractive and intelligent businesswoman all by herself. She had to be okay with being alone before she got involved with another man. If a woman wasn't happy in her own skin, she could never be happy as part of a couple. She'd depend too much on the opposite sex to feed her ego. And Jacquie's ego was so big, she couldn't fit it under the hood of this big Jag.

Jacquie felt every bit of her loneliness fill her heart. She hated being alone. Hated not having a man. Hated Spin for making her promise not to date. She wished she could retract it, go back to having sex for fun. Life was too short. Pleasures were too wide and too enjoyable to live like a recluse.

But as Jacquie turned into the drive of the Sunrise, she hated to think that maybe Spin was right....

Maybe she wasn't capable of going solo. And what did that say about her? Did she have such a fear of herself that she couldn't stand the woman she'd become?

Dammit. She didn't want Spin to be right.

Once she had Spin back in her room, Jacquie broke the frosty ice. "Are you sure you're up to going to the picnic tomorrow?"

"What?" Spin made an adjustment on her hearing aids.

"About tomorrow. Are you sure you're up to going to the picnic?"

Lying back on the bed, Spin gave an audible sigh of tiredness. She looked unwell. Feeble. "I wouldn't miss it."

"I'm thinking about missing it." Jacquie mused on the various reasons why, then spoke the one at forefront of her mind. "I have no desire to run into Lucy Carpenter at the picnic. I heard she's been riding on Drew's boat with him. I think they're dating."

"It's not your concern anymore, Jacquie."

Jacquie swallowed and tasted bitterness. She'd

loved Drew in so many ways. Seeing him with another woman was like salt in the wound.

"I want to find out more about this Mackenzie," Spin said, sitting up taller on the bed.

That was another thing.... Jacquie knew damn well who Mackenzie was, and it chapped her hide knowing the whole truth, yet being one big outsider on the entire deal. Several times, she'd almost dialed Drew to ask him how that had all played out—how had he managed to get Mackenzie to come see him? And for the summer.

Jacquie felt cheated for not yet being introduced to Mackenzie, when she was the only one in Red Duck who knew who the girl was. Sadly, she and Drew just didn't swim in the same circles anymore.

A burn of tears threatened and Jacquie tried to stave off the empty ache in her heart. She wasn't so much missing Drew these days, rather, missing being with someone who cared about her.

"I heard that young girl is a love child Drew had with Sophia Loren."

"Sophia Loren?" Jacquie snapped. "Loren is old enough to be Drew's grandmother."

"But she was a real dish back in her day. I always wanted to be her."

Jacquie glanced at the many photos of Spin as a young woman, displayed in various places around the tiny room. There were ones of Spin by the Boise courthouse, and others of her and Wally with a fish or dead animal, hunting and fishing.

Spin had been really pretty.

"I'm tired, Jacquie. I need a nap."

Jacquie went to her, put a hand on her arm. "Okay. I'll pick you up at six tomorrow."

She nodded with her eyes closed, looking pale. Frail. Aged. Her thin skin like parchment.

Before Jacquie left the room, she gave the sleeping woman a fond smile.

"Matt, move the cheese spread over there. And Jason, I think the asparagus pasta should go here."

As her sons made the necessary changes, Lucy placed her hands on her hips and assessed the table.

She'd borrowed a folding picnic table from Sue Lawrence for the Fourth of July picnic at Big Eddy's. Several days ago, Lucy had had an inspiring idea on how to drum up more business. To date, her clients included Drew, the Dickensons and the Gentrys. Word of mouth went only so far; food to mouth went further.

Lucy had spent the last several days cooking and preparing dishes she knew were crowd pleasers. It had cost a small fortune to buy all the ingredients, and then the time to put everything together. But in the end, she was certain that having a table set up, and offering free samples at the town's biggest summer gathering, would be worth every dime and minute she'd invested.

"Can we go now, Mom?" Matt asked, nabbing a butter cracker, which, thankfully, he didn't swipe through her feta and roasted garlic paté. "I want to watch the guys set off firecrackers."

Dusk wouldn't descend for another couple hours, but already the boys were down by the water shooting off smoke bombs and devil rays.

"In a minute, honey."

"But, Mom," Jason complained, looking over his shoulder as if he were trying to be nonchalant about his actions. But it was obvious to Lucy he was looking for Mackenzie.

"Jason, come here."

A worried expression crossed his face. "I didn't do anything."

"I know you didn't. Matthew, come, too."

The boys rounded to her side of the table, but before she reached under the tablecloth, she put her hands on their shoulders.

Jason was the first to speak, his tone sarcastic and low. "Gary's not coming."

That thought hadn't crossed Lucy's mind—at least not at the present time. Last week, Gary had called the boys and said he'd be coming to Red Duck for a visit. She wouldn't count on him being here until he actually showed up at the house, but he had promised the boys. She could only hope he'd follow through. The fact he'd bring Diane with him wasn't something Lucy looked forward to, but she was an adult and, for the boys' sake, she had to be civil. Even if it was to the woman their father had had an affair with.

"As far as I know, your dad's still coming." Lucy's reassurance was met with lukewarm reception. "I have something I want to tell you boys." She affectionately squeezed their shoulders. "I'm very proud of you both for doing such good jobs. Matt, I didn't think you'd keep up with the dog walking, but you have."

Yesterday, she'd picked Matt up at Ada's and taken him out to lunch—just the two of them. She'd spent so much time helping Jason pull himself together that she'd had to stop and realize she had a younger son who needed her attention just as much. Over French fries and chicken strips, Matt had told her the latest about every dog that came through the groomer's.

"Yes, ma'am. I like it."

"You're a good boy." Then she turned to her oldest son, his hair spiked in a short summer cut. She swore he'd grown an inch taller in the last few days. "Jason, you've really proved yourself lately. Taking the initiative for the job at Woolly Burgers, going to the Sunrise and helping. Staying out of trouble. I appreciate the effort. Thanks."

"Sure, Mom."

"So because you've both been on your best behavior, I got you something." She grabbed the large bag of fireworks she'd bought at one of the stands in town. "Here. Just don't hurt yourselves when you set them off."

"Bang-o-rang!" Matt squealed, rifling through the

items. "We got whistlers, rockets, speed freaks, turn-abouts! Wow! Thanks!"

He gave her a big bear hug, compressing her ribs as hard as he could with fond affection.

"You're welcome."

Jason was less physical these days. Lucy couldn't remember the last time her son had hugged her. She knew the likelihood of him doing so with his friends around was slim to none, so she simply smiled.

"Thanks, Mom." Jason took the bag, and he and Matt headed off to the shore.

Lucy laid out her personal chef brochures and set business cards beside them, then gave the table a last glance. Everything looked inviting. She'd done what she could. Now it was time for the food to speak for itself.

In short order, friends and acquaintances she'd made in Red Duck came over to sample. Sue hung around and enjoyed the roasted portabello mushroom melts with Gruyère.

"Delicious, Lucy. Dave would love these."

Lucy and Sue had talked about her cooking for them, but Sue was proficient in the kitchen and liked to do the cooking herself. Of course Lucy knew that just because she had friends, that didn't necessarily mean they would hire her.

"I'll give you the recipe." Lucy cracked the top of a bottled water. "Just don't tell anyone. Especially not Raul Nunez."

Sue laughed. They'd joked plenty about Raul in

the past, how he'd slipped just a little on the personal chef monopoly. Lucy wasn't going to give up. This was her home now. Free enterprise.

The afternoon wore on, and Lucy and Sue visited. Dave came by a few times, tasted items, then went back to the group of men playing football on the beach, Drew among them. Drew stood out a head above the others, tall and muscular, wearing a white tank top and khaki shorts. Barefoot, tan and chiseled, he made tackles and outran several of the beefier guys.

Lucy couldn't help watching him for long moments. If she had any sense, she would have kept her gaze moving right along. But when it came to Drew, she rarely took her own advice.

Busy with his friends, he didn't come to her table, and she hated the fact that this disappointed her. He'd already hired her and had eaten her cooking, but she had hoped he would at least stop by to say hi.

Clyde Cooper dropped by for a sample once, then twice, and by the fifth time, Lucy got suspicious.

Being discreet, she followed him along the edge of trees to a picnic area not in use. Hiding behind a spruce, she saw Raul Nunez at the redwood table— five empty paper plates in front of him. The off-duty deputy left, and Lucy waited a few seconds before walking quietly forward.

Raul was examining her crustless quiche bites, taking the side of a fork and flaking the egg and vegetables. He brought a taste to his mouth, smacked his lips, then shrugged.

Leaning forward, and talking loudly into his ear, she said, "It's the wasabi paste." No harm in revealing just that small detail; he'd never get the other ingredients right.

The plate and fork flew into the air, and Raul let out a scream like a woman, hand over his heart. Quiche dumped into his lap, a mess of egg and red peppers on the coarse black hair of his legs. "C'hew gave me a freakin' heart attack!"

"Oh, I'm sorry," she innocently replied.

He jerked his head toward her, a scowl on his swarthy face. "I don' tink you're that sorry."

"So, do you like the quiche? It's different, isn't it?"

"No comment."

Lucy had to laugh. "It's the best."

"The Raul does quiche, too."

"I'm sure."

"C'hew don' want to know how much better than yours it is. I use a different cheez. Richer. More full-bodied."

Lucy simply sighed with indifference. Inside, she seethed at the gall of the man.

Raul could make her so mad. His arrogance was as big as the whole damn dam.

"Well, you come back over and help yourself to whatever else I have left. But it's been going fast." She waved at him. "I'm all out of brochures and I have two consults next week."

He glared.

"Happy Fourth of July," she added, while walking away.

There was a confidence in her stride, and the smell of success tasted every bit as good as a piece of fine milk chocolate. This was the first time she'd taken the upper hand with Raul and beaten him at his own weasel game, and it felt delicious!

Not long after her triumph, the campfires were lit and dusk began its slow descent. The sky was awash with pink as ribbons of clouds reflected the sunset.

Dotted along the sand, flames flickered and sunless air took on a slight chill. Children ran with sparklers, and Lucy noticed her boys were with the older kids, starting to set off the bigger fireworks.

Rubbing her bare arms to warm up didn't provide immediate relief so she snagged her car key and went to get her sweater from the Passat. She made her way up the dirt trail to the parking lot, which was now deserted. Everyone was at the shore, ready for the big show. Sounds of laughter drifted to her ears. The pops and explosions of fireworks filled the night.

For the first time since coming here, she felt really good about her decision. She knew she wasn't home free yet. Jason was doing well, but he could be influenced by the wrong crowd. Her business was picking up, but not thriving. Yet she'd made some friends and had started to fit into this life. These were all important achievements.

She didn't like the narrow-minded gossiping, but

she supposed that could happen anywhere. Within the small perimeter of Red Duck's city limits, she just happened to notice it more.

"Hey, Lucy. P. J. Guffy said you put on a good spread," Drew called out, and she turned toward his voice. "That's saying a lot for a guy who puts Bugles on his bar as beer snacks."

In spite of herself, Lucy laughed at the silly comparison. "I've never been told I was better than beer snacks."

"Sugar, I'm sure you're better than just about anything." The murmur of his voice washed through her, making more shivers.

She'd promised herself she wasn't going to do this—let him get her heart skipping beats. He did so without even trying, and she sensed he knew that.

Needing space between them, she took a step back, resting her butt against her car. She hadn't had the chance to talk to him alone in what felt like forever.

That thought had her pulse skittering.

She could get her heart into a lot of trouble if she fell for this man. Drew did things on his own terms. He made it known he was available, but only when he felt like doing the chasing. She wasn't expert enough to gauge his moods or read him all that well. But she had gathered this much: he wasn't the type to date because of loneliness. He kept busy, led a full life. Didn't need a wife, but he liked being in the company of a pretty woman.

In spite of her boys and her growing business, she hated admitting she was lonely. The nights were the hardest. Lying in bed all by herself, missing the security of a man's arms around her. Snuggling in close beneath warm sheets. The feel of a wide hand on her behind, cupping her next to him. The length of a man settled between her legs, desire burning between them. That ability to have sex whenever she wanted, because the man beside her was committed to her…was in love with her.

Lucy flushed. She looked into those hazel eyes of Drew's and willed herself not to want to kiss him right now.

"You're beautiful," he said into the night. Leaning forward, he pressed his hips to hers, pinning her to the car. "I think about you."

She couldn't find her voice. The moment felt surreal. She thought about him, too. But her thoughts were usually scattered and disjointed. Mostly, she was talking herself out of him.

She started to say something, tried to think of some snappy response, anything to make her come across as unaffected by his words. It wasn't good to show a man he could have her without hardly trying—at least that's what she'd read in one of those self-help books after Gary's affair.

"Well, I think—"

But any comment she would have made was cut off as Drew's mouth settled over hers.

Inhaling deeply, she could actually feel the heat

radiate from him and seep through her clothes. This was real. All those times she'd imagined him kissing her were nothing compared to having him here.

She softly groaned against his lips, opening her mouth and welcoming his tongue. If she hadn't been up against her car, her knees would have given out. Sensations ignited her body, and she came alive in ways she hadn't felt in a long time.

Her hair brushed the curve of her neck, and she wanted him to bury his face there, to kiss her skin, then go lower to the swell of her breasts.

She felt her nipples harden, straining in the lace cups of her bra. Those big, suntanned hands of his slid ever so slowly down her bare shoulders, her arms, then caressed her breasts. The firm pads of his thumbs rubbed her nipples, making small circular motions.

Her hands explored the strength and contours of his back and the thinly ribbed white cotton stretched taut against his frame. She seriously thought about yanking his shirt off.

Lucy shook, her fingers aching to release the button from his shorts and...she could feel the bulge pressed against her. She wanted to run her hands over his thighs, feel him bunch the fabric of her top and lay the flat of his palm on her skin.

Slip a hand down her shorts and put his finger...

She stood on tiptoes, eyes closed, and kept her lips on his. In his arms, she forgot all reason, didn't think about consequences. It was dangerous, but also exciting.

Right now, all she could feel was the burning heat from Drew's body, the burning need to have him inside her.

She felt the rough khaki of his shorts rub against the bare skin on her thighs, a light friction that caused a groan to work up her throat. His right hand slipped behind her to bring her closer. His hard hand felt sinfully good kneading her butt, and she didn't care that he was working on the hooks of her bra with his other hand. She sucked in her breath, let out a gasp when her breasts came free and he rolled a nipple between this thumb and finger.

She had to touch him. Everywhere. His neck, back, shoulders, waist and thighs. Then her palm settled on the fly of his shorts, exploring and learning.

Drew's hands fitted into her underarms as he lifted her up on the trunk of the car, spread her thighs and settled in between them. She hooked her legs around him, keeping him close as she lay back on the window glass. Her sweater had come off at some point. There was no recollection of it even being on.

Breathing hard, she had to close her eyes a moment and get her bearings.

This was crazy insane. They were in a parking lot. Anyone could walk up and see, even if the faded light from the restrooms gave off little illumination. The fact was, they were out in public.

But she didn't care.

He went to lift her top off, to fully expose her to

the night air. The sound of laughter came to them; someone was walking up the hill to the parking lot.

Yes…she did care!

"I can't." They were the hardest words she'd ever had to say, or so it felt at this moment.

She sat up, putting herself back together. She pulled up the straps of her bra, redid the hooks. Her panties were wet from her arousal, and embarrassment flooded her.

Pushing him away, or rather pushing herself off the trunk of the car, she tried to stand on steady legs. Not an easy task. She faltered, and Drew was there at her side to put an arm around her waist.

"Don't touch me." She couldn't think clearly when he was so close. He stepped away. "I don't mean never again. I just mean, not right this second. I have to…" She smoothed her top down, found her sweater and slid her arms into it, even though she wasn't cold anymore.

"Lucy," Drew began, then he saw the kids coming into the lot.

"Hey, Coach!" Brownie ran ahead. "We're getting Ryan's Wiffle ball and stuffing it with beehive-bombs."

Ryan snorted with excitement. "We're going to light it and I'm hitting a high hard one over the lake."

"Yeah!" Nutter confirmed. "We're going to watch it blow up. Wanna come see?"

"I'll be down in a minute," Drew said, casually shifting his stance. Lucy's gaze dropped, and she saw that Drew wasn't easily forgetting where his hands had just been. Neither was she.

It was a good thing the area was dark or else things would have been a lot more awkward than they already were.

"Where's Matthew and Jason?" Lucy inquired lightly, trying to sound nonchalant when her heartbeat still raced.

A hasty answer was supplied by Ryan. "Matt's getting the beehives lined up and Jason's with Mackenzie."

"Where with Mackenzie?" Drew turned to the boys.

"Just sitting in some chairs by the water," Nutter replied. "He isn't hanging out with us. He wants to be with *her*."

"Score!" Ryan hollered from the depths of his parent's minivan. "Dude, I have two of them!" His fists were raised into the air, a Wiffle ball in each hand.

The boys ran in a pack back down to the beach.

Lucy crossed her arms over her chest, a shield to ward off the impulse to press herself to Drew once more.

Instead of doing something she'd regret, she said in a light tone, "Jason and Mackenzie have spent most of the day together. Maybe you'll have to give me her father's phone number so I can feel him out about the idea of his daughter with my son." She gave a soft laugh.

Only Drew didn't see any humor in what she said.

His expression closed off and his body grew taut. It seemed like a clash of emotions fought for dominance on his face. She couldn't read his mind, but wished she could. Whatever his thoughts, they were troubling.

"Drew, what is it?" she asked, putting a hand on his shoulder.

His voice was dark when he said, "She's mine."

Not fully grasping the meaning of his words, she questioned him with her gaze.

Drew looked her over, as if trying to decide what to say, how to say it. Lucy sensed he was struggling, but finally he made a decision. His next words were strong, and with them came a clarity that all of a sudden made perfect sense.

"Mackenzie is my daughter," he said.

Twenty-One

Lucy didn't respond in what felt like forever, and for a second, Drew regretted telling her the truth.

He'd been thinking about it for a while, ever since he saw Mackenzie and Jason were interested in each other. Call it a hunch, but he'd trusted Lucy the first time he'd met her. With her boys at Opal's that day, it was evident she had a good heart, and was a grounded person. In the two months he'd known her, he'd seen her acting fair, being honest and always determined. He couldn't think of anything he didn't like about her.

"But she said her father was a truck driver," Lucy finally said.

"I'm her real father. Bobby Wilder was someone her mother married when I denied getting her pregnant." The words were hard for him to speak. He knew good and well they made him sound like a jerk. And he had been.

"You denied it?"

Drew took Lucy by the hand, walked her to the cliff where a picnic bench overlooked the lake. "Sit down. It's a long story."

She did, slowly lowering herself onto the bench, hands folded in her lap.

The July night was still and cloudless, and the stars were hazy from gunpowder smoke lingering in the sky. They'd yet to set off the big aerials paid for by city funds. Everyone was still busy setting off their legal fireworks bought at the local stands.

Turning toward him and meeting his eyes, she waited.

Drew fought to form the words. Besides Caroline and Lynette, only Jacquie knew most of the whole story. But when he'd told her, he'd left pieces out, glossed over some details that, at the time, were too painful for him to talk about.

Being with Mackenzie, having her here, trying to reconnect with her, he had been reexamining all his choices, going back as far as childhood and high school. He realized now that the pattern set up for him as a kid had influenced the decisions he'd made as an adult. It didn't let him off the hook for all the stunts he'd pulled, but it explained things he hadn't fully understood about himself.

"I was a hero jock in high school and not smart enough to do anything else." He shrugged, painting a portrait of a ballplayer who hadn't taken his books very seriously. "Why let school interfere with my education?" He laughed, trying to see humor. "I barely passed my classes, but I got a diploma. I went straight from Alhambra High into the bush leagues. I had a natural talent and had played most of my childhood. T-Ball. Little League. About the only thing my dad ever encouraged me to do was hit baseballs."

Drew rested his forearms on his thighs and knitted his fingers together. He let his mind go, and it was as if he could see his past in front of him. He saw himself as a little kid in the front yard of their rambler with its single car garage, his dad pitching a plastic baseball for him to hit with a plastic bat.

"My dad wasn't good at anything. He changed jobs a lot, was never content with one thing. It drove my mother nuts—literally. I don't think they ever loved each other. One day she just left. It hit me pretty hard. But I got over it." Pausing in reflection, Drew said aloud, "You know, out of all the people in Mackenzie's life, I probably know best how she feels. My mom left me and I had to cope without her. Just like my daughter's had to cope without me. Weird. But she doesn't know that about me. I haven't told her."

Shaking off those thoughts, he went on. "I moved through the minors fairly quickly, doing a lot of partying. I'm not proud of it, but that was just the way it was. Shit happened. You get caught up in a different world. Women are always available. Drinks are always in your hand. You don't pay for anything and life is good. Then when the Cincinnati Reds stroked me a check for some serious money, I thought I was really something."

Lucy bit her lower lip.

"I had some good years. When we were heading for the play-offs there was one game riding on me, and I remember standing on the bump. Sun in my eyes blinding me. My knees were shaking, palms sweating, and my stomach was in knots. I knew I couldn't let the team down. I got us out of the inning with only one hit, and we won the game." Drew's memories rose at once, and he relived all those glory days. "If it hadn't been for sports, I don't know where I would have ended up."

"You would have done something useful with your life," she said optimistically.

He wanted to share her faith, but he couldn't. He knew himself too well. "In '87, I had my agent get me out of that Cincinnati deal so I could come home to L.A. The Dodgers signed me on, and the next year, we won the Series. It was sweet. I was on the top of my game, the winning pitcher, an MVP nod. Life just didn't get any better than that. Unless it was at the bottom of a Patrón bottle."

In his mind, he tried to conjure the taste of tequila, the burn of it against his tongue, the heat in his mouth, the way it went down his throat. He couldn't really remember. And he was glad. Every once in a while, he thought about having a drink, but he knew it only took one. He'd already had a half-dozen chances—and that part he recalled very clearly.

His life had changed for the better since becoming sober. He lived well, lived healthy. He lived for the moment, rather than the glory. The blackouts were gone, the mindless sex with women he couldn't remember, the lifestyle that was too large, the way he felt like death in the morning.

Being who he was now actually took less effort. He liked who he'd become, but even so, he knew he could bring back a little of the old Drew Tolman anytime he wanted. That bad boy, the dude who could make anyone smile. He sort of liked that ability. It was flattering when women stopped, when they smiled. It was like living *la vida loca*, but without a hangover.

"Remember that show *MacGyver?*" he asked, gazing at the lake, watching ripples of water glistening in the starlight. "I was asked to have a guest role on it, but I showed up drunk, got in a fistfight with one of the cameramen and was escorted off the set."

Lucy's brows rose as she digested that news.

Drew exhaled, wondering if she'd ever talk to him again after tonight.

"I was paid big money to be a certain kind of man. A public figure. A sports star. I wasn't a robot. I was a man who had warm blood, and sometimes it got hot in there running through my veins. So I started drinking. A lot.

"The alcohol kicked my ass and I never minded sleeping on other people's floors. I woke up, didn't know where I was. The drinking started to affect my performance. I couldn't accept it was my own destructive behavior that was doing it. Denial. You learn that in AA."

Her eyes remained on his, dark pools of emotion, and if he wasn't mistaken, empathy. He didn't deserve hers, but he appreciated it.

"I was officially in a slump. Drinking daily. I over-analyzed every pitch. I started getting a little nervous entering a game. I got no velocity on my pitches, and hitters started hammering on me. I was brought into the front office, reamed out by my manager, by the bean counters, by everyone associated with the club. Being taken down verbally like that sucked. But I didn't quit drinking.

"That fall, my girlfriend called me an alcoholic and I told her she was full of it. She quit seeing me, and I drank more to put her out of my mind." Drew rubbed his temple, made a face. "It was almost spring training and I wasn't worth a crap physically. I'd lost weight and the trainers called me into the camp and told me I'd better knock it off. I couldn't even remember the schedule for Vero Beach, but I knew I had to be there in a month. So I quit drinking. I needed to prove to myself that I could do it. And I did."

"That's a good thing." Lucy looked him in the eye, her tone one of encouragement.

"I quit for all of a few months, then I was right back. We were at Vero Beach, training. And that's where I met Caroline. Mackenzie's mother. She was pretty, blond, a nice smile. She worked at the hotel where we stayed. I got her to come to my room and we were together the whole summer while I was there."

Lucy looked at him with heightened interest. "Well, then you had to know Mackenzie was yours."

"I didn't know any such thing. You want to know how many times I've had women tell me I got them pregnant?"

"No."

He felt like a shit, but he said it anyway. "Dozens. And you know how I know that none of them could be telling the truth?"

"Oh, I don't know, Drew. You tell me." For the first time since she'd sat down impatience rang in her words.

"I used a condom every single time. I don't care how far gone I was, I *always* made sure I didn't get anyone pregnant."

"Condoms fail."

"Apparently this one did."

"When did she tell you?"

"She was two months pregnant when she called me. We'd already gone back to L.A. to begin the season, and I told her she was wrong about it being mine, that there were any number of guys in that hotel who could have been the father." With his heartbeat slamming in his chest, Drew waited for Lucy to tell him he was a jerk.

He relived that conversation with Caroline, knowing now the life-changing pain he had caused her, the humiliation to her family and sister. To this day, he struggled to forgive himself. Maybe he never would.

Lucy stared at him, licked her lips, but said nothing.

"You can say it. I was a jerk."

"You were."

For some reason, that validation made him feel better.

"Obviously, at some point," Lucy said, "you told Caroline she was right."

"While I never saw a physical resemblance between me and Mackenzie, I guess I did half-ass believe she could be my daughter. I never threw any of her photos away, and I kept a couple in my locker. But booze clouded my judgment and it was years before I could admit to myself that Caroline had always been telling me the truth." Drew dug into the past, a dark pit of recollection. "Mackenzie was seven when Caroline brought her to spring training camp and asked me to come into the bleachers and meet her. I refused."

Lucy sucked in her breath, and it almost felt good to feel her disdain. It opened the wounds again, made him *feel* raw. There were days now when he forgot about how painful it must have been for Caroline, and it was good to remind himself of that, to feel what she had felt. Perhaps in a way, Caroline was vindicated when he hurt, when his actions cut deep into his heart and made him accountable.

"Yeah, I know." Drew stared into the sky. "I did

go see Mackenzie when she was twelve, looked into her face and knew in my gut she was mine. Still, I wanted a paternity test. Caroline told me to go to hell." Swallowing, he said in an uneven voice, "And I did, literally, when the drug scandal broke wide-open and my name was everywhere."

"Steroids."

Drew gave a wry smile to cover the humiliation that surrounded him. "That's an easy thing to believe, isn't it? Hell, sometimes I wish." Rubbing the rough bristle of a day's growth of beard, he said, "I left baseball because I couldn't hit a ball, I couldn't throw one and I sure as hell couldn't function as a player or a man. I was a raging alcoholic. So I walked. Cost me a small fortune to break my contract with the Dodgers and check into the Betty Ford Clinic under an assumed name."

"So…you didn't do drugs?"

"Alcohol is a drug."

Thoughtfully lifting her brows, she said, "Yes, I suppose you're right."

"I am right, Lucy. I'm an addict." Although he told very few people those words, they were still difficult to speak. Being addicted to something said he had no willpower, was a failure. Even sober, he would always be an alcoholic, always have the predisposition to overindulge.

"I haven't had a drink since 1998."

"Do you think about it?"

"Sometimes," he answered truthfully.

The sky was suddenly alive with fireworks bursting in colorful showers, bombs going off, rockets glaring and popping. For a long while, the two of them sat there in silence and watched.

Drew had a lot to think about. There were many old wounds that he still needed to heal. A bleakness settled into his heart. He wondered if he would ever be whole again.

Lucy finally spoke through the noise of fireworks. "And what about Mackenzie? She was twelve when you saw her. When did you see her again?"

"She was fourteen. I'd gone through the program, was able to live with clarity, and I wanted to tell her that I was sorry, that I knew she was my daughter—that I didn't need a test. I apologized to Caroline, to her sister, Lynette, and I told them I wanted to make it up to everyone involved. But it was too late. Mackenzie didn't want anything to do with me."

"I'm sorry. But now she's here."

"Yeah. Since her mother passed away, Mackenzie's had it pretty rough. I don't want to mess her up any more than I have." Drew shrugged in resignation. "I never got married. Sixth sense, I guess. I knew that Mackenzie would be a part of my life and I didn't want to have to tell my wife that we'd have a knock on the door one day and it might be my daughter. I felt like one more complication in my life would be too much, and it wouldn't be fair to anyone I got involved with."

"I've wondered…."

"What?"

"Why you were forty-six and you'd never married."

"That's why."

"I thought that maybe Jacquie—"

"Jacquie's a good person. I know she comes across otherwise, but she's a good person. She knew about Mackenzie. She's been a friend to me in unexpected ways."

Lucy's gaze lowered; she looked at her hands. "Do you miss her?"

Drew answered truthfully. "Sometimes I miss her friendship, but I don't miss the stress of our relationship and the direction it was headed." His voice grew strained. "What about you? Do you miss your ex-husband?"

Her lashes flew up. "Good grief, no!" Then she grew suddenly very quiet. "Well, yes…yes. I miss the ideal. The whole thing about being married forever, having a fiftieth wedding anniversary and growing old together. I feel cheated because he cheated on me."

"Do you ever talk to him?"

"I try and avoid it. He's supposed to be coming up to see the boys, but I'm not holding my breath. Divorce is horrible enough without an absentee father. Being there as a parent is huge, and the kids suffer when that doesn't happen." She drew in a breath, looked at him. "I'm sorry. I wasn't referring to you."

"It's okay. You're right. I know what I did with

Mackenzie will have a lifelong effect on her. Caroline and I were able to talk about it. She was an amazing woman and, at the time, I was too stupid to see just how wonderful she was. She did a great job without me, and I am very fortunate she raised my daughter for as long as she did."

"So what are you going to do now? Have you and Mackenzie talked about anything?"

"I don't know how to bring it up."

Warmth swam in Lucy's eyes. "Just talk."

"Timing's been off. I don't want to upset her."

"Drew, I think she's already upset."

"Yeah. I guess."

Lucy reached out, took his hand and held it. He absorbed the warmth and comfort she offered, accepting the gesture more readily than he'd anticipated. The night grew brilliant with reds, yellows and blues. Down on the beach, the "Star-Spangled Banner" played.

A tightness settled in Drew's chest, his heart, his lungs. His daughter was on that beach, she was here, in his life. But he didn't know what to say to her, how to talk to her, what to tell her.

"Drew…" Lucy's voice pulled at him and he met her eyes. "Why don't you just start by saying, 'Mackenzie, I'm your dad and I love you'?"

Jason tilted back on his lawn chair, the sand beneath his bare feet cold when he dug his toes in. Trying to act cool, he drank a sip of cola, gazed at the sky and watched the fireworks, ignoring Mackenzie, who sat next to him.

They'd been talking about stuff. Like how it was to live in Florida and what there was to do. Jason never knew that swamp swimming could be fun. The way Mackenzie described it, everyone went into this big pond fed from a swamp. They had a tree rope and swing, sometimes someone brought beer and they had a few. She said she never did. She'd tried it once and hated it.

She was different than anyone he knew. Maybe it was the way she talked. He loved the sound of her voice, the way she said words. He couldn't figure out how she took the same word as him and made it sound pretty.

"So what is it ya'll said you did for fun in Boise?" she asked, breaking into his thoughts.

It was cool he had her all to himself. The guys had been too busy being pyros to notice Mackenzie. A part of Jason had wanted to set off some more rockets, too, but he found he'd rather sit by Mackenzie and just smell her. She smelled nice. Like sun and sand and wildflowers.

"We hung out at the skateboard park, my friend Brian's house and just…you know." If she didn't drink beer, she sure wouldn't have smoked pot. He didn't want to tell her he had.

"No, I don't know," she said in that accent he liked.

"Just stuff. Hanging out, listening to CDs and talking about things."

"Like what?"

"Just things." He shrugged, lowering the lawn chair. He had to sound rad, like hotties loved him. "Girls."

She laughed, and the sound of her girlie voice made him smile inside. "Now ya'll are talking about the same things we do. Boys." She grew quiet a few seconds. "Do you have a girlfriend?"

That she'd flat out asked sort of tripped him up. He wasn't sure what a good answer would be. He thought a minute before replying. If he said yes—then he looked like a jock who had it going on. If he said no—then he looked like a benched loser.

"Do you have a boyfriend?" he asked, wondering which answer would work for him.

"I did." When she spoke, he heard *Ah did.*

For some reason, he really liked to listen to her, and he didn't care what she had to say. But her answer did get his attention. She didn't have a boyfriend now.

Maybe he didn't want to know, but he asked anyway. "What happened?"

"He was messing around on me with my best friend."

Jason's eyes narrowed. "That bites."

"I thought it was deplorable."

Deplorable. Was that a Southern word? He wasn't sure what it meant—other than it was something she didn't like.

"What'd you do?"

"I came here to get away from him and forget."

Taking another drink of cola, he swallowed. "So is Drew like your uncle or something?"

She grew real quiet, her face becoming a shadow in the night. Her eyelashes were long against her cheeks, her hair soft around her shoulders. She had on a white sweatshirt, unzipped, and her legs were still bare. They were long and smooth and tan. Her pink lips shimmered with gloss that she'd recently put on. He wondered if it was that flavored kind. He'd never kissed a girl in his whole life.

While he liked Mackenzie—a lot—he didn't know what to do with her. He wasn't ready for girls. His stomach felt like there was too much carbonation in it, like he'd eaten one too many hot dogs with too many chips and dip.

"No, he's not my uncle." Mackenzie's voice grew whisper soft and he almost couldn't hear her. "He's my daddy."

Jason wasn't sure he'd heard her right. "He's what?"

She looked at him, her eyes sad. "If I say it again, promise me you won't tell anyone? I swear to God, Jason...I don't know why, but I have to tell somebody in this town or I'm going to go crazy." It almost seemed as if she was crying, but no tears fell down her pink cheeks. "I don't have anybody here to talk to...."

"You got me," he said, then before he chickened out, he took her hand. Just for a second, just a light squeeze. To his horror, he found his palms were damp with sweat, his throat tight.

She blinked, one tear slipping free, and his reaction was one he would never have imagined. He wanted to touch that single tear with the tip of his finger and wipe it away.

"He's my daddy."

"Drew Tolman?"

"Yes. He never believed my momma when she told him I was his daughter. But now he's sorry, so he wants to be my friend."

Having his dad walk out on him, Jason was all too familiar with what it felt like not to have a dad in his daily life.

"What a shit," he blurted, gazing around the beach and trying to spot Drew.

"Don't," Mackenzie hushed. "Keep your voice down. Don't make me feel bad for telling you."

"I guess I'm pissed for you because my dad walked out on me and my brother to live with his girlfriend in Meh-he-co."

"Is that in Idaho somewhere?"

In spite of his anger, Jason smiled, his heart warming. He did like Mackenzie's innocent questions. They made him feel funny. His skin grew hot. "No. Mexico, like south of the border. He forgets we're even around."

"I'm sorry for ya'll."

"I'm sorry for you," he replied. "So what are you going to do?"

"I don't know."

"Do you like him?"

Her pretty face grew thoughtful. "I'm trying not to. But there are times when he says something to me and I know he's real sorry for everything—even though he hasn't said it." She toyed with the white string of her sweatshirt hood, absently tugging down one side, then the other, her lips pursed. "I don't know what I'm going to do about him."

Journal of Mackenzie Taylor

We walk through this big house and we don't talk to each other. We do, but we don't. It's always polite.

"Do you want orange juice?"

"Yes, thank you."

"Do you want to go out on the lake today?"

"I'd like to."

"Want to ride the four-wheelers?"

"Do you?"

"If you do."

"Okay."

I don't know how to talk to Drew. He's not acting normal. He's too nice, too pleasing. He doesn't show happiness or anger. Just neutral, like he's not sure who he is around me.

The other day, he let me drive the Hummer to Opal's for our breakfast and when I ran up the curb and accidentally into the pole and cracked the front head-light glass, he didn't even yell at me.

Aunt Lynette would have taken off my hide. I wasn't paying attention. There was the cutest dog being walked by Jason's little brother and I turned my head to see it. The tiny thing looked like a pug-dog and beagle mix.

But no, Drew didn't yell at me.

I wish he would have.

If we don't start yelling at each other soon, we're going to go stark, raving mad in this house.

I called Aunt Lynette and told her that I'm not sure I can last for the whole summer. She's okay with me coming home whenever I want.

I don't know if I really do.

Part of me wants to stay and get this over with. For seventeen years, I've been missing my daddy, but I haven't wanted to admit that to myself.

Maybe deep down, I knew I didn't belong to Bobby Wilder. When I found out he wasn't my real dad, I had momma change my last name to hers.

When I look at Drew, I see myself and it scares me. Sometimes he calls me "sugar." That's what my momma called me and he knows that was her word. Whenever he says it, I think of her. And now whenever I hear it, I'm going to think of him.

The other day, he let me hit baseballs in his batting cage, and he watched me slam them. He said I had a real nice swing.

That made me happy.

Now why can't I always be happy around him? I think maybe I'm just waiting for him to say he's done with me and he'll send me home.

Maybe I should leave before he leaves me.

Again.

Twenty-Two

Lucy had two clients to cook for in one day—something that didn't happen often and, when it did, made for a very long day. But she wasn't complaining. Business had been slowly picking up. She now had six full-time clients.

She started in the morning at the Waterhouses', spent three hours there, and now she was finishing at Drew's. The house had been quiet up until thirty minutes ago, when Mackenzie had come home and gone into her room to listen to music.

When Lucy worked on food preparation, she didn't socialize with the family. Generally, she was in the home alone while everyone was either at work or school. That's why she had the homeowner's keys, got familiar with the pets so they didn't snap or claw at her, and even knew the gardeners and other service people who happened to be working on the property.

In a way, working for people made Lucy feel she had extended family, and she felt more and more at home in Timberline.

The Waterhouses had two adorable schnauzers and she'd been given permission to give them dog treats. The Dickensons' large Persian cat liked to curl up on the bar stool and watch her.

Lucy wiped the countertop, getting ready to prepare the last dish of Drew's choices. It was a side. Portabello mushrooms with Italian sauce, artichoke hearts and feta cheese.

As she scraped the gills from mushrooms, Mackenzie wandered into the kitchen.

"Hi," she said, walking toward the refrigerator and grabbing a bottle of Coke. Drew kept the commemorative kind, and he had an opener on the side of the countertop.

Mackenzie knocked the cap off, then took a long and satisfying drink. "My momma used to put mint leaves into the bottle and she called it a Dixie cola." She took a seat at the long counter. "She made that up so I'd feel special when my grandpa Earl came over and drank a mint julep on the porch. I liked to sit in the white wicker chair by him and watch the wind ruffle his whiskers. He kind of looked like a Civil War general."

Smiling, Lucy couldn't help but warm to Mackenzie. The young girl was very open with her feelings, and the expressions on her face were genuine and real. "Your mother sounds like someone I would have liked." As she said it, she wondered how Drew could have walked away from Caroline. Lucy didn't like how that felt in her heart. Torn in two...

"Everybody liked my momma. I miss her."

"I'm sure you do." She felt the need to steer the conversation away from Mackenzie's mother. "Both my parents are still alive. They live in Sun Lakes, Arizona. Shoot, I need to call my mom and check in. I haven't called in a couple of weeks. I've been busy, but that's no excuse."

"Do you cook for a lot of folks?"

"Six people."

"You must like to cook and all. My momma said that anyone who could read, could cook. I can, but I'm just not a natural at it."

"What do you like to make?"

"I can do all right with a grilled cheese. Sometimes I burn it if I have to use this stove. Ya'll use gas. We have an electric range back home and it doesn't get this hot." Mackenzie's brown hair was thrown into a ponytail, its glossy mane dusting her bare shoulders. Her summer tan was rich and golden. She wore a lavender tank top with a scoop neck, and hoop earrings, a silver ring on her right hand. "I know how to bake cookies."

"What's your favorite kind?"

"Chocolate chip. Do you bake?"

"Not too much."

"Do you ever get sick of your own cooking?"

"Sometimes." Lucy brushed olive oil on the

mushrooms, then put them in the oven for ten minutes to broil.

"I miss my aunt Lynette's grits and gravy." Mackenzie absently took up the pen that rested by a notepad. She doodled pictures. "Drew cain't make anything. We order in or we eat out, or we eat what you cook for us."

Lucy leaned her back against the counter. Knowing that this girl was Drew's daughter put a different light on things. She had had a rough upbringing, and Lucy wasn't sure how she could forget the truth. She more than liked Drew, but the mother in her wanted to protect Mackenzie from further hurts. Lucy had raised her sons from babies and couldn't conceive of ever leaving them or denying them. That Drew had was a hard pill to swallow.

She'd promised Drew she'd keep his secret. And she'd meant it. But right now, a part of her wanted to tell Mackenzie that Drew was trying to be a better person, that he wasn't the same man who'd fathered her. It had been a long journey for him and he wanted to make amends.

Setting the record straight wasn't Lucy's business, so she kept her mouth shut. Or she would have if Mackenzie hadn't asked, "You like Drew, don't you?"

Lucy was momentarily taken aback. That wasn't just a casual question, but Lucy treated it as if it were. "Everyone likes Drew."

"You like him like a boyfriend."

Suddenly, Lucy had ten different things to do. She got out the feta and began to crumble it.

Do I like Drew Tolman as a boyfriend?

The question echoed inside Lucy's head.

Yes, I do.

She'd known that for a long time now, but she hadn't wanted to confront the idea. Because she did want him in the worst way—a sure sign of sinking. She knew she'd drown in his arms, and that was the surest way to bring her heartache.

He was the town's bachelor boy, a man with a full plate right now. A daughter he was trying to bond with, an ex-girlfriend he was getting over… Add in a new woman? Disaster.

Lucy had had one disaster in her life in recent years: Gary's leaving her. She couldn't deal with another so soon. That was why she had purposefully put off dating and getting involved with someone else. Already, she felt the threads tightening, pulling, bringing her toward a vortex of emotions and complications she wasn't sure she was capable of handling.

This was new territory.

"Do you?" Mackenzie questioned.

Pushing aside the feta, Lucy kept her back to Mackenzie. "I think he's a fun person to be around. You can't help but like his way with people, don't you think?" She turned toward Mackenzie in the hopes that the young girl would see Drew's merits and maybe soften toward him.

"I think he's a charmer," Mackenzie said flatly.

"And I think I'm probably crimping his style, so maybe I should go home."

"Oh, no!" Lucy quickly replied, then bit her lip. "I don't think you're crimping anything where Drew is concerned. What gave you that idea?"

"I don't know." The teen grew quiet, then lowered her chin. "I guess I'm just homesick, and I'm thinking it's better I leave before I get left."

Lucy came around to Mackenzie, stopped, wasn't sure if she should put her arm around her or not. In the end, she did.

The young girl smelled like floral body splash, and it reminded Lucy of the fact that, at one time, she'd wanted a daughter really bad. But over the years, she'd settled in with her boys and was now used to having sons. Even so, holding this soft-skinned young lady who smelled like a woman brought unexpected tears to Lucy's eyes.

"I think you should stay," she whispered, wondering if Mackenzie would stiffen at her touch. She didn't. "Talk to Drew if you're having a problem."

"I don't know how to talk to him. All he does is act nice to me, and I'm going to scream if he doesn't tell me to cut it out when I do something I shouldn't."

Pulling slightly back, Lucy gazed into Mackenzie's eyes. "What do you mean?"

"Lately I've been doing stuff to make him mad, but he hasn't taken the bait. If he were a crawfish, he would have snapped on to my line by now, but Drew doesn't feel anything."

"Oh, that's not true, Mackenzie."

"Yes, it is. I accidentally busted out the light on his Hummer and he didn't say diddly about it. Now if I'd've done that with my momma's car, she would have given me holy heck."

"Well, maybe Drew didn't care."

"He cared. When we got home, I heard him on the phone with the dealership, making an appointment to have it fixed. In case you haven't noticed, Drew's a neat freak. Nothing's out of place in this house. It's not lived in. I walk around and I feel like I'm in the middle of a museum. It ain't right." Mackenzie's voice cracked. "I miss my bedroom, my things, treasures and stuff that I have. I hate this house. It's nice and everything, but it's like we're all glass inside it and we're going to break. I mean…look at this kitchen. You don't think it looks plain? There's nothing on the counter, there's nothing personal. Nothing stuck on the refrigerator with magnets. All that's personal in this house are the baseball things. I don't see any pictures of anyone."

Lucy had thought about that as well. Drew did seem to isolate himself from everyday details that didn't have to do with his former baseball career. There weren't any photographs of his parents, nor of Mackenzie.

The timer for the portabellos went off. Mackenzie sat taller and Lucy slowly released her to go to the oven. As she set the mushrooms on a pad to cool, her mind went a few different ways.

Knowing both sides, Lucy thought maybe Drew and Mackenzie needed to get real with one another and lay all their cards out on the table.

This young girl was hurting and Drew held the key to a lot of answers for her. He was keeping quiet, unsure how to unlock the mystery that was Mackenzie. They were at a stalemate.

Unless…

"Where's Drew?" Lucy asked, feeling a hot spark of something leap into her pulse with a lively punch. She had an idea that might backfire, but she was going to do it—even if Drew came unglued.

"He's in town at some meeting for the Park and Rec committee because of the baseball play-offs coming up. We had lunch at Opal's, and I almost kicked him under the table—he kept asking me if I was okay, if I wanted dessert, if I wanted to go to the lake, if I wanted to take a ride on the four-wheelers, if I wanted to hit some baseballs in the batting cage." Mackenzie's eyes grew large. "I wanted to hit *him*…"

Tears shimmered in her hazel eyes, and Mackenzie pressed her full lips together. "He's not really a family friend," she began.

Lucy shook her head, not wanting to put Mackenzie through that. In a flash decision, she simply said, "I know."

"I guess everybody knew but him. My grandpa Earl knew it, my momma knew it and my aunt Lynette knew it and…well, now that Drew accepts it… I…"

The tears began to fall, and Lucy saw Mackenzie's frustration on her face. She held her close, tightly, and didn't let go.

Mackenzie was a soft crier. She didn't make noise, didn't shudder. Probably the time for that had passed, and now it was just a lonely release of pent-up sadness.

"When's Drew coming home?" Lucy asked, brushing her lips over Mackenzie's silky hair, then letting her go.

"We're supposed to go to a movie in Hailey tonight. He said it started at six." Mackenzie wiped her cheeks, then glanced around. "See what I mean? This house is a mausoleum. He doesn't even have a box of Kleenex anywhere. Toilet paper just ain't the same."

In spite of the somber mood, Lucy laughed. "Oh, Mackenzie. You are so wonderful. When my ex-husband left, I went through every box and had to resort to TP a couples of times. I agree with you on the toilet paper—although the two-ply is a lot better than the single."

"Drew's got two ply. He only buys the best."

They both burst into laughter.

"I heard about your husband. Jason told me."

Lucy nodded. "It hasn't been easy for my boys."

"And you." Mackenzie talked while walking down the long kitchen hall. Her voice carried from the bathroom and she came back with a long streamer of tissue to blow her nose. "Ya'll seem like you're doing a good job."

"I'm doing okay."

Mackenzie was smart beyond her years. What they said about girls maturing faster than boys was true.

Disregarding the unfinished side dish, Lucy took in a firm and deep breath, her heartbeat racing. "Drew won't be back for hours. I have an idea. I don't think he's going to like it, but that's the whole point."

Drew turned into his half-circle drive, the radio blaring. His mind was places other than Margaritaville and wasting away. He had a mind-blowing headache. The school board was on a rampage about funding sports equipment for next year's season; Drew said he would take a cut in pay to keep the boys in gear. The powers that be were "considering" it—but no guarantee. They had to vote on it.

The other meeting he had today ran longer than expected. The city budget for next year had been cut by twenty percent—Little League would be affected. And he'd just found out Ryan had sprained his wrist falling off his skateboard. He'd told those boys to go easy on the other sports while they were heading into play-off contention. They'd been having a marginally good season, and now this.

Cutting the motor, Drew sat in the Hummer a long moment. He didn't feel like going to the movies. All he wanted to do was sit in the hot tub, smoke a cigar and veg out. But he'd promised Mackenzie they'd go to a movie, and he had to make a good showing of trying to be a good dad. But, damn, it was difficult.

This was harder than he'd thought.

She'd been really pushing him lately, almost intentionally, as if she was trying to get a rise out of him. He didn't want to yell at her or anything, but he could only take so much.

He'd gotten his cell phone bill in the mail, and had a heart attack when he saw she'd text-messaged $396.00 worth of messages. Who knew that many damn people? He'd questioned her about it, but only mildly, not wanting to rock the boat. She said she hadn't realized she'd sent that many. He suggested she just pick up the phone and dial the number after 7:00 p.m. instead. She'd replied that texting was much funner.

So Drew let it go.

Then he came home and she'd left dirty dishes all over the kitchen counter. Leftover scrambled egg on the plates, empty milk glasses, dirty pans and utensils in the sink, and the butter had been left out on top of the stove and had melted from the heat of the pilot light. He cleaned it all up, didn't say a word, when he'd really wanted to lay into her but good and tell her he didn't live like a pig.

He liked things neat and uncluttered. Simple. Basic. Keep it neutral. Don't personalize. Open. Nothing closed off. It stemmed from his childhood and not wanting to feel suffocated. The way his dad changed jobs and his mom's moods swung from hot and cold, Drew had always needed space—wide-open and with nothing in his way. He liked a clear view. Uncomplicated.

Opening the SUV's door, he tugged in a tired breath. This movie playing in Hailey was some teen comedy, and he really wasn't in the mood. If he'd been a drinker, he'd have had a shot to take the edge off and release the tension of the day. But those thoughts were long since gone and he'd turned to other things for self-medication.

A glass of orange juice gave him a bit of a sugar rush, and was almost just as good. He wasn't much for drinking pop, not without rum in the Coke, so he'd all but given up soft drinks.

Drew let himself inside and was thinking about drinking the juice straight from the carton, when he paused in the entryway and gazed around. For a second, he thought he'd come into the wrong place.

"What the f—"

That last word was never uttered, fading before he even got the door closed.

The main living area was decorated with white mini holiday lights—over the windows, on top of the bookcase, by the wet bar. The two leather sofas that faced one another had throw blankets over them. He recognized both the lights and throws—they were his. The lights only went up at Christmas, and he didn't do it himself. He paid someone. The soft yarn throws had been given to him, or maybe he'd bought them—he couldn't remember, but he didn't like them sitting out on the furniture. They only cluttered. As far as he could remember, he'd never used either. They'd been in the linen closet for years.

The expensive coffee table sitting between the couches had two boxes of facial tissues on it, and the focal point was his pitcher's glove, the same glove he'd had dipped in bronze and engraved with the date he'd retired it. The glove's pocket wasn't that deep, but it was filled to the brim with peanut M&M's. This was his No Hitter glove he'd earned at a team dinner. It had a place in his trophy cabinet, not on the damn coffee table.

Peanut M&Ms were his favorite, but he'd never set a bowl of them out.

On top of the fireplace mantel were rows of frames. About a dozen of them. And filled with pictures. He went over and looked. He froze. Those pictures he'd kept of Mackenzie all these years—they'd been put into the frames. Drew's gaze went down the line of photos, pausing as he found one of Sheriff Roger Lewis and Deputy Clyde Cooper.

"What the hell?" he said aloud. He picked up the picture frame and saw the bend in the paper. He recognized it as a cutout from the town's local travel brochure that included a brief bio on the two lawmen. Looking farther down, he found a framed portrait of Opal's Diner from the same brochure, then one of Ada in front of Claws and Paws.

Not sure which way to go, Drew found himself headed for the kitchen. It smelled as if Lucy had been here, the aromas of chicken and garlic filling the air.

Once in the kitchen, he paused and took it all in. He wasn't sure what to hone in on first—his highly prized, valued and autographed baseballs that were now residing in the fruit bowl as if they were a bunch of apples—or the collage of things stuck onto the front of his refrigerator with magnets.

He stopped at the stainless doors, gazing at everything. There was a grocery list with several items listed:

Kleenex
Lip Gloss
Fun

There were cutouts from magazines on the refrigerator along with household things. Pictures of dogs, cats, an Armani suit taken from the pages of *GQ*, a seascape, a perfume bottle, a Hummer ad. Then there were pizza coupons, a grocery checkout receipt, the schedule for the Wood Ridge Little League, a picture that he'd never seen of Mackenzie—of her sitting on the back porch with her elbows on her knees, smiling.

He slowly pulled it off the fridge and studied her features, swallowing tightly.

Glancing over his shoulder, he wondered where she was. Had she done this? And why?

The countertop was filled with more stuff. A large chunk of white granite rock. He had a ton of those rocks on his property; he'd paid dearly to get most of them excavated when he'd put in his hot tub. There was writing on the rock. He checked it out.

"This rock was picked by Mackenzie Taylor."

Then she had dated it.

Leaning closer, Drew found an old photograph of himself as a boy, standing out in the baseball field of Alhambra. He wore his peewee outfit, a bat resting on his slender shoulders. He stood with a cocky tilt to his hips. Hell, he must have been all of eight.

Unbidden, a smile curved his mouth.

The picture frame that housed it had rows of elbow macaroni glued around the perimeter.

Where had she found this black-and-white photograph taken with his dad's old camera? Drew wouldn't know, unless it had been shoved into the very first baseball rule book he'd been given. That might have been it. He kept that book, among others, in his trophy case, never revisiting the pages.

Another box of tissue was over by the toaster—the toaster that he kept in a utility drawer. He only took it out when he needed it, not wanting crumbs on the counter. He noticed the blender, the mixer, the cutting board and napkin holder were now all in plain view.

What was up with the flowery boxes of Kleenex?

Turning back to the baseballs, he got more than

a little torqued up to see them in that fruit bowl. His blood pressure rose, his pulse thudding in his ears, and he was reminded of his headache. Those were signed official balls and not to be messed with. Each had its own plastic case and stand. They were priceless. And to be thrown in a bowl like this—

"Mackenzie?" he called out, stymied by the changes. "Mackenzie, are you home?"

He told himself not to get pissed, not to let the frustration of the day erupt to where he felt himself losing control. But looking around this house, at the stuff that had been moved and put out of place, he wasn't happy about it.

"Mackenzie?"

He walked down the hallway toward her room and knocked on the closed door. When she didn't answer, he opened it.

She sat on the bed, her iPod earbuds in place. Looking up, she raised her brows as if to ask: *What?*

He motioned for her to pull the plug on her music. She slowly removed the earpieces, wet her lips and waited.

"What in the hell happened to the house?" he asked, damning himself for using profanity. But he was really trying his best to keep it together here. "It's all screwed up."

"I made a few changes. I noticed you don't keep a lot of your personal things out."

"Yes, I do," he countered sharply, then gritted his teeth.

He remained rooted in the doorway, gazing at his daughter as if she were a stranger. The idea hit him full-blown and hard: he realized she *was* a stranger. She'd been here for two months and he didn't know her any better today than he had when he picked her up at the airport.

"No, you don't. You keep stuff hidden away, put on a shelf or inside a cabinet, and you don't use it. I thought you might like the house this way."

"I don't need a picture of Roger Lewis on my mantel."

"He's your friend. So is Opal and everyone in town. They all like you—I thought you might want to remind yourself you have friends who'd like to come over for a party, maybe."

Roger Lewis and Clyde Cooper over here for a party? Off-duty, those two guys sat around eating beer nuts and bullshitting about lame things. Why in the hell would he want their pictures up, much less have them over?

He had no response, didn't know what exactly to say. Wasn't it obvious he preferred it one way? If he'd wanted the things out, he would have put them out. But he didn't want to hurt her feelings, so he let it go. He simply didn't have an answer right at this time, and so he stalled.

He asked, "What's with all the Kleenex?"

Her response was spoken so softly, he almost thought he didn't hear her correctly. "In case you have to cry."

A long moment passed before he said, "I don't cry."

Mackenzie's chin lowered, her mouth a thin line as she looked at her iPod and scrolled through the pictures. She ignored him.

The seconds ticked off, slowly and hard. One, two, three, four. Then ten, fifteen. He'd never known just how long a second measured out until now.

"Are you mad at me?" she finally asked, her hazel eyes lifting to his and locking on to his face. Waiting. Wondering.

He was royally torqued, but he wouldn't let her know that. "It's not that I'm mad…I just like my house a certain way. But I'll take care of it. I can put the stuff away."

"Get out," she snapped, and his brows shot up.

"Mackenzie?"

She scrambled off the bed, went to the door and took it by its edge. Her cheeks grew red, her breath came out in a whoosh and she flicked her hair from her shoulders. "Get out of my room! I'm calling Aunt Lynette. I want to go home. I hate it here. I hate you!"

The door was slammed in his face before he could say another word.

Twenty-Three

"Pull over, Spin! You assured me you remembered how to drive a car!" Jacquie grabbed on to the dash of the Jaguar as Spin took a sharp corner, tire rubber burning.

The hundred-and-three-year-old woman sat in the driver's seat, spindly and tall, her gnarled fingers gripping the steering wheel. "I do remember."

"It doesn't seem like it!"

Spin signaled for a right turn, but made a left onto Cherry Hill and onto the highway toward Timberline. "It's like sex. Once you do it, you never forget how."

Brows arched, Jacquie asked, "When was the last time you had sex?"

"About fifty years ago."

"Holy shit."

Jacquie hadn't intended to let Spin drive her car, but Spin had been really under the weather lately, so she'd wanted to pick the old girl up and let her do something fun. They'd had to miss the big Fourth of July celebration. When Jacquie went to get her, Spin had been in bed, not feeling too well. They'd had to take her to the hospital for tests. Her age was definitely setting in and she'd been deteriorating. Although the physicians weren't allowed to tell details, they alluded to the fact that Spin probably wouldn't last until Christmas. That very thought caused a stab of fear in Jacquie.

What was she going to do without Spin?

The woman had snuck into her life and filled her world with a presence Jacquie never could have anticipated. Spin was full of B.S. and stories and humor. If it hadn't been for her DUI, Jacquie would never have met Spin. In a roundabout way, she had Drew to thank for it. If he hadn't stood her up on her birthday, she wouldn't have gotten plastered.

Sometimes life worked out weird.

Spin inadvertently crossed the double yellow line, squinting through the car's low windshield. She almost wiped out another car.

In the side mirror, Jacquie caught a glimpse of Raul Nunez's Caddie swerving before gaining control.

"Spin, I think you should pull over so I can drive now."

"I want to take you to me and Wally's fishing spot. It's not that much farther out of town. We're almost there."

While she didn't want to deflate Spin's balloon of rebellion, Jacquie couldn't help saying, "You probably don't remember the turnoff."

"I most certainly do. It's mile marker 4, right by that old yellow pine that has the funny branches."

Jacquie couldn't recall any funny pine trees.

Since Spin was determined, all Jacquie could say was, "Just go slow." Then she got out her cigarettes, lit one and put a slight crack in the window to vent the smoke.

Thank God they'd reached the highway and there wasn't any real traffic. Every once in a while, a camper or RV passed, or a minivan. Local campers. The area surrounding the Red Duck city limits was filled with vacationers.

The town's population had swelled in recent months, and that was good for Jacquie's business. People who had money got the bug to buy a vacation home, or even relocate. The odd thing was, lately Jacquie just hadn't had a good game. She usually thrived in July and August, was like a bitch in heat going after clients and closing deal after deal.

Lately, she'd been finding excuses to leave the office more and go spend the day with Spin.

Spin slowed the car, easing off the accelerator. "There it is! I told you."

Funny…Jacquie had never noticed the broad tree with odd-shaped upper branches, as if it had been struck by lightning. "Well, where's the road?"

"Right here." A small cutoff was tucked into the sage, and a dirt road loomed ahead.

"Hell. We can't take my car on that rutted road.

We'll bottom out." Jacquie pulled in a deep drag, chewing on her fingernail.

"No, we won't." With amazing dexterity, Spin navigated the tires carefully over the compacted earth, its talc raising in a rooster tail behind the Jaguar and coating its glossy paint. Jacquie would have to take it to the car wash when they got back to town.

Not too far in, Spin turned right to a spot that was hidden by a growth of sumac. Jacquie wasn't real up-to-date on the local flora, but she did recognize poison oak and a few of the basic Idaho plants. She'd never have guessed this place was here.

Jacquie was a hotel woman. Give her a turn-down service on a set of high-thread-count sheets, and a chocolate on her pillow. She didn't do the camping thing. No shower, no way. Bugs, no thanks. Fishing, never tried it. Even growing up in Cheyenne, there'd been a slice of civilization that she'd found quite comfy.

Spin cut the large engine, but forgot to put the gear column in Park. The car died in Drive. Jacquie reached over and fixed it while Spin got out of the car, oblivious to her mistake. It was like she had to be here, had to see the old fishing grounds.

Getting out of the Jag herself, Jacquie was glad she'd slipped into a pair of flats today. Normally she wore heels to give shape to her long legs. Today she'd worn low mules and white capris with a black top.

"Be sure to remember where the turnoff is,

Jacquie. I want you to be able to show Morris where this is."

"Yeah, sure, Spin. I'll show Morris." Jacquie merely placated Spin.

"Did I tell you Morris is a lawyer?"

"You mentioned it."

"And that he's my great-nephew?"

"You mentioned that, too."

"He's a fine man."

Anyone named Morris would have to be a fine man because he sure wouldn't be might-tee-fine in the looks department.

Walking toward the edge of a mossy creek, Spin glanced at Jacquie and pursed her lips. "Put that damn cigarette out. You'll torch the whole place to smithereens and then the memory will be gone."

She crushed the cigarette's cherry against a rock, made sure it was completely out, then joined Spin, taking her by the elbow. "I don't think you should be walking all the way down there. It looks too steep for you, Spin."

"If you keep hold of me, we can make it."

Jacquie didn't want to, but Spin gave her a pleading look. The woman had nostalgia written in her eyes. Evidently this was a special place for her, and she might not ever get the chance to come back. "Okay, Spin. Hold tight."

The embankment wasn't as steep as Jacquie had thought, but little pebbles slipped into her shoes, making it uncomfortable. Once at the bottom, she situated Spin on a bleached boulder that was warm from the sun. Feeling better about things now that Spin was safely here, Jacquie shook the rocks out of her shoes.

"So you and Wally came here fishing, huh?" Jacquie made a panoramic sweep of the area, noting the quiet beauty and interestingly enough, appreciating it. A magpie squawked from a tree; the trickle of running water was actually soothing.

"All the time. This was our spot. We did everything here, if you get my meaning." A far-off look glazed Spin's eyes.

"Yeah, I get it."

Rather than being on sacred ground, Jacquie was standing on sexual ground. The thought brought a smile to her mouth. Not in a bad way, but fondly. Knowing Spin was reflecting on being intimate with her husband was a nice thought.

And God knew, Jacquie lacked sentimentalities like that.

She'd given up on Drew, that dream having died. Oddly, he hadn't been that hard to let go of once her mind accepted the fact that it needed to end. For the past year, she'd really been trying to put a square peg into a round hole. Her and Drew, they just weren't real compatible in the long haul. She wouldn't have known what to do with Mackenzie if they'd ever committed to one another.

Jacquie wanted a man who was okay without children. Maybe they would do some traveling, just be together for the sake of being together. Of late, Jacquie realized she just had to have a man who was mad for her. She didn't think that was detrimental. Just honest.

Speaking in a faraway voice, Jacquie asked, "How come you and Wally never had kids?"

"Selfish." Spin readjusted herself to sit more comfortably. "There's nothing wrong with two people only wanting to spend time with one another."

"Not very many people would admit that."

"They should. Wally and I were in love. We fulfilled each other. I had my career and he had his. It worked out for us." She gazed at the trees. "Morris never had children, either. He's divorced."

They sat quietly for a long time, just listening to the sounds of nature, the whisper of trees.

"Jacquie?" Spin's distant voice broke into Jacquie's thoughts and startled her.

"Are you okay?" She was by Spin's side, looking down into her weathered face. Oh my God, she hoped like hell she had cell service out here in case Spin needed help.

"I'm fine, Jacquie. I'm better than fine." She smiled, a deeply satisfying smile of utter contentment and knowing peace. It was as if the aches and pains that had been troubling her had subsided and she was years younger.

"Don't scare me, Spin."

"I won't, Jacquie."

Jacquie sat down next to her, inhaling the fragrant

air and the rich ground. The musty scent of moss and the floral hint of flowers somewhere in the brush.

"Jacquie…?"

She turned toward Spin. "Yeah?"

"Thank you for being my friend. I love you."

A lump formed so swiftly, so quickly in her throat that Jacquie felt light-headed. At no time in her entire life could she ever recall those three words meaning so much. They were altogether potent and meaningful, deeply moving and utterly heartfelt.

For long seconds, Jacquie almost couldn't compose herself.

Tears sprang to her eyes, but she took Spin's hand. "Back at you, girlfriend."

Raul didn't care that he'd almost been run off the road by that polished silver Jag of Jacquie Santini's. Psycho-nut-ball Realtor. Raul had better things to do than to trouble himself over a near-miss with a car. For one thing, he had some serious gloating to do.

He'd just scored the coup of the century and, quite possibly, of his life: the personal chef gig for Hollywood's hottest gay couple—movie producers who were in town through Labor Day.

Beating out that Lucy Carpenters for the job was a rich reward, given the hellacious month he'd had competing with her. She thought she was pretty smart at the Fourth of July. But she didn't have the know-how to land the really influential clients like the Raul did. He knew the ins and outs, the best way to do things. That was why he was the best. The *only* personal chef to hire.

But he hated to admit that Lucy had given him a buck for his bang…a run for his money, as you say.

He found out she'd interviewed before him and the men liked her food choices—they'd told him so. They raved about her diversity and flare. Adored her as a creative woman and wanted to all but flambé her with compliments.

After so many years in the biz, Raul knew how to turn himself into a human chameleon when necessary. Today he'd become the gay chef, the man who "understood" what being gay in today's society was all about. Feminizing his language and walk, his savoir faire, had been easy. Raul had seen *The Birdcage* a dozen times.

Being faux fruity had been his meal ticket.

The producers thought he was *fabulous*. They gave him air-claps and they'd cinched the deal with a champagne toast and limp-wristed handshakes.

Thank you, Lord Jesus. Raul crossed himself again, something he had been doing just as that Jaguar raced toward him.

Never count too many blessings.

On that thought, he crossed himself once more while driving on Main Street toward Sutter's Grocery to stock up on supplies.

Score one for the Raul.

Matt sat at the kitchen table with his mom and brother, all of them eating dinner together. It was

nice his mom had made them their favorite—
homemade mac and cheese, chicken and carrots.

They hadn't been eating together as much since
coming to Red Duck, what with Mom having to
work, and Jason being at Woolly's.

Things had changed a lot. Sometimes Matt got
bummed out about it. He wished they were a family
again, with Dad at the table, Mom and Jason and
him. And they were all goofing off and talking about
what they did all day at school or work.

But this wasn't bad. He loved his mom. She was
a good mom and she'd been doing good for him and
Jason. The house they lived in was fixed up pretty
nice, even though the porch was busted. He'd gotten
used to no Internet and no cable. Their TV only
tuned in ten channels. But he never had any time
to watch it, anyhow.

Ada had him walking more dogs over the summer,
since people were here on vacation. When he thought
about it, Matt figured he was a pretty lucky kid to live
here all the time. He liked it. When he was in town,
the trees on the mountainside seemed like they
jumped out at him. The air smelled like fresh laundry.
The ski runs looked neat even without snow. He liked
the metal lift chairs dangling from poles. There were
the regular guys who sat outside, in front of the Mule
Shoe, when he walked past and they always said hi to
him.

He liked Bud, the guy who owned this house. Bud
had given him five bucks the other day, just because

he felt like it. Matt bought some comic books and candy.

Jason was doing better. He liked hanging out with Mackenzie. She was pretty. Matt knew his brother liked her. All the guys on the team thought she was hot.

Taking a drink of his milk, Matt wrinkled his nose. He didn't think girls were hot yet.

"Jason, do you think you guys will make the play-offs?" Matt asked.

"Doubt it." Jason shoved a big bite of mac into his mouth. "Now that Ryan wrecked his wrist, we're screwed."

Their mom frowned. "I don't think that's a good word choice, Jason."

"But it's true. We're screwed."

His mom frowned again, but she didn't say anything more. She'd come home from Drew's house and had been real quiet. Maybe she was tired from all the cooking. But she didn't act tired while taking off her shoes and putting on her slippers. She'd acted funny, like she was waiting for someone to come over at any minute, or maybe like she had to leave at any minute. She seemed anxious, glancing at her cell phone.

When it rang, she jumped.

"That's going to be Mackenzie," she exclaimed, rising to her feet.

Then Jason said, "Well, then it's for me."

But Matt was too quick and he grabbed it, since it was the only phone they had in the house and maybe it was for him. Sometimes he had boys from the team call him up and want to go to a movie or sit out at the ice cream place and eat scoops of chocolate fudge.

"I got it, Mom!" he hollered, scraping his chair legs from the table, then speaking into the mouth piece. "Hullo?"

"Who's this? Mattie or Jason?"

"Dad!"

"Hey, Matt. It's your dad."

Matt flopped into the overstuffed armchair and dangled his legs. "What're you doing, Dad?"

Glancing at his mom, he saw her expression of wonder, as if she was thinking something bad.

"Just sitting here thinking about you and Jason," Dad said. "I sure miss you boys."

"We miss you, too, Dad. We're going to see you this Friday. I already got my ideas for what we can do. We can go fishing in the river—Bud said we can use his tackle, and I can take you to Ada's and show you the dogs and then we can have burgers at Woolly's and make Jason clean up our table—"

"Shut up," Jason scowled, but with a smile. "I'm not cleaning up after you guys." Then his brother got quiet for a sec, as if he was trying to decide something. "Tell Ga—tell Dad I said hi."

Matt felt better. "Dad, Jason says hi!"

Their dad replied, "Tell him hi back."

Kicking his feet to the side of the chair, Matt asked, "So what time are you going to be here?"

"That's why I'm calling." His dad didn't say nothing for a long time.

"Dad?"

"Matt, I won't be able to come up." Matt's heart sank into his stomach. "I'm having a little bit of a financial problem down here. I can't seem to get the money for an airline ticket up that way. You know how it goes. I've got to pay child support and that about taps me out. But I'm thinking of you boys all the time."

Matt didn't say anything, and maybe the look on his face said everything. Because his mom came over to him and took the phone. Matt let her. He went back to the kitchen table, sat down and gazed at Jason. "Dad's not coming."

Jason's nostrils flared. "Effing bastard. I knew it."

Their mom went outside, onto the porch, but Matt wasn't even interested in listening. He had a stomachache now.

After a couple of minutes, she came back inside, stood in the doorway and folded her arms across her chest.

"I'm sorry."

"It's not your fault, Mom," Jason said, looking up at her with his chin down. "Gary's an ass."

"Jason, I really don't think you should say that."

"I don't care. It's true."

Matt wished he could cry, but in a way, he just didn't feel like it.

"Okay, I have an idea." Mom came toward them,

her brown eyes happy even though her face was sad. "Let's get out that old tent we have and pitch it in the yard. I call campout-sleepover, and we'll even make a fire to roast marshmallows."

"Yeah!" Matt smiled, a surge of excitement hitting him.

Even Jason shrugged with a half smile. "But, Mom, last time you put that tent up for us, it collapsed."

"I never claimed to be perfect." She set the cell phone on the counter, put her hands on her hips and gave them a loving glance.

Matt fought tears. He jerked to his feet, put his arms around his mom's waist.

"I think you're perfect, Mom."

Even Jason got up and hugged Mom. It was just the three of them, but that was okay. They loved each other.

Twenty-Four

The plan must have worked.

Lucy woke up early, sunshine streaming through seams in the thin tent and blinding her. She put one of the pillows over her face and closed her eyes, her body sore from having slept on the ground. She was getting too old for this.

The boys were still out like lights, each a lump in sleeping bags zipped up tight, with shaggy hair sticking out of the openings. They'd stayed up late, toasted marshmallows, talked about the new school year, which classes they wanted to take. The things they'd been doing over the summer, and baseball.

Sleeping with her cell phone close by, Lucy had expected Mackenzie to call to say the plan hadn't worked, that Drew didn't care and they hadn't talked things out. But they must have.

Grateful, Lucy smiled in spite of feeling as if she'd

slept on a pile of rocks. Checking the time on the front of her phone, she had to squint.

Almost seven.

Dragging herself out of the sleeping bag, Lucy left the boys and went inside to put on coffee. She padded into her bedroom and sat at the vanity, gazed at her reflection and frowned. She looked awful.

A quick visit to the bathroom to wash her face, brush her teeth and brush her hair into a ponytail had her feeling better. Thankfully, she'd taken a shower before bed, so her legs were shaved and smooth for a pair of shorts and a tank top. Already, the day's heat seeped into the cabin. It was going to be a hot one.

Lucy sat back at the vanity and applied marginal makeup. A little blush and mascara, a light coat of lipstick. She preferred pink. She swiped on deodorant and sprayed apple blossom body splash on her neck. Inhaling, she looked at herself, satisfied. Almost content to the degree that the past had been left in the past. No longer was Gary able to affect her. His not showing up was not surprising. Was it going to ruin her day? No. Was she going to feel guilty about it for her boys? Yes…

That's why she'd camped out with them last night. But in the past, she would have brooded the rest of the day and thought about how she could get Gary back, and make him suffer the way she was suffering.

But the funny thing was, she no longer suffered.

She'd finally hit neutral. What Gary Carpenter did and who he did it with was no concern of hers, and his actions weren't going to bother her.

Lucy slipped on a pair of flip-flops. Today she intended to give the house a cleaning. Dusting, sweeping, shaking out area rugs and scrubbing the bathroom.

The sound of a car pulling into the yard caused her to glance out the front window. A deep-gray-and-chrome Hummer had pulled up next to the lilac bush.

Drew Tolman was here.

Going to the door, Lucy wondered what made him show up all of a sudden. He'd never come over, she'd never invited him. Living in a teardown wasn't exactly a place she wanted to have company visit. She'd been thinking about finding some place permanent, but that was a long way off. Maybe by Christmas she could save enough for a small condo. The odds were unlikely, but with prayer and luck, it might very well be doable.

She went out to the porch, one hand on her hip and the other shading her eyes. "Hey, Drew," she said, her voice sounding sleepy. His name was the first thing she'd said since waking. And it felt good to say it.

"Morning." He glanced at the tent. "Rough night?"

She smiled. "The boys and I had a campout. They're still in there sleeping."

Drew looked too good in a pair of khaki shorts and a white linen shirt that hung to his narrow hips. His face was tanned, as were his muscular arms. A hint of stubble shadowed his jaw, as if he'd shaved just before bed, but not this morning. He had on black leather flip-flops.

Pocketing his SUV keys, he came toward her. "I know it's real early. Is this a bad time?"

"No. I'm making coffee."

"Good, I need some."

On closer inspection, he didn't appear as if he'd rested well. Maybe it hadn't gone well with Mackenzie last night. Lucy's initial thought when seeing him was he'd come by to tell her he and Mackenzie had had a great night, connected and come together. Now she wasn't so sure.

"Come in."

No longer did thoughts of her run-down residence fill her mind. There was something wrong. She had women's intuition.

Drew stood in the kitchen as if he didn't know what to do. He had that helpless-man look on his face, something she never thought she'd see there.

Absently putting her hand on his shoulder, she said, "Sit down. How do you like your coffee?"

"With cream, but milk's fine."

"I've got vanilla creamer."

"That works."

She put everything out, let him pour the amount he wanted. Taking a chair next to him, she drank a sip of coffee, let the flavors wrap around her tongue, and tried to anticipate what he was going to say.

"What happened?" she finally questioned when he didn't start blabbing.

Drew pinched the bridge of his nose, rubbed the center of his forehead, then gazed at her through his fingers. "Mackenzie went a little nuts yesterday. I think she has that shit you call PMS."

However Lucy thought he'd word it, saying "shit you call PMS" hadn't been part of the equation.

"I figured you'd know about this teenage girl stuff, since you were once her age." Drew dumped creamer into the black depth of his coffee and then stirred.

Keeping her rampant emotions in check, Lucy tried not to think the worst, but she had a bad feeling. "What do you mean, she went a little nuts?"

"I came home yesterday and she'd messed up the whole house with my stuff. She got into my baseball things, put the baseballs into the fruit bowl, framed pictures of Opal and Roger and put them on the mantel." Drew shook his head. "Just some weird stuff. And she had Kleenex in all the rooms in case I cried. Hell, I think it's so she can cry because she's whacked out on hormones. She hasn't been herself lately. She's been doing things—almost as if to piss me off—and it's working. She's leaving dirty dishes out, crap like that. I've held it together because I don't want to lose it with her. It's a hard situation. I mean, she's my kid, but I don't want to parent her."

"Why not?" Lucy asked curtly, then pressed her lips together. "Why aren't you being her dad?"

He looked as if she'd just spoken a foreign language. "I am."

"Well, if she's doing things in your home that are disrespectful, you have to tell her no."

"Yeah but, Lucy, she's dealing with the death of her mom. She doesn't know me. I just want to be her friend for now. You know, keep it even. No tension."

"It sounds like you're having tension."

He sucked in a breath that hissed between his teeth. "You're right. So what do I do?"

Lucy toyed with the spoon in front of her, her eyes cast down. "Why were the changes in the house displeasing to you?"

"I don't know, they just were. I like things one way. Neat and organized." Drew lifted his cup. "I've lived a certain way for so long it's not easy to change."

Keeping her temper, she tried to speak without displeasure in her tone. "How do you know your way is the right way? What makes Drew Tolman think that living a sterile life without photos on the walls and personal objects in the kitchen is a way to live? What's wrong with having the refrigerator covered with magnets and life—pictures, receipts, take-out coupons?"

"I don't like clutter on my fridge, okay? I just want—" But he stopped himself, scowled. "How'd you know about the fridge?"

Lucy bit the inside of her lip, the truth weighing her down. No way out. "I was there. I helped her do it."

Drew tilted his head. "You did what?"

"She was upset with you, Drew, so I—"

"Upset with me? I haven't done jack. I've been keeping my distance, haven't tried to pressure her or make her talk to me." A dark gleam landed in his eyes. "I've taken her places, done the father-daughter things and hoped she'd forgive me."

"Have you asked her to?"

"Yeah, as a matter of fact, I did. This past February when I went to Florida I took her to a spring training game at Vero Beach. I told her I was sorry for everything."

Lucy's dander rose and she spoke from personal experience. "Being sorry and asking for forgiveness are two different things. I could burn your dinner and tell you I'm sorry, but if I did wrong by you, that would require me asking you for your forgiveness." The stirring of a headache built, and maybe she wasn't as "done" with Gary as she'd thought....

Sometimes, out of the blue, something got her worked up, and she remembered all too well what it was like to deal with a man's ego. In this case, Drew's was getting in his way.

Playing with the spoon's handle, she formed her words. "I told you that my ex-husband cheated, then walked out on me two years ago, and in that time, I have made my peace with him. It wasn't an easy thing to do. Bitterness is a hard thing to let go. Gary has never once asked me to forgive him. And he was the one who wronged me. In his mind, he said he was sorry for how things happened, so he gets a clean slate. I can tell you, Drew, there's a whole different playing field between those two words. You live for baseball. Think of being sorry as a foul ball and forgiveness as a line drive."

He stared blankly at her, as if he didn't know what to say.

In a strong tone, she advised, "I suggest you ask your daughter to forgive you."

Drew made a check of the time on the dial of his watch, then adjusted the band, looked at her and the surrounding room. "It isn't going to be easy."

"Nothing worth having ever is."

"She's going to tell me to go to hell."

"I think you've been living in it for the last seventeen years."

He raised a brow. "I'll have to tell her about the alcohol."

"She's a smart lady. She won't judge."

"She might."

"You'll deal with it."

Clearing his throat, he uttered remorsefully, "She told me she wants to go home."

"It's not too late to change her mind."

"She's stubborn."

"I wonder where she got that from?" For the first time since Drew had come over, Lucy smiled at him.

Drew made a face—at himself. A roll of his eyes, a grimace, a soft snort of self-disgust. "Yeah. Maybe." He stood, tall and broad-shouldered, then dragged a hand through his hair and smoothed it away from his temple.

She walked him toward the door, but he turned to her before they reached it.

One minute she was behind him, the next she was in his arms and he was kissing her softly on the mouth. The move was sudden and unexpected, disarming and wonderful at the same time. She'd been too surprised to linger and taste, but the warmth from his lips caused her heartbeat to lighten, flutter. Her arms wound over his shoulders, her fingers cupping his neck.

Against her mouth, he whispered, "Thanks, Lucy. I think you are amazing."

His words of validation brought the burn of tears to her eyes. For a long time after Gary, she'd thought herself unattractive and unworthy. It felt good to be reminded she was important. She'd come to that conclusion on her own, but it felt really great to be told she had worth. And especially by Drew.

"Thanks." She gave him an encouraging smile, one that she hoped he could carry with him and remember as he talked to Mackenzie. Part of her wanted to be there to mediate in case things got ugly; a part of her knew it wasn't her place. Sometimes things had to get a little unpleasant before they could be fixed. This was one of those times where everything that either of them had ever felt needed to be spoken. Too much time had passed when things had been kept inside.

Drew brushed his warm fingers over her cheek, then traced her lower lip with his thumb. "You're a quality lady."

The affirmation warmed her to the core, heated her skin with a blush that threatened to overwhelm her. This was a side of Drew that she'd never seen, that probably few people had seen.

He had a huge heart. For the first time, she realized that even a big man could feel vulnerable. Fear rejection. Want to walk away from pain rather than face it.

"I gotta go," he said, and took the keys from his pocket.

She watched him pull away, her heart swelling with a feeling she'd thought was long since dead. She'd known from day one that she had lust for Drew Tolman. No doubting that. But now something else flickered to life. She hated to even acknowledge it.

So she didn't.

Caroline Taylor had never contacted Drew demanding child support or recognition for Mackenzie. Over the years, as Drew rode the elevator higher into the majors, she could have cleaned him out for some serious cash. A court would have made him take a paternity test, but she hadn't been like that.

When she told him she was pregnant, she'd knocked the hell out of his curve ball. She deserved a whole lot better from him, but the past was the past and he couldn't change what had happened.

In those days, he'd spent half his time in the bar and half his time on the ball field. After too many drinks, he reasoned that even if Mackenzie was his daughter, she'd be better off without him.

But deep down in his core, the center of his soul, he'd known the truth from the very day Caroline had called to tell him she'd missed her period and the test strip confirmed her suspicion. He would always remember the tone of her voice, that helpless quiver to her words.

Even to this day, recalling it made a stab of conscience and self-loathing spear his heart. Caroline wasn't a liar. That's why he never threw any of Mackenzie's pictures away and hadn't been fully able to talk himself out of having a daughter.

To Caroline's credit, she'd done an amazing job. Who Mackenzie was today, even the little rebellious streak in her, she owed to her mother. With all Mackenzie had been through, it was a wonder she stood tall and strong. Losing a mother, and even a stepfather, only to find out your real father denied you—nobody should have to deal with that.

All Drew could do was thank God he'd had the opportunity to make things right with Caroline before she passed. When he'd started sending her money, she'd accepted it, but they hadn't discussed their heated conversation so many years ago before Mackenzie was born. That night Caroline had told him and he didn't own up, she'd left him without a backward glance.

It wasn't until two years ago that Drew flew to Florida, and he and Caroline met in private. They finally cleared the air about what had happened. She was a saint, never once raising her voice at him. The only time he'd ever seen her lose her temper was the time she'd told him to get off her porch.

Drew pulled into his driveway, got out of the Hummer and headed toward the front door. The rapid-fire *pop* of the Iron Mike spitting out baseballs pulled his attention. He changed direction, and at the side of the house he saw Mackenzie inside the cage, helmet on, taking some swings. Holding back, he watched.

She had a perfect stance, a good pivot on the balls of her feet. She held the bat at the right angle, took a swing and made contact. The ball flew into the cage with a metallic ring. Her smile was one of pure satisfaction.

Pride surged through Drew, his pleasure intense. Seeing her determination, the way she held herself with an effortless grace and speed, reminded him of himself way back when.

Readying for the next pitch, she kept her form steady. A ball sailed toward her and she sliced the air, chasing after leather and hitting it hard. If she had been in a Little League field, that one would have been a home run.

He went to her, stood outside the cage with his fingers curled in the chain link. "You sure can hit a baseball."

Without making eye contact with him, she replied, "I can do a lot of things you don't know about."

She missed the next ball, her concentration broken. Another pitch came and she threw her whole upper body into it, fouling the ball away.

"Mackenzie. I want to talk to you." When she didn't acknowledge him, his confidence faltered and a natural reaction was to build up his defenses. He wasn't sure if he had what it took to make things right with her.

"It's a free country."

Drew went to open the latch on the batter's gate. "Let's turn this thing off. You're liable to get hit on the head."

"I can hit a baseball and listen to you at the same time," she challenged, taking a swing and this time ripping one hard.

"But I'd feel better—"

"I'm sure you would. It's always about what makes you feel better, isn't it?"

"That's not the truth and I think you know it."

"I don't know anything."

Sweat dampened her brows. The golden tan on her cheeks was enhanced with blush. A mottled line of perspiration showed on the back of her sand-colored tank top. She had on white shorts and white tennis shoes. She wore his wrist guards. When she gritted her teeth to take a bite out of the air, slicing a chopper, she looked just like him.

It sort of freaked him out, put a dip in his blood pressure. But not in a way that made him want to run. He wanted to hug her in the worst way.

"Mackenzie," he said, his voice scratchy. He cleared his throat so she could hear him over the noise. "I know I've been a shit to you for most of your life."

"You were a shit to my mom," she countered.

"Well, Caroline and I got things settled."

"I know. She told me. She told me to give you a chance."

"I'm glad she said that."

"I wish I'd never come—" she reached for a ball, took a swing, but missed "—out here. It was a bad idea. If Brad hadn't two-timed me, I would have spent the summer in Florida with Aunt Lynette."

There were a few implications here: an unfaithful boyfriend. So did that mean Mackenzie had had sex with him and then he'd gone out and had sex with someone else? The scenario paralyzed Drew. He couldn't think about his daughter making that choice, and he hoped Caroline would have talked to her about responsibilities. He'd bet his Cy Young Award she had. Something else struck him—her being here didn't have anything to do with him, but rather she'd used him as an escape.

That reality stung. But he had to own part of it. He'd done her wrong, and she owed him nothing. Even so, he recognized the hurt that nicked his heart.

"Who's Brad?" he asked, tempering the father-instinct in his voice. If the kid had even laid a hand on her...

"Nobody."

"How come you ran away from nobody?"

Mackenzie abruptly stepped out of the batter's box and a missed ball slapped the wire of the cage, falling to the ground.

Hand on her slight hip, she glared at him with hazel eyes. "He was my boyfriend and I never did *that* with him since I know that's what you're thinking. Maybe if I had, he wouldn't have done it with Misty Connors, but I'm over him so I don't care anymore." Blowing the hair off her forehead, she wiped her damp skin with the back of her hand. "I shouldn't have told ya'll why I came. Momma said bad manners are no excuse to give bad manners in return. I didn't mean to tell you that's why I changed my mind, but now that it's out, you know."

"I'm not mad."

"Of course not."

Ball after ball methodically hit the chain link. Drew opened the gate, went inside and turned the machine off. Facing her, he tried to form the right words. "Mackenzie, I have to ask you something."

Her chin rose, defiant and on guard.

"I know I wasn't around when you were growing up. I'm sure when you found out who I was, it was a shock to you."

She released the bat and it made a sharp noise

hitting the ground. Her breathing seemed to catch in her throat. "When I saw your name on my birth certificate, I flipped. I knew exactly who ya'll were—I'd been looking at your picture on the Wheaties box that morning when I was eating my breakfast!"

Unsnapping the strap, she removed the helmet and set it down. Her hands shook as she smoothed her hair from her face. "I don't know if you know this, but my momma always encouraged me to love baseball, and she even told me she had known some baseball players when she worked at the motel. She especially pointed you out when Dodgers games came on the TV. She did that so when the day came and she had to explain you were my real father, I'd have good thoughts about you—like it would almost feel as if we'd been friends." Her hair was flicked over her shoulder with a terse move. "When I was twelve and I saw you walking up our steps, it was like that Wheaties box come to life."

A long span of time stretched between them. He wasn't sure what to say, how to say what he had to. The tension between them was thicker than the August air.

"I should have come sooner," he finally said, then explained, "Your mother brought you to Vero Beach when you were seven."

"I know." *Ah know.* The Southern vowels were punctuated by her distress.

"She wasn't how I remembered. She'd developed into a fine-looking woman, not that girl I'd met so long ago. She'd grown up, gotten rid of some of her shyness. She came right up to me in the locker room and she said, 'I have your baby daughter sitting in the bleachers and I want you to meet her.'"

"Why didn't you come out?"

"I couldn't." Drew's response was spoken fast. His mind raced, trying to organize thoughts to clarity. "Meeting you would have been more than meeting a seven-year-old little girl. You would have expected me to be your dad. I couldn't deal with it."

"And how do you think that makes me feel?"

"Mackenzie, I'm so sorry. Back then, I was a full-blown alcoholic. I didn't know the upside to a bottle from looking at it down the neck. Every night I got trashed, and every day I played baseball better than the day before. It took years before it caught up with me, but at that time in my life, I wasn't any good to myself, so I sure as hell wouldn't have been any good to you."

Her full lips almost formed an obvious pout, a stubborn streak with a defiant downturn of the corners. "So you never did those drugs like the newspapers said?"

"No, Mackenzie. Never."

She digested that news. "What made you come see me when I was twelve? Were you still drinking?"

"I'd been sober for two years, but that didn't mean I thought with a sober conscience. The behavior of an alcoholic is still there even though they're not drinking. It's taken me some time to heal. Your mother kept sending me pictures of you throughout

378 Stef Ann Holm

the years, and it was when you were twelve that I saw something that scared me. I knew you were mine— the photo of you standing by the rosebush with your hair on your shoulders and that expression on your face, the look in your eyes. But I needed scientific proof, so I asked her for that paternity test."

"She told you to go to hell and get off our porch."

"So I didn't come back for two years."

When Mackenzie had been fourteen, he'd returned to Kissimmee and he'd waited for her to come home from school. Caroline had been at work, so he'd sat on the porch alone.

Mackenzie had walked up, seen him and stopped. Gone was that look of wonder and hope that she'd given him when she'd been two years younger. This time he'd been met with resentment and distrust.

"When I saw you there, I was mad at you," she said.

"You had every right."

"But when you started talking to me about the trouble I was having in school, I knew Momma must have told you, and I wondered why she was even telling you my business if she was so angry with you."

"Caroline kept in touch with me throughout the years, and when she said you'd been struggling, I knew I had to come see you and try to make things up."

He blamed himself for hurting her so bad that she might never recover as an adult. To Caroline's credit, Mackenzie had never had issues with drugs or alcohol. A true testament to Caroline's well-grounded parenting skills.

In a lifetime of mistakes, Drew felt worst about how he'd treated Caroline and Mackenzie. It was the one thing after becoming sober that he knew he needed to go back to and correct.

Mackenzie shifted her weight, put a hand on her hip. "I remember you said sometimes adults make mistakes that fall back on children, but it's not their fault."

"I did."

"Do you realize you said I was a mistake?"

Drew felt the breath knocked out of him. "Mackenzie, I never."

"Yes, you did. You said I was a mistake." Mackenzie's chin rose, a quiver in her lower lip. "How can I ever forget that?"

"I didn't mean it like that. I'm sorry."

"Sorry, sorry, sorry! That's all you've ever said!" She balled her hands into fists. "I wrote you letters! After you came to see me the first time, I wrote to you. I wanted you to be my dad."

Drew had received her letters, but he hadn't responded. He didn't know how to. He'd been dealing with stuff from rehab, but having a brain messed up from alcohol abuse was no excuse. If he could throw a baseball, he was capable of picking up a pen.

After those first few letters, her enthusiasm changed and she'd wanted to know how come he was so rich while she and her mother lived in a two bedroom house?

In Drew's mind, he felt it best not to reply, because

ultimately, he would just let her down. But because of Mackenzie's long letters, he did start to send Caroline money. He had more than made up his financial responsibilities.

Only once did Caroline ever threaten him—that was when Mackenzie had been entering her senior year and Caroline wrote to ask if he could pay for college. For some reason, he never got that letter. To this day, he didn't know what had happened to it. So Caroline called him and the first words out of her mouth when he answered was, "I'll see you in court."

After he'd calmed her down and got her to believe he knew nothing about her letter, he'd agreed about the college tuition. Mackenzie needed that education and she had to go.

Even when Caroline got sick with cancer, any hope he'd had of having a mock family was nixed. He would have gone to see her in the hospital, but she was adamant he stay away. She didn't want his memory to be of her dying. Up to the end, Caroline never displayed a bitter hatred toward him—and she had every right. She only wanted what was best for their daughter.

The hot sun beat down on his face and a bead of sweat trickled down his neck. Lucy's words came back to him, reminding him of the differences between actual remorse and actual forgiveness—even if what he'd done had been entirely wrong.

Sorry and forgiveness *were* two different things.

His eyes burned from the lack of sleep last night.

But if he was being honest with himself, he'd admit they burned from the hot sting of unshed tears. He knew there was no hope, could feel it in his heart. "Mackenzie, when I think about all the birthday cards I never sent, the phone calls I never made, no Christmas gifts, no regard for you whatsoever when you were growing up—I don't deserve any chance you might give me."

He couldn't even beg for one. He didn't have that right.

"I do want to ask you something, though." He swallowed the saliva in his throat, blinked hard once, then twice. "If you can't, I understand, but it has to be said. Can you forgive me?"

Mackenzie glanced away, unable to look at him. He knew it, and didn't blame her. Bees droned in the nearby brush, their sound so loud it was deafening. Someone down the street was mowing a lawn. Life moved on. And here they stood. Stagnant. And he was helpless to fix it.

"After Bobby left…and then I found out who you were, my reality was no longer real." Mackenzie's soft voice carried to him and she met his gaze. He saw years of fear, loneliness, hope and despair, a deep longing, rejection, fondness, and something else. He couldn't dare to probe deeper in case he was wrong.

Tears spilled from her eyes, coursing down her cheeks. She cried without noise, the sight going straight to his heart. "All I ever wanted was someone I could call Dad—who *knew* he was my dad. Bobby knew he wasn't. *You* knew you were…but you never—" Her voice cracked. "You never said you wanted me to be your little girl."

Drew took a step closer. So close, he smelled her skin. That distinct scent that he'd come to know as Mackenzie. Flowers, shampoo, a certain lotion. It scented her sheets, the bathroom, his house. It was something he'd never forget.

He wanted desperately to draw her into his arms and hold her tight, but he wasn't sure.

"Momma always told me," she said, wiping at her tears with her fingertips, but they fell faster than she could catch them, "to give you a chance if the day ever came. She wanted me to have you as my father. Not Bobby. Even when she was dying, she said that me and you needed to be together and I really was someone's little girl."

Drew almost couldn't speak. "Well, I'm the one." His throat clogged. "I am your dad, Mackenzie, and you're my little girl."

She began to sob, her shoulders shaking from the effort not to lose control, but it was too late. She buried her face in her hands, crying hard and standing there as if she was going to break.

He made a decision. He brought her close, enveloped her in his arms and held tight. She didn't try and get away.

Mackenzie cried and cried. And he realized he was crying, too.

His nose tucked into her hair, that Mackenzie

scent that was unique to her alone. There'd been moments in his life that were priceless to him, but he would trade them all for this one. Seventeen years had been a long time to reach this point.

Whispering against the strands, he dared to say, "Mackenzie, I love you."

For long seconds, she didn't reply. Then, with her wet cheek sticking to his shirtfront, she said, "I forgive you, Daddy."

Twenty-Five

As the summer wound down and fall approached, the stores on Main Street advertised back-to-school clothes. On Overlook Dam, Labor Day was the final blow-out for docking and good times, the last call on coolers of beer, football, wakeboarding and gossip served up in warm weather.

Lucy lay out on the bow of Drew's boat, face and body toward the gloriously warm sun. Eyes closed, she listened to water lapping against the hull, the laughter of children, Lloyd as he went on and on about who was constructing a gigantic house in the Knolls, the purr of outboard motors as they cut through the lake, the wet-rubber squeak of a blow-up seal that Lloyd's fly-swatting grandson was trying to stay afloat on.

The various sounds were that of life in Red Duck, Idaho. The flotsam chatter of a resort community heading back to normal after a full summer season.

Lucy was actually looking forward to the population thinning back down, even though that meant she'd lose some customers when they returned home. She'd gained several year-rounders over the last month, and her day planner was full enough that she'd started breathing easier.

"What are you thinking, sugar?" Drew asked, his voice close to her ear.

Lucy opened her eyes, shading them against the blinding sun. Drew crouched beside her, his hair damp and his upper body glistening with water. He'd been swimming with Mackenzie, and water dripped off his body, spilling onto the terry cloth of her towel. She was roasting and the cool droplets felt good on her heated skin.

"Hmm," she responded, noncommittal. Earlier, she had been thinking about him. Fantasizing. She'd been watching him before lying down, eyes fastened on the way his back muscles bunched up and smoothed as he moved to tighten the cleat ropes, as he pitched a baseball to the boys and when his arm lifted to run a hand through his hair. She'd caught herself staring at his thighs, the strength and sinewy cords of hard definition in them.

His face had strong features. His thick, dark brown hair was made for a woman to sift her fingers through. His hazel eyes were a combination of golden flecks and olive-green…. Whenever he looked at her, she caught herself going from zero to lust in all of a few seconds.

Until today, she'd never noticed that he had creases at the corners of his eyes when he smiled. His face was tan, his mouth wide and his smile white.

"That's not an answer," he replied, his voice whiskey soft and filled with a drawl that was to die for.

When he touched her naked shoulder, she was shocked by the sensations that rocked through her body, the blood that rushed to all sorts of places that had been calm just a second ago.

She lied and said with a carefree tone, "I'm not thinking about much of anything. But that water dripping off you feels real good on me. It's hot."

"You're hot."

Laughter rose from her throat before she could stop it.

His hand cupped the curve of her shoulder, slid down her arm, and his flat palm laid on top of hers.

The atmosphere between them became charged and reckless. Lucy wanted to fill the silence, utter something witty and fun, but the words wouldn't form.

She'd never been a flirt, but she found herself taking chances, saying and doing things around Drew she hadn't done around other men. Through the years since her divorce, no man had ever interested her to the point of distraction.

Drew distracted her, made her crazy-nuts with carnal thoughts of ripping his clothes off. Resisting temptation had been a increasingly hard to do these past few days.

Something had been building between them, dangerous and exciting.

The hard calluses on his fingers were a stark contrast to her own soft hands. With a will of their own, her fingers curled into his and cinched tight.

His shadow fell over her bikini-clad body, the pungent scent of musk and man filling her senses. She wanted to bury her hands in that hair of his, and would have if nobody had been around. She had to get hold of herself.

"Want to go swimming?" he asked innocently.

"Yes, I think I better cool off!" She let go of his fingers.

Drew held out his hand for her, but she didn't dare take it. She practically flew off the boat and dived into the chilly water.

The shock of icy-cold after the blistering heat did her traitorous body good, muting the groan that had gotten stuck in her throat. She needed a bracing swim to clear her thinking.

She swam around the floating dock to where her boys were.

Mackenzie and Jason stood at the edge, Mackenzie wearing a string bikini and looking adorable. "Ya'll want to go wakeboarding?"

Matt was with them. "Can you do it goofy-foot?"

"What's that?"

"You put your other foot in front—the one that feels funny," Jason explained.

"How do ya'll know what that is?"

Jason stood in front of Mackenzie, put his arms out without touching her. "Okay—do this. Fall forward like you're going to go flat on your face. Don't worry, you won't. If you do, I'll catch you."

Mackenzie giggled. "I don't know about this." She smiled, leaned toward Jason, then her left foot came out in front of her so she wouldn't fall.

Matt said, "Your right foot is your goofy foot. So if you wakeboard goofy, you gotta put your right foot in front."

The kids went to round up Drew to ask him if he'd take them all out. He got Dave Lawrence to ride along as flagger.

As Lucy pulled herself out of the water using the stair handles, she watched Drew and Mackenzie. The two seemed to have synchronized moves, a testament to their father-daughter relationship. Jason and Matt sat on the back leather seat, and Matt waved to her as Drew fired up the loud motor.

Drew had a camera with him. He took a random snap of the kids on his boat, then aimed toward her. She gave him a roll of her eyes, a parade queen wave and shake of her head. He'd been taking a lot of pictures lately. He said seeing Roger Lewis on his mantel wasn't exactly the way he liked to start his morning. He'd admitted to getting used to all the personal touches, though. He wanted current photos of family who meant something to him. Already, many of him and Mackenzie were placed throughout the house.

As Drew motored away from the dock, the sight was one that Lucy wouldn't soon forget. Drew and his daughter. Mackenzie elbowing him when he was sifting through CDs to play and she didn't like his selection. Lucy's two boys checking out the high-tech wakeboard. Smiling. Happy. Innocent.

There was no other way to define it: Contentment in the purest form.

Mackenzie was leaving on Wednesday morning, and school started that coming Monday for Jason.

This summer had probably been the best of his life. It hadn't started out good at all. Him being hacked off at his mom for making him move up here. But he'd figured out that Red Duck wasn't all that bad. In fact, he kind of thought it was rad now.

He missed Brian and the guys, but he'd made a couple of new friends here. Nutter was a dumb-ass, but he was the funniest guy he knew. Ryan and Brownie were fun to hang out with. His boss at Woolly's wasn't too bad, but he'd quit that now that he was going to start school. His mom wanted him to focus on getting better grades this year. He was gonna try.

One thing that he decided not to change was taking food to the Sunrise. Jason hadn't seen that one coming. He liked it over there. He'd gotten used to the old people, liked a guy named Beansie. He was an old cowboy and he told Jason cattle drive stories.

His mom had said they could go car shopping this

week *and* get him a cell phone. Badass! He was getting another truck he could fix up. He couldn't wait.

They'd packed up everything from the dock, and Drew's boat was back on the trailer hitch. Everyone stood around in the ramp parking lot, saying, "See you next year," even though they'd still see each other in town. Funny how this place was like one big family.

At first, Jason hadn't liked that about Red Duck. But now he though it was neat that people cared about each other. Even that gorilla-hairy guy who talked so much—Lloyd. He'd brought a plastic grocery bag filled with garden tomatoes to the Sunrise just because he had extras. And Opal, she was real nice to Ada, the dog groomer. Spin was funny when she'd sometimes swear. Jacquie was okay, too. She'd been hanging out at the Sunrise a lot. At first, he hadn't liked her, but he'd seen her with Spin, and Spin was real happy to have the company.

As Drew and some of the dads got talking, Jason went up to Mackenzie, who stood by the Hummer.

"So...hey," Jason muttered, unable to really think of anything good to say. He wanted to give her a hug goodbye, but there were people around and he was self-conscious.

"Hey," she replied, smiling back at him.

She had the best smile ever. And he could listen to her talk for hours.

"So what are you gonna do when you get home?"

"I'm going to take a semester off before going to

college. Me and my dad are going to take some trips together and get to know each other better." The pink sunglasses she wore covered her eyes. He wanted to look into them in the worst way. "He wants to take me to California. I've never been. We're going to Disneyland." Her smile was perfect, just like a chewing gum commercial. "I'm going to college in January. I told him I would. That's what my momma wanted."

"What are you going to be?"

"I don't rightly know yet. Maybe a photographer."

"You'd be good at it."

She laughed. "I don't know about that. I've only been messing around with my dad's camera. It's fun to doctor the pictures up on the computer."

Jason looked at his feet, the chunky rubber sandals and his big toes. He felt awkward and clumsy. Lifting his chin, he said, "Well, I liked hanging out with you this summer."

"I liked it, too. We should call each other sometime."

"Yeah. I think that would be cool."

"Or e-mail."

"We're getting the Internet. My mom figured out the house can be wired for it."

Mackenzie slipped her glasses off her nose. She stood barefoot, her feet perfect and toenails painted pink. He tried to put her out of his head because he knew that they probably would stay in touch for a while, then stop.

Sixteen and seventeen might have only been a year apart, but she was out of high school now, while he had two more years of tardy bells and morning announcements. He'd been held back in the first grade for being a slow reader, so he was just a junior.

"Thanks for taking me around. I liked watching you play ball. Too bad you guys didn't go to the playoffs." She sounded genuinely sorry.

"It's okay. I wasn't really into it that much this year, anyway."

"I think I'll get on a college softball team."

"That'd be good."

Jason felt as if all his muscles were too tight for his bones. This was effin' awkward. All of a sudden, he was shy around her and was struggling with what to say. It sucked.

"Well…" She looked over her shoulder at Drew, who was headed toward the Hummer. "It looks like we're leaving."

"Yeah."

"It was nice meeting you, Jason."

"Yeah."

"We'll call. You have my number."

"Yeah."

She grinned, then gave him a hug he wasn't prepared for. Into his ear, she whispered, "I'll bet all the girls are going to have a mad crush on you."

Then she pulled back, waved and went around to her side of the SUV.

Jason watched her drive away, and he kept a stupid slap-happy grin on his face.

Oh yeah. She thinks I'm a stud.

He and Mackenzie Taylor weren't destined to be boy- and girlfriend, but she sure knew how to make a guy feel like he could get any girl he wanted.

The Hailey Airport, small as it was, didn't allow anyone, not even if your name was Hemingway, to wait with passengers beyond the security checkpoint.

Mackenzie stood next to Drew, her backpack over her shoulder. He felt strangely nervous. Part of him wished she never had to leave; part of him knew that she had a life in Florida.

About a dozen passengers waited to board her outbound flight. He could see her gate through the security area. She had about five minutes left and then she'd have to go through.

"So you'll call me when you get to Salt Lake to change planes." His voice sounded unintentionally clipped.

"I said I would. Don't worry. I know how to change planes all by myself." Brows raised, she gave him a placating smile, one filled with light teasing that warmed him to the core.

"I know, sugar. I just want to make sure." Drew shifted his weight from one foot to the other.

Earlier, he'd given her some cash so she'd have plenty of money to buy something to eat in the airport.

He'd even bought a *Seventeen* magazine for her when she was in the ladies' room. She'd looked at him as if he was silly, but she'd taken it and given him a hug.

"So you're all set?" he asked.

"All set." She patted her backpack. "I've got the money and the magazine, I have my iPod and my journal inside."

"You going to write something on the plane?" he asked.

"I don't know." *Ah don't know.*

"About me?"

She grinned. "Maybe."

"Well," he said, not understanding why he was suddenly so self-conscious about letting her go. Maybe a part of him worried she'd never come back. That her trip had been a fluke, a one-time deal. Something not to be repeated. But they'd made plans and he was sure she wanted to head out to Disneyland and do some other things with him.

Just the same…

He reiterated, "So, Disneyland this fall."

"Count on it."

"Great. And maybe some camping in the spring. I've got a tent. It's been awhile since I used it, but I have all the gear. We could take the boat up, find a good spot."

"That would be fun."

"Cool. Good."

She laughed. "I'm coming back. I promise."

He nodded, his throat feeling dry, and he licked

his lips. Over the PA speakers, flight attendants made an announcement that Mackenzie's flight was ready to board.

"I better go."

"Yeah…"

Smiling, she gazed into his face. "Thanks for everything."

He gulped, shook his head, his eyes momentarily closing. "No, *thank you*. Thank you for giving me a chance."

"Thank you for giving *me* a chance," she said, with such grace and warmth, it was all he could do not to crush her in his arms.

"Well…" she said, her smile waning and emotions swimming in her eyes.

Drew reached out, held her firmly, kissed the top of her head, the soft strands of her hair. "You be good, Mackenzie."

"I will, Daddy."

Daddy.

The word was like a balm. It soothed old wounds, made him feel as if he were the best thing on the face of the earth.

"Love you." He spoke into her hair.

"Love you, too."

They broke apart; he brushed her smooth cheek. "You're so pretty, sugar. You tell those boys to stay away from you."

She laughed, a honeyed sound. "I'm not looking for a boyfriend right now."

"Good."

Her flight was called once more and she had to head through the security check. She gave him a final hug and he squeezed her firmly, but gently. Backing out of his arms, she waved, walked to the clearance area and put her backpack on the conveyer.

Drew didn't move until he watched her wave from the doorway to the boarding ramp. And not even then.

He waited until the small plane taxied and left his view. Only then did he turn around and head home, already missing his little girl.

Journal of Mackenzie
~~Taylor~~ Tolman

From the airplane window, I can see the town of Red Duck disappearing like a small speck in the distance, and somewhere on that gray ribbon of road, my dad is in his Hummer, driving to his house.

He's going to find Momma's letter on his bed, just where I left it when he wasn't looking. It was a letter she wrote to me just before she died, saying she thought it would be a good idea if, when the time came, and I said it would be okay, that I took Daddy's last name.

Momma said I'd had hers for a long time, and she didn't mind sharing and letting me use Daddy's once he and I made our peace.

Momma always hoped we would. I wish she could know right now that we worked things out. I think she does know from Heaven.

I left Drew a note saying I'd like to take Tolman as my last name.

I think my dad will say it's okay. In fact, I know he'll be happy about it. Me, too.

He's going be fine and so am I.

Twenty-Six

The last week in September, the annual Little League dinner at Woolly Burgers wasn't as lively as it had been in past years, since the team hadn't gone to the play-offs. But the boys still got achievement awards from their parents and coaches. It was just an off season this year and Drew looked forward to the next one. Before this summer, he would have been bummed out about it, taken on some pressure over not producing a better outcome. But he realized it didn't matter.

There were so many more things to life than baseball.

"Are you heading out?" Drew asked Lucy as she left her boys with Nutter's parents.

"Yep. Jason and Matt are spending the night with Nutter and I have the house all to myself tonight. I may just have to stand in the middle of the living room and stare at the ceiling." She laughed.

He smiled at her, liking the way her teeth contrasted with the darker lipstick she wore. She had on a sleeveless, form-fitting white dress with a scoop neck. It looked nice on her. Some of her tan had faded, but she was a strikingly beautiful woman no matter what her skin tone.

She'd pulled half her hair up into a claw; the rest spilled over her shoulders. The rich brown color had brightened from the sun and strands were highlighted a reddish-bronze.

"You just don't know how noisy your house is until the kids leave. I never get a day off." She fitted her purse on her shoulder. "I'm always on duty."

She didn't say it with bitterness, but rather fondness. And with a hint of anticipation about not being a parent tonight, but a woman who was going to go home and enjoy her surroundings without parental responsibilities.

"Bye, boys," she called, waving to them.

"See ya, Mom!" Matt was trying to juggle three baseballs at a time. They fell to the floor and then Jason tried.

Lucy went toward the door and Drew followed. "I'll walk you to your car."

The outside air was warm and lazy.

"Actually, I came with Sue and Dave. I told her I was going to walk home." Lucy gazed at the horizon. "It's so nice out."

An Indian summer had crept into September, the day filled with a warm breeze. The sunset was heavy with fall colors, the sky aflame with an orange-and-red wash.

The muted golds reflected on Lucy's face. He remembered what her body felt like next to his, the way her breasts looked in her bikini top. The scent of her perfume hung in the air.

His heart raced as he thought about how she'd feel up tight to him, flesh to flesh. How it would feel to run his hands across her body right now, the smooth cotton of that dress. Her back and waist, then her butt.

She glanced at him, her eyes darkening as if she was having a thought she struggled with. "How'd you get here?"

"I drove. I can drive you home if you want."

"Okay."

The drive to Lucy's house was short, and neither of them said a word. They didn't have to. He cut the engine, went around to open the SUV door for her. She hopped down and didn't look at him.

Lucy could feel the soft cotton of her dress move over her skin as she walked to the porch. A delicious sense of anticipation surged through her body. She stopped at the door, turned to say something—then cut herself off.

Drew leaned toward her, brought his face over hers. She felt her backside pressing into the screen door, and that was the last conscious thought she had as Drew's mouth covered hers.

They kissed, quick yet lingering.

After a minute, she managed to get the lock open and let him inside. She kicked the door closed with her foot, stood a distance away from him and tried to figure out what exactly was going on.

She knew exactly what was going to happen. And she wanted it to. But she just hadn't known when or where.

"Can I get you anything to drink?" she offered, the words lame even to her own ears.

He made no reply. He just looked at her as if she were the best boat on the dock—something he wanted. Quite badly.

Her face was flushed and she pushed aside a stray lock that had come loose from her hair claw. She threw her shoulders back and forced herself into a calm she didn't feel.

Anxiousness churned in the pit of her stomach. Her smile wavered a little. She had a hard time concentrating when he looked at her. She hadn't been with anyone other than her husband for nineteen years. Nobody since her divorce. This was new.

It must have showed.

He pulled her to him and murmured, with his face in her hair. "I can leave."

"No," she said, clinging to his shoulders, not wanting to let him go. Her hand slipped into his jeans and she found him straining against the fabric. "Stay…."

He reached under her dress and began to stroke her thighs and then in between her thighs. A moan rose from her throat when his fingertips reached into her panties. It had been a long time since a man touched her intimately, and she arched her back as the feeling rose and rose. She shut her eyes tight and grabbed on to the front of Drew's shirt.

"Don't stop," she whispered.

Her head started to spin; her mind reached places she'd long since forgotten about. She let herself go, riding the feelings that rose. Suddenly, she let out a cry as a burst of pulsing heat pleasured her body.

Her breathing grew jagged; her legs went numb.

Drew scooped her into his arms, carried her down the hall. She pressed herself to him, eyes closed.

He set her on her feet and undid the nylon zipper of her dress. He pulled it over her head. The dress landed on the floor.

She moved her face to he could kiss her cheek, the corner of her mouth. He stroked her bare back and she shivered.

A dozen different thoughts went through her head. She didn't want to talk about anything, but she had to say something.

"Drew…I haven't been with anyone since Gary, and when he had the affair, I made sure that I was okay." That was the best way she could phrase it without coming right out and saying she'd had a panel of STD tests run on her.

"I know what you mean, Lucy." He brushed her hair from her forehead. "I did the same after me and Jacquie."

She nodded.

"And when Mackenzie was fourteen, I got a vasectomy."

That news pulled Lucy slightly out of the moment. "You did?"

"I should have done it years before." He kissed her neck softly, his mouth warm. "So I'm okay…if you're okay with everything."

"I am…." She reached out and undid the buttons on his fly, then helped him shrug out of his jeans. He kicked off his shoes. She undid his soft shirt, and the fabric flowed like a teal-blue river onto the floor.

His callused fingers unhooked her bra and peeled her panties down her legs. His roughened hands felt every inch of her, working over her breasts, both nipples between his fingers, then softly down her stomach.

He laid her on the bed, kissed the curves and dips of her skin until she felt as if she had no bones. She melted into the duvet cover as his mouth found the underside of her breasts, the crook of her elbow and the dimple of her navel. She shivered deep inside herself, the sensations almost overwhelming.

She arched her back, waiting for him, wanting him.

Her hands skimmed across his skin, so smooth and cool, like fine marble on a summer's day. His muscles felt like slabs of steel, and bunched and tightened when he moved. In spite of wanting this to last forever, she moaned, impatient. She'd waited so long to feel like this with someone. With Drew.

She kissed his shoulder, the curve of it where the skin was too delicious for words. Her heartbeat raced as she reached out and wrapped her hand around him. He pulsed, that part of him thick and hard, heavy in her hand.

Then he entered her, finally, filling her as she pushed up to feel him deeper inside her. The tip of him reached a place that rubbed a spot she'd never felt before. Her legs wrapped around his thighs, and the pleasure intensified as he moved back and forth.

Her body danced to the rhythm he set. Back and forth until she felt the release that had been building inside him. She chased it, found one of her own, her hands splaying his back, holding him close.

She wrapped herself around him, letting the sensations linger, pulse and reach the ends of waves until she could begin to think a little more clearly.

She already knew she wanted him. Again. And again.

He moved onto his back and took her with him, still joined. He kissed her fingertips. She kissed his mouth. Softly. Tenderly.

Gazing into his face, she uttered the first thought on her mind, completely ludicrous. "Hello." Her voice was a mere whisper.

"Hey, sugar."

She smiled at him, at them still locked together. A myriad of rampant thoughts rained through her mind.

From here, were would they go?

Drew tucked a piece of her hair behind her ear,

causing her to shiver with longing. "I think we should go out on a date," he said in a long, audible breath. "Dinner. At a restaurant."

The absurdity of his timing broadened her smile. All summer, they'd been eyeing each other, interested, touching, kissing—and it had never crossed her mind to go out on a date with him. Sleeping with him—yes.

She knew beyond a lingering shadow of doubt she did want to get to know him much better. All the complexities. They'd done this backward. Physical first. But she wouldn't have changed anything. Sometimes life worked best unscripted, and this was what had felt natural and right to her.

"I'd like to go to dinner with you, Drew," she said, running her fingertip over his brow, then caressing his cheek.

"There are things I want to know about you, Lucy. I want to learn who you are. Everything. What your favorite thing to cook for yourself is, what you like to do for you. Where you like to go. I don't even know if you have any brothers and sisters, or if your parents are living."

"I'd like to share all that with you," she said softly, not wanting to move.

He murmured, "But I don't want to talk about it right now. I want to kiss you. Touch you. Learn your body."

His arm slipped tighter around her waist and she felt a pull of wild abandon spring to life within her. Something she hadn't felt in too many years.

Twenty-Seven

Jacquie had been contemplating giving up smoking. What the hell. She'd given up sex—a major accomplishment for her. So how tricky could nicotine be?

Tricky, she mused as she gnawed every last ounce of flavor out of a stick of peppermint gum.

Cigarettes were readily available at the grocery store. But, she also reasoned, so were single men around the dinner hour. And she'd gone right through the checkout without one man in her cart, so there was hope. All she'd gotten at the grocery these days were single-serve frozen dinners and expensive wines. So with the right willpower, she could forgo the cigarettes.

Then again, a cup of coffee or a glass of wine just wouldn't have the same taste without a cigarette.

A decision like this was too much to contemplate at the moment. There was always a New Year's resolution. If she made hers on the 30th, maybe it would stick better than last year's on the 31st, which had not.

Walking the polished linoleum floor of the Sunrise Trail Creek Seniors Home, Jacquie thought about their class today. Salsa dancing. Good Lord, but it was going to be a hoot watching Spin shake her skinny ass.

Jacquie turned the corner into Spin's room.

"Spin, you wouldn't believe the morning I've had. My stupid cell died and this fabulous listing of mine—" She cut the sentence off.

Spin's bed was empty.

Not just empty-unmade, as if she were in the restroom or in the dining hall…but empty of her favorite floral-print linens. Empty of Spin's rose-colored, twin-size chenille bedspread, her TV pillow, her pink fuzzy slippers.

Panic welled in Jacquie. Her chest constricted and she felt as if she was suffocating.

No, no, no!

Running out of the room, she went to the nurse's station and found one of the familiar charge nurses for Spin's unit.

"Hi, you know me. I come here all the time," Jacquie said in a rush. "I'm looking for Fern Goodey-Leonard. She's tall, skinny as a broom handle and…"

The nurse's expression was one of sympathy.

Jacquie refused to acknowledge it. *No!* She continued in a fast slur of words. "Her bed's not made the way she likes it. Where are her sheets? And what h-happened…t-to her s-slippers?"

Jacquie's shoulders began to quake, her body trembled. Tears splashed down her cheeks, onto the front of her blouse, wet spots on the fine silk.

"I'm sorry," the nurse said, her mouth creasing with empathy. "They tried to call you this morning to tell you, but we couldn't get hold of you."

"Spin…" Jacquie let go of the sobs. "Ohmygod… Spin."

Jacquie lifted her chin, her vision blurry. The nurse's gentle tone had been placating, but Jacquie's pulse threatened to pump out of control.

"She died in her sleep," the nurse murmured. "She wasn't in any pain and she lived a good, long life. Everyone here loved her." Even the nurse got a tissue and blew her nose. "She was a real kick in the pants."

The words simply refused to register. All Jacquie knew was that the best friend she'd ever had in her life wasn't in her room, in her bed, with the television blaring with a *Bonanza* rerun.

Vaguely hearing herself talk, Jacquie said, "We were supposed to have salsa lessons today."

"I'm so sorry," the nurse said, sympathy etched on her young face. She went to a white cabinet, came back with a large manilla envelope and handed it to Jacquie. "She left us instructions to give this to you on her passing. She also has something in the art room for you. We left it just as it was."

Unable to speak, Jacquie took the offered envelope and walked numbly down the hallway.

Grief had never been one of her strong suits.

When her mom died, Jacquie hadn't done well at the funeral. She didn't like sad or depressing things. Which was why she sometimes filled herself with artificial happiness, anything to rid herself of lonely realities that, at times, were too much for her.

Without Spin, Jacquie didn't know how she would have gotten through her breakup with Drew. Oh, hell…she would have done it, she was strong. But my God…Spin.

Spin…you saved me.

Jacquie gulped hard, yielding once more to the compulsive sobs that shook her shoulders. Her hand grabbed the hall railing. She couldn't move forward. She had to lean into the wall for support, her cheek against the cool surface.

She'd known this day would come. And yet, no matter how much she'd told herself she could deal with it, she couldn't face the pain of losing someone who'd meant so much to her. Who'd actually taught her to value herself more than a relationship, to place her wants and desires before that of a man.

If she'd just jumped right into the next affair without healing from the last one, she never would have understood that she was worth the wait for the right man. That even with her faults and flaws, she was worthy of being loved and cherished for who she was, not who someone wanted her to be.

Thank you, Spin.

Once in the art room with its multitude of

windows flashing in sunshine, she went to the corner where Spin's easel was set up. All the paint tubes and the waxed-paper palette were just as she'd left them; a canvas was on the easel, but covered with a paint-smeared cloth.

Using just her fingertip, Jacquie slowly lifted the cloth and took a peek underneath. Seeing mostly an area of candlelight-white on the canvas, she lifted the cloth higher until the entire painting was revealed and the cloth fell to the floor.

Even Jacquie Santini knew what the Lord's Supper was.

The painting was blotchy and some areas not sharp, as if filled in by sections. But the spiritual feeling was there, godly, dominant and meaningful.

Fresh tears fell down Jacquie's face, her heart melting into a puddle of nothing. Emptiness. Loneliness. Despair. They hit her all at once.

"Spin..." she uttered, her voice cracking.

Jacquie lowered herself into a chair and rested the manilla envelop on her lap. Swallowing hard, she stared at the painting.

After a long moment, she opened the envelope and took out the contents. Sheets of papers. On the very top, a letter. Handwritten. Spin had kept her good penmanship, even in her declining years. The woman had perfect form on all the curls and loops, the legibility still impressive.

Unsure if she could read the letter yet, Jacquie gazed out the window and recalled her first meeting with Spin. The veranda, the pond and geese.

Hot tears silently stole down Jacquie's face, her neck, into the collar of her blouse. She dug into her purse for a tissue and couldn't find one. She ended up using the easel cloth to wipe her nose.

She began to read the letter, slowly…blinking several times to clear her vision….

Jacquie—

If you are reading this, then that means I'm gone. Don't ruin your makeup and cry for me. I was old. I lived a long time. Now I'm with my Wally and we are happy to be back together.

I left you my painting. It was a bitch to finish, my eyes just not what they used to be. It's the Lord's Supper and it gave me comfort knowing I was painting Jesus as we know Him on earth. I'm almost anxious to see what He looks like in Heaven. It will be one of my defining moments, right up there with Willard Scott putting me on the TV.

Morris Leonard, my great-nephew, will be handling my estate. I know I've said I wanted my ashes baked into a loaf of bread and fed to the pigeons, but that was just a load of bull. Morris knows where I want to be buried.

There is one thing, though, that I'd like you to do for me, Jacquie. You'll need to take a drive to Boise. On my art desk is a tube of geranium-red paint. I want you to paint lipstick on Judge Har-

rison's statue. Right in the kisser. That man was a sexist asshole and deserves to be painted like a woman.

Well, that's about all. The other papers in here are case transcripts I had representing women who struggled for equality back in the old days. You'll find their stories interesting reading. They paved the way for you to do a woman's job in what was once a man's world.

You are a fine woman and I am proud of who you are, Jacquie. You've come a long way and you're ready for the next chapter of your life.

I give you my full blessing. You'll know what I mean when the moment arises.

With all my love,
Fern Goodey-Leonard

With her head down, Jacquie watched as her tears splattered onto the letter, fat drops of love, gratitude and fondness for a real lady of quality.

"Did you set out the cheez?" Raul asked, his voice respectfully low.

Lucy nodded, motioning to the platter of cheeses and fruits on the reception table. "All that's left is to light the candles in the chafing dishes."

Raul and Lucy were the only two in the large banquet room at the Elks' Lodge. In light of Fern's death, they'd called a truce and had catered the reception together. Lucy couldn't recall whose idea it had been—hers or Raul's.

They'd been at Sutter's Grocery in the bread department, Raul eyeing the same loaf of focaccia that she'd been ready to nab, when word fanned through the store that Spin had passed away.

When Raul's and Lucy's groceries were being rung up in two different lines, their eyes had met and they'd agreed to combine forces and do this one last thing for Spin.

"It looks good," Raul remarked, his complexion appearing more olive-toned in his all-black suit with black shirt. "What is that over there?"

"Chicken broccoli bake. Simple, but a crowd pleaser." Lucy gazed at several of the dishes Raul had set up. "What's that?"

"Pork Chops Olé."

She examined the hot dish. Its top was sprinkled with melted cheese.

"It's nothing special," Raul said. "Any moron could make it. I got the recipe off the soup can."

Lucy smiled. "Slumming, Raul?"

"C'hew know how it goes. Sometimes simple is better. Spin was a simple lady."

Nodding, Lucy gave a sigh. They lit the chafing candles to keep the hot dishes warm, and made one last check of all the foods. "Well, I guess we should go to the funeral now. I can drive—"

"No, no—I can drive," he insisted with a slight bow. "I'm a gentleman and I insist. Besides, c'hew haven't lived until you've experienced a Cadillac with velour upholstery."

Trying not to let him know that his humor put a lightness in her heart, Lucy said somberly, "All right, Raul."

Fern "Spindly" Goodey-Leonard's funeral was simple, yet a classy goodbye from those who'd known her. People had come up from Boise to join all of Red Duck in the Chapel of the Woods Funeral Parlor to pay their fond farewells.

Jacquie hadn't been able to give a eulogy. She just wasn't up for it. She had the director of the home read the meager words she had typed on her computer and printed. They were almost an embarrassment. Expressing how she felt about Spin wasn't easy to convey in a written statement. The feelings in her heart didn't easily translate into words.

Spin had a plot beside Wallace Leonard in the old Timberline cemetery, not ten spaces down from the town's famous writer who had committed suicide in the early 1970s.

There had been one time when Spin had had Jacquie take her to the cemetery to visit Wally. They'd stopped into Sutter's Grocery and bought bouquets for the urn, and Spin had gotten down on her knees and lovingly arranged the carnations and mums. At the time, Jacquie had even asked her why she wanted to be cremated and not laid to rest by Wally. Spin never gave an answer. She just put that familiar smile on her face, crooked lipstick and all.

So now Jacquie knew the whole story.

416 Stef Ann Holm

Spin was a romantic and there was no way she'd end up as pigeon crap on a statue. She wanted to be by her Wally.

The very idea was so poetic that Jacquie had a moment of feeling sorry for herself that she'd come to the funeral alone, without any male prospects in her life to take a journey with over the next fifty-some-odd years. That she even let the thought hit her, for a mere second, was so wrong.

Jacquie slipped her sunglasses back on, her black gloves blurring in her vision as she covered her eyes. She'd been crying all morning and looked like death warmed over herself.

The weather had finally turned cool, with a bite to the air that had arrived overnight.

The graveside gathering began to thin, and people returned to their cars. Jacquie had already said her goodbyes in private, and now she simply smiled at the opening in the ground, where Spin's dark wood casket had already been lowered. She gave the quietly serene scene her best parting nod and turned toward her Jaguar.

Inhaling the clear air, she forced herself to rise out of her sorrow.

At the edge of the road, a man in a classic black suit waited by her car. He had clipped-short dark hair, and smoky sunglasses covered his eyes. She'd seen him at the chapel. He'd remained in the last row and, if she hadn't been mistaken, he'd stared at her throughout the service. At least he'd been looking whenever she glanced behind her. But God only knew. Her man transmitter was screwed up. It had been so long since she'd even tossed her hair over her shoulder to get a man's attention. For all she knew, he was looking to buy a house and wanted her card.

As she made her way to him, she realized his shoulders were quite broad and impressive. He was very tall. Handsome in an elegant way. Yet he didn't come across as brash or arrogant. She liked that about him.

"Can I help you?" she asked, her work voice coming into play. If he were a prospective client, she was going to tell him this was a wholly inappropriate place to discuss real estate.

"You're Jacquie."

"Yes, I am." She gazed at him through the tinted lenses of her sunglasses, knowing he could see her roving eyes taking in the angle of his jaw, the dark slashes of brows just above the frame of his own sunglasses. When he removed them, she was fascinated by a pair of unique gray-blue eyes.

"I'm Spin's great-nephew." He extended his hand. "Morris Leonard."

"Oh." The word squeaked out between Jacquie's lips. "She's spoken about you."

"She told me all about you, too."

Jacquie wasn't sure she liked the tone of that. Speaking about someone in a casual reference and telling them all about a person were two different things.

"She did?" Jacquie blurted, unsure what to say next.

This man was delicious, and if she didn't watch herself, she'd be sticking herself to him like chewing gum. It had been far too long since she'd gone without. But she'd made Spin a promise and she'd kept it.

Morris smiled, his lips made for kissing, his perfect white teeth disarming her resolve and tearing it down a notch. Or two. Or three. And four. "My great-aunt was a hoot. She called me up weekly and told me about the two of you."

"She did?" Rarely did something baffle Jacquie, but this had her confused. "What did she say?"

Morris simply grinned. "A lot."

Jacquie's breath solidified in her throat, caught, held, and she fought to remember to inhale, then exhale. "I'm afraid you have me at a disadvantage. I'm not sure what this is all about."

"I'm not exactly sure, either. Other than she spoke very highly of you and she told me not to talk to you until after the graveside service. She said she didn't want you distracted from crying over her."

"Distracted? Did she really say that?" A flash of indignance lit into Jacquie. She'd been overwrought, damaged, upset. That Spin would ever suggest she'd come to a funeral and be distracted—

But she had.

Shit on a stick. Spin had been right. The very irony...

Jacquie raised a gloved hand to her cheek and the words in Spin's letter came back to her. Then, unbidden, she began to smile. Wider, bigger, broader, until she was laughing. And laughing so hard she almost peed her pants.

"Oh, you old bird," she said with complete humor. "I get it now."

Then, gazing at Morris, for the first time in months she let the old Jacquie come out and play. "Morris, how often do you get up to Red Duck?"

"Apparently not often enough."

"My thoughts exactly. There's somewhere I need to take you. Spin wanted me to show you her and Wally's favorite fishing spot. And after that, I know of a fabulous place for dinner and drinks. We'll give a toast to Spin. She'd like that. I know it for fact."

The warmth that spread through Jacquie was a welcome tide, and long overdue. Her gaze settled on Morris Leonard like that of a cat who'd been denied a bowl of cream forever.

It felt good to feel sexy again. To allow herself to purr and be a female who appreciated a handsome man. On that thought, she let herself smile.

Jacquie Santini was back in business.

Lucy had been sewing new curtains for the living room. It had taken her the better part of yesterday to measure and cut everything into the right dimensions.

She'd worked out a deal with Bud Tremore that was too good to be true—but it was true. For whatever reason, Bud agreed to let her stay in the teardown. She'd proposed she pay for the land on a lease-to-own basis, since that was the only value the property had. It was an incredible arrangement. He was in no hurry to move his RVs and she'd gotten used to them, anyway. But the house needed major improvements and she'd been determined to make this a home for her and the boys. So she'd been painting and fixing things up on her days off.

The master bedroom was complete. With Drew's help, she'd installed new floor molding, applied a coat of beige paint to the walls and refinished the hardwood floors—a process that had taken her far longer than she'd anticipated. The smell of varnish still lingered in the house. She bought rose-print fabric for her vanity skirt, hung some oval mirrors and had herself a nice place to put on her makeup.

Leaving the kitchen table, where her sewing machine was set up, she went into the kitchen to pour another cup of coffee. There was a coolness to the room and she was glad she'd had Jason chop a bunch of firewood into kindling.

She took her cup into the living room, threw some slivers of wood into the iron stove and sighed with contentment as the flames licked and sparked over the dry timber.

She caught a glance of her reflection in the window glass. She wore her favorite peach sweater, black jeans and little black-beaded slippers. Smiling to herself, she thought this was a nice day to be in Red Duck.

The boys were in school—Jason having driven

them in a used Toyota truck she'd picked up for a reasonable price. She had the house to herself, and she was cooking for two clients tomorrow, so it would be a nice payday.

Remembering she needed a different spool of thread, she went into the bedroom where she kept her sewing things in the closet. As she rifled around for what she needed, the phone rang.

She'd had a land line installed for the Internet, the old wall phones still in place and now working. The boys thought it barbaric that she didn't buy a cordless, but the three-prong jacks for the corded phones would have to be converted, and she thought they lent a nice touch as is.

"Hello?" she said into the receiver, the handset heavy.

"Mrs. Carpenter, this is Mr. Summers, the principal at your son's school."

Principal. School.

Dread worked up Lucy's spine. Not again. Please, no.

"I'm calling about an incident we had today during break."

Lucy felt sick to her stomach.

"Your son and a few other boys were discovered out in the parking lot—"

—smoking marijuana—

"—with a box of tarantulas."

The ringing in Lucy's ears ceased. "Excuse me?"

"They were in the back by the Dumpster and

betting money to see whose tarantula would kill the others."

"What?" Lucy blurted, not able to connect the dots. What was Jason doing with tarantulas?

"Nobody got hurt, and from what our science teacher told us, a tarantula sting is no worse than that of a bee's." The principal went on in a half-amused voice, almost as if he were reflecting on an old schoolboy prank he'd once done. "I've seen a lot of things, but this was a first. We're making all of the boys stay after school with desk-cleaning detention. Just wanted to let you know."

Relief pooled in Lucy. Thank goodness it was nothing more than this, and if she allowed herself, there was a warped humor in the whole thing. Tarantula fights? A total boy thing that she would never understand, but it did give her a smile. "I do appreciate the call," she said with a shake of her head. "I'll talk to Jason when he gets home."

The line grew quiet, then he said, "Ms. Carpenter, I'm Mr. Summers at the middle school. I'm calling about your son Matthew."

"Mattie?" Lucy exhaled a huff of breath, then a delayed laugh. "Oh, I just assumed..." She let the thought trail, her laughter increasing. "I'm sorry. It's just that...never mind."

Some days, she just never knew what was going to happen, and this was one of them. She'd take tarantulas over pot any day. An astonishing sense of fulfillment washed over her. She'd come a long way. So had the boys.

They were all going to be okay.

After hanging up, Lucy remembered the thread, but the phone rang once more.

"Hello?"

"Hey, babe." Drew's voice warmed her to the core. "What are you doing?"

Lucy loved it when he called, loved hearing the sound of his voice. She sat on the floor and settled in to talk to him. "Just thinking about how great my life is." She lay on the hardwood, propped her slippered feet on the wall and stretched the phone cord through her fingers. "It feels good to have it back."

Epilogue

As far as Roger Lewis was concerned, Opal had the best set of gams on a woman he'd ever seen. They were as thin as twigs, but they had a real shape to them that he admired. They'd been going out for three weeks now, and he was after her flirty-girl trail like a bloodhound on a scent.

If he believed the rumors, they were engaged. Roger couldn't go that far, but as he leaned back on his bar stool to watch his gal head on over, the thought did pop into his head. He had been waiting a long time to nail her.

"Hey, Rog," she said, settling a smooch on his mouth right in front of everyone.

"Hey, Opal."

"The day I've had. Ada let loose on me that if Drew brings her any more biscuits, she's going to kill me." Opal parked her behind on a stool. "She's gained ten pounds on the South Beach."

Raul rolled his beady eyes. The new couple were nauseating, ruining his appetite for what was already bad buffalo wings.

"And they call this bleu cheez dip?" he complained, poking a wing tip into the white puddle of dressing.

"You ought to cook for High Country, Raul." Clyde made the suggestion. "Give this lounge some class."

"I don' cook for no restaurants. The Raul is a private chef and the number one best cook in all of Timberline. I always will be and don' you forget it." Cocky arrogance marked his tone, but the truth was the truth.

Although Raul would never admit it to anyone, Lucy Carpenters was very talented when it came to culinary expertise. After Spin's funeral, Lucy and he had formed a kind of respectful thing for each other's chef business. That wasn't to say the Raul didn't retain his mythological status in town, because he had savvy and looks—he just glanced the other way now and then and let Lucy shine.

Lloyd Zaragoza scooped a big wad of blue cheese onto his hot wing and munched the skin right off the bone. "Mighty good eats. Did I tell you that I heard some news about Jacquie Santini the other day?"

All eyes leveled on him.

"She got married. To that lawyer fella. Morris Leonard."

Opal lit an unfiltered, blew the smoke away from the group. "He was related to Spin, wasn't he?"

"Great-cousin three times removed," Clyde stated.

"I thought he was her nephew," Roger said.

"Who the hell cares?" Lloyd grumbled. "I'm trying to tell you a story." In between licking his fingers, he related, "So anyway, this is what I heard. She married that Leonard guy and opened up her own real estate company in Boise—Santini Properties."

"It sounds like a magic show," Raul suggested.

"That was Houdini, you lug-head," Lloyd growled.

"Santini. Hoodini. It don' make no difference to me becuz in La Puente, you don' need no magician to make your Cadillac disappear. Jess a Slim Jim."

Opal laughed, cuddling up to her sheriff. She loved a man in uniform. He put a hand on her thigh and she winked at him. Bud Tremore made a face. He was probably jealous, the old coot.

Talk drifted over the tabletop like streams of Opal's cigarette smoke. Drew and Lucy were always good for conversation, but they had turned about as dull as the floor in the Mule Shoe. They acted like a normal couple around town, never doing anything scandalous that anyone could tell, and always holding hands and kissing.

Trying to keep the conversational attention focused on him, Lloyd exclaimed, "That Jacquie is a piece of work. Seems like just yesterday she got arrested for painting red lipstick on that statue of Judge Harrison down in Boise."

"I-gad, I remember that," Clyde mused aloud. "I

think it was that Leonard fella who sprung her from the jail. Bail was something like a thousand clams."

"Four hundred," Raul said.

Opal chimed in. "She got out on a bond that was five hundred dollars."

"No, it wasn't." Bud adamantly shook his head.

Then a big debate ensued and suddenly everyone was talking over everyone as they all remembered the story a little differently.

It was just another day in Red Duck.

REQUEST YOUR
FREE BOOKS!

2 FREE NOVELS
FROM THE ROMANCE/SUSPENSE
COLLECTION PLUS 2 FREE GIFTS!

BOB206

STEF
ANN
HOLM

32222 LEAVING NORMAL	___ $6.99 U.S.	___ $8.50 CAN.	
32086 PINK MOON	___ $6.50 U.S.	___ $7.99 CAN.	
66949 GIRLS NIGHT	___ $6.50 U.S.	___ $7.99 CAN.	

(limited quantities available)

TOTAL AMOUNT	$ _____
POSTAGE & HANDLING	$ _____
($1.00 FOR 1 BOOK, 50¢ for each additional)	
APPLICABLE TAXES*	$ _____
TOTAL PAYABLE	$ _____

(check or money order—please do not send cash)

To order, complete this form and send it, along with a check or money order for the total above, payable to MIRA Books, to: **In the U.S.:** 3010 Walden Avenue, P.O. Box 9077, Buffalo, NY 14269-9077; **In Canada:** P.O. Box 636, Fort Erie, Ontario, L2A 5X3.

Name: _____
Address: _____ City: _____
State/Prov.: _____ Zip/Postal Code: _____
Account Number (if applicable): _____

075 CSAS

*New York residents remit applicable sales taxes.
*Canadian residents remit applicable GST and provincial taxes.

MIRA®

www.MIRABooks.com

MSAH1006BL